✦ The Road and the Star

The
Road and the Star

BERKELY MATHER

NEW YORK

CHARLES SCRIBNER'S SONS

TO
WYNNE AND PETERJON

❖ The Road and the Star

1

THE mist was rising in layers from the dark river as I approached the bridge, turning the flaring torches of the linkboys outside the playhouse to a smoky orange. No plays were shown here now—the Puritans had closed the theater—but a few roisterers still lingered outside, while more were congregated in the tavern opposite. A screaming slattern waving a feathered hat darted under the nose of my tired horse, causing it to shy and rear. The owner of the hat pursued her, cursing and bellowing, while his companions, from the playhouse entrance, howled ribald encouragement after them both. It was a common trick of the bawds to draw pursuit from the main road to the stews that debouched from it, in order to market their raddled wares to the undiscriminating, and while thus engaged to give opportunity to the footpads and cutpurses to rob their victims. This one, however, lacked fleetness, and she tripped and fell headlong in the brimming gutter, tattered skirts and petticoats flying to disclose the absence of decent covering beneath. The bereft owner of the hat drew his sword and applied the flat of it vigorously to her bare rump before recovering his muddied property, she shrieking vile abuse the while. I was glad of the diversion because it drew the attention of the Watch who normally posted themselves at the bridge and noted the comings and goings of travelers across the Thames, for these were troubled times and the grip of the ailing Cromwell, for a time relaxed, was now tightening again.

I was to meet Pengelly a mile the other side and half that distance short of the Pied Raven, and I was already an hour late because the Watch at the turnpike at Highgate, to the north of London, had been more vigilant than that here, and I had deemed it prudent to detour to a more distant and discreet entry point. These, too, were Englishmen, I reflected bitterly, even as I was, but now they were greater enemies than any who threatened from across the seas. I sighed; then, as my horse's hooves cleared the planking of the bridge and became muffled on the muddy surface of the road the other

3

side, I felt my spirits rise a little. Perhaps, after the meeting tonight, things would emerge a little clearer. Perhaps, if this man of Pengelly's was not, at best, a vainglorious boaster, at worst, an *agent provocateur* and an instrument of treachery, and if he could produce the letter itself or even a sworn copy of it—but I had had enough of these idle ifs and buts. They had bedeviled me all through the long journey south from Yorkshire and were even now clouding my judgment. Tonight would prove or disprove my doubts and thereby resolve me in my future course. Tonight *must*, because in the dim half-world of politics and intrigue in which I had unwittingly enmeshed myself, I had little time to devote to the affairs of my estates, and soon, in addition to my other cares, would be added those of a financial nature. Tonight I must be fully committed or fully withdrawn.

My horse shied again, and from the shadow of the hedgerow I heard a muffled cough. I reined in, and my hand sought the pistol in my saddle holster, then a low voice said "Barleycorn," and I breathed more easily and answered "Beechmast." A dark figure emerged onto the road and I saw the glimmer of a white face beneath a wide hat as a man looked up at me.

He said, "It would be best to dismount here, my Lord Bemforth, and proceed across the fields on foot. There are some strangers at the Pied Raven whom Master Pengelly views with a certain unease."

"My horse—?" I questioned.

"Will be attended to," he assured me, and I saw other figures move up behind him. I dismounted stiffly because I had been in the saddle constantly since before dawn that day, except for such brief rests for my nag that common humanity demanded. My hand brushed the butt of my saddle pistol again as I dropped to the ground. I drew it from its holster and slipped it under my cloak. This man had the password and the name of Pengelly came easily to his tongue, but I had long reached the frame of mind where I trusted nobody fully.

A hand came out of the darkness and took the bridle.

"Feed him, rub him down, and muffle him against the chill," I directed. "He and I have come far, and hope to go farther."

"That will be done, my Lord," the first man said. "But your dressing valise? You will need that."

"I will not," I said shortly. "I tarry here but two or three hours before moving on." There was naught in my valise except a change of clothes and my simple toilet requisites, because a wise man carried nothing on the highroads that could incriminate him. The man bowed, turned and plunged through the hedgerow, and as I followed him I heard the faint clopping of hooves as my horse was led off in the other direction.

There were three of them in this party—the man who had spoken and who now led, and two others who fell in behind me. I knew a faint uneasiness which did not, as yet, amount to suspicion, but my soldiering in the cause of his murdered Majesty had bred in me a mislike for strangers close on my heels in the dark. I stepped aside and motioned them to precede me, which they did readily enough, and we marched thus across the uneven pastureland, our boots swishing softly over the dew-laden grass and setting up swirls of wraithlike mist.

We walked for what I judged to be half an hour, with our right shoulders pointing at the polestar, which told me that we were moving westward and parallel to the Thames. Twice we closely skirted farmhouses, and each time I heard the barking of dogs and I felt my unease increasing, because this way led to country that I had every reason to know but not like. The Pied Raven was too close to danger for comfort and peace of mind, in all conscience, but this path was one to the lions' den, and may that noble beast forgive me if I miscall him. We were making direct for the manor house of my Lord Carstone.

Almost as if my doubts were transmitting themselves through that chill night air, our guide halted, turned and muttered something to the men ahead of me, then walked back and fell in beside me.

"Your forgiveness, my Lord," he said. "The password and Master Pengelly's name I was perforce to mention back there in order to assure you of my worthiness, but it is not safe to speak too freely near the roads. The hedgerows sprout ears like blackberries in October—"

"Where is Pengelly?" I demanded.

"Taken, my Lord," he answered, and I detected, before all feeling went numb, a tremor in his voice.

"Taken?" I echoed blankly.

"This forenoon," he went on. "By Sir Christopher Jarvis, the High Constable, and lodged in the Tower. It is said that his attendance in the Star Chamber is arranged for tomorrow."

I shivered slightly as an icy hand seemed to clutch at my vitals. Though the Star Chamber had been officially abolished these fifteen years or more, tales were beginning to be whispered again. The rack, the Maiden, the boot and the hot pincers had, it seemed, only been in temporary eclipse, and all trials that had ended at the block on Tower Green had not been public ones. Soft tappings were being heard once more in the still small hours on doors of manor houses and hovels alike, as the Black Riders of Carstone and his jackal Jarvis bore glumly silent men away into the night, leaving the sobbing of women and children behind them—and it was putting a strain upon the loyalty of even such sworn King's men as myself. Did the younger Charles across the sea know what his supporters here were enduring?

I forced my whirling thoughts back to present reality. The man was talking again, but I cut him short.

"Where was he taken?" I asked wearily.

"At the Tavern of the Porter's Knot," he answered, and my heart sank still further. That disreputable alehouse almost in the shadow of the Tower of London had, we had thought, been a safe place of assignment. It had three entrances—one that was open for all the world to see, though the high-stomached would perhaps think twice before entering, and two that were not. It was in the midst of that area which was becoming known by the name of Alsatia, a resort of criminals and prison sweepings. The landlord was a one-legged master's mate who owed Hugh Pengelly a service. Yes, it had been safe, we thought, and I know that Hugh had kept certain papers there.

Once again the man seemed to divine my unspoken thoughts. "They found nothing there, my Lord," he said, "even though they searched from cellar to rooftop."

"Where do we go now?" I demanded.

"To a safe place—a house nearby—"

"Whose house? We are nearing the manor of my Lord Carstone."

"It was always the way of Master Pengelly," he said quickly. "He chose his hiding places in the shadow of the walls of his enemies—"

I nodded slowly. That was true enough. I had known him in his disguise as a coastwise mariner sit and drink in their off-duty hours with the Yeomen Warders of the Tower who used the Porter's Knot as a drinking den, but this seemed to be stretching his theories a little far. Carstone maintained his manor like a garrison, and it was said that he kept a small army of over two hundred men here. The man went on, "We go to the house of Stephen Laidlaw, a minor steward in my Lord Carstone's service—and one who has no cause to love him." And that tallied too, because I knew Laidlaw, an honest enough man, though I was unaware until this moment that Pengelly had had privy dealings with him. But I was still uneasy. This man had said that Pengelly was not due before the Council of the Star Chamber until tomorrow. That meant, with fortune, that he would not be put to the question until some hours later. We had often discussed this, Hugh and I. How long could a reasonably brave and resolute man hold out against the torturers without breaking—and naming names? We had agreed, after much disputation, on four-and-twenty hours. Come what may, if one was captured one would have to muster every inner resource and take what they served in the dim dungeons of the Tower for one full round of the clock. In that time, it was to be hoped, the others could scatter and get under cover—warning yet others in the process. That way, and that way alone, could we hope to keep some remnants of our party intact—to live and reform and fight another day.

But surely, I thought, Carstone, who had once been one of us, would know of this unwritten compact? What if Pengelly had gone straight to the dungeons? What if he was even now a broken and bloody wreck, whimpering out our names? Could one blame him? Not I, for one. There is a point beyond which no quivering flesh and bone and blood can be expected to stand steadfast, no matter how strong the spirit. Religious men, both Catholic and Protestant, we had been told, had certain inner funds of faith and resolution that strengthened them to go further along this ghastly path than others—but we were not particularly devout. We were not martyrs in the service of a Higher Cause. We were ordinary men, perhaps loving freedom a little more than some of our fellows but otherwise no better or different, who wished to topple a clique of canting humbugs and restore our rightful monarch to the throne. Yes—if Pengelly had broken already it was but a matter of hours before all of us were in the net—and there were things I had to do quickly to save what I could from the wreckage.

As I reached this decision we came up against a thick high yew hedge, and our guide skirted it to the left until we came to a gate. As we went through and up a graveled path which led to the dark bulk of a medium-sized house, I saw shadowy figures close in on us, and once again my fingers sought both pistol and sword hilt, but the man in front heeded them not, and we went round to a side door which opened off a stone terrace. He knocked softly—once, twice, thrice—then again more quickly. The door opened before us and we went through into pitch darkness, then, as the door closed once more, I saw a faint chink of light under another door ahead. It opened and I saw Laidlaw on his knees at a fireplace, burning papers. He straightened as I entered, and turned towards me. His face was strained in the dim candlelight.

"My Lord," he said in little above a whisper. "Thank God you have arrived in time. This is a sorry business."

I said, "How much do you know, Laidlaw?"

"Little enough," he answered. "Master Pengelly was seeing his agents at the Porter's Knot when Jarvis and his jackals pounced. All who were in the tavern were held, in order, no doubt, that none should escape to give warning—but we had a standing plan for that—a man who watched from a house opposite whenever Master Pengelly was within, and who received a signal from the landlord through the taproom window. The warning reached me two hours later—as fast as a swift horse could bring it—and I have done certain things, as were my orders."

"Such things as?" I queried.

"I have warned all on the lists of Master Pengelly," he said, "and I have burned such papers here as might compromise the rest—as far as they lay within my knowledge. I have messengers standing by to go out to those on your list if you will let me have it."

Then, and only then, did my unease turn to the stomach-chilling certainty that I had walked into a trap. Master Laidlaw had made his first mistake, because there *were* no lists. That had been a cardinal principle agreed upon amongst us. No names were ever to be committed to paper. Each of us knew only the man immediately above us—and ten others whom we recruited ourselves and who were thus below us. Each man was therefore a captain of ten, and the structure reached upwards and downwards, but never laterally. Under torture, or defection through baser motives, we could only betray our captain and our own ten lieutenants. They, in turn, could betray others, but, if the rule of four-and-twenty hours of courage and fortitude held, this would take time and enable more and more to scatter, hide and, God willing, reform on another pattern later. But the names of our ten lieutenants were never to be communicated to another, however trustworthy we might deem him. In such sorry case as this, one warned one's own ten by word of mouth if it were possible, or by a privy means of our own devising if it were not. In the case of my own ten, who were all lodged in and near York, this was simple. A nosegay of dried herbs had to be hung in the window of one of them—a locksmith in the Shambles. My duty therefore was clear. Having secured what information I could of the fate of my captain, Pengelly, I had now to return to the north with all dispatch and warn them. That, and, until further orders reached me, nothing more. If Laidlaw was one of us he would have known this. These thoughts ran through my whirling brain in less time than it has taken to set them down. I nodded my agreement and hoped that my face did not betray me.

"I have five," I told him.

"Not ten?" he asked quickly, and that told me that he knew something of our structure if not of our procedure.

"I have not yet recruited my number," I answered. "That, as you must know from Master Pengelly, is the purpose of my visit to London—to make my band up to its full strength from disbanded soldiers who served under me in the King's cause."

"Of course," he agreed gravely. "My Lord must forgive me a certain absence of wits. I have been sore pressed these last few hours. The names and lodgings of the five then—for there is little time left."

A modicum of truth in a welter of lies can be more confusing than pure fabrication itself. I looked my surprise. "But surely you know that the names are ones we contrive ourselves and have no bearing on a man's real identity? Lodgings? We are forbidden to communicate them even if we know them. In the case of my own five I know them merely as"—and this was a self-imposed drill prepared for such a contingency as this, so I reeled off the names without hesitation—"Owen, Noah, Foremast, Cog and Spring-flower—two pikemen-ensigns, a one-eyed sailor, a master caliver-maker and a runaway felon from the Medway galleys, branded on the right cheek but the mark hidden by a full black beard. I have to see them all tomorrow forenoon by prearrangement from our last meeting."

"Where?" he asked, even as I got my last words out.

Again I didn't hesitate. "Where else but the Porter's Knot?" I shot at him. "You should know that. You should know also that Springflower is suspect by Master Pengelly, though I am disposed to trust him until his guilt is proved further. He is to have his chance to clear himself tomorrow—or be dealt with by Foremast in the mud below the Tower—as near to Traitors' Gate as prudence will permit—as a warning to the others."

But I was not dealing with a fool. He refused to fall into the trap by pretending to knowledge he did not possess.

"No," he said. "Master Pengelly had told me none of this. You know his wont. He tells nothing that is not a matter of pure necessity. So you are to see them tomorrow? At what hour?"

"They will assemble before noon—as strangers to each other—and will follow me separately and with discretion into an inner room when I arrive. If I am not there they will come again the next day—or again the next. If I do not appear on the third day, then something is amiss, and all will go to ground— The normal procedure in other words," I finished impatiently.

How much of this he was believing I could not tell, but it was clear that he was bedeviled by some doubts and consequently was disposed to play the game out further. He nodded again.

"I see," he said slowly, then smiled faintly and with apology. "But you must be fatigued, my Lord—and I have not offered you refreshment." He looked past me at my erstwhile guide and I turned and followed his glance. The other, seen more clearly, was not such a good choice as Laidlaw, who was every inch the decent, earnest, honest steward striving desperately to carry out the little understood wishes of his fallen captain. The guide was a ferrety-faced ill-visaged gallowsflower, shifty-eyed and besmitten with the pits of the gaol-pox across his tallow-hued face, but withal a powerful man, still wearing his broad brimmed hat and mud-bespattered black riding cloak. Laidlaw said, "Meat, bread and wine for my Lord, Gardle—then see that a bed is prepared for him."

"There is no time for that yet," I fumed angrily. "Get me my horse here—there is gear hidden in the saddlery which I must now destroy before I think of rest and refreshment."

I turned wearily to the burnt paper–bestrewed hearth as if to warm my hands, my eyes flickering sideways just long enough to perceive a faint nod from Laidlaw to Gardle.

"Of course," agreed Laidlaw. "But that will take some little time. My Lord can refresh himself while we await its arrival."

All this was gaining me some much needed leeway and was, I reflected grimly, cutting down, however pitifully, the four-and-twenty hours I might soon be praying and groveling for. I resolved to go yet further along the twisted path of mendacity.

"This, of course, will affect the stuff from Stamford Bridge," I said, and I felt Gardle, who had turned to the door, hesitate and turn back again.

"What stuff is that, my Lord?" Laidlaw inquired innocently.

"God's teeth!" I shouted. "Surely you know that the muskets, pikes, shot and powder—" Then I bit it back and mumbled, "Well if you haven't been told it is best that I say nothing in case you, too, are taken—"

"God forfend," he said fervently. "I fear I would talk early. I am not a brave man. My heart beats strongly for the cause, but I know my limitations—which is why Master Pengelly told me so little—but now, unfortunately, with the exception of yourself and Gardle here—I am the only link with these other stout fellows. A grave charge lies heavily on us all, my Lord."

I yawned mightily and shook my head slowly with a great weariness that was not all feigned. "The horse," I said, "Get me that cursed horse—and do not let me sleep until it arrives. That cypher

remains a millstone round our necks until I have seen it burned."
And this time Laidlaw could not quite conceal his reaction. I felt the
faintest lift of hope. Papers *en clair* they might hunt for themselves,
but with the bait of a cypher they would want me and it together
—and there might yet be the forlornest hope that I could, under
cover of searching in the nag's harness, blast the nearest of them
with my pistol, swing to the saddle and make a dash for it into the
night.

Laidlaw said sternly, "Don't stand there like a 'mazed goose, Gardle. Get my Lord's horse brought with all dispatch—and tell them
in the kitchen to send food and wine."

Gardle went quickly, and as he opened the door I saw that some
of the others were standing without in the hall, which hamstrung any
hope I might have harbored of overcoming Laidlaw in his absence
and making good my escape on foot. I lowered myself stiffly into a
fireside chair, yawned again and lay back, tilting my hat forward
over my eyes and stretching my booted legs to the dull embers.
Laidlaw stood regarding me for a moment or so, then went softly
from the room.

In spite of my tautened nerves, torturing doubts and creeping
fear, nature must have had its way, and, notwithstanding my injunc-
tion to Laidlaw, they let me sleep until food was brought to me
some time later. I fell to hungrily and felt my strength return mo-
mentarily—but then it receded as quickly, and I knew a great hol-
lowness in my vitals as Gardle staggered in with the furnishing of
my horse—saddle, blanket, valise and, worst of all, my empty pistol
holster, which plainly told them of what I had stuck in my belt
beneath my cloak. He dumped the gear on the table and stood back.
Laidlaw said softly "If my Lord pleases—"

With a hunk of broiled beef in one hand and a cob of bread in the
other, I belched and cocked an eye at the saddlery.

"Bring in the martingale and escutcheon," I grunted. The latter
was a sizeable leather pad, brass studded and with my crest embossed
thereon, which rested on the horse's chest and through which the
martingale straps were threaded. Laidlaw motioned impatiently at
Gardle, who turned and went out again. I rose from my chair with
the air of one who looked for a place to throw the discarded gristle
of the meat, and moved casually to the heavily curtained window. I

drew back one of the drapes and saw a low leaded mullion the other side, against the diamond panes of which the rain was now beating furiously. I stuffed the bread in my mouth and reached for the catch, and Laidlaw moved quickly behind me. "My Lord may throw it in the fire," he said—and I saw the small pistol in his hand. I nodded, turned back, threw the gristle in his face, kicked him hard in the belly and again to the side of the head as he went down gasping and spewing wind and rheum, then sweeping the candles from the table, I leapt at the window, taking it bodily with its frame in my headlong flight.

I landed crashing in the mud of a garden bed below, my cloak torn and rent by the broken glass, and the noise of my egress blended with heavy footsteps from within, and confused shouting, then the explosion of a musket over my head which near burst my eardrums. I rolled sideways in the mud, gained my feet and hared blindly away in the pitch darkness, came up against the yew hedge, burst through it and rolled down into a filled brook the other side. Behind me pandemonium was unleashed and I heard howled curses, blows and more shots as they obviously milled round in the darkness, mistaking, I hoped, friend for foe. I crawled out of the brook and ran on—first across a cart track, then a harvested field, into some woods which impeded me sorely, and then eventually on to a highroad, which I crossed hastily and thereafter avoided.

The sky, now heavily clouded, helped me none in my directions, but I eventually came to the banks of a river so big that it could only be the Thames, and I knew, since I was to the south of it, that London must lie away to my right. I blundered along in that direction, falling ever and anon into drainage ditches that were cut at intervals from the fields that breasted the banks, until I was muddied and soaked from head to foot, and savage temper was bidding fair to over-rule both fear and discretion. I cursed aloud my own stupidity at falling so easily into their trap. Why had I accepted so blindly their command to surrender my horse without further proof of their good intent? I should have pistoled the knave when first he challenged me, and spurred on into the night. I thought I had served a hard apprenticeship as a plotter, but I had walked meekly straight into their mesh.

Had Pengelly been taken, I wondered, or, terrible thought, had he defected—like the foul Carstone? Was the band even now broken, or was it only I who had drawn their suspicion? I dismissed the last. They obviously knew something—or how would they know of Pengelly's connection with me—or of our rendezvous at the Pied Raven? Or the passwords? Or of the Porter's Knot? No— something had gone badly amiss—something that stank of treach-ery. I had one chance now—one pathetically slim chance—and that was a ship out of London Pool to Amsterdam, and connection once more with our friends in the Lowlands. To return to York was out of the question. I would be taken long ere I reached there. The warning to my ten worried me not a little, but I comforted myself with the thought, that was more than a hope, that Carstone's men were still in ignorance of their names, else why should Laidlaw have been at such pains to elicit them from me? I permitted myself a wry grin as I pictured their quest for Owen, Noah, Foremast, Cog and Springflower. That much I owed to Pengelly. When inventing names, he had always told me, err on the side of the unusual and outlandish—and have them ready in advance, with minute details of their manners and appearance—

Well—only one thing for it now. I must reach the Pool, and hard by it the shop of Watley, the rascally, but to me—I fervently hoped—reasonably trustworthy old soldier from my Civil War campaigns, who could hide me in his filthy cellar while he procured seaman's clothes for me and approached some Hollander shipmaster who would be willing to augment his cargo profits by a little man-running across the North Sea. Fortunately I carried in a bag beneath my shirt forty golden crowns. What would happen after that I was too dispirited to conjure upon—except that I knew with sickening certainty that my estates would be gleefully escheated forthwith by the Commissioners for Distraint. Still, I reflected sourly, what use would my broad acres be to me without a head upon my shoulders? I was, temporarily at least, my own man—but a bare three-and-twenty, strong and lustily built—with a knowledge of field soldier-ing—had commanded my mixed company of horse and dismounted pikemen from the age of sixteen—was the bearer of a good if now sorely tarnished name—had forty crowns in my pocket—a sword, pistol and *main-gauche* poniard at my side, the wit and skill of their use—and those were always saleable—and there was aways tomorrow.

It was at this point in my deliberations that I came hard up against the fowlers' barge that was drawn up on the muddy bank. The current, here tidal, was strongly on the ebb and flowed therefore in the direction I wished to go. The barge was waterlogged and rotten, and when I searched inside it I found no oars, but at least there were loose deckboards that would serve as such. It was but a small thing, and I made shift to turn it over and so rid it of the water it contained, then I heaved and shoved it through the mud until it floated. I clambered in and paddled clumsily into midstream where I settled shivering in the stern sheets and let the current do the rest.

❖ 2

COLD and exhausted though I was, I must have slept again, because I remember little of that drifting journey downstream except for some anxious moments when I was challenged as I went under the center span of the wooden bridge. A gruff voice hailed me in the darkness but I crouched down under the gunwale and made no response. Then the cursed boat had to foul the piles of the bridge and I heard scurrying footsteps on the planking above as the Watch made for the stairs which led down to the lower staging. I pushed free frantically and was once more abreast the rushing stream when someone cut loose with either a musket or a caliver, and there was a roar and the dark air around me sang with the angry bee noises of the heavy charge. But, as God willed it, they could have had but one piece between them, and by the time they had reloaded it I was once more swallowed up by the darkness of that rain-lashed night, untouched of hide though shaken of nerve.

My next recollection was in the cold light of a miserable dawn as the wretched boat, now nearly awash through her divers leaks, nosed gently into some steps near Blackfriars. Soaked to the skin I climbed painfully out and kicked her back into the current, then turned and climbed the steps to the narrow alley above. I could have wished to have been carried farther, as Watley's chandlery was still a mile or so downriver on the other bank, but beggars being ill choosers, and the sight of a waterlogged boat carrying a scarecrow under London Bridge being one that could not have failed to draw unwelcome attention, I accepted my destination and went in search of some sort of shelter to dry my clothes a little and make much needed repairs to my appearance before venturing further.

At the top of the steps I stumbled over a bundle which stirred and spat curses at me, and peering into the gloom cast by the overhanging buildings which nearly met above the alley, I saw a hideously wrinkled face framed by lank and dirty hair emerging from a tattered heap of rags and straw. As I stepped over the creature, a skinny hand shot forth and grabbed my spur strap. I tried to kick free but the grip persisted.

"A groat for a poor old woman with neither piece nor sup within her belly this two days or more," she whined.

I shook my head, for charity sat ill within me at that moment, but still she clung to my boot, so, since I had no stomach to do the wretched creature real injury, I felt within the placket of my breeches for a small coin, which was a mistake of judgment, for as she heard the clinking she sprang upright and transferred her clutch to my arm. She peered up into my face and cackled shrilly.

"Oho, my bonny buck! A gentleman of substance, is it?—taking the river way to quit the tables?" I realized that she took me for an absconding blade from the secret gambling hells that not even the Puritans had been able to stamp out.

"Just that, mother," I answered. "And with but three groats between me and the debtors' pillory—here, take one of them and let me go—"

But the clink of money to one of her ilk is like the scent of blood to a tiger. Her fingers twisted into the cloth of my torn cloak and her voice rose louder and shriller.

"A groat, is it? A groat for a poor old woman as starves without bite nor sup nor shelter—rolling the gold 'uns through the night —and him with silver spurs and pockets lined"—and immediately there was a rush of padded footsteps from out the stinking entries between the buildings, and a cudgel thwacked down over my be-draggled hat and jounced off my shoulder, and other hands were now tearing at me. I swung free of my cloak and in the split moment that it gave me, drew my sword and got my back to the wall.

There were four of them—footpads and worse—obscene and stinking beasts of the sewers, the old woman their bellwether who summoned them with her cries when fat enough victims passed their lair. A cudgel across the head, a knife across the throat, a quick stripping of the still twitching corpse, and Father Thames received on his broad bosom another of the nameless things he carried each night to the sea. I thrust quickly, twice, and two were down and the others had scurried back to their holes within the twinkle of an eye, but now there were stirrings as other of the refuse came to life beneath bundles of rags, fustian and straw. Verily I had stirred up a nest of vile hornets. I grabbed my cloak and rushed on, the rabble at my heels, emboldened by their very numbers—and like a fool I found myself in a cul-de-sac, but at the bottom of it was an open house door and a woman squatted over the drain outside. She arose hastily and darted inside as she saw our pell-mell approach, but I had reached the door before she had time to close it in my face, so I threw my weight at it, upending her in the process, darted inside and slammed it shut. My questing fingers found the drawbolts, and, as the mob hurled themselves at the stout timber, I managed to shoot them home. The woman glared up at me from the floor.

"I mean you no harm," I shouted above the noise outside. "Let me tarry awhile until these dung wasps have dispersed and I'll pay you well."

She arose then and peered closely at me in the light of a dim tallow dip on the wall. She was middle-aged and unlovely, but withal of a certain buxom strength and I saw that she was more angry than afraid.

"A pretty thing!" she said indignantly. "Rump-ending a woman from her morning prayers. Pay me, will you? Show me the color o't." But then she glanced down and saw instead the color of my sword which I still held unsheathed, and it was becrimsoned half its length. It disturbed her not one whit. She shrugged and said, "An Innsbruck blade. *They* cost more than a bauble—and if you've pinked a brace or two of them out there I'll take your credit at its value. Wait."

She darted up the rickety stairs that led from the narrow hall in which we stood, grabbing as she went a large iron kettle that hung over a blackened fireplace, burning her hand and cursing the while. Outside, the rabble were pounding at the door and bidding fair to crash it in. The woman went to the half-landing above, thrust open the window and poured the boiling contents of the kettle down upon them. Shouts and curses turned to shrieks and howls as this unfamiliar element assailed them from above, and the pounding ceased as they withdrew to a safer distance and contented themselves with hurling paving stones and filth at the house before withdrawing with many a bloodcurdling threat. The woman gave as good as she received in this wordy battle, then closed the window and came back down to me.

"To tarry awhile, is it?" she asked.

I nodded. She turned back to the stairs, motioning for me to follow. At the top there was a passage and from it led many doors into what must have been very small rooms, for it was not of great length. She walked down the passage, listening at some of the doors and tapping at others, and receiving in reply divers muffled protests, until at last satisfied, she kicked one of them open. She beckoned me to approach and then held out her palm and demanded two shillings. I paid her and she spat upon the coins for luck and thrust me through.

The room was the length of a tall man and little over half in width, and the space was taken up entirely by a soiled pallet bed from which a sleepy trollop half rose and cursed us both. The woman answered in some thieves' argot which I did not understand, slammed the door and left us.

I looked down at the girl. She was little more than a child but already the aging marks of the bawd were upon her. She had fair tousled hair, angry blue eyes, and skin which should have been rosy but which now had the pallor upon it of one who saw the sun seldom. She spat at me and cursed vilely again.

"A pretty cull," she snarled. "Five sailors and a Smithfield porter —and now a muddied ploughman. Is a girl to get no sleep? What did you pay the old slut?"

"Two shillings," I told her.

She groaned. "All night—or is it all day?" I realized that the poor soul had no means of telling one from the other, because this foul hole was windowless and was lighted only by a lamphouse, a glass-fronted box which ran the length of the passage from room to room and behind which candles guttered.

"I want naught of you," I said, "except a place to rest awhile." And I fumbled for a silver groat which I threw to her. She made no attempt to pick it up. She just looked at it and laughed harshly.

"And hell's good that will bring me," she said, "with neither purse nor placket to keep it." She threw back the blanket which covered her and I saw she was mother-naked. "We have to give the old devil the extras, or take a beating from her bully if he finds it in a search. Rest, you say? Little of that in this plague pit."

I stood and regarded her, there being scarce room for my booted legs between the bed and the wall. I was near to death with fatigue and my sodden clothes hung heavy upon me and their chill struck clean through to my very bones. There was nothing for it. I dragged them off until I was as naked as she, dropped them into a heap, tucked my pistol and bag of crowns under the ragged straw palliasse, and pushed the girl to the wall.

I have slept in haystacks and betwixt silken coverlets—but never as blissfully as on that strumpet's malodorous but wonderfully warm couch. I awoke once and that was when the door was kicked and the whoremonger demanded a further two shillings as my hire had been expended. I paid and gladly, then went to sleep again.

When next I wakened it was through surfeit of rest. I stretched and yawned mightily. The girl was sitting up beside me with a basin of mixed stew and oaten porridge on her knees. She wiped her mouth on the back of her hand and offered me her spoon civilly enough, and in spite of the fetid air of that cell, which a privy bucket in the corner did naught to allay, I was glad to accept her invitation to both a share of her food and a quartern of small ale. The food, though rough enough, was solid and refreshing and I fell to with a will until I realized I was eating this poor creature's rations. She said, however, that there was enough and to spare, so in short order we cleared the bowl together. I noticed then that my clothes had been hung around the walls of the tiny room in order to give them some chance to dry, and I remarked upon this gratefully. She shrugged and said it was a pity to let good clothes rot and spoil, thereby telling me that it was not in any way due to her kindness, but her sharing of her food with me had touched me, and I tried to draw her into conversation, but she would have none of it.

"What is your name?" I asked her at last.

"Fifth-on-the-right-hand," she answered.

"That is not a name," I protested.

"It suffices," she said drearily. "Ask for me by that if you should want to see me again."

"How came you to this place?" I persisted.

"Mind your own cursed affairs," she told me, and thereafter would answer none of my questions. I gave up after a time, and rose from the bed and started to don my clothes. I had no idea of the hour, but I had had enough and more of this place. I felt under the mattress for my bag of crowns and pistol—but they were not there, nor was my sword upon the floor where I had left it. I turned upon her grimly, but she had been watching me and she reached down under the blanket and hauled up both the money and handgun from some place near her knees.

"I moved them as you slept," she said. "None but a fool places treasure under a whorehouse mattress. The sword I could do nothing about because she had seen it, and she knew you had small money in your breeches."

"I am mightily obliged," I told her. "Why did you do this for me?"

"You have paid four shillings for the use of me for two nights," she answered. "You have not mistreated me except to snore like a bull in my ear, but I am still not obligated to answer your foolish questions. Take your crowns and pistol and be thankful you are alive."

"Do you wish to leave this place?" I asked her.

She answered me with a filthy word, but I persisted until at last she burst forth passionately.

"How can I, you fool?" she spat at me. "I have taken the bond and here I stay until I have earned my quittance—like all the other cattle in this byre."

"Why did you take the bond?"

"What business is that of yours? I mislike questions. They are asked only by fools and the impotent. The others rut upon my carcass, pay their tally and go. Those I understand."

"Do you wish to leave?" I demanded again.

She did not answer, but turned her face to the wall, and I saw her shoulders heave. I was dressed by this time in my shirt, breeches, and boots. I reached over and grasped her by the bare shoulder and pulled her from the bed—then I draped my cloak over her and took her by the wrist.

"Stay close to me," I commanded, and opened the door. She did not answer, but I saw hope fighting with the fear and wonder in her eyes, and she followed me without question.

We went along the passage and down the stairs. At the bottom, the woman of the house was sitting drinking with three gallows-flowers. They rose as one as we came down upon them, but my pistol caused them to tarry. I advanced upon the woman and struck her down with a blow to the head, then kicked the three men into file so that the pistol's charge would deal with all impartially. I said, "My sword and poniard. I shall count three."

They broke into cursing and reviling. I raised the flintwheel of the pistol, blew upon the priming and said "One." Two started to speak sweet reason but the other, the furthest in the file, was of tougher mettle and he started to edge towards the door. I said, "Two," and my finger tightened. The nearest man gibbered and pointed to a corner closet. I motioned the girl to look within, and she returned with my sword, poniard and belt. I pushed her ahead of me to the door. I hesitated for a moment, thinking to send her back to take the clothes and shoes of the unconscious whoremonger, but in that instant the boldest of the three men decided to make a run for it, no doubt to summon help. I pressed the trigger, and since a bell-mouthed horse pistol spreads the charge wide, it was sufficient for all, and we burst through the door, leaving them weltering and kicking in a bloody heap.

I had had no means of judging the full passage of time and I was mightily relieved to find that it was night outside. Dragging the girl behind me, we sped up the cul-de-sac. The thunderous report of the pistol had roused the neighborhood, and doors and windows were opening and heads were emerging. We ran on to the steps at which I had landed, and then along the sea wall that bounded them, then found more steps that led upward. I did not know these parts but I judged we were somewhere between Blackfriars and the Fleet. The girl, clutching the cloak about her naked form, shoeless, no doubt long without exercise, at least of a nature that would assist her running, was in sorry plight, and she was gasping and breathing hard. I stopped when I deemed it prudent, and drew her into the dark angle of two buildings. And then, and only then, did I consider my own plight.

Here was I adrift in London, Cromwell's officers on my track, no doubt with a price upon my head, the block before me, and now cumbered to boot with a naked whore. Had I not been the principal in this sorry farce I would have laughed. As it was, I cursed long, loud and bitterly, at Fate, my folly and myself. The girl regarded me solemnly, peering up into my face through the gloom. I asked her our whereabouts, but she shook her head and shrugged. "It is all Alsatia," she said, "but I have not been abroad since I came here."

"If I gave you two crowns could you fend for yourself?" I asked her.

She said, "Let me stay with you. I can earn five shillings a night —and pick a pocket with the best of them. I would not be a drag at your heels."

"No," I said firmly and fumbled for my pouch. "Take your money and go."

"Where to? The gallows?" she spat at me. "An absconding milliner—naked but with gold in her hand—and a litter of corpses behind her? What chance would I have outside Alsatia?"

"Inside then?" I said.

"To another rutting den? I'll take the river first. Why did you not leave me where I was, you wind-blown braggart? Keep your crowns." She flung away from me and turned back down the steps to the river, and for a moment I knew great relief—then shame overcame me.

"All right then," I called after her. "I will get you some gear wherewith to cover yourself, but after that—"

But she did not heed me. She just walked on down the steps, and at the bottom she threw off my cloak, standing once more mother-naked—a slim, pitifully young and slight figure against the cold mist-enshrouded river, dimly seen in the errant gleam of light that came from an upper window of an overhanging house. Had she glanced once behind her I would have known that she but tried to force my hand by threat, but she didn't. She looked up at the dark sky for a moment, swayed slightly, then fell forward and clove the smooth black surface of the water.

I reached the spot ere the sound of the splash had died, and before the eddy caught her form and whisked it out into the stream I had dropped to my knees and caught her floating hair. I hauled her back onto the slimy steps, she fighting desperately to slip from my grasp. I struck her hard across the face, less from anger than from the need to bring her sharply back to her senses. The blow had its effect. The fight went out of her and she drooped, head down and shoulders asag, and I heard her quiet, hopeless sobbing. I snatched up the cloak and wrapped it roughly about her, cursing her savagely the while, then, my arm around her, I led her back up the steps into the labyrinth of stinking alleys that formed the pestiferous purlieus of this unlovely place. Round us as we walked, I felt rather than saw that the night had a hundred eyes. Muffled forms stirred uneasily under heaps of rags and straw, and every nook and cranny held huddled figures seeking what shelter there might be.

We walked on and up, I with my sword drawn, she sobbing piteously. I had no thought of anything in those first moments but to find some shelter, however inadequate, where we might sit and be out of sight while I racked my muddled brain as to what I was to do next. I had no exact idea of our whereabouts or in which direction we were moving, except that it was away from the river, but soon I saw that we had emerged from the narrow alleys and were in a broad highway, and that the houses the other side were of more seemly appearance than those through which we had been slinking, and that the ground floors of them were formed of shuttered shops. And then above the pointed gables I saw the soaring spire of old St. Paul's against the cloud-racked sky, and I realized that we had come out of the stews into the end of Cheapside. It was dark and deserted at this hour, but I knew that we should have to be careful, because now we were in the district of the merchants, and the City guilds employed their own Watches—strongly armed bands of stout men who gathered in all suspicious characters and impounded them in the bridewell until morning, when they were haled before the Lord

Mayor and his Aldermen—and God help those who in the broad light of day still remained suspect. They had a pretty habit of nailing rogues and vagabonds by one ear to the pillories at Cripplegate, and charging them with such unsolved crimes as stood upon their lists, the wretches remaining held fast until they had confessed through desperation, taking the prospect of anything from the prison hulks of the Medway to the gallows themselves as a more immediate release from their present discomfort.

I bethought me then of Watley and his shop, and since I now knew my position, I turned right and eastwards and we crept along in the shadows.

We met no living creature other than a lean and starving cat that crossed our path, until rounding a corner I saw two smoking torches ahead of us in the middle of the street, and the sound of cursing and hammering came to us. I pushed the girl quickly into an entry and strained my eyes through the darkness.

A heavy coach stood at an ungainly angle, tilted over to one side, and two men strained and heaved at the axletree while a third made shift to replace a rear wheel. Two others held the torches while yet another pounded upon a shop doorway with a noise to wake the dead. As we watched, a window above was opened and a nightcapped head and a hand holding a candle emerged—then a second hand, pointing something that gleamed dully in the dim light.

"I tell you again—be off with you lest I discharge this piece among you," the nightcapped one shouted angrily.

"Of your charity I beg of you," pleaded the pounder. "We have shed a cursed wheel and it is too much for our efforts to get it back again. Give at least the lady shelter while I send for help."

"None but rogues are abroad at this hour," said the other, "and none but fools open for them. Be off I say—or share a capful of leaden slugs between you."

"I am an honest merchant of St. Albans," protested the other, "by name of Master Josiah Culperton of the Guild of Cordwainers—All know me there—"

"Then in the name of God get you hence back there," shouted the irate householder, "and let honest folk sleep."

"We travel to Tilbury for the wedding of our son—" began Master Culperton.

"A formality dispensed with by his father I doubt not. Go!" And the head was withdrawn and the window slammed again. Then I heard the lady's voice raised in peevish plaint, and I saw her, wrapped in a rich traveling cloak, standing in the shadows to one side, and she berated her ill-starred spouse for their misfortunes, and he in turn set about the coachman, two guards and two torch-bearers, and there was discord among them which rose noisily to the heavens, but the wheel remained still sundered from the coach. Master Culperton then kicked the torch-bearers and drove them to help, and they had to lay their flaring links upon the flagstones where they immediately extinguished themselves in the mire. I turned to the girl and whispered to her to creep forward past them and to wait for me some distance in advance. I whipped my cloak from round her and stole up upon the woman, brought the heavy wet folds of it down over her head and shoulders, snatched her up and bore her off into the night. Her screams and struggles were like those of three she-cats in a bag, but they were muffled by the cloak and, thank God, the noise that the would-be wheelwrights were making drowned all but their own.

I ran on with her through the pitchy darkness until a white arm came out and grasped mine and led me down an alley. I halted at last, thankfully, for Mistress Culperton was no easy weight, then between us, the girl requiring no commands, we tugged and pulled at tapes, buttons and fastenings until we had the good dame stripped to her shift and bare feet, I hissing divers threats into her ear the while if she made outcry.

The girl gathered up the garments and ran on. I left my cloak draped over the lady, spun her rapidly three times and then pushed her further down the alley where she sat heavily in the open drain and bewailed dolefully. I hurried after the girl and we halted not until we had put a good half-mile between us and the alley, then, in the shelter of an archway, she donned the stolen clothes—hose, petticoats, dress and cloak. The shoes were large for her, but better than none, and I think our spirits rose from that moment because I heard her laughing softly, and, uneasy though my fortunes lay, I could not forbear to join her.

We walked on towards London Bridge, and now I was greatly worried again because the Watch here, at both sides, was stricter than anywhere else in London, and Watley's shop lay on the other bank. I considered that it would be better to cross in the broad light of day when many people were abroad, than to attempt it at night, but that meant finding a place to lie hid for some hours.

Dawn was breaking coldly when we came once more to the river, and I saw a low tavern opening for the custom of early watermen and the market porters who were now beginning to stir. I thought awhile, then entered—the girl on my heels but keeping to the shadows. I asked an ill-visaged tapster who was emptying slops through the door if he had room to spare—staggering and belching slightly in the manner of an all night roisterer with his doxy looking for a berth to sleep. He regarded me suspiciously, as indeed he had every right to, because my apparel was slashed and muddied, my hair awry and my beard sprouting like an autumn stubble field, but my good sword, poniard and leather giving the lie to all. However, a proffered crown and a lewd wink seemed to reassure him, because he grunted and took a tallow dip from over the chimney piece and led us off through the taproom and up a narrow flight of stairs and finally to a small bedchamber. I told him to bring me a jorum of hot brandy, but he sneered and said that rum, ale and Rhenish wine was all they had to offer. I settled for the first, and when he had brought it, the door having no key, I wedged it shut with a worm-eaten chest of drawers and turned to the girl.

She was sitting on the edge of the bed, smoothing and examining with great satisfaction the texture of her newly acquired apparel. She looked up at me and smiled, and with some shock I realized that clothed she was a different creature. Unclothed and in more salubrious surroundings than those in which we had recently moved, I would have had little to cavil at had I not been so preoccupied with my own affairs, but now, with the greater assurance that decent covering gave her, she was another person entirely. The tired harlot's scowl had lifted from her face, and her brief immersion in the Thames seemed to have imparted to her a freshness that she lacked before. Her blue eyes were no longer angry, and her corn-colored hair, tousled though it was from the salt water, had come to new life. She was, in fact, although I had little enough interest in her at that moment, an exceedingly beautiful girl. For want of something to say, since my regard seemed to be troubling her, I asked again her name.

"Cloda," she told me in a low voice, dropping her eyes and once more smoothing the cloth of the cloak. I wondered somewhat, for it was an outlandish enough name for such an unconsidered scrap of Alsatia flotsam.

"Cloda what?" I asked.

"Cloda St. Bride," she told me.

"From what fine parish register did you cull that?" I scoffed.

"None," she answered me simply. "I was found in an osier basket on the steps of St. Cloda's in the parish of St. Brides, and it is the custom of the poorhouse dames to name foundlings thus. I could be thankful I was not found on the steps of St. Sepulchre in the parish of Newgate." And I felt a churl.

"How came you to that brothel?" I asked.

"By divers means," she said. "The agent came in my eleventh year."

"What agent?"

She looked up at me, and in her eyes was that sort of gentle patience that one saves for the foolish questions of a child.

"The indenture agent," she explained. "The gentleman who takes the wenches from the poorhouse to be bound in service to the good folk of London."

"And he bound you to that?"

"No. I was bonded to a milliner who treated me well enough, but she was taken in debt and my bond was passed to an innkeeper. His wife did a trade in hats and bonnets snatched from the unwary by the bawds, and I spent long hours and learned my trade refurbishing and stitching them so that they could be sold again. She did another trade as well, and men were admitted privily by night to the garret where five of us slept—when we could. But she was taken by the Watch for trading without a license and pilloried—and we wenches were sent to the House of Correction."

"What age were you then?"

"Full grown," she answered. "Twelve years from my foundling date, but the dame once told me I was near six months old at that time. Say twelve and a half."

"And what are you now?"

She pondered for a time. "I spent a year in the House—carrying sea coals from the brigantines in the Pool to the houses of the merchants in Eastcheap. Then the steward at one of them made me tarry one day, bathed me and kept me for a time at the top of the house. But he ill-used me so I ran away over the roofs by night, and was seized by the Watch a week later as I stole a quartern loaf from the stall of a baker." She counted on her fingers. "That would make me thirteen and a half then. The House would not take me back as they said I had become by my waywardness a hissing and a byword. The Aldermen therefore sentenced me to the Medway hulks for two years, but I served only six months before the hulkmaster consigned me by the list."

"What does that mean?" I asked.

Again she looked at me in some pity, as if I should know of such simple things. "When a woman died she was struck from the prisoners' list and the seal and sign of hulkmaster, parson and apothecary entered in the register in certification of such—then the parson read the burial service over her and she was consigned to the ebb tide in a decent shift of sailcloth and with a weight at her feet. It was always done at night because of the unrest it occasioned among the still living. It was a simple matter, if the parson was befuddled—they drank much to ward off the gaol-fever—to drop a weighty bundle into the tide, and keep the real body until the next day—and then record another death, giving to it the name of yet another woman who was then 'consigned to the list'—which means smuggled ashore privily and sold to a bawdy house."

"And that is what happened to you?"

"Yes—as I say, after six months. That would make me fourteen plus the months that I was in that place. I do not know how long that may have been, because it was not possible to tell the passing of day into night. Food came, men came and sometimes the bully took us out in the darkness to walk a little so that we did not lose the use of our legs. It may have been another year—so that would now make me fifteen."

The manner in which she told me all this chilled me to the vitals. She did not pity herself nor did she seem to bear anger against Fate or the vileness of men who had used her so for profit. She recounted it solely to answer my idle question of her age, each dreadful happening being just another milestone in her short span. Then the chill passed, and it was replaced within me by a seething rage that these things could happen in our England that we called in our smugness "Merrie."

But my rage helped me no whit in the solution of my present problem, which primarily was to flee London and was now so sorely complicated by the addition of this girl whom I knew in my heart I could not just abandon if I wanted peace of mind in the future. I stood looking down at her, rubbing the stubble on my chin thoughtfully, and she, knowing only one intent in men, smiled at me shyly and started to divest herself of her clothes. And I do not use the word shyly mistakenly, because there was in this child a shyness that partook of innocence, as if even the foul traffic to which her body had been subjected had left the inner part of her unsoiled. I let her complete the removal of her outer garments, then I motioned her to get between the sheets, and I arranged the coverlets over her. She looked up at me and in her gaze I detected a compound of wonder, puzzlement and perhaps even some little pique that I was thus rejecting her, and I was moved by some strange impulse to bend over her and kiss her on the brow as one would a child, as indeed she was. I said softly, "Sleep, Cloda. I must have time to think of our next move."

The look in her eyes was replaced by one of fear.

"You will not steal away?" she begged.

"I promise," I told her. The fear passed and once again she smiled, sighed contentedly and felt for my hand, and then in an instant was asleep.

 3

SHE was still sleeping some hours later when the sun was fully risen and the street below was abustle. I stood by the window and watched the traffic that crossed London Bridge from the Kentish side—lumbering coaches from the Dover Read, farm carts from the fields and orchards, horsemen, laden porters, shrilly chattering market women, soldiers marching to and from the Tower, sailors from the ships below us in the Pool and occasionally a sedan chair daintily picking its way through the crowd from the substantial merchants' houses in Southwark. They made a motley picture and

one which at any other time would have held my interest, because
crowds have always drawn me. They interested me now, in fact,
though not for any entertainment I drew from them, but rather as a
means to an end. I could see the bridge and the houses that were
built along both sides of its entire span, and the guardhouse and
wicket barrier that controlled this end of it, and it worried me to see
that though the Watch, through necessity, could do little to check
everybody coming with the main stream from the other side,
they scrutinized the few travelers moving south from this bank very
closely—questioning and looking at papers, and in some instances
taking an unfortunate wayfarer or two inside the guardhouse itself
—from which few emerged thereafter. Yes, the checks were on
rigidly and if my description had been circulated I would have little
chance of crossing undetected.

I moved into the corner of the casement and craned my neck and
peered downwards at the river steps that lay immediately beneath
the tavern. It was a place for watermen though none seemed to be
plying for hire and their boats were pulled up onto the slipway, and
when an obvious shipmaster approached a group of them they
shrugged, shook their heads and pointed to a guard post that overlooked them—then a corporal of Yeoman Warders came down and
led the protesting mariner off. So that way was closed also. I cursed
and turned away from the window. The girl had awakened and she
was watching me.

I said, "You have clothes now, and I can give you money, so you
can go your way."

She shook her head and I felt my temper rise. "Damn you," I
swore at her. "What more do you want?"

"Only to stay," she said simply.

"You cannot stay. I have to cross the river—and the checks are on
the bridges and the watermen are being watched. I shall have to
swim tonight—"

"None but a fool would attempt that," she said. "At high water
the current would sweep you away—at low the mud flats would
trap you the other side. Keep me with you and I'll take you across
dry-shod."

"How?" I asked, not believing her but impressed withal by her
calm certainty.

"With the Black Angels," she told me, and I fought down an impulse to box her ears for her impertinence. She scrambled from under the bedclothes and joined me at the window and peered down towards the bridge. "They should be going back by now."

"What in God's name are you talking about?" I growled at her.

"We will have to leave our beautiful clothes—" she began regretfully, then broke off and pointed. "There! There are some of them now."

I followed her outstretched finger and saw naught but the crowd still surging this way past the guardhouse, and a string of grimy scarecrows going in the opposite direction and carrying empty baskets on their heads. "The sea-coal porters," she explained. "They carry it across this way in the mornings from the brigantines the other side, deliver it to the houses and then go back—"

And even as we watched I saw the sense of her suggestion. The scarecrows, mostly women, girls and young boys, but with a few men among them, were shambling through the wicket without so much as a glance from the Watch.

"Mostly from the House of Correction," she told me. "Those are the ones in fetters—but often the numbers have to be made up with paupers from St. Botaud's almshouses."

I glanced down at my own clothes and then at hers. "But how?" I began.

She looked sideways at me slyly. "Do I stay?" she asked. I did strike her this time, but it was a buffet in high good humor.

"You little devil," I said. "All right—you stay—until we reach the other side. After that I make no promies."

"Pay the tally and let us go then," she said, and began hastily to dress. "They all have to be back the other side before noon or the Watch put them into the bridewell and they are beaten and lose their evening meal."

"How do you know all this?" I asked.

"I have been one of them," she laughed ruefully. "Once I took an absconding debtor across under promise of a shilling. The son of a harlot absconded again—but he didn't get far because I told the Watch the other side and he was brought back and nailed by the ear to the stocks. You have nice ears," she finished meaningly.

The taproom was crowded when we went downstairs, and the

assembly was entirely male, but Cloda elbowed her way through them without concern, the strings of her bodice loosened beyond the point of modesty, hair tumbled and awry, and when a sailor thrust a questing hand into her bosom she smiled sweetly, took his heavy gold earring between finger and thumb and twisted, and we made good our exit amid his howls of agony without undue notice —just another strumpet completing her night's work, and her client trying to make himself inconspicuous. Outside we turned left, away from the river. "Follow me, but not too closely," she muttered.

She led me some distance back towards Eastcheap, and then signed to me to wait before diving into a low doorway beside an archway that led through to an open yard where coal and kindling wood was heaped high. She was gone some time, and I was beginning to toy with the idea of taking advantage of her absence and making good my departure, when she reappeared. She jerked her head at me and turned back into the doorway. I followed her along a low passageway that was indescribably filthy with coal dust and worse and which led into a dark kitchen. An old woman, who fitted her surroundings like a sow its sty, sat in the corner picking at a pile of rags, which she sorted into three heaps in some order of merit known only to herself. She dropped her task as I entered, and sidled crablike towards me. She felt the texture of my doublet and the quality of my high riding books, gabbled toothlessly and returned to her corner. Cloda was already undressing again.

Minutes later we were clad in foul rags that stank to high heaven and the very touch of which prickled my skin, and the old woman was clawing handfuls of soot down from the chimney, and I had at least the mordant satisfaction of seeing that my clothes and those of Cloda were accorded the honor of a fourth pile unto themselves. My sword, of course, had to join them, but in spite of the old woman's protests I retained my poniard and pistol, which I managed to bury beneath my tatters together with my money belt. Then she plastered us liberally with the soot from head to foot, taking, it seemed, a vast enjoyment in this part of her task—and finally she presented us with a treble-bushel basket apiece which Cloda showed me how to balance on my head.

We went back to the bridge and I was vastly relieved to see that the only notice we drew from the hurrying crowds was that of fastidious avoidance. At the wicket we joined another party of scarecrows with whom we shuffled across the bridge. One of them, a young woman, tried to engage me in some thieves' argot which I did not understand, but this contingency was immediately covered by Cloda who claimed me as her bully, whatever that may have meant, and threatened to cut from the unsavory person of the other those portions of her anatomy whose absence would have made her even less desirable. With an adroitness that I could not forbear to admire, she then drew the others into the quarrel, which, by the time we had gained the opposite bank, was threatening to break into mayhem, and under this diversion we managed to slip by the bailiffs from both the House of Correction and the almshouses and escape into an alley opposite. She looked up at me and grinned impishly through her black-grimed mask, her teeth even whiter by contrast.

"You keep your ears," she said, "but if another speaks to you in the cant don't stare at her like a boiled fish—just growl, spit and swear. Where now?"

We were within a scant two hundred yards of Watley's shop, and I was glad to reassert my ascendancy by leading the way to it, she following this time meekly on my heels.

He was leaning against the doorpost sunning himself when we approached—a giant of a man with a livid cleft diagonally across his face from hair-roots to chin where a billhook had taken him outside Utrecht some years before. He cocked an eye at us and told us to be off for a pair of gallows-cheating thieving black devils, and being a man of ready wits he kept up his abuse even after I had muttered my name to him, breaking off only to tell us to collect the coal baskets from the yard at the back of his house. Thus furnished with an excuse for entering, we went round to the back entrance where he was waiting to admit us. Without a word he led us through the yard and into a small stable where a large and angular roan mare eyed us viciously as we passed. Watley threw open a door leading to the forage barn and stood aside while we entered, doffing his Flemish cap and bowing civilly, whereupon the ill-conditioned wench, thinking he was making a mock of us, pulled a face and flirted her ragged shirt at him up over her bare behind, and Watley, old soldier notwithstanding, was scandalized.

I said, "Can we rest here awhile, Sergeant?"

"As long as my Lord wishes," he answered promptly, "though London will be a good place to be quit of before long. Four hundred guineas is a lot of money and—"

My urgent signs stopped him at this point, but he had already said more than was discreet, although the girl appeared not to have heard him as she was drinking from a water butt at the end of the barn. I drew him back into the stable and we lowered our voices.

"They've hauled a netful," he told me, "and the criers have been calling those still at large—your honor amongst them. Four hundred guineas on your head—and branding and banishment for any who give you aid and comfort."

"I'll not imperil you then," I said, and I tried to make it sound brave and disdainful because I thought I detected a broad hint in his tone, but he cut me short and assured me stoutly that his house was mine, and the broad of his rump to the treasonable rats who sought to harass me. I took him at his word and told him that I required sailor's garb and his good offices with a Hollander shipmaster to procure me passage to any port in the Lowlands. He pinched his lip then and looked doubtful.

"Sailor's garb is easy enough," he said, "but a ship, English or foreign, presents difficulties—" and he started to list them on his fingers. "Item. Under general proscription such as this, all ships are stopped and searched from keel to topmast off Greenwich. Item. Fugitives involve the shipmaster and every member of his crew in the full penalties—plus escheatment of the ship. Item. Any shipmaster betraying you would qualify for the reward. Item—"

But I stopped him there. It made doleful hearing and I knew it already. Once the criers had been abroad all seaborne rat-runs were stopped. They had been quick. My mistake lay in not crossing to the south bank that first night. Unreasonably I felt my rancor rising once more against the girl. I turned and scowled at the forage barn door. He followed my glance.

"*That* one should be dealt with without delay," he said. "Whores are chancy cattle at the best of times."

"I owe her something," I told him.

"I'll see that it's paid—as soon as it's dark," he assured me. "Then your honor's best course will be on foot to one of the other ports. I know a smuggler in Romney who'd be loyal and helpful—for one guinea more than the reward."

But I shook my head firmly. "Romney maybe," I said, "but the girl must come to no harm. Keep her here until I'm clear. I'll pay you."

"Not for a knapsack of gold crowns," he swore. "Even if she didn't sell you to the criers there's my old woman to be thought of. She'd have the rafters down around my ears."

"You needn't tell her," I suggested, but he looked at me in pity.

"My old woman served her time on the mattresses of Mother Blanche in Amsterdam. She's got a nose like a ferret for one of her own kind. There's nothing so virtuous as an ex-strumpet."

"Then the hell with you for a loud-mouthed, faint-hearted rear-rank runaway," I ground at him. "Get us some clothes if the guts haven't fallen through the trap of your belly, and we'll go our way."

He was reasonable enough in spite of my ill-merited insult. I couldn't blame him. Life was hard enough for a worn-out soldier, and I was asking him to risk all he had built from nothing in a few short years; his home and his modest business. He said, "Listen, my Lord. You were young enough, God knows, but you were a good captain to us fellows in that ill-starred campaign. I'd do a lot for you, but there's limits. I'll get you clothes for sure, and I'll give you a name in Romney—but take my advice and travel alone, by night and in the shadow of the hedgerows. A woman'll hobble you even if she doesn't sell you—"

And then Cloda grasped his arm from behind and spun him round, and a gob of spittle took him fair in the face. He swung full-armed and struck her down onto the dung-littered cobblestones under the very belly of the white-eyed, flatten-eared mare. I dived forward and pulled her clear of the thrashing hooves before she was pounded to a pulp. I had to hold her tight because she was fighting like a vixen to get at Watley again. I threw her onto a bale of hay and sat on her, and a venomous stream of gutter filth came up from under my seat until I stopped the flow with a fistful of straw. She lay quiet then, her eyes darting hate at him from out of her coal-grimed face.

"Perhaps your honor sees what I mean now," said Watley drily.
I said, "Get us some clothes, Sergeant, and a bucket of water and
we'll go."

He hesitated, then shrugged and sighed with some relief, and
went out. I released Cloda.

"Let us go now," she said, "before that half-groat barrack weasel
does that which he was discrediting *me* with, and brings back the
criers and Yeoman Warders."

"He wouldn't do that," I said positively.

"How do you know?" she spat at me. "Your sort are pigeons for
plucking in the hands of such as he. Why didn't you tell me you
wanted to take ship? I could have arranged it without leading you
into this sort of trap."

"How?" I asked for the second time.

"Down river with the randy Dutchmen," she said. "Me working
our passage in the forecastle, you as my bully collecting the shillings
outside."

"Carrying a coal basket across London Bridge is one thing," I told
her. "Facing a trained rummage at Greenwich is another."

"Not if the crew is with you," she assured me. "The sailors get a
flogging from the shipmaster if they are caught carrying women
aboard, so they'll hide you and then put you ashore when they wait
for the tide at Gravesend—or we could make a bargain to be carried
on farther if you've a mind. I know, I tell you—I *know*."

And high-stomached as I thought myself in those early days I
think I would have accepted her offer had I foreseen what lay ahead
of us, but I'd had enough and to spare of harlotry and filth by this
time, and besides I had no wish to take her farther with me than I
could possibly help—although I realized that I could not in decency
leave her here either. I shook my head and sat on the bale, elbow on
knee, chin on fist and stared into the gloom of the stable, my tired
brain cudgeling itself impotently. She seemed to realize that her
arguments were falling upon stony ground so she accepted it with
the philosophy of her kind and settled down at my feet and left me
to my futile thoughts.

No, Romney it would have to be, I decided at length, and since
there was no haven for her here I would have to take her with me,
contriving somehow to slip away and leave her once we were clear

of the city. It seemed scurvy repayment for what she had done for
me, but what else was there for it? Anyhow, what call had she on
me? I had brought her out of that pesthole but I could not be
expected to keep her for the rest of my uncertain days, and where-
ever I left her she could not possibly be in worse plight than when I
had rescued her.

I was no nearer a better solution than this when Watley returned
late in the afternoon with clothes, a bucket of warm water, strips of
linen and a bowl of ashes and fine sand wherewith to cleanse ourselves. For me he had a countryman's rough fustian jerkin and
smallclothes and woolen hose, together with clumsy but serviceable
leather shoes, and for Cloda a gray kersey gown with a cottage-
wife's wimple. He also had bread, meat and a quart of ale, and to do
him justice, he would accept payment for none of it. He had more
news too, and this he imparted to me as I scrubbed at my dirty
carcass. Pengelly, it seemed, had named his ten, of which I was high
on the list, and of that ten, eight had already been taken and they in
turn, poor devils, had yielded to the question, so that nearing a
hundred had been arrested and taken to the Tower, and the process
was still going on. It would be sorry few of us who would escape
the net this time. Much, no doubt, could be discounted, but as
Watley recounted to me the names that the criers were at that
moment calling in the streets of London, I realized with sinking
heart that there still remained more truth than invention in the
doleful tally. Yes—the wolf had struck and the sheep were
scattered—those that were not already in the dungeons. And it was
no salve to my pride to learn that the blood money on my head had
been increased by a further six hundred guineas and that I was now
a very valuable prize indeed.

"I will give you the address of the man in Romney, my Lord,"
Watley told me glumly, "but I had rather you didn't use it, because
he will sell you now for anything above a thousand and one guineas
—and you'll go to the block doubting me."

"I promise I won't do that," I answered, "but at the same time he
would have to trust me for the thousand and one. I can raise funds in
the Lowlands but I'm a man of straw here."

"He and his kind trust nobody," he answered. "Take it then, but
for God's sake don't let slip to him who you are. Say rather that

you're a felon escaping the gallows with a price of twenty golden crowns upon you. I could let you have that. His name is Gil Bardock and you'll find him at the fisherman's hutch close the Fledged Cygnet—a low alehouse on the hard at Romney." He felt inside his doublet and drew out a small leather bag that gave forth a clink. I waved it aside but Cloda's hard little paw shot in between us and grabbed it.

"We'll take it, and thank you kindly, barrack weasel," she said, and gave me a meaning look as I turned angrily upon her.

Watley smiled sourly. "The strumpet is better versed in such things than you, my Lord," he said. "Take it as she says—and tell her to teach you some of her thieves' cant on the journey down. It might help to lend a little credence to your story—but watch her—and take your belt to her occasionally. Her sort understand little else."

She assailed him with filthy language until I had perforce to cuff her, whereupon she turned the rough edge of her tongue upon me, the more so when I took the bag back from her and returned it to Watley.

"I have enough for my immediate needs," I told him, "and we have taken too much from you already."

"You fool!" she shrieked. "Carrying some of his gold he is less likely to sell you to the Watch once we have taken our leave." And then I cuffed her again, harder this time, and she retired into a corner and sat sulking. Watley gave me a meaning look and withdrew. I unbuckled my belt and drew it through my fingers significantly.

"Stay where you are, you wicked creature," I told her grimly. "If I catch you listening at the crack of the door again I'll beat you to within an inch of your life." Then I went out and joined Watley.

"Leave her to me, my Lord," he begged me earnestly. "She can only bring you grief. She'll slit your purse or your throat or both while you sleep, and then sell you, because the price on you is dead or alive. All whores are dangerous; this one the more so because she has a certain low intelligence. She's right, you know. A thousand guineas could be a great temptation to a man such as I—but if I intended to collect it I would not first give you twenty gold crowns which the Watch would certainly appropriate to themselves when they arrested you."

He watched me closely as I struggled on the horns of dilemma. I owed nothing to her really. I had brought her from her foul prison when it would have been easier to have left her there, and she had but squared the account in bringing me safely across the river. I would have to cast her adrift sometime before I took ship abroad. She now had clothes and money— If she were taken with me she would be punished as an associate. It was more logical to send her on her way here in London which she knew, than in the country which she didn't. No, there was no question about it, but . . . but . . .

I said, "If I go my way alone you'll promise me that no harm will come to her at your hands?"

"None whatsoever," he assured me, but he said it too readily. I knew that he would take no chances on her betraying me and involving him through pique, and knowing what the consequences would be to him and his I could not really blame him. But I couldn't do it. I was now inwardly cursing her as a millstone around my neck but I still couldn't condemn her to a slit throat on the mud flats below London Bridge. I sighed and shrugged hopelessly.

"We'll go on together, Sergeant," I said. "My thanks for what you have done. I hope that one day I may be able to make some small repayment—" and I cut short his protests and turned and thrust open the forage barn door.

We saw the open window at the same time. Watley cursed savagely and darted for the door to the yard, drawing a knife from his boot-top as he went, and I followed close upon his heels.

It was pitch dark outside and there were a thousand places in that cluttered yard where she might have been hidden. "Guard the gate," Watley hissed at me, and slipped off into the shadows. The gate stood ajar and as I strained my eyes into the blackness of the lane outside I thought I heard a slight movement ahead of me, but though I explored its length, slipping and stumbling on the wet cobblestones, it availed me nothing. I went back and joined Watley. He was badly frightened.

"She's away to the Watch," he chattered. "I know it—I know it."

"Why should she wait until now?" I demanded impatiently. "She could have betrayed me a dozen times in the last two days."

"Did she know the price on you?" he asked. "Of course she didn't. You didn't yourself until I told you in her presence, fool that

I was." There was something in that, and I felt my stomach turn, but I sought to reassure him.

"I don't think so," I told him with a certainty which I did not feel. "But we can take no chances. If I'm caught I shall deny all knowledge of you. Good-bye old friend—"

I gripped his hand and sped away up the lane.

"Turn left at the top," he whispered hoarsely after me. "Take the Hastings road through Tonbridge—then left again at Robertsbridge and across the marshes—" But I was already on my way and his words died behind me in the darkness.

A chill misty rain was falling, for which, miserable though it was, I felt grateful because it had caused all with wits and a place to shelter to withdraw from the narrow streets. I was unfamiliar with this part of the city but I knew my route lay south from London Bridge, and I soon found myself on the main highway which ran from it to the village of New Cross where I remembered the Hastings road divided from the main one to Canterbury and Dover. Once on it, I set out resolutely at a smart pace until the houses each side of me had thinned and then ceased altogether and I was in the open Kentish countryside which sloped gently here up to the heights of the distant Weald.

But the smart pace did not last long because soon the paved road gave out and I was floundering in the mud that was deep rutted from the heavy coaches and farm carts that used this main artery to the city during the hours of daylight. It was some sixty miles to the coast near Romney, I remembered. Three days, I reflected ruefully, because I could not hope to make more than a bare infantry march per day in this going. I plodded on, trying to ignore a patch on my right heel that was being worn raw by my clumsy shoe, and the icy rivulet that was running down my spine under my sodden doublet, cursing Charles and his selfish companions in exile and all fools such as myself who allowed themselves to be drawn into the murky byways of political intrigue—who wasted their patrimony chasing the will o' the wisp of idealism on behalf of the ungrateful and the treacherous—and generally feeling very sorry for myself.

It was when I was kneeling for the third or fourth time to ease the chafing worsted away from my sore heel that I heard the soft squelching in the mud behind me. There was time to do naught but drop flat and roll backwards against the legs of the follower, my hand flying to my hidden poniard. A scuffling heap fell forward across me, and my head was enveloped in folds of wet cloth, and then I found myself fighting with a wildcat that cursed and swore shrilly. I struggled free and stood up, my poniard now in my right hand—and for a moment I was tempted to use it on her and so divest myself of this unbearable encumbrance once and for all.

"So much for your promise, my bonny flash cull," she spat at me.

"I have promised nothing I have not fulfilled," I said wearily. "Why can't you leave me alone? This way you'll bring death to us both."

"Keeping me with you is your one chance of avoiding death," she flashed. "What do you know of the alleys and byways, my fine Lord Bemforth?"

"How do you know my name?" I asked, startled.

"Because the criers were calling it under our very window while you snored at the tavern—with your description and even what you were wearing when you flew the trap," she answered.

"Then if you know that you must also know that I am a hunted man and that my head is already forfeit if I am caught," I said.

"Small loss if you use it to no better advantage than at present," she retorted.

"Why did you not collect the reward while you had a chance?" I asked.

"I didn't—and I *did* have the chance, as you yourself say. Let that suffice." She wiped wet mud from her face with her sleeve and then took my arm. "Come, let us be going. The Watch patrols these roads for some miles and it will be well for us to be the other side of Eltham before daylight."

And since there seemed naught else for it other than to slit her throat, I shrugged and let her fall into step beside me.

"You'll live to regret this," I growled.

"I'll *live*—that's all that matters," she answered. "So will you if you'll let me help."

✧ 4

DAWN found us well short of Eltham, and the fault was mine and not hers. As a cavalryman and an idle young devil to boot, my feet were tenderer than a nun's virtue, and those cursed shoes were playing the merry devil with them, rubbing them raw in a dozen places, and try as I would my pace got slower and slower. And now people were abroad, afoot and ahorse, and we were being eyed strangely because we were an ill-assorted couple to be traipsing the highroad at this unearthly hour. We halted under the gibbet at Catford crossroads and I swear that the three felons who hung upon it in tar and chains looked not one whit more miserable than I felt on that bleak November morning, and the smudged handbill that was pinned to the foot of it, calling on all loyal and God-fearing subjects of the Commonwealth for their assistance in apprehending a list of twenty traitors with my name at the head of it, did nothing to raise my spirits. That proved that the hue and cry had reached this far at least, and I knew that it would be rash to risk calling at villages, farmhouses or hedge-taverns for rest and refreshment. But at the same time we had to get under cover, so we settled at last on a haystack some distance off the road, burrowing deep into it and huddling close together for warmth. And there we stayed throughout that livelong dragging day until darkness fell again and I deemed it safe to go on.

My feet were still giving trouble, but Cloda ripped off strips of her petticoat, and together we bound the worst of the raw patches, which eased them somewhat. But we were famished now and I realized that we would have to find food before long if we were to keep up anything like pace, so when we came to a mean and solitary tavern squatting back in the hedge, I told the girl to wait while I explored its possibilities. I fumbled under my doublet and produced the smallest coin I had, which unfortunately was a gold crown.

"What will you do?" she asked. "Just go in like a marquis and call for the best the house can offer?"

"Mind your own cursed business," I told her savagely.

"I am," she answered coolly. "I, also, am hungry. Put away your golden piece, you fool. A scarecrow like you with jingle such as this could only be a footpad. If you have one crown you are like to have another, and would therefore be worth the rolling for it if there are men in there. Even if you hadn't any more, a rogue or cutpurse is worth three gold crowns if delivered to the parish constable, so you would still be bonneted. Leave it to me."

"What will *you* do?" I asked.

"Get food," she snapped. "I've traveled this road before—or one like it." And before I could stop her she had slipped away.

I waited some minutes and then saw her looming up again through the shadows, and she was empty-handed. "Not that one," she said. "Just the landlord and his vinegary-faced old bitch of a wife—and a bell-mouthed blunderbuss on hooks over the chimney piece." So we trudged on and she reconnoitered the next two taverns, rejecting both for reasons of a similar nature, and I was fast losing what little remnants of temper I had left when we came to the fourth inn—bigger this time and on the outskirts of a village. It was one that I would have passed by because a coach and several farm carts stood outside, and an ostler was leading a steaming horse up and down while its rider refreshed himself within. But it seemed to hold no terrors for Cloda. "Walk on through the village," she muttered to me, "and wait for me at the first milestone the other side."

I was past arguing by this time, and truth to tell this seemed as if it might be a heaven-sent opportunity of getting rid of her, so I nodded my agreement. "You'd better take some money," I began, but she was off towards the inn before I could give her any.

I walked on through the deserted village street and I did not stop at the first milestone, nor the next, but I heard hurrying footsteps behind me before I had gained the third, and I was in the act of slinking into the hedgerow when she came up with me, panting and breathless—and this time she had half a quartern loaf and a heel of cheese. She upbraided me for not waiting where she had told me and in defense I mumbled something about her being a long time.

"From handing over his horse to stealing this from the kitchen, laying me in the stable and then seeing me on my way again, a scant five minutes," she said. "He was an ostler, not a cockerel."

Outraged pride welled up within me and fought against my hunger, but it was an unequal contest. We sat in the ditch at the side of the road and ate the wages of sin to the last crumb.

We trudged on again through that night and sought shelter next morning in a hayloft, setting out once more when darkness fell. Cloda prepared to earn our supper in Tonbridge but this time I forbade her. She railed at me. "What does it matter, you fool?" she said. "So much water past the mill, nothing more."

I declined even to discuss it, loftily, so then she mocked and ridiculed me until I lost my temper and sent her reeling with a cuff to her ear. But far from quieting the baggage, this only made matters worse, because she then seemed to assume that I was jealous, which put her in high good humor. She clung to my arm and teased me until I was near to heeding Watley's advice and taking my belt to her. We were now in the center of Tonbridge, and it being a market town of some substance, there were people about and we attracted no little unwelcome attention—two mud-stained figures in soaked and tattered clothing, one striding moodily and silently, the other capering like a mad thing around him—and in the end the inevitable happened and we were stopped by the town Watch.

There were four of them, the parish constable and his three runners—large and stolid men in leathers and half-armor, armed with halberds, short-swords and an air of authority that brooked no nonsense. I felt the hair at the nape of my neck prickle. The constable asked me my name, whence I came and where I was going, and like a fool I stood there stammering because Pengelly's training deserted me just when I most needed it. But the girl's quick wits came immediately to my aid. She dug me in the ribs and shouted, "If there was less ale in you there'd be more room for civility. Answer the gentleman." Then she turned to them apologetically and said, "A poor tinker and his woman, kind sirs. We mean no harm."

"Name and where from?" demanded the constable again, impatiently, and because they happened to be the two uppermost in my mind I said quickly, "Gil Bardock—Robertsbridge," and could have kicked myself thereafter.

But they seemed grudgingly to accept it. They eyed us without favor, the constable rubbing his chin in deep consideration as if weighing the duty of arresting us as idle vagabonds against the trouble of conveying us to the town bridewell, as has always been the way of officers of the peace the world over. Cloda smiled timidly at them, then sniffed and wiped her eyes on her muddy sleeve pathetically, and that seemed to tip the scales, because the constable told us gruffly to be gone and not come this way again as Tonbridge was a respectable town that did not welcome the vicious and the idle. She bowed and scraped and called down blessings on them and took my arm and pulled me on our way, but I could feel their eyes on our backs for some time even after the darkness had swallowed us.

And the wretched girl began once more to give herself airs and graces because of her timely rescue of us from my tongue-tied predicament.

"See?" she taunted me. "What would you have done without me then? I handled those bully-boys as to the manner born—with you standing there looking haughty like a marquis insulted by his underlings. If I hadn't wept and made them feel strong and of importance at just the right minute, you'd even now be feeling the weight of their staffs across your hinderparts in the parish lock-up."

"Be silent, woman!" I commanded angrily.

"And then they'd have found your money—and they'd have taken you for a cutpurse—and these chawbacon justices sentence to the gibbet even quicker than they do in London," she went on without heeding me. "And in the matter of food—"

"Have done with that," I said, really stung on the raw, and she laughed uproariously.

"Go on your way," she said. "But this time wait at the *first* milestone as I told you."

I grabbed her arm. "Listen," I ground out at her. "Go and hawk your wares if you wish. That is your affair, not mine—but don't expect me to be waiting at the first or any other milestone."

"But we must eat," she protested.

"Granted," I answered. "But this time *I* shall procure the food." She pretended lewdly to misunderstand me and told me that her marketable value would be higher than mine even in Tonbridge, and she shrieked with sheer delight when she saw that she had reduced me to speechless wrath and indignation.

"Go," she said, gasping. "You'll be the death of me. I will try and beat even last night's time."

But I would have none of it and she realized that I really meant it. "What does it matter?" she asked scornfully. "A business transaction—over in a moment and forgotten."

"Your affair," I repeated. "But I have not yet descended to living off a woman. I shall *buy* food."

She railed at me and called me a canting prig, but I heeded her not and when we came to an inn on the farther edge of the town I strode haughtily to the front door, she clinging to my arm, now badly frightened.

"No—no—" she begged. "Not here—if you must, let us go on to a smaller tavern—and one outside the town where we can escape across the fields if aught goes wrong. I know these things—I *know*, I tell you!"

But in I strode, purblind fool that I was, to find myself in a taproom full of yokels who looked up from their ale pots and stared at me. And to cover my confusion I stared back at them arrogantly, which was not the right thing to do, but the truth of the matter was that at that time I had very little experience of things and people outside my own immediate circle. On my estates in my father's time, and certainly in my own, none questioned my authority and ascendancy. In the army it had been the same. In the murky world of secret politics it had not differed. I had my place in the scheme of things—a place that was mine by right of birth. Now, for the first time, I was stripped of all inherited privilege and I felt myself naked and inadequate and I reacted accordingly. Too loudly I ordered ale and bread and meat from the landlord, conscious, even as I spoke, that my voice and accent were not of those parts—and then, to cover up the awkward staring silence that followed, I made the mistake of mumbling to the landlord half-apologetically and asking once again more civilly for refreshment. But Cloda was right there at my elbow, ready to cover my gaucheness again. In the twinkling of an eye she had pulled her skirts up above her knees and she had gone into a rude but lively dance, accompanying her steps with as bawdy a song as I ever wish to hear, which pleased the company mightily, and within minutes ale pots were pounding out the time on the rough wooden trestles and I heard the landlord mutter with resignation, and ale, bread, meat and cheese were forthcoming. I fumbled for the wherewithal to pay for it, but before I could reach my money she had grabbed me by the arms and had whirled me into her obscene dance.

"No money, fool," she hissed under cover of the din. "We sing for our supper." And she broke into another song about the idle apprentice and his master's wife which would have brought a blush to the face of a brass monkey. I knew this one because I had often heard the troops singing it on the march, so I joined in, and that went down with the company even better than the first. And so we ate and quaffed and clowned and sang to the great content of all present, and I remember wondering through a haze of ale how a wench who had lived the life of this one could remain withal a creature of such beauty, for now that I could observe her under full light, that was what she was. Her golden hair flung wild and lustrous as she whirled in her dance, and there was a color to her cheeks that was brought to full flush by two days in the fresh air and rain, and her eyes sparkled wickedly and her lips framed her white teeth in a generous scarlet. Yes, she was a beauty . . . a beauty with all the poignancy of a blossom that has been trampled in the mud and slime but which has still retained the delicate strength and resilience to turn its face to the sun and rise again when opportunity presents—a piece of porcelain that has been fouled by greedy, grubby fingers but needs only the wipe of a damp cloth to bring it back to its pristine purity.

I was a little drunk by this time, and accordingly sentimental. I think I had even reached the stage of daydreaming. When sanity returned to this realm of ours and I could go back to my estates I would take her with me and hand her over to my Aunt Clarissa, who would teach her the domestic virtues—and eventually she would marry some upright, stalwart young yeoman, and this life would be behind her forever.

I could see myself as the kindly lord of the manor visiting her trim neat farm, she at her spinning wheel with the patter of tiny feet around her, and in her eye all the gentle gratitude in the world for what I had done for her—

It was her scream that brought me back to the present. A young blood had entered, in brighter garb than would have been deemed prudent nearer Puritan London. He stood just inside the door, swaying gently and smiling at her, one hand caressing his trimly curled moustache. He was evidently known because the landlord came forward obsequiously and several of the rustic company had got to their feet and were bobbing and knuckling their forelocks. He was a youth of single purpose—a purpose that had no doubt seldom been crossed, because he stepped forward and caught her by the wrist, spun her round and threw her over his shoulder, turned and made for the door again. The company, though robbed of its entertainer, howled its indulgent and sycophantic approval—and she, shameless baggage, instead of scratching his lascivious eyes out, merely snatched off his gorgeous hat and planked it on her tousled curls and winked at them all, and I realized that her scream was one of only mock terror. She knew what was going to happen and it worried her not one whit.

My gentle idyll dissolved into a mist of red. I lumbered to my feet and made after them, and she, seeing me, signaled frantically to ignore them, but I was beyond sweet reason or discretion. I grabbed him by the arm and spun him around. He gawped at me in amazement and then merely grinned again.

"Ah, are you her bully, my honest fellow?" he inquired, and he felt within his pouch and flicked me a small silver piece. I pulled Cloda from his shoulder with one hand and planted the other violently on the end of his nose. It squelched like a strawberry and he staggered back, hit the wall and slid down. For a second there was a horrified silence behind me. I seized Cloda by the wrist and shot through the door and out into the darkness—and then pandemonium broke loose, but as often happens in these cases, several of them tried to get through the door onto my heels at one time, and the ensuing jam gave us the few seconds we required to gain the outer darkness. We crashed through the hedge the other side of the road and crossed a stubble field in a blind run, and then we were in a thick wood. I dived for a patch of dense undergrowth and pulled her in with me. We lay panting for a moment or so and the pack thundered past us in full cry, and when I deemed it prudent we emerged and moved to a flank—and kept moving until we had put a good two miles or so between us and that ill-starred inn.

She was furious. "You fool!" she shouted. "Is that the way you carry your ale? What caused you to do such an idiotic thing?"

But I was sober again now and was not disposed to discuss it further.

"A pouch full of gold," she grumbled, "and as ready for the plucking as a ripe plum."

I told her savagely to shut her mouth, and because my cursed feet were bothering me after the run in that heavy mud, I led off to a haystack and sulkily burrowed into it. She followed me and stood behind me still railing.

"Was it the gold that worried you?" she demanded. "I'd have handed it to you afterwards."

Something snapped within my rage-fogged brain. I straightened and hit her once more—hit her much harder than I intended— a brutal blow that struck her to the ground. On the previous occasions they had been mere cuffs such as one would give a naughty child. If she had reviled me or even uttered a cry I do not think I would have felt the slightest pang of remorse—not then certainly—but she did neither. She lay on the wet ground and I saw her white face staring up at me through the darkness and I felt the most brutal of churls. I stooped and raised her, and then I am not certain what happened except that she was in my arms and we were buried deep in that fragrant hay, and for the first time I realized that she was two people in the one body, if I make myself clear—the little harlot I had lain with naked but had not wished to touch—and this strange girl, Cloda the gay, the brave, the beautiful. The analogy of the blossom in the mud came back to me as she really gave herself, probably for the first time, and all memory of the squalor that had touched the other Cloda was, for that hour at least, blotted out.

 5

But I cursed myself for it thereafter. All hope of leaving her, except by the meanest stealth, was now shattered. In vain I tried to explain my position to her as we walked on through the night. If

I were taken by enemies in England I was a dead man, and any proved associates of mine would be attainted also. Then I must not be taken, she told me simply. That would only be a matter of time if I stayed here. Spies were everywhere. Then *we* must not stay here —wasn't that why *we* were walking to Romney?—to take ship for foreign parts? Exactly, but that was where the rub lay. Once in those foreign parts I would have to take up my trade for a livelihood—and my only trade was that of soldier. All the easier, she said. There was always a place for a woman behind an army and there would alway be a warm corner for me when the fighting was over. She could cook, wash and mend—*and* earn her living in my absence. She would never be a drag, and she asked nothing of me—except to stay with me.

And thus it went on throughout the livelong night until the warmth that had been engendered by that brief interlude was dissipated, and once again I felt naught for the baggage but a resentment that she should thus be proving a millstone about my neck. So, when dawn came upon us near the village of Robertsbridge, my mind was steeled for what I felt I must do, however scurvy it might seem, in the girl's own interest as well as my own. I finally shrugged and pretended reluctantly to accept the inevitable, and I told her it was upon her own head and not to blame me for aught that might befall us in the future. The silly creature was overjoyed and she flung her arms about my neck and swore I would never have cause to regret my decision.

We found yet another barn and laid low through the day once more, but when darkness fell again I pleaded that my feet were now in worse state than ever and I groaned dismally when I tried to stand upon them. She said that there was naught for it but to stay there for a time and that she would go on into the village for food. I pretended to argue fiercely against this but she would not listen to me, and eventually she set out through the darkness. I gave her some time, then wrapping twenty of my golden crowns in a piece of rag torn from my shirt, I left them upon an upturned bucket and stole out. It would be idle to pretend that I felt aught but a cur at what I was doing, but for the life of me I could see no alternative.

I judged that she would try to follow me to Romney once she discovered my duplicity, so I abandoned all idea of going there and decided to retrace my footsteps back towards Tonbridge and from thence to one of the Medway towns where I would try to take passage with a Dutchman, since the Lowland ships used these ports as frequently as they did those of the Cinque, so once on the road I put my best foot foremost and I did not pause until I had come to the crossroads at Flimwell. I remembered passing a small tavern here the night before—just a hedge alehouse—and there had been a gypsy encampment nearby and some charcoal burners' huts, and it was, in short, the sort of place a ragamuffin such as I could use without arousing undue curiosity.

Late as it was there was a chink of light showing from one of the front windows, and I went forward thankfully, raised the latch and went in boldly.

I saw him the second I entered and the recognition was mutual, because he dropped the pot of ale he was holding, shouted and dashed forward, drawing his sword. I spun round and made for the door again, but it was too late. There were others there also and they fell upon me tooth and nail, and somebody fetched me an almighty buffet across the head with a wooden stool.

I lay on the rush-strewn floor and looked up at the ring of faces that surrounded me, and took no comfort from them because besides the young blade whose nose I had punched the night before, there was also the parish constable and his runners. Boots crashed into my ribs and then I was hauled to my feet and slammed back against the wall. The young coxcomb sat on a table, hand on hip, regarding me with a malicious grin.

"Our thanks to you for not taking your carcass out of our parish, my bonny bucko," he said. "It will make a pretty garnishing for our stocks. Where's the strumpet?"

I made no reply. The constable smote me on the back and said, "Answer Sir Robert when he addresses you, knave."

I whined something about her going off with a soldier to Chatham and I was inwardly praying that they would not search me because the twenty crowns I still had upon me, not to mention the costly Toledo poniard and Flemish handgun, were sufficient to hang me as a cutpurse unless I could account satisfactorily for them. But my prayers were not answered. The runners patted me all over and the arms were found forthwith, and then, their faces turning even grimmer, they stripped me to the buff and discovered my moneybelt, which was of the finest Moroccan leather with a clasp of gold, and altogether a most unlikely piece of harness for such an unsavory gallowsflower as I appeared then.

They exchanged looks. Sir Robert counted the gold and sat on the table edge weighing the belt in the heft of his palm, regarding me closely.

"Garnish our stocks, did I say?" he said quietly. "You can amend that to our gibbet, my friend. Have you aught to say about this?"

"Naught, that you'd believe," I told him, my heart sinking—for never was a man in worse predicament. If I disclosed my real identity it would mean a quick passage to the Tower and the block—if I kept my mouth closed I had no doubts upon my fate either; a speedy trial before the local justices and a noose at the end of it. I found myself speculating upon the melancholy alternatives. The former would be the more honorable, no doubt, but that is all it had to commend it. I would, I was certain, be put to the question before the Council first—and who knows under torment what I might be driven to disclose—and what others I might thereby involve? No—better to die as a nameless felon and at least have the sour satisfaction of the trouble I'd be causing them in their continued search for my Lord Bemforth. As I reached this conclusion I sank to my knees under a shower of blows from the constable and his minions, and I realized that young Sir Robert was speaking to me and that I had not answered.

"Your name, varlet?" he yelled at me. "Or do you crave a flogging before hanging for being mute of malice?"

I didn't, so I quickly supplied the one I had given before and told them I was called Gil Bardock.

"Take him to the bridewell," Sir Robert directed, "and bring him before the Bench tomorrow."

They dragged me out and somebody produced a sorry nag from the tavern stable, and I was mounted on a wooden packsaddle with my hands tied behind me and a rope running from one ankle to the other under the horse's belly, then the Watch led out their own horses and we set off back to Tonbridge at a fast trot, I, stirrupless, bouncing like a pea upon a drum and cursing my fate and my own rank stupidity.

The bridewell was a low stone building on the edge of the market place in the center of the town, where a bridge carried the highroad over a small canal that debouched into the headwaters of the Medway itself. There were the normal instruments of rustic justice set up outside it—stocks, a pillory and a ducking-stool on the end of a long pole, while a tall gibbet reared its grisly height from the bank nearby. They pulled me from the horse, and the constable unlocked a heavy iron-studded door, and I was unceremoniously kicked through it, falling forward down half a dozen steps in the darkness to land in a heap on a bundle that wriggled and grunted. The door slammed to behind me.

I sat up and strained my eyes in the pitchy black, and an aggrieved voice cursed me for a clumsy ox. I gave as good as I got but my heart was not in it, so I rolled over in the foul and evil-smelling straw wherewith the floor was strewn, as far from my fellow prisoner as I could get, and lay under a crushing weight of misery through the rest of the night until the gray dawn crept through the barred window above us.

The other man was a hulking young countryman who told me he was awaiting trial before the justices for poaching game on the estates of one Sir Robert Manforth, and for want of something to take my thoughts off my own immediate plight I asked who that might be. He cursed and spat.

"A poxy young churl who has recently inherited from his father," he said. "Lord of the Manforth manor, what's left of it."

"Young, moustached, and dressed like a French whoremonger?" I asked.

"That's him," he nodded, and then stared at me and chuckled. "Him as whose nose you swiped for him two nights ago. I was there," he went on, "and was took by the gamekeepers two hours later with a brace of fat partridges in my pouch."

The nose-swiping at least secured my standing with the country-man who was civil enough to remove the ropes from my wrists. He told me his name was Jem Groombridge and that he was a black-smith's striker when he was not poaching. He told me many other things, among them the fact that we would not be going before the justices that day as it was market day.

"Not as it matters," he said morosely. "It's all settled before you goes up. What've *you* been lagged for?"

"Nothing," I lied, "other than Sir Robert's nose."

"That'll do to be going on with," he told me. "Raising hands against the gentry is serious. That should gain you the next two Lady Days on the hulks, that should."

They brought us no food or water all that day, although we did not lack for either as Jem, being a local man and one of some popularity, spent his time clinging to the bars of our overhead window which opened into the market place at ground level, calling to friends of his and enlisting their sympathy in practical form, and we were showered with bread, cheese, cold bacon and pasties. This gave me an idea and I suggested to him that he should ask one of the more trustworthy to bring us a stout file wherewith to cut our way through the bars that night, but he would have none of it.

"What? Wander the roads a masterless man for the rest of my days? Me that can earn six sovereigns a year at my trade in this very town?" he demanded, scandalized.

"Small use your trade will be to you on the hulks," I retorted. But he shook his head knowingly.

"Not me," he assured me. "That young cockerel hasn't a feather to fly with. The old man left him little enough, and he's seen that little off long since, what with his wenching and quaffing round the inns and stews of these parts. Randiest young stoat in Kent he is, and up above the buckle of his hat in debt. He'll bond me with the justices, he will."

"What's that?" I asked him.

He looked at me with incredulous pity. "How long have you been legging it on the highways?" he asked. "Don't you know what bonding is? He'll take me on bail to be of good behavior for two years, me being answerable to him for that time—then he'll hire my labor out to any who needs it and pocket my wages."

"That's slavery," I said indignantly.

"That's as may be," he answered, shrugging. "I'd liefer do that than go to the hulks to be branded. So would any other man of sense. Ask any of the two dozen he's got on the same lay."

"You mean he makes a practice of it?"

"That and other little ploys," he answered. "He'll list a man in the trainbands, send him for a soldier or before the mast as a sailor —or a wench to the joy-houses in Chatham—all according to how the market is crying at the time. Him and the Watch is in it together."

I began to see a ray of hope for myself and it must have shown in my face, because he shook his head. "You'd be worth naught to him," he said. "Only tradesmen."

"But I've soldiered," I told him.

"So has many another man—for King or Parliament. There's disbanded soldiers by the score wandering the countryside at this very moment, cutting purses and throats. That's the quickest road to the noose, that is."

"And I've sailed the seas," I said.

"Keep that to yourself too," he advised. "English ships is rotting along the whole length of the Medway—and there's as many sailors on the lag as soldiers. Only the Dutchmen are prospering at present. Where have you been, cull, that you don't know this?"

But I did know it. He was, in his crude unlettered way, only putting into words what had been happening right from the death of Elizabeth. Each ruler in turn had been equally to blame: the dull James, the saintly Charles, and now the pig-headed Cromwell. Yes, the ships rotted, and the common men of England were being exploited like cattle, and hunger stalked through the land—and we who tried to bring back a King who might conceivably change these things were being hunted down and butchered.

I turned in sickness to the barred window and clung there looking out in the gathering darkness.

And we had been so close to it, I thought bitterly. The letter that had come into the possession of Pengelly—from the French Ambassador, pledging Louis's support when the time came. Copied and printed in broadsheets and spread the length and breadth of the country it might have heartened the people—but somebody had sold us, and now we were just plotters either trying to make for the rat-runs as I had been doing, or whimpering each others' names under the torturers' pincers in the dungeons of the Tower. I felt the black bile come up into my throat. I dropped from the window and slunk into a far corner, and then I think I must have slept.

It was midnight when they came for us because I remember hearing the nearby church clock striking the hour. The door thudded back softly and I saw a shadowy group of men file in, one of them carrying a darkened horn lantern. I sat up and recognized the parish constable. He came towards me and stirred me with his foot, and from the far corner I heard the sleepy protests of Jem as he received the same treatment. I wondered wretchedly if they had decided to dispense with the mockery of a trial and whether I, at least, was bound for the short walk to the nearby gibbet. Knowing that it was futile, I struck out at the men who clustered round me but I was beaten to my knees and then to my face, and booted feet kept me pinned down while my hands were bound tightly behind me. I cursed and reviled them until I was gagged with a fistful of the filthy bedding straw and a strip of rag, then I was hauled to my feet and a cloak was thrown over my head and the sudden cessation of Jem's frightened bellowing told me that the same had happened to him.

Shoved forward by the men, I went up the steps into the night air and I felt the slippery cobblestones of the market place under my feet as they urged me on towards the spot where I judged the gibbet to be. But then there were more steps, down this time, and I was thrust forward to fall with a hollow thud into a boat. A hand gently felt for the shape of my head under the cloak, then the darkness was split by a searing sheet of brilliant orange flame, or so it seemed, and I remembered no more until I came to muzzily to find myself lying on the bottom boards in a couple of inches of icy water, and there was a rhythmic clatter, creak and thump of oars above me and the musical passage of water past the planking against my ear.

How long we had been rowing I have no means of telling, but it went on for an unconscionable time after I regained my senses. Swathed and blinded as I was by the folds of the cloak it seemed to me to be hours before we eventually brought up against what I rightly judged to be the side of a ship, and I heard a soft hail from far above us. A rope smacked down over us and hands fumbled about me and I felt it being tied under my arms, then the cloak was whisked free and I was plucked from the bottom of the boat like a sack of chaff and borne swiftly aloft to the noise of a creaking block. Above me I caught a glimpse of yards and rigging black against the night sky, and far in the distance a solitary light twinkled on the shore. I was swung inboard and dumped in a heap on the deck, and as I started to scramble to my feet a boot kicked me flat down again, and I had wit enough to stay quiet thereafter until another similar bundle to myself was dumped down beside me. Low voices conversed over the side but try as I would I could not hear what they were saying, but then the thump of oars came to me again and receded as the boat pushed off and rowed away. More hands hauled us both to our feet and we were pushed across the dark deck and dropped through a hatch, I first and the other bundle on top of me, and the fall was one of many feet which knocked the breath from my carcass. I had one last sight of a square of night sky far above me before the hatch cover was bumped back into place, and then there was more darkness, as dense as that under the cloak. Beside me I felt the other bundle stirring. I chewed at the foul straw in my mouth and managed to spit some of it out past the rag until at last I was able to speak.

I said, "Jem?" but received only a gabbled mumble in return until he also managed to clear his mouth a little, and then he moaned forlornly, "But I was willing to be bound by the justices to that whore's son. Why send me to the hulks?"

But that was a question I could not answer. All I was concerned with then was getting the ropes on my wrists free because they had been tied so cruelly tight that my arms were paralyzed in an agonizing numbness. I rolled and twisted until my back was towards him and told him to do what he could to loosen them, but try as he would with his teeth, it was hopeless. Then I turned again and tried to loosen his, but with the same lack of success.

Above us feet were pounding the deck, then we heard the creaking of a windlass and a wet and soggy rope snaked down over us and I realized that we were like to be buried under the incoming anchor cable as it came up overside and down through the hawsehole. I warned Jem and we struggled to our feet and did our best to keep clear of it. Around us there was a frightened shrill squeaking and I thought I saw the pinpoints of tiny eyes as rats scurried to and fro. Then finally the creaking ceased and no more rope came down, but the pounding of feet continued overhead, and the same passage of water past planking came to me as that I had heard previously, only greatly magnified.

"It's not a hulk we're on, my friend," I said to Jem grimly. "This is a ship—and we're under way."

"But why? Why?" he moaned. "I'd a been bound—I'd a given no trouble—and there's me woman about to bear a child. Why? Why?"

And he kept up his plaint until I told him roughly to shut his mouth. I was standing by this time, leaning against the rib of the ship and I could feel a rusty bolt embedded in the stout timber behind me. I moved my position until my wrists were against it and then I started to saw, and I think it was that which saved my reason in the remainder of those dark hours. I sawed and sawed, lacerating my wrists but not caring, until at last the bonds fell away in a mess of frayed rope and blood.

It was another hour before life came back to my arms, and by now the hatch cover above us was rimmed in a sickly line of gray light and there was a movement under the ship that told me we had gained open water, and soon the movement was replaced by a heaving and a pitching which bothered me little but incommoded poor Jem considerably, and to his sum of woe was added that of seasickness. I worked on his bonds until my fingernails were cracked, broken and bleeding, and eventually got them free, but he was not grateful—he asked only the boon of death.

And then at last, the hatch cover was thrown back and a round face looked down on us and grinned, and a can of water was lowered on a line and some hard biscuit and stinking salt beef was dropped to us—and the hatch was replaced.

From the waxing and waning of the light round the hatch cover, and the food that was lowered to us twice each day, I judged we were in that hell-hole four days, during which we ran through a violent storm, before we once more sailed into calm water. Poor Jem was near to death the whole time. I did what I could for him, even to chewing up morsels of weevily biscuit and beef and forcing the paste into his mouth, because I had once been told that prolonged seasickness on an empty stomach will eventually slit a man's guts like the blade of a knife. He was not grateful, and he reviled me weakly, but in times of deep despondence such as this, a creature in worse shape than oneself is a great comfort, and in trying to save the stupid creature's life I drew strength.

It was broad daylight when they eventually lowered a ladder for us. I had the very Devil's own job to get Jem up it, but at last we struggled into the weak morning sun—and then I gasped with unbelief because I was familiar with this place and recognized it immediately. There were tall gabled buildings crowded down to the waterfront, and neat stone piers and jetties, and behind them in the open fields I could see the whirling sails of huge windmills, and the country was flat and over all was a scene of ordered bustle—and I knew we were in Amsterdam. My heart rose and I turned and smote Jem a mighty blow between the shoulder blades which was meant to raise his spirits but which only succeeded in bringing him to his knees, so weak was he.

Around us the crew were engaged in the myriad tasks of berthing ship, and when I attempted to speak to hurrying sailors in my fluent though faulty Dutch, they shoved me roughly to one side and heeded me not. And then I saw the shipmaster on the poop, so I hurried aft to him and said politely, "Mynheer, I wish to speak with you."

He turned and grinned at me amicably, then kicked me in the stomach until I was rolling in agony in the scuppers, and continued with his task of berating his sailors. I returned to Jem.

"Don't worry, my friend," I told him. "I know where we are now. I have friends here."

But he had seen the treatment meted out to me by the shipmaster, and he was not impressed. We sat on the hatch and waited until the ship had been brought to anchor and the sails brailed up and made snug, and then, judging the time to be more propitious, I approached the shipmaster again and once more addressed him. I told him I was Lord Bemforth and that if he would have a message conveyed ashore to a certain merchant whom I knew to be in touch with Prince Rupert, in whose cavalry I had once served, I would be greatly obliged. He said, "Yah, yah—me I am Yeesus Gryste—soon I send an angel ashore for you. Out of it." But this time I avoided the swinging boot.

Boats came alongside us then, and two sailors hustled us both to the gangway and pushed us down a ladder into one of them, and the shipmaster joined us, but we had made the mistake of sitting in the sternsheets, so he booted us both forward.

We were rowed ashore and landed on a jetty, and soldiers in half-armor and Dutch casque helmets took us over, and the shipmaster handed them a paper.

"Yem Groombridge—blacksmith; Yil Bardock—carpenter," I was mystified to hear him say, and the soldiers hustled us across the jetty and into the door of a large building, along a passage, down some steps and into a huge cellar-like room.

The room was full of men and boys and, as we entered, a babble of tongues assailed us, and from my soldiering days I recognized many of them as German, Low German, Flemish, French and even English. We stared into this Babel, and then the soldiers, pushing us roughly forward, withdrew and left us standing.

✵ 6

NEARBY I heard a man cursing vilely in English, so I approached him and asked him civilly if he would kindly tell me in what place we were and what was afoot? He stared at me for a moment or so and then asked me if I had any money—which of course I had not. The man shrugged and lost interest in us, but I was angry, so I reached out and caught him by the arm and spun him round to face me.

I said, "Your pardon, good sir, but I would be obliged if you would answer my question, and thereby save me the necessity of twisting your neck for an ill-conditioned lout." Whereupon he used more filthy language but deemed it imprudent totally to ignore my query.

"This is the Company clearinghouse," he growled, "and you'll find that it was easier to enter than it will be to leave—save on their terms—and now, if you can't lend a man the wherewithal to wet his festering whistle, at least let go his pox-ridden arm, damn and blast your pestilential eyes."

Another English voice in the crowd said approvingly, "That's right, Reverend, put the bell, book, and candle on the scurvy louse," and I saw that the man whose arm I held was wearing a filthy black scholar's gown and the tattered remains of clerical bands about his neck. His face was puffy and bloated, his eyes bloodshot and red rimmed, and his matted hair hung in greasy elf-locks about his shoulders. One side of his face seemed to have been frozen by a stroke into a ghastly vulpine grin while the other was afflicted by a tic which made it constantly start and twitch, causing his tongue to dart in and out of the corner of his mouth like the fork of a serpent. Never in all my life, I decided, had I seen so evil a countenance. But at least he was English, and his voice, profanity notwithstanding, was that of an educated man, so I shook his arm sharply again and said, "Answer my question, sir!"

Behind me I heard Jem say in tones of great surprise, "Parson Saunders, as I'm a living sinner!" and then go off into shouts of bellowing laughter. The man swore horribly again and said, "Groombridge, you son of a whore—lend me a groat for a dram of schnapps before I expire before your eyes." And to my amazement Jem dug into his rags and produced from some privy pocket a silver shilling. The man pounced upon it with his free hand, wrenched loose from me and wormed his way through the crowd to a small barred postern window in one corner, through which I could see a fat *vrouw* at the tap of a huge barrel. She passed a leather drinking jack through to him and he drained the contents of it at a draught and returned it for replenishing, and only when he had tossed this off also did he return to us, wiping his slavering chops with the back of his hand. Jem said in a low aside to me, "The parson of our parish—until he was called upon for an accounting of his evil ways, and he flew the byre with the quarter's tithes."

The man evidently caught the last few words of this because he smote Jem heavily on the back, "Don't poison an act of Christian charity with lies and calumny. I didn't prig your cursed tithes because Sir Stinking Robert, who is the patron of the living, had forestalled me," he shouted, and added, "What brought you to this hell-hole, anyhow?"

Jem started to catalogue his woes and misfortunes but the disreputable clergyman was not really interested. He turned to me, his tones somewhat mellowed by his two draughts of liquor, and said, "Your pardon, sir, for my earlier rudeness, but I have an affliction of the lights and liver that manifests itself in a shortness of temper until such time as I take my morning medicine. You ask our whereabouts? This is the clearinghouse of the Dutch East India Company, and however much you may argue to the contrary, you are here of your own free will, having signed a covenant with them to serve them zealously and faithfully for a period of seven years in their new colony at the Cape of Good Hope, or Kaap Stad, as the bastards call it, which is at the hinder end of the continent of Africa and may God strike it and them with the black pox, and the Devil fly away with 'em." He finished on a hiccup.

I begged him to tell me more, and nothing loath to display his superior knowledge he said, "All a papal conspiracy. The Spaniards having, with the Pope's approval, arrogated to themselves the gold and treasure of the Americas and all the New World to the West, the Dutch, who are just as great a race of pestilential thieves and rogues, have had to look elsewhere for easy pickings, so they've gone East. The East India Company they call 'emselves—the *Dutch* East India Company, as distinct from the bonny band of brigands which that bedizened old whore of ours, Elizabeth, licensed many years ago for the same purpose—the Honorable *English* East India Company. It's a long voyage from Holland to the Indies so they've established a fort and a dock at the Cape of Good Hope where their ships might break the journey, rest and revictual, and from whence they can mount expeditions against the pirates that infest the route. They've found the Cape to be a fruitful place in itself so they have expanded beyond the purlieus of the fort and dock, and they are settling and farming and planting vineyards in the hinterland. For that they need people—more and more people—farmers, artisans, craftsmen, laborers. They have enslaved the few miserable blackamoors that inhabit the place, but those heathens are untutored as yet, so we are the torchbearers of culture and enlightenment. By the shipload, my good sir—by the shipload."

I began to see light. It was the infamous bond-slave system. We ourselves had started it in England to populate the new colony we had founded in the Americas in the face of Spanish opposition. Virginia we had called the place, in honor of our spinster Queen, and we shipped out the offscourings of our prisons to labor and die in its fever-ridden swamps.

"But Holland is not a large nation," went on the clergyman, "and they could not stand an indefinite drain on the more intelligent sections of their communities, so they recruit from neighboring countries. You sign a bond with 'em and they advance you fifty gold crowns. Then you work diligently for seven years, at the end of which time you can claim burgher status and a grant of land out there—and be assigned bondsmen to work it for you, and even a wife if you're minded—or a further sum of fifty gold crowns and a passage back to Europe should you so elect. The ships arriving here from those parts are singularly empty of returning wayfarers, so one assumes it is either a paradise out there, or that few live to exercise their options."

"I signed no bond," I told him. He chuckled grimly.

"You tell them that," he said. "They might even show it to you. There it'll be, all down in the clearest double-Dutch—in your name, or somebody's—listed by your trade and with your witnessed mark on it in receipt of your fifty crowns—all legal, honest and above-board. They have agents who arrange these things for 'em." He cleared his throat and spat. "I've assisted a few unfortunates myself along the road—parishioners fleeing injustice—then I fell out with my partner, Sir Stinking Robert Manforth, God rot the black-hearted bastard's soul, and I was fool enough to accept his invitation to dine with him one night to straighten out our differences. I woke to find my nose being nibbled by a rat in the hold of a ship, and I have subsequently learned that my name is Michael Angel and my calling that of shepherd. He has a pretty sense of humor, Sir Robert."

We remained in that place for three days, our company swelling hourly by the addition of some of the most villainous charac-ters I have ever seen. Not a few had managed to retain secreted about their persons small sums of money, while others made shift to sell items of their wretched clothing through the postern window, and were thus enabled to maintain the lively trade in liquor that never ceased throughout the livelong day and night. Never have I seen such scenes of vile debauchery as in that pesthole, for the spirits they sold seemed to madden rather than stupefy, and fights were constantly breaking out between some, while others sat in groups and howled obscene choruses, with yet others in furtive coteries in the darker corners of the chamber, engaged in shameless and disgusting activities with a band of simpering youths who had once formed a company of strolling Bohemian players. Twice a day our guards fed us, like animals, on buckets of sour bean porridge, heels of moldy cheese and loaves of coarse black bread, and it was then that bedlam reached its peak of screaming, cursing, fighting and clawing, for there was barely enough provided for half our number, and the stronger therefore despoiled the weaker.

More by the bond of common language than any other reason, the lapsed parson, Jem and myself drifted into a company of three. Other Englishmen tried to join us but since they were all manifestly gallowsflowers of the lowest order we resolutely closed our ranks against them, establishing ourselves in one corner and beating off any who sought to violate our privacy. I tried to send out messages to my merchant friend, or any other known sympathizer who might conceivably aid me in rejoining Prince Rupert, now in Germany, but I had no success because I had no means of writing and, of greater moment, no means of bribing any member of the guard.

So there we remained until the third day, when soldiers entered and a fat Dutch captain tried to read our names from a long list but had to abandon his endeavors because of the outcry. They merely counted us then and drove us out through the heavy doors to the jetty, and I found myself blinking gratefully in the pale winter sun after the gloom of that underground chamber.

My first thoughts were of escape, but our captors were taking no chances. A treble file of soldiers lined the short route from the door across the jetty to the water's edge, and they were armed with drawn swords and halberds, standing close-drawn shoulder to shoulder. One poor wretch did in fact try to break ranks and make a run for it but he was cut down by a stolid-faced Frisian before he had taken his third step. We were herded onto a barge, bluff-bowed, wide-beamed and deep, so that even standing, our heads were below the level of the gunwale, and soldiers took up their positions on the short foredeck and poop, armed with crossbows and bell-muzzled calivers, and it needed no military eye to realize that they could have picked off one or mown down many had they been given cause. Sailors then hoisted a large spritsail and we cast off and headed out into the stream.

We sailed for about an hour before bringing up under the counter of a huge galleon whose sides towered above us clifflike and were pierced by a myriad of gunports. We were herded up the gangway under the flailing butts of the halberds and the pricking of sword points, and once again some desperate fool tried to escape, this time by jumping from the top of the gangway into the narrow space of water between the two vessels, and sinking out of sight. He must have swum clean under the barge but it availed him nothing because the soldiers were waiting when he broke surface, and two calivers boomed as one, blowing him clear of the water like a leaping salmon, to sink again in a bloody mass. We were driven across the deck and down into the hold and the hatches were clapped to over us, then after a further wait of some hours, we heard sounds from the deck above us that betokened our departure.

I shall not dwell upon that ghastly voyage, because each day was so like another in its deadly dragging monotony that details have become blurred and merged, and even now I hate to look back upon it. We suffered storms and intense cold in our dark wooden-walled prison at first, and to our other miseries were added those of the seasickness of the majority of our number. Later it became warmer, then hot, then hellishly so, until we could only lie flat and gasp like landed fish in the well-nigh suffocating stench of that place. For the want of something to occupy my mind I had made a tally of our wretched company. One hundred and fifty of us had emerged from the dungeon. Two died even before embarking, in the manner I have described, and another thirty-odd during the voyage—some of seasickness early on, some of the ship fever in the heat—at least half a dozen in bestial fights among themselves below decks, and two spectacularly by leaping overboard during the hour's exercise we were allowed in batches on such days as the weather was fair; so when we eventually made harbor again there were scarce a hundred of us left—filthy, gaunt, half-naked ghosts—bearded, long-haired and sunken-eyed.

It was a wide and sheltered harbor in which three ships of a size comparable with our own lay at anchor, together with many smaller ones. It was a brilliantly sunny day, and a clean wind blew in from the sea, and the distant shore looked peaceful and enticing with its small cluster of cool white buildings and pretty church on a hillock

—and dominating all a huge flat-topped mountain. So this was the Cape of Good Hope, I reflected, and grinned sourly at the irony of the name.

Our arrival was evidently an event of some moment because guns boomed out in salute from the shore and the other ships, and we answered with a like number, then across the water we saw a host of small boats making for us, headed by one bigger than the others, rowed by twelve richly liveried oarsmen each side, flying an emblazoned banner and covered astern with a brilliantly-hued canopy. Now that we were safely anchored in still waters, the gunports had been opened and the stronger and more nimble of us were enabled to climb from the fetid depths of the hold and peer out on the scene. The stately barge was evidently that of the governor or some similar high functionary because there was a great deal of palaver at the gangway as several portly *mynheers* and their ladies came aboard, and the sound of fanfares and the crash of presented arms came to our ears.

No doubt because of our sorry appearance, we were not disembarked before darkness had fallen, and then we were marched through the deserted and silent streets to a long low wooden building which was completely surrounded by high palisades, and the next morning huge cauldrons of water were heated on fires in the open yard, and for the first time those of us who were of a mind to do so were allowed to clean and disinfest ourselves of the lice that throve upon our emaciated frames, and Hottentots, as they called the black men who thronged the place, came among us with scissors and razors and ridded us of our matted hair and beards. Those who were too sick or dispirited to avail themselves of this heaven-sent opportunity were dealt with by the Hottentots like so many sheep at shearing time. Then we were given shapeless garments of coarse unbleached cotton—just pantaloons and shirts and rough leather sandals, with woven straw hats to protect our shaven skulls from the fierce sun—and finally we were fed with an abundance of boiled corn, meat and wooden buckets of milk, which put us at first in good heart but soon upset our shrunken and unaccustomed bellies.

Clerks and overseers then arrived to supplement the soldiers who had until now been superintending us. They were armed with lists and there ensued a period of confusion and much Dutch cursing as

they endeavored to sort us out, their task not being made easier by
the fact that most of us were unfamiliar with the names under
which we had been bonded. But finally, by dint of bellowing, kicking and thumping, we were segregated by groups according to our
alleged callings, which meant that our party of three was split, but
this worried "the Angel," as the parson was now called, not one
whit. He slipped away from his fellow shepherds and joined my
group, stoutly averring that he was a carpenter, and calling for Jem
to do the same and eschew the blacksmiths.

We stayed in this place for a further two days, during which time
our numbers were steadily depleted by groups being assigned to our
new masters and led away, until finally our turn came and seven of
us—myself, the Angel, Jem and four stolid Germans—were sent in a
party to the shipyards.

The work was not too arduous and consisted for the most part in
splitting baulks of timber with adzes and wedges into planks of a
size and shape suitable for repairs to fishing boats and other craft,
and since the Germans, at least, were skilled, and the Angel was
adept in roaring and cursing officiously when the fat Dutch shipwright was nearby, he managed to give the impression of experience
and zealousness and soon came tacitly to be accepted as a master
craftsman and was put in charge of us, a position which he exploited
to the full.

It was curious to observe the effect of hardship upon him. While
it had taken toll of the meager resources of most of the other
wretched prisoners, it had merely stripped from him a good deal of
obese grossness and he stood revealed as a man of great physical
stature. His enforced abstinence from strong drink had also
benefited him, and the nervous tic was not now so frequent or
noticeable. Mentally too he was a man to be reckoned with, his
naturally evil cunning being sharpened and reinforced by wide reading and an Oxford degree in philosophy and divinity. God knows
what had led the ruffian into the church, except that it was well
known that there was much corrupt trafficking in livings in those
days.

Jem also was improving in condition and was accepting his fate
with the resignation of his kind. Our food was rough but wholesome and ample, the air clean and fresh, the sun hot, but not unbear-

ably so, and our muscles thrived on the work we were called upon
to do. Our treatment was not harsh, in fact the shipwright often
came in the evenings to sit and talk to us in the airy loft above the
slipway in which we slept, and sometimes he would bring a small
stone bottle of schnapps, and clay pipes in which to smoke the tobacco that was now being carried to all parts of the world from the
Virginian plantations, a habit which I had not yet acquired but to
which the Angel and Jem were very partial. He, the shipwright, was
himself a freed bondsman who had been out in the colony for many
years and now had no inclination to return to the Low Countries.
He had a certain amount of English which, with my smattering of
Dutch, was sufficient for our converse. He told us much about the
system.

"Iss goot," he used to aver gutturally. "Food goot, wine goot,
schnapps goot, black vench goot. You don't vorry, mein friendts.
Just work goot for seven year then the governor set you free and
you grow a big belly like me and live like a lord. Ver' goot." And
the Angel used to assure him earnestly that that was the sole ambition of the three of us, until the latter, beaming paternally upon us,
had betaken himself back to his neat white-painted house outside the
shipyard, then he used to lie on his back and curse horribly.

" 'Iss goot' is it, you square-headed, pig-begotten Dutch bastard?"
he would swear. " 'Iss goot' for you, no doubt, with your liquor and
your pipes, your fat-arsed mattress of a wife and your stud of little
black girls. Seven years? Great God Almighty!" The absence of
women was for him, I think, a greater trial than that of liquor, and
much of his conversation was made up of lascivious reminiscence.

"Remember Mistress Halketh, Jem?" he would ask.

"Her as was the wife of the parish clerk? Aye, plump little pigeon, none the less comely for being almost a Puritan, with her gray
gown, white cap and collar." And transported for the moment back
to his Kentish home, Jem's eyes would water.

"Small black mole on her right rump surrounded by teeth marks
—mine. Planted there last Lady Day in the vestry. Very pleasant,"
the Angel would say musingly, and Jem would stare at him in
shocked incredulity.

We were allowed a measure of freedom during the daylight hours
in that we could move without let or hindrance within the confines
of the town, marked men in our outlandish garb, despised even by

the Hottentots, and I took full advantage of every minute of my scanty leisure to explore the place, because the thought of escape was never far from my mind, hopeless though it appeared to be.

Behind us to the north rose the steep sides of Table Mountain, beyond which, we were told, stretched countless thousands of miles of parched hinterland, waterless desert, dense jungle—all teeming with wild animals, poisonous reptiles and cruel and savage natives with a partiality for white flesh. On all other sides lay the sea, but having traversed it once it was at least a familiar element, and it was on that which I concentrated. I would lie hour after hour at night, conferring in low tones with the Angel on the possibility of stealing a fishing boat and secretly vitualing her from the store within the yard, and slipping out of the harbor one dark night and running north.

"The wind blows constantly from the south," I would say, "therefore it is favorable to us. We would sail only at night, stealing close inshore during the day, hiding from passing ships in bays and inlets—reprovisioning with what we could hunt and snare, and re-filling our barrels from fresh streams."

"Can you navigate?" he asked me once.

"What navigation is necessary? We keep the polestar above our bows, the wind behind us and the whole continent of Africa on our right hand, then, if I remember my maps, comes Spain—"

"And galleons laden with dons and Jesuits who would bear us ashore and broil our arses at the stake for the good of our souls. Go on, my little soldier, what next?"

"Then, still keeping the land to our right hand, we go on along the coast of France—"

"Whose whore-begotten inhabitants love us like the Devil loves holy water. What next?"

"Then the Lowlands—"

"Which gave us such a hell of a welcome last time—"

"I have friends there."

"I noticed the bastards showering you with adulation and pledging you in cups of gold." He spat. "Showers of shit and the rough ends of their halberds."

"All right then," I said angrily. "What do you intend to do? Rot here for seven years?"

"Trust in the Lord," he answered, rolling his eyes in mock piety.

"He will provide. He had better—if he wants his bloody tithes back. Yes, seven years if necessary—then I'll be a burgher, turn Dutchman and become the predicant of that church of theirs up on the hill—and drink my fill and bed their wives and daughters. It's population they want out here, is it? By God, they'll have no cause to complain of *my* services."

I am not a religious man, but there were times when I shuddered and wondered why he was not struck down in his foul blasphemy. But he wasn't, and he flourished like the green bay tree, and withal waxed in the favor with our easygoing master who was convinced that in the Angel he had a loyal and diligent servant, working like ten men and beating and reviling the unfortunate Germans for laziness. And it wasn't long before he was promoted from wielding an adz, and the shipwright entrusted him with the account books and ledgers, which he kept meticulously in a neat and clerkly hand—and from the ledgers it was but a short step to the keys of the chandlery stores, and a merry harvest it was thereafter. If a fishing-smack master came in for fifty guilders' worth of work upon his boat, the Angel would debit him with thirty, taking ten in gold for himself, to the great content of them both. A hundred guilders' worth of ship's stores became eighty in the account, with yet another ten in the pocket of the Angel, until he had a goodly sum put by in a privy place known only to himself. Then it was an easy matter to purchase sailor's clothing and to steal out at night and roister in the waterfront taverns and brothels.

In justice to him I must hasten to admit that he was free with his ill-gotten gains and he offered to outfit us both also, but I declined at first, not from any excess of virtue, but because each man to his own aim, and mine was solely to escape, though Jem gladly joined him, and the pair of them would return morning after morning before dawn, giggling and hicupping. Then it occurred to me that therein might lie the furtherance of my dreams, and I allowed him to procure for me a mariner's doublet, hose, trunks and Flemish cap, and finally one night I climbed the wall with them—and there, had I but known it, lay our undoing.

✧✧ 7

I HARBORED no set plan as I dropped over the wall that night, other than that of reconnoitering the waterfront for a ship on which to stow away. That in itself, I thought, would present no great difficulty, but I would have to be careful not to leap from the frying pan to the fire. A ship to England was of course the last thing I wanted. One to the Lowlands, although that was my ultimate destination, would avail me little either, because if the shipmaster handed me over to the authorities I would be certain of being sent back here, in worse plight than I was now. Spain was a country to be avoided also, unless one wished to make the uncomfortable acquaintance of the Inquisition. France, I decided, would be my safest wager. True, the English were disliked there, but not quite so rabidly as in Spain—

The Angel undoubtedly guessed what was running through my mind because he growled to me as we set off down the lane to the waterfront, "Listen, Gil my young friend, you return with us tonight. Fly the byre and these Dutchmen will be around the ears of us others like bees."

I said, "The Devil take you. I'll do what I have a mind to. Do you think for one moment that you could stop me?"

"I alone, no—but with Jem here ranged beside me we'll lay your skull open and carry you back if need be," he assured me. "I have not labored these months to arrange things comfortably just to see them disrupted by a hotheaded young fool. Accept the gifts that heaven sends you—drink your fill and have a woman, and then come back with us like a sensible man." And Jem rumbled his agreement.

Outnumbered and wanting time to watch and observe without their eyes upon me, I pretended to be persuaded, and I even gave my promise that I would not entertain any idea of escape, at least for that night, and after a walk of some ten minutes we came to a low tavern in a lane near the Grand Jetty.

The place was crowded because the harbor carried more ships on its broad bosom that night than ever before. A large Dutch East Indiaman had put in that afternoon, straight from Amsterdam; another lay there awaiting a favorable wind to sail in the opposite direction, having recently arrived from the Spice Islands; a Portuguese galleon lay at anchor farther out, and to make up the tally there must have been a full half-dozen dhows from Araby—strange ghostly craft, low-lying and rakish with a single mast carrying a huge triangular sail, which traded down the eastern coast of Africa carrying slaves to this port and guns and powder back to their own.

There must have been well-nigh a hundred sailors crowded into that stifling low-raftered taproom, many smoking their reeking tobacco pipes and filling the place with a blue haze, and all quaffing the eternal schnapps and the fiery local wine. There was a babble of many languages in which Dutch and Portuguese was by no means predominant, but this was not strange, as the flag of a ship did not of a necessity determine the country of its crew. A shipmaster picked his sailors when and where he could—which was something I had learned on the voyage out here and was a fact I intended putting to good use.

We found with difficulty a space against the wall where we could lean and survey the scene, and the Angel, whose Dutch was fast becoming fluent, grabbed a Hottentot pot-boy by his woolly hair and ordered schnapps and pipes for the three of us, with the air of one who knew his way about. This potent and aromatic spirit has never been to my liking, and I was still holding my first glass scarce tasted in my hand while the other two were pledging each other in their third. Leaving them, I started unobtrusively to circulate through the tight-packed crowd, my ears acock for any snippets of information I thought I might turn to my advantage. The Portuguese galleon interested me not a little. She was the first of that flag, it appeared, which had used this port for some considerable time. Neighbors of the Spaniards notwithstanding, the Portuguese were an easygoing and tolerant people who traded to most European ports. This might be the answer to my problem. But then I heard from the conversation of two men that she was bound to the East and might not return for a year or more, so I relinquished the idea for the moment, though I decided that it was one which I might well bear in mind for the future, should more Portuguese ships come in, bound the other way.

Well satisfied with the little I had learned, and feeling in my first experience of temporary freedom more cheerful than I had for many a long day, I returned to the others. They were in converse with a ratlike Frisian in military uniform, the Angel doing most of the talking, the other winking and leering, and Jem listening with mouth asag and drooling—and about them all was an air of deep conspiracy. The Angel drew me into the circle.

"A little diversion," he chuckled, "and one none of us will take amiss. Guess what cargo that big Dutchman brought in from Amsterdam this afternoon?" He lowered his voice still further and nudged me in the ribs. "Wenches—two hundred and more—*white* wenches—Dutch, German, Flemish, Huguenots—all on the bonded lay, the same as us poor devils." He smacked his lips. "All of 'em booked for the beds of freed burghers, very correct and seemly, with the Dutch parson ready to marry 'em off in coveys to sober and God-fearing grooms who have been of good behavior for seven years. Odd's faith, they do 'em proud out here. Some for every taste, so the Corporal here tells me—short, tall, skinny, fat; fair, dark and middling; ugly, pretty; but all young and possessing one feature in common."

I shrugged, not greatly interested. We had heard of these shipments before. Our female counterparts, recruited, poor souls, in much the same way—from the prisons, the brothels and the poorhouses—but despoiled of even our scant privilege of election to return to Europe at the end of seven years. Theirs was a term for life, because only freed burghers who contracted to stay here were permitted to marry.

The Angel went on, "At least they *say* they all have one feature in common—but you know these damned Dutchmen. Cheat their own flesh and blood they would, given the chance. The Corporal here says the soldiers and crew on the way out did their best to ascertain that all were as per bill of lading—but he's not prepared to take his bible oath upon it. They did what they could—but there was a lot of wenches and not many soldiers and crew—and a man can't give of his best on salt beef and weevily biscuit alone, can he Corporal? Here, you black bastard, more schnapps for the Corporal!" He grabbed a passing pot-boy. Jem guffawed and capered like a clown and I saw that the drink they had taken so quickly was making itself felt upon them both.

I said, "What of it? I'm going back to the yard."

He took me by the arm and regarded me sorrowfully. "Gil, my hearty, where's your sense of public duty? How can you contemplate some poor fellow bondsman being short-delivered at the altar tomorrow? No, my cocky, we go up with the Corporal here who's in command of the guard at the barracoon where the fillies are stabled for the night. Inspectors in the interests of fair dealing, us. Inspectors of—" He broke off. "Lay hold of him, Jem, till I get back. Don't let him get away." And he was off through the crowd.

I shook off Jem's hand. "Let go damn you. You'd best come back with me, unless you wish to finish up at the flogging post or the gibbet. That fool's drunk enough to lead you into anything," I hissed.

"C-can't d'sert a comrade, Gil," Jem hiccupped solemnly. "Goo' feller. Greatest ram in all Kent. But two hundred of 'em!!! He can't manage that in one night. Got to help." He grabbed my arm again in his huge blacksmith's paws, and try as I would I could not shake him off this time short of doing him serious injury. I had no wish to go with them—again not through any excess of virtue, but the very thought of that meat market appalled me. And then the Angel returned bearing two large stone jars of schnapps. I was in a quandary. Drunk and on their own, the Lord knows what mischief they might finish up in. With them, there was the chance of my getting them back to the yard before too much harm was done. It was neither loyalty nor love for the ill-conditioned louts that kept me with them in the end, but just the thought that if they were taken I might be involved as well, which would be the end of my chances of escape. Unwillingly I trailed along.

Outside, the Corporal halted and held out his palm, and the Angel put down his jars and fumbled for some golden guilders. The Corporal counted them and shook his head firmly, and then ensued a long and acrimonious chaffering until the Angel gave him some more—and eventually we set off up the hill to the compound where we ourselves had been confined on arrival.

We crept along in the shadow of the palisade until we came to a dark spot on the side farthest from the guardroom, where the Corporal left us with sundry grins, winks and nudges, promising us to be back with the keys of the rear gate in some minutes. And there we waited, the Angel and Jem indulging in ecstasies of anticipation and having alternate recourse to one of the stone jars.

They descended upon us in a silent swoop from round the corner of the palisade—five soldiers led by the Corporal, with unsheathed swords and halberds at the ready. Jem was in the act of raising the jar to his lips at that moment. He swung it and I heard the Corporal's skull cave in like an eggshell. He fell, bringing down the two men immediately on his heels. I jumped sideways to miss the thrust of a halberd directed straight at my belly, and as the point embedded itself deep in the palisade behind me, and the wielder's jaw loomed palely before me, I punched viciously with all my force, felling him like an ox. Jem struck again with the jar at one of the men who was rising, and again I heard that sickening crack. The Angel had pounced on the dropped sword of the Corporal and he ran the other through with it. The remaining men swerved and raced back into the darkness shouting blue murder, and in the distance I heard the alarm bell tolling wildly and the shouts of the rest of the guard turning out.

The road we had come by was now barred to us, and there remained only one other way open, which was down a steep slope to the waterfront. I grabbed the arms of the other two and we took it at a breakneck run, stumbling, falling and then regaining our feet in the darkness, behind us the tumult growing louder, and swelled now by the screams of women in the compound.

"The bastard told that much truth, at all event," grunted the Angel. "God rot his treacherous soul. Selling us for the escape reward, eh? I apologize to the Devil for sending such to him."

We gained the waterfront, but only to run into the arms of the Watch who were hurrying towards the scene of the outcry. They called upon us to halt, but we turned in our stride and set off the harder in the opposite direction, which unfortunately for us lay away from that part of the town in which the shipyard was situated.

But beggars could not be choosers, so we sped on with the heavy-booted soldiery pounding behind us, and some fool twirling a rattle with a noise fit to wake the dead.

And now other bells were ringing, and windows in houses each side of us were opening and burghers' heads were emerging, and someone, somewhere near, discharged a musket. On we went, gasping, puffing and retching with the effort, until I thought we'd finish on the top of Table Mountain itself, and we had to stop before the Angel expired of apoplexy. The sounds of our immediate pursuers had died behind us, but the clamor in the town was rising apace.

"Naught for it but to work our way back by a circuitous route, regain our roosts and hope we've not been missed in the meantime," said the Angel, in the tones of one discussing a foul break in the weather that was due to no cause of his. " 'Twill be the gallows else—you randy pair of stoats."

But that was easier said than done. We had ever and anon to diverge from our track to evade parties of searching soldiers who seemed to be rounding up all wayfarers and bearing them off to the market place—and several times we lost ourselves completely, until at last we knew all hope had gone because we could not possibly regain the yard before dawn, which was when we were roused for work.

We found ourselves at last by the Grand Jetty, and boatswains' whistles were shrilling and there was a cursing in many tongues as ships' officers sought to round up members of their crews and get them out of harm's way before some were lost to the Watch. And this seemed to me to be my deliverance. If I could gain one of those ships in the confusion, and hide somewhere until she sailed—

I started to creep away from the others in the darkness, but then, when it came to the point I found I could not do it. I had cravenly deserted one already since I had been a fugitive, and that guilt had seldom been far from me. I turned back and pushed through the crowd to them and told them my plan. The Angel demurred at first because he still had thoughts of returning to the yard and trusting to his silver tongue, but finally he nodded grudgingly—and it was only just in time because the Watch, swelled by nearly the whole garrison, were trying to prevent the sailors from leaving, in case the guilty ones were among them.

"Three honest Dutch soldiers foully murdered!" I heard an officer shouting. "None leaves the shore until all have given an account of themselves. The Burgomaster has ordered it!"

But fortunately that spurred the ships' officers to greater efforts, not wishing to lose half their companies, and it thereby made our task the easier. We linked arms, ducked our heads, pushed through to the boats and tumbled into one of them. It was overfull already, but under the pummeling and shouting of the boatswains, we were shoved off and I found myself tugging at an oar.

Clumsily and in ragged and unsailorly fashion we rowed out into the darkness, and then somebody brought a rope's end into play round our shoulders and we made better shift, and yet another, with better wits than the rest of us, took the tiller and steered into mid-harbor. I could not tell which ship we were making for, nor did I greatly care. We now had an excuse for being aboard whichever it was. When order reigned again we could claim to be from another ship and loudly complain about so cavalierly being herded aboard this one. All we had to do was to get below out of sight until she sailed.

We hove to under the gangway of a galleon, and trailed up to the deck above. I waited just outside the circle of light cast by a dim lantern hanging in the shrouds, until the Angel and Jem came aboard, grabbed their arms and drew them away into the darkness. Then we sought an open hatch and descended into the pitchy gloom below and hid beneath some coils of cable.

We sailed with the dawn but not with the approval of the Dutch authorities ashore, because we heard a gun boom out from the fort, then another and another—until finally we were actually struck by a roundshot which, although it did little damage to us at that extreme range, put the fear of the Devil into some of the crew, because we heard a great outcry above. And then we were clear of the harbor, and Jem was sick again.

Deeming boldness our best tactics I insisted on them both coming up on deck with me in order to make our plaints, but we had no immediate cause for alarm because as soon as we emerged, the boatswain bore down on us with a torrent of cursing and drove us to an enormous rope on which men were hauling. We did not understand his language, but that mattered little. We grasped the idea and hauled also—then, when our hearts and lungs were pounding fit to burst, he drove us to another task, and then to another and another, until, when the sun was high at its meridian, Table Mountain was but a speck behind us, and I rejoiced greatly—but then I looked at the sun and from it deduced north, south, east and west—and saw that we were standing in a northeasterly direction—and I noticed for the first time that the ensign we flew at the mizzen peak was not the Dutch one, but was plentifully besprinkled with saints and crosses.

We were on the Portuguese ship and were sailing for the Indies.

I imparted this information to the Angel and Jem. It meant little to the latter at first, but the Angel cursed loud and long, and accused me of deliberately hoodwinking them, until I told him to roast in hell and withdrew upon my dignity.

The Capitano, as they called their shipmaster, then had all the crew mustered under the break of the poop, and great was the confusion that reigned for some time, because what I had been hoping for had indeed happened. They found they were many of their own crew short, but manifestly had several new members, though on balance they had lost a dozen men. This put the Capitano into a towering rage. He was a small dark man with flowing black hair, white flashing teeth, one eye and two enormous gold earrings. He addressed us passionately for some ten minutes or so, gesticulating to heaven, drawing off his feathered hat and jumping on it, crossing himself fervently and finally weeping. If more of us had understood the language he was employing, his speech would no doubt have made a greater impression upon us. However, it was then translated by various officers into as many languages and finally into English, in which it was greatly abbreviated.

"Capitano say you no damn good. Capitano say this very nice ship. Capitano say you no work he hang you on the rope by neck. Capitano say he want you to be happy. Damn rogues."

Looking back I don't think we were *un*happy. The weather was fine, the sun was warm, the sea of a blueness that I would not have believed possible in nature had I not seen it with my own eyes, and daily there was some new wonder at which to marvel. There were fish that flew like birds, breaking the surface in silver darts and then skimming the wavetops gracefully for great distances before plunging into them again. There were other fish which played round the thrusting bows of the ship, huge monsters that leapt and twisted and sported by the hour and which a sailor who spoke a little English told me were called dolphins. And there were others, yet bigger, as big almost as the ship itself—and these spouted water like fountains, high into the air. And then there were great white birds with wings that spanned wider than those of the biggest eagles I had ever seen, which appeared to hang motionless in the sky day after day, but which were actually following us at our own great pace. These were albatrosses, and it was said that they were great bringers of good luck to all ships that they followed thus. It was certainly true in our case, because the wind remained fair day after day and the sea smooth.

Short crew notwithstanding, the work was not unbearably hard and we were not driven as were the wretched sailors on the Dutch ship, and never once did I see a man flogged. The food was adequate even if strange to our Northern palates, and this was agreeably supplemented on many occasions by fresh fish which the men caught on lines which they trailed astern. But I must confess to a certain nervousness which assailed me from time to time at the very immensity of that vast ocean. I did not feel this so much on the voyage out to Cape Town because on most days that we were allowed to come up on deck one could catch a glimpse of land away to the east, and this in itself was comforting. I could remember the geography I had been taught at school also, and the two globes, terrestrial and celestial, that stood in the library at home, could visualize the land mass down which we sailed, and knew that at the end of it there was a town—as civilized in many respects as any part of the Lowlands in which it had its roots. But here we were sailing across a vast uncharted ocean, and I knew that there was land only many thousands of miles away in any direction—and that those lands were little known.

And then one day there was a cry from the masthead, and all the crew crowded to the rail and peered in the direction the lookout was pointing—and we saw a boat, if indeed it could be called that. It was little more than two logs roughly shaped and bound together with ropes, and from its side projected two arms or branches at the ends of which was yet another and smaller log which appeared to balance it on the waves. It had a stumpy mast supporting a long curving spar on which was set a sail of some strange weave. A man sat crouched at the stern, steering the rude contrivance with a paddle, and two others stood balancing themselves against the boat's motion, hauling in on a fishing net. They were small and brown and naked except for cloth about their loins. They waved to us and we raised a cheer, and I felt a great admiration for their courage in being such a great distance from land in this frail thing.

That was our first knowledge that our long ocean passage was drawing to a close. Next day we saw many similar craft—then on the next came the long drawn out cry of the lookout at the masthead, and before us, no more than a cloud upon the horizon, was the faint blue outline of land.

I NEED but to close my eyes for one moment to recapture my first sight of that strange coast. Between us and it were cruel reefs over which the surf boiled whitely. Beyond the reefs, across the smooth lagoon, gleamed a golden beach that stretched unbroken on either hand as far as the eye could see. Behind the beach rose the jungle in a brilliantly green and seemingly impenetrable wall of tangled undergrowth over which swayed the graceful heads of the palm trees. Far in the distance I could see the outline of mountains. A gentle inshore breeze, scarce enough to flutter the sails, did little to temper the murderous heat of the sun which blazed down upon us from out a brazen sky.

We turned north and sailed parallel to the reef for two days, the coast unchanging and seeming to go on forever, seeing no habitation other than occasional fishing villages rudely built of sticks and mud, huddling at the edge of the jungle, until at last we sighted a break

in the reef, and then we beat back and forth for some hours until
the Capitano deemed the tide and wind suitable for an entry. With
the ship's barge rowing ahead of us, and a leadsman therein sounding
the depths, we felt our way in gingerly under top and headsails
alone, the little Capitano handling the great ship very skillfully and
boldly in a passage that was fringed with jagged rocks and was at
times so narrow that a man could have almost spat its width.

We glided across the lagoon, looking down into water so crystal
clear as to enable us to count the sea shells glinting on the sands
beneath, and to follow the darting courses of myriads of brilliant
fish, until all was spoiled by the outfall of a muddy river that fouled
its pellucidness. We turned into this river and saw before us a place
where the jungle bent back in a clearing within which was a small
whitewashed fort and near it a village somewhat larger than those
we had seen hitherto. The Capitano caused a gun to be fired, and as
its roar rent that still heavy air, the jungle came to startled life and
clouds of strange and beautiful birds rose above the trees in loud and
raucous plaint. But that was the only response, a fact which seemed
to puzzle the Capitano greatly, because I could see him in animated
converse with his officers on the poop.

The sailor who spoke English leant on the bulwark beside me. He
was a man of some intelligence who had made this voyage before,
and he seemed troubled. This was one of a string of Portuguese
trading posts, he said, and was, or should be, a hive of industry.

"One Captain-Governor," he told me, "and fifty Portuguese soldiers, and a priest and clerks—and many natives. They know when
the ship comes. They know for many days because they have a
means, these dark people, of sending news long distances up the
coast. Usually there is much excitement and they salute us with
guns and come out in boats to greet us. But now, today, nothing
except the birds. Why?" He crossed himself. "It can only be the
fever."

The officers came down from the poop then and selected from us
a party to go ashore, and since the Angel, Jem and I were three, at
least, whose curiosity overcame their nervousness, we pressed forward and all were armed by the boatswain with a miscellany of
muskets, crossbows, swords and halberds. Twenty of us made that
first landing, led by the Capitano himself.

The prow of the ship's boat bit into the muddy bank and we swarmed over the gunwales and followed the Capitano across the clearing to the fort. Its stout wooden door stood open and as we marched through into the small courtyard my soldier's eye saw naught amiss—except its very desertion. All was neat and in good order, the flagstones swept clean, and twelve small cannon standing in their embrasures on the walls, with round shot and canisters of grape in pyramids beside them, lanyards coiled and ramrods laid across trails as if a master gunner who knew his trade had but recently drilled upon them. On the left of the gate was a small chapel, and through its open door we saw white cloths and the glint of rich plate upon its altar. Under the walls were open-fronted sheds piled with sacks and bales of corded timber which gave off a rich and aromatic variety of scents and which I learned later were spices and sandalwood.

The main building of the fort was square and rose in three stories to a flat roof, which was surmounted by a squat watchtower with a flagstaff from which fluttered bravely the flag of Portugal. The lowest story contained storerooms and magazines and the armory. The doors were close-bolted and locked, but through the barred windows we could see that here, also, all seemed to be in order. Wooden stairs led up to galleries surrounding the upper stories, the lower of which contained the barrack rooms of the soldiers, and my heart warmed to the absent Captain-Governor because I could not have faulted one detail of their furnishings and appointments—cots in line, armor and accouterments hanging uniformly on pegs in the walls, and all of a perfect cleanliness. We went on to the top story which was apparently the quarters of the commander himself and his officers, and here again there was naught to cavil at. They were furnished richly but not extravagantly, and in one room papers and books were set out with pens, ink-horns and sandboxes. The Capitano advanced quickly on the table and took up a heavy book which stood open. He commenced to read aloud to his officers, and the English-speaking sailor translated to me in a low aside. It was apparently the Captain-Governor's log, and the date of the last entry was but three days earlier. It set out the daily unremarkable happenings of the post, making no mention of pestilence or other calamity, and it closed with the news that they were aware of the arrival of our galleon upon the coast, and awaited our appearance with the liveliest pleasure and anticipation, and then there was a Latin inscription giving thanks to God. In another book was a tally of the cargo they had ready for us—spices, sandalwood, sugar, ivory, silk and bales of cotton cloth, and it appeared that it was a goodly total, the fruits of a full year's garnering.

We left the fort then and followed the path across the clearing to the native village. Here again all was silent and deserted, and although not as scrupulously clean as the fort, there were at least no signs of confusion or disorder, nor indeed even of hasty departure. There was food in cooking pots arranged round dead fires, clothes spread out to dry on the banks of a small stream, filled water jars on the lip of a well, a child's toy in the form of a roughly carved ox lying in the dust, and before a hideous six-armed idol under a spreading tree, offerings of rice and fruit and of flowers that were scarce faded.

Deeply troubled, the Capitano led us back to the fort where he and the officers drew apart in low converse and we others sprawled in the shade speculating upon the strangeness of all this, the unease of our superiors now communicating itself to us also. We went back on board then, and later the Capitano had us all mustered and told us that he had no explanation for the desertion of the post ashore, but that next morning he would load the cargo that was ready for us and then sail on up the coast calling at other posts en route and arranging for this one to be regarrisoned from their resources.

We set anchor watches, and I well remember that night, sitting on the forecastle under a blazing canopy of stars that hung so low and clear that one felt able to pluck them from the dark skies, a soft offshore breeze bringing the rank scent of the mysterious jungle to my nostrils, the ebbing tide making quiet music along the ship's side.

We set to work as dawn streaked the eastern sky, our total company of eighty divided into three parties: one unshipping ballast from the holds in order to receive the cargo, another breaking open the piles in the sheds and preparing one-man loads, and the main body carrying to the water's edge and ferrying to the ship.

Looking back, one cannot but admire the cunning of the fiend in thus disposing of our force in one strung-out and unarmed line.

The attack came at mid-morning when the men were already near exhaustion in that terrible heat. I was working near the gate of the fort with another man, swinging loads onto the shoulders of the straggling line of porters. I heard the volley of musketry and thought for a second that it came from the ship, but then I saw several of our men fall, and a line of yelling figures burst from the edge of the jungle and charged across the open ground. They dropped flat, and a second line emerged and fired over their prone bodies, then both lines dropped their muskets, drew swords and fell upon the few dazed survivors strung out across the open ground. For a moment my companion and I stood dumbstricken staring at this swift and horrible carnage, then the nearer of the charging line of figures wheeled and raced towards us, and we came back to life quickly and turned tail and ran for the fort. There were a dozen or so of our men working there, and they had come to the arched gateway to see what was amiss. We gained the entrance a few scant steps in advance of our pursuers, and I shrieked to them to swing shut the gates, which we managed to do with the split of an infinitesimal second to spare, and we heard the thump of the bodies of our pursuers and the clang of their armor the other side as they brought up short against the stout wood. Desperately I sought for the wooden bar which closed the gate, but it was nowhere to be seen, so we strained with our shoulders against the pressure the other side and for a time managed to withstand it. Heaving with all my might I gasped to the man beside me to find the bar, but he understood neither English nor Dutch—and then reinforcements joined the others outside, and the gates sprung back sharply, carrying us with them. I traveled in their full arc and my head came crashing against the stone side of the archway and I remembered no more for some time.

When I came to I was in semidarkness and there was a crushing weight upon me. I tried to move but found I was wedged tight. Something warm and wet was dripping down over the back of my head and round into my eyes and almost blinding me, but I could not move my arms to wipe it clear. Then, as full comprehension returned, I realized that I was lying on the ground in the flat-crushed space between the opened gate and the side walls of the archway, and that there was at least one body on top of me. My face was pressed hard against the wood of the gate itself and I could see with half an eye through the crack between the bottom of it and the ground. Bare brown feet in leather sandals were passing to and fro the other side, and I could hear a gabble of voices in an unknown guttural tongue like no language I had heard hitherto. Then the pressure on me was eased a little as I felt the gate swing to a foot or so. There was a ghastly thud on the body above me, then another, and more wetness cascaded down over me. Then through the widened aperture of the gate I saw brown white-clad men going round and stabbing and hacking at the bodies of my late shipmates. In the distance a drum started to beat in a throbbing rising crescendo and the brown men gabbled again and hurried out past the gate, and their voices died away in the distance.

I lay there for what must have been an hour at least, scarce daring to breathe, before venturing to crawl out. I stood swaying in the archway fighting down my rising gorge. Around me lay those of us who had desperately striven to hold the gate, and in a ghastly line stretching from the fort down to the landing place lay the others who had fallen in that first volley and charge. The galleon, under headsails and mizzen, was slowly dropping downstream towards the open sea. That much I saw in that first second, though it took a much greater time to realize exactly what had happened.

The sun was sinking below the western horizon, and the short tropical twilight was fast drawing in before full comprehension came to me. Behind me was a low insistent crackling which for a time meant nothing to me until I felt the heat on my back, then I turned and saw that the wooden sheds and the interior of the fort itself were burning fiercely. I moved slowly away from it and forced myself to walk the distance between the fort and the landing place, looking at each still figure in turn in hope that some at least still lived, but with a sick realization that brought neither relief nor gratitude with it I was forced to accept the conclusion that I alone survived among those ashore. Thirty-two I counted in the line, with Jem among them, and at the landing place a further group of ten which had no doubt formed the crew of the barge. With the men in the fort—fourteen up there I had counted—it made a total of fifty-six dead, and if I had had any doubts about the fate of the odd twenty or so who had been aboard the galleon, they were resolved by some other partly submerged bodies I saw farther out in the shallows.

The fort had now become a blazing pyre, the flames leaping high and lighting up the whole compound, then farther down the river round a bend that had been hitherto hidden from me, I saw a second fire—and staring through the gloom I made out the shape of a smallish vessel hard aground on a sandbank and burning fiercely down to the waterline.

I became conscious of a torturing thirst, and remembering the well in the native village, I turned and wearily made my way back across the clearing. They, whoever the fiends were, had not deemed it worth the trouble to set fire to these poor huts, and things were as we had seen them on our arrival. I drank my fill, then stripped and bathed, scrubbing madly at my body to try and rid it of the filth and clotted blood wherewith it was covered—and it was while I was thus engaged that I caught in the corner of my eye the movement of something white at some distance to one side of me. My heart turned right over and I stood paralyzed of all movement save the uncontrolled trembling of my limbs. Slowly I turned my head and strained my eyes in its direction, and I saw that it was the figure of a man—in white—advancing slowly towards me in the light cast by the burning fort. Then as I realized that he was alone and did not seem to be bearing arms, my manhood reasserted itself and my groping fingers found a loose rock at the coping of the well. I spun round, my hand upstretched with the rock poised to strike. I struggled to get my constricted throat muslces under control.

"Hold! Hold, you fiend, or I'll dash your brains out," I croaked, hoping dully that while the words themselves might mean nothing to him, my attitude would.

The man stopped dead in his tracks a dozen paces from me.

"Praise God!" he quavered. "Praise God for the sound of honest English again. Say something more, m'dear—even if it's only to threaten a poor old man with death." And in his speech was the rich burr of the West Country. I dropped the stone in open-mouthed amazement. He came a little closer and I in turn advanced to meet him, only to recoil in horror.

He was, as I said, in white, but his costume consisted only of a scanty loincloth, the rest of what I had thought was clothing being his own skin, which even in that dim light I could see was of a dead, dull, encicatrized scaliness. He was emaciated, stooped and bent nearly double, and he leant upon a staff, grasping it with a hand that lacked fingers. His hair was of the same linty whiteness as his skin, as was his straggling beard, and both grew in patches. Even his eyes appeared white. There was no color about him at all save in the red bowl which hung round his neck on a string. But it was his face that struck terror to my heart and near turned my bowels to water. The nose was gone, leaving only a hole, and the ravages of his foul disease had already started on the corner of his mouth in the form of a hideous ulcer. I had never seen one before, but I had heard travelers' tales and knew my Bible. This was a leper.

He saw the revulsion in my face even though I tried in common humanity to fight it down.

"Aye," he said bitterly, "the white blight." Then he cackled shrilly. "But it takes longer to carry a man off than the *red* blight which seems to have stricken your shipmates asore this day. How comes it that you're alive, young laddy-buck? Is Weaver losing the sharpness of his tooth, God rot his soul?"

"Who are you?" I asked.

"Dan Nancarrow's the name," he answered. "Though I ant heerd it used this twenty year and more. But *you* talk—*you* talk. If you only knew what music it was to an old man's ears. How came you to be on the Portygooser—you an Englishman, and o' the quality by the voice of you?"

"I sailed in her from the Cape of Good Hope," I told him. "We arrived on this coast a few days since, and here yesterday. Our captain found the post deserted, and he was loading the cargo when we were foully attacked by brown men this forenoon."

He wagged his head. "Aye, aye, aye, I could tell *you* all that," he quavered.

"Then in the name of God who were they?" I shouted.

He lowered himself creakingly into the grass and scratched himself. "Them? Oh them was Mekranis—there's some as says they eat human flesh, but that's larrup-a-likens. Followers of Mahound the Prophet—Mohammed as some calls him. Come from the dry coasts up north, they do. Fierce fighters and nasty people to cross, but good enough friends to them as they like—provided you keep the whip hand on 'em. I had that on 'em all right, till I was took with this. Turn whiter 'n me they would if they thought they'd displeased me. Pigs, it was. They hates pigs. And I kept the skin o' one in the lazaretto special. Any larrup-a-likens from 'em and I'd hang 'em from the yard arm with a strip of it for a collar. Didn't like that, you see. Stops 'em from going to heaven."

"Why did the fiends attack us?" I asked.

He cackled. "Attack you? What do you think? Because it's their trade to. Every man to his trade, laddy-buck. Fox takes a fat goose, you don't ask why he done it. It's his trade to."

"You mean they're pirates?"

"Pirates if you like—but that ant the seagoers' term for 'em. Gentlemen of the Middle Passage *we* call 'em."

"Is there no power out here to deal with them?" I demanded.

"There's some as tries. The Portygoosers up here, the Dutchmen down below. They catch a dhowload of 'em from time to time—mostly younkers just astarting the trade. The Portygoosers burns 'em in front of their church up the coast. The Dutchmen flay 'em slowly. Don't discourage the others, though. It's their trade. Ever see a neater lay than that today? Never lost a man, they didn't. but that was *my* idea, not Weaver's. Had it years ago, but never got the chanst to work it."

"Who's Weaver?"

"The black-hearted trollop's bastard who was my mate. Shipped together for years we did—me as master. Then I come in for this, and they set me ashore here with a barrel of salt beef and a cask of Dutch strong waters and leaves me to rot. They toss me a scrap in passing from time to time—like a dog a bone—but they won't let me near 'em, won't talk to me." He brushed what might have been a tear from his horrible eye. "Gets lonely, see. Me as taught the piddlegullion his trade."

"You mean that this man Weaver is one of those people?" I demanded.

"One of 'em?" he said querulously. "He's the captain of 'em now. But *I* learned 'em—an him—their trade. He'd never of thought of that today. Bribed the cook boys in the fort to hocus the wine casks as soon as we knew the galleon was signaled. Sleeping like angels, some of 'em, and them as wasn't was attended to later. Drove the villagers off into the jungle. Laid up in the trees until the Portygoosers were all working, strung out in a line. Attended to 'em, then laid 'em aboard up creek from the dhow. Burned the dhow. And now he's taken the Middle Passage in the galleon. Sailing back along the way Frankie Drake first came, says he is—right across the Pacifico to the Amerikies—and round 'em onto the Main—with a crew of Mekranis. But he can't navigate like me."

"How long have you been here?" I asked amazed.

"Near twenty years as far as I can reckon. Stayed ashore with some little black turtledoves and got left, we did—me and Weaver. Then we fell in with the Mekranis and learned 'em their trade proper. But the Main—that was where we learned *our* trade—was always acalling, and this was what we planned to do some day." He wiped his eyes again. "But now I been left, and the jungle's a cruel hard place for an old man."

"Where do you live? *How* do you live?" I asked.

"I've got a hut near here, and the people leave food out for me." He leered. "They're obligated to, lest I put the blight on 'em. There's two ways never to go hungry in this land, young laddy-buck—go mad, or get the blight. Both ways you're what the Mekranis call 'accursed of Allah'—Allah being their God, see—and all the Mahounds have got to look after you or the same'll be visited upon them." He cackled maliciously, and watching him, fascinated, it occurred to me that he was accursed twofold because his swift changes from tears to laughter, from fawning amiability to venomous spite, could indeed only be madness.

And now he was wailing again. "Poor old man, that's me. Poor old man as nobody wants. Poor old man with the blight upon him and all his friends run off into the jungle, God damn and blast their poxy black hides. How'm I to get me victuals now, eh? Can you tell me that, young laddy-buck?"

But I couldn't, nor did I care. My only concern was to put as much distance between myself and this ghastly creature as I could force my legs to accomplish. I felt for my garments which I had been trying to wash, and started hastily to assume them, whereupon he set up a loud outcry.

"And now *you're* acutting of your cable, eh? *You're* going to slip off and leave a poor old man. *You*, a white man, behaving like these dirty black heathens here, going to leave me—me as hasn't heard a soft word from one of my own kind all these long years." He struggled to his feet and stumbled towards me, his fingerless hands outstretched. I skipped nimbly round the lip of the well, putting the bulk of it between us and at the same time snatching up the stone again.

"Keep off!" I cried. "I do not wish to do you harm, but by God, come near me and I'll brain you."

He stopped then and stood cursing me horribly. "You dirty young varmint you," he spat. "All right, I'll keep off—and what do *you* do then? Where do you go? Through that jungle, with its striped cats as big as oxen, its serpents a cable in length? And what do you eat? Do you know them fruits as is poisonous and them as is not? Do you know them blackamoors as will help you and them as will kill you as soon as look at you? You don't. Do you know the junglee bolee—the language of these parts? You don't. What are you going to do without me, young laddy-buck? Where'll you go?"

That gave me pause. He was right. Much as I loathed this awful apparition I still needed him. In the dying light of the smouldering fort he saw my hesitation. He chuckled.

"Now, on the other hand if we sails together comfortable, lee to weather, I can teach you a lot. You've got no trouble about your victuals. These blackamoors'll be back afore long and we'll live off the fat of the land again. They'll build a hut for you if I tells 'em, and I promise I'll not lay a hand on you—you can't catch the blight unless you're touched." He was sidling towards me now, a half step at a time, and suddenly it dawned on me what he intended to do. The filthy creature was going to touch me, to lay upon me the curse of his disease, to make me one of his kind so that I would stay here until I dropped to pieces, sharing and thereby lightening his misery. I had heard tales of Catholic priests who had done that voluntarily, but I was not of the stuff whereof they were made. I was a badly frightened man whose flesh was creeping with horror, and this thing, apart from his leprosy, was evil—vile.

I turned and fled blindly.

I sped across the clearing, and behind me I could hear him shrieking wildly. I came to the river bank and felt the mud gripping my ankles but I waded onwards, knee-deep then waist-deep. Then I was swimming, and soon I felt hard sand beneath me and I emerged onto the opposite bank. His yells were dying in the distance, but I still pressed onwards and found myself on the beach. Heavy though the going was in the powdery sand, fear and horror still lent wings to my heels and I did not stop until some hours later I fell exhausted and merciful oblivion enfolded me.

 9

I AWOKE to feel the hot sun beating down upon my back. I was lying face downwards in the sand, the gentle waves of the lagoon lapping close on one hand, and the jungle looming green on the other. I rose stiffly and gazed back the way I had come the night before, but saw nothing but my own footsteps stretching, it seemed, to infinity. The water of the lagoon looked clean and inviting, so I stripped off my clothes and plunged in. I emerged greatly refreshed, but thirst was again troubling me so I set out in search of fresh water and was fortunate to find a shallow stream crossing the beach from the jungle. I drank my fill, then sought the shade of a palm tree where I sat and considered my position.

From what I remembered hearing on the galleon, the Portuguese had a string of such coastal trading forts as this, though at what intervals I knew not. I did know, however, that we were to sail north after we had loaded, so it was a reasonable assumption that if I kept walking in that direction I would eventually come to another of them, and here I could give the melancholy tidings of the fate of my shipmates, and hope that they might have the means of pursuing, finding and dealing with the fiends who had brought this upon them.

Rested and now more at ease since I had come to a decision, I set out along the beach, having the wit this time to walk at the water's edge where the sand was firm. My clothing consisted now only of a tattered shirt and breeches, and I soon had to remove the former and wrap it round my head as some protection from the blazing sun. It was as well for me that we usually worked nearly naked on the galleon so that now my feet were reasonably hardened and my skin tempered against sunburn.

Hour after hour I tramped. I did not suffer from lack of fresh water as tiny streams crossed the beach from the jungle ever and anon, but soon my belly was crying out for food. I thought of seeking wild fruit in the jungle, but that availed me nothing, the undergrowth being bare of everything except leaves. But relief was at hand.

The beach curved here, out of my line of vision, which was why I did not see the village before stumbling upon it. It was of the same type as those we had seen from the ship—just a huddle of mud huts round a fresh water stream. Some small dark naked children played upon the sands, and they stared at me wide-eyed as I approached, then they uttered shrill cries and ran in terror to the shelter of the huts. A group of women mending fishing nets in the shade of the palm trees left their task and flew to the children and gathered them up, retreating then into the undergrowth from out of which they regarded me with every evidence of terror.

I stood in the open and held up my hands to show that I bore no weapons, and I put on what I hoped were gentle and conciliatory expressions, finally opening my mouth and pointing to it and rubbing my belly. They chattered among themselves for some time, then an old woman, bolder than the rest, came out of the undergrowth and brought a pot from one of the huts. She came a little way towards me, put the vessel down on the sand and then retreated rapidly. It contained a mixture of cold rice and fish, and I fell to ravenously. This evidence of my hunger seemed to reassure them a little, because they came out of the jungle timidly, and the old woman picked up something which looked like a skull and neatly chopped the top of it off with a large and heavy knife, then proffered it to me. I took it and bowed my thanks but must have looked my bewilderment because I heard giggling among them. The old woman made signs of drinking. I did so. The skull-like object was a large nut with a fibrous husk and a hard shell, and it contained a white flesh and a clear liquid which was cool and delicious, and I then recognized it as coming from the palm trees I had been passing all day.

Replete and refreshed at length, I pondered my next move. There were no men here so I assumed that they were all away fishing. The women, shy and timid though they were, were kind and compassionate, but I wondered how their lords and masters might receive a stranger on their return. It would perhaps be safer to go my way before they appeared. I therefore thanked the women as graciously as I could in sign language, and continued along the beach. A small boy ran after me and handed me some fruit which resembled yellow Dutch sausages close together on a central stalk. Again I looked puzzled and the child gurgled with delight and showed me how to peel them. These also I found delicious—and I rejoiced because I had seen many such growing on a smaller type of palm than those which bore the nuts. I was now aware of two types of most agreeable food which grew in abundance all around me.

I walked on until nightfall and then threw myself down under a palm tree and slept again, but not as soundly as in that exhausted coma the previous night, because I was tortured by the stings of insects which beset me from the darkness, and I was aware for the first time of the frightening immensity of the jungle. I gazed wistfully aloft at the nuts on the palm tree next morning, at a loss to climb the tall smooth trunk, but then I saw some which had fallen to the ground. I had no knife but I contrived clumsily to break some open with a stone; then I found some of the other fruit, but these were green in color and not so agreeable in taste, so I searched for some of the yellow ones and indeed found them on the same tree, concluding therefore that they were both of the same species but some were ripe and some were not. I was learning apace.

And so I continued for several days—how many I have long lost count of. After that first encounter I did not risk calling again upon the natives, but thereafter kept a sharp lookout, and when a village appeared in the distance, I took to the jungle and skirted it. My fruit diet, though after a time monotonous, was at least adequate, and once or twice I was able to vary it when I came to outcroppings of rock and managed to knock shellfish from them.

And then suddenly that seemingly interminable beach came to an abrupt end in a muddy swamp in which strange trees grew with their roots in the water, and through which a broad and sluggish river flowed to the sea. It was, I judged, somewhat more than a mile or so in width here, and that was more than I cared to risk swimming in my present weakened state, so I turned inland and traced its bank until it narrowed somewhat, and finally I came to a well-defined track that led down to a ford, which I crossed.

The track led on for some miles through the close crowding jungle, then I came to signs of habitation; first some rude rice cultivation in which women were working, then some mean huts, a native idol on a stone plinth, and finally a Calvary with the figure of Christ on the cross. I knew I was near a Portuguese settlement, but I was not prepared for the size and importance of it when it burst upon me.

I rounded a bend in the track and found myself on a broad road that led to the sea, and on each side of it were irrigated rice fields and groves of palm trees, and across them in the distance rose a town of sizeable proportions, clean white- and yellow-washed buildings with two large churches rising in their midst, one of which, from the scaffolding around it, seemed still unfinished. I set out towards it and almost immediately ran into a small group of natives before I could seek cover at the side of the road, but to my relief they took scant notice of me, passing me with scarcely a second glance and no break in their chattering. Then, as I stared at them, I realized why. I was dressed in a manner not unlike their own. My head was bound untidily in dirty white cloth, and my breeches had disintegrated to little more than a swathe about my loins that barely preserved decency, while the sun had burned my body to a brown almost as deep as theirs. Greatly heartened by this I strode on until I reached an open market place in the center of the town.

It was a noisy, bustling place set out with stalls, piles of fruit and nuts on the ground, fish on squares of woven matting, bales of many-colored cloth, eggs, chickens, gourds, pottery and brassware. Natives of many kinds and degree were there, some near naked and as black as the Hottentots of Cape Town, others of lighter shade in cool white garments, others in rich silks and some, to my horror, dressed like the Mekranis who had attacked us. And there were also Portuguese there—soldiers mostly, with here and there a black-robed priest. I approached a soldier and bowed respectfully and said, "Sir, do you perchance understand English?" But he merely looked at me with raised eyebrows, put out his hand and thrust me aside and continued on his way; and much the same thing happened with the next two I accosted, until I bethought me of approaching a priest, but never having spoken to one of this ilk before, I was nervous of doing so. Then I saw an elderly and scholarly gentleman walking slowly and meditatively in the shade at the side of the market, and I tried once again. He, also, stared at me, but not as rudely as the soldiers, and he nodded his head in affirmation.

I said, "Sir, I am an Englishman. I sailed in a Portuguese galleon —the *Santa Elena*—and some days ago we were beset by Mekrani pirates down the coast and all were killed except myself. I have walked here with the tidings."

I had to repeat it slowly again before he grasped the import of it, then in great excitement he signed to me to follow him. He led me across the market and up a broad avenue to a gate in a high white wall. It opened into a cool courtyard on three sides of which were high pilastered buildings with green-shuttered windows and ornate balconies. The courtyard was surrounded by flower beds in the midst of which a fountain splashed musically, and from somewhere came the cooing of doves. He ushered me into a cool darkened hall, signed to me to wait and then hurried off. He returned in a few minutes and led me along a passage into a large room. It was richly furnished, and portraits of dons in ruffs and breastplates, together with those of beautifully appareled women, hung round the walls. A man sat at a carved table, writing with a quill on a vellum scroll. He looked at me sharply as I entered. He was of middle age, dark and handsome, with carefully curled moustaches and a small pointed beard. His eyes were black and piercing.

He said, "Speak."

I repeated what I had already said to the older gentleman. The man said in precise though heavily accented English, "And when did this happen?"

"Five or six days ago, Sir," I answered. "I regret that I have lost exact count of time. At first I was not clear in my mind."

"Your name?"

Without hesitation, I said, "Gil Bardock," because that was the one which came fresh to me.

He motioned me to sit in a chair the other side of the table because, unaccountably, I had started to tremble violently and in spite of the heat I suddenly felt intolerably chilled. I sat heavily, and he said, "Tell me all that happened. From the beginning."

I recounted to him our arrival on the coast, our landing with the Capitano, the desertion of the fort, the attack upon us by the Mekranis, my encounter with the leper, and my march along the beach. He heard me through without interruption, then he spoke rapidly in Portuguese to the other, and together they took my elbows and helped me from the room. And I needed aid now. All strength had suddenly drained from me, and my knees had turned to water. I dimly remember walking with them down more passages and out once again into the sunlight, then through another garden and finally into a long high room with beds arranged in a row on either side, and there was an old white-robed priest there who mumbled over a rosary. Then we were at the side of one of the beds and I was looking down at a man whom at first I did not recognize even though he smiled weakly up at me and said, "Bardock, my friend." It was the sailor who spoke English and for some reason I found myself weeping. Then I remember no more.

I hung between life and death for three weeks, ravaged by the alternating fires and chills of the jungle fever, and heretic though I was to them, those monks of the Hospital of Blessed Joao Albuquerque could not have nursed me back to health more tenderly. When at last I could sit on the shaded balcony, they told me all that had happened. My friend the sailor had been with the party on the galleon that fatal day. They saw and heard the attack upon us but could do little to help us immediately because both the ship's boats were at the bank, and their crews were overwhelmed before they could return to bring help. Then, as they tried to run out and serve the ship's guns, the dhow had silently closed on the other side of her, and grappled and laid her aboard, and all the Portuguese were massacred except my friend who, sorely wounded, dropped unseen into the water and managed to gain the bank opposite that on which the fort stood. He crept away through the jungle and later that day fell in with fishermen. Speaking a few words of their language, he managed to persuade them to bring him swiftly by water, upcoast to this place, the town of Goa, and he had reached it some days ahead of me. He had now died though, poor fellow, but he rendered me a kindly service before doing so, telling them that I was a man of education and good character, well thought of by the Capitano and the officers, who had joined them in Cape Town through the brutal blundering of the Dutch and through no fault of my own.

I stayed on there for a further two weeks after I had been allowed to rise from my bed, gaining strength daily. Several of the hospital monks spoke a little English, and many more French in which I was reasonably proficient, so I passed away the idle hours picking up some rudiments of Portuguese, having, of necessity already acquired a sailor's smattering on the galleon. Then one day they brought me clean garments in the cool local cloth that they sensibly wore here, and the Governor was kind enough to send me a chain of gold for my neck and a good Toledo sword, deeming me no doubt on the sailor's word, a gentleman—and I was much touched by the gesture. I was taken before him—and found that he was the dark man who had first questioned me—dom Francisco da Fonseca.

He received me most cordially and thanked me for the slight service I had been able to render the authorities in thus making my way here with news of the dastardly attack upon the post, for although the sailor had arrived before me, the poor fellow was in such bad shape that they had thought him to be raving, and had accordingly not given his story full credence until mine had confirmed it. Since then, while I had been so near death, they had sent soldiers down in small coastal craft and given the dead decent burial and were now rebuilding the post.

Having thus brought me up to date on events, he then questioned me on my own personal history, courteously and in no way indiscreetly probing into my private affairs. I was tempted to tell him the whole truth at first, but the path of deceit, once embarked upon, is not an easy one to abandon, and I also realized that Charles Stuart the younger was not regarded in a friendly light by Portugal and Spain, so I dissembled and stuck to my false name of Gil Bardock. I was the younger son of a country squire in the county of Yorkshire, I told him, trained in the military arts, with some learning but a short purse, and I had left my home to seek my fortune as a gentleman-adventurer in the Virginias, but my ship had been driven far to the south during the Atlantic crossing and I had finally found myself in Cape Town, where, as he already knew, I had been pressed aboard the galleon by mistake.

He accepted my story without question and expressed his regret at the inconvenience that had thus been thrust upon me, with such sincerity that I felt a deep inward shame at my own duplicity, but I soothed my conscience with the knowledge that at least I was harming none other by it but myself. He then begged of me to regard myself as his guest and promised to arrange passage for me back to Europe at the earliest opportunity.

"But that, I regret, will be long delayed," he told me. "Only two galleons a year come out to Goa from Lisbon, so it will mean a wait of six months at least—and even that might well be protracted because then we will be in the season of the monsoons, and tempests could well put many more months upon the passage."

I assured him that I understood perfectly, and thanked him for the great kindness I had received at his hands already—and then, with expressions of mutual regard, he had me conveyed to the quarters they had put at my disposal.

My chambers were in a cool pavilion in the gardens of the Governor's palace, and they faced outwards across the sea. They were plainly but comfortably furnished, and from the high vaulted ceilings hung heavy matting fans which were kept in motion by cords pulled by relays of natives outside. They had provided me with a servant, a young Indian who told me his name was Gupta Rao. He of course spoke no English and but few words of Portuguese, but he was an intelligent youth and right from the first moment he presented himself to me I found I was picking up a few useful words in his language.

And soon thereafter I began to make a serious study of the language, or rather of three languages, because in teaching me Urdu, which was the lingua franca of all this vast and mysterious land, the language teacher, *munshi*, had perforce to teach me also Portuguese, which he spoke fluently though stiltedly; and while walking through the bazaars of the town, I learned much of the second language of these parts, which was called Konkani. I learned also some of the history of this interesting place. Goa was even then being called the Rome of the East, and its influence was spreading wide. It had originally been a Hindu city of some importance; then it had fallen under the influence of the Mohammedans, led by their king Yusaf Adil Shah, who used it as a port for the entry of Arab horses from the land of the Mekranis, and as a departure place for the devout of his own religion on their pilgrims' way to their holy city of Mecca.

Then, in 1510, had come a handful of Dominican friars from Lisbon who had built the cathedral and then the hospital. And after them came another and a greater missionary, one Francis Xavier, whom the Pope had recently canonized. Close on his heels came the Jesuits and with them the merchants and the soldiers, and they had established their trading posts up and down the coast and become rich. But the Portuguese, wiser than their cousins the Spaniards, did not strip the lands of their wealth and transport it all back to the mother country. They used it to build and expand, and they brought order and justice with them instead of the intolerable cruelty of Spain. Goa now almost matched Lisbon itself in importance, and its inhabitants of all races and colors shared equal status with the citizens of the mother country in much the same manner as the subjects of Rome's overseas colonies in earlier times.

But now their expansion was being threatened by the recently arrived Dutch, who had established themselves in similar manner to the south, and between whom and the Portuguese there existed only the most tenuous and uneasy peace. All this I learned in those early months, and more. I learned of the interior of this mighty land. It consisted not merely of the dense jungles that fringed the settlements. Beyond them were mighty mountain ranges, and after them came the plains and great rivers, and there were many kingdoms there, and cities and fortresses—and then more mountains, and far beyond them was the Road.

It was the Road that I never tired of hearing about. The Road that led from China itself, across the mountains and the deserts, right to Europe. The Road that had been traversed by Marco Polo. The Road that bore the silk, the gold and the precious stones, and was watered with the blood of many thousands. Much of it, as told by the munshi on those furnace-hot afternoons, was no doubt pure allegory, but nevertheless the stories gripped me in a vicelike fever, and I spent much time in dom Francisco's study, poring over the terrestrial globe and tracing the Road's probable route, because, I was assured, it had never been committed to map or chart. And I would lie on my bed staring up at the ceiling and traveling in fantasy those endless leagues, taking with me pack-trains of horses bearing the riches of all Ind, and raising en route an army such as that of Alexander the Great when he came down that same Road in the opposite direction. It was a pleasant time-passer and one that never palled.

Indeed it became more than a time-passer; soon it was an obsession, and the arrival of the galleon that was eventually to take me back to Lisbon, instead of an impatiently awaited deliverance, became a cloud upon the distant horizon which irked me sore.

I was lying thus upon my bed one afternoon, and I think that in my mind's eye I had traversed the whole length of the Road. I was now crossing London Bridge, to the northward this time, and not carrying a coal basket, with a whore by my side, but at the head of a fierce but disciplined cohort, all of us mounted on Arab steeds, and banners and bunting were flying and the whole populace was astir and cheering, and I knew my King awaited us at the Palace of Whitehall—

Dom Braganza, the old secretary to whom I had first addressed myself, entered and I swung my feet to the floor and stood up. He begged me to be seated, and took a chair himself, and I remember feeling irritated at this interruption of my roseate if idle dream. I expected some learned discourse in Portuguese, he gently correcting my grammar and atrocious accent—or perhaps one in Urdu in which I was now outstripping him—but this time there was an air of seriousness about him and he came to the point at once.

"Dom Gil," he said, "I bear from the Governor a request—no, call it rather at this stage an inquiry. Do you feel it in your inclination to grant him a boon?"

"I grant *him* a boon?" I shook my head. "After his kindness and great courtesy that would be unthinkable. Please command me."

"No," he said positively. "This could not be a command. This is something that should not even be *asked* of a guest—but necessity is driving. We expect reinforcements from Lisbon on the next galleon, but in the meantime our garrison is at a low ebb, so many of our soldiers being laid low at this time of the year with the jungle fever."

He paused, and I could see that he was picking his words, with care. "Word has reached us from Aligarh that they are in particularly bad plight there"—Aligarh was the fort at which we had been attacked—"and the Captain can muster no more than a dozen fit men—and farther down the coast two Mekrani dhows have been sighted—"

"Go on," I said breathlessly.

"We can spare a hundred men from here and we have a caravel which is armed with six brass cannon—we have also a skilled ship-master—but the soldiers are Indians and we lack officers. The Governor wondered if—"

But I was already struggling into my doublet and buckling on my sword.

"Take me to the Governor, dom Braganza," I begged.

✦ 10

WE took the inner passage—that is the one between the reef and the shore—since the caravel drew only three feet of water, and Lobo, the shipmaster, knew the coast as none other in Goa. We had a hundred sepoys—Marathas from the hinterland—and a Portuguese master gunner, Pereira. This latter had once been the most skilled man in his craft in the whole of the East Indies, but drink and opium had brought him low, and he was assigned to me only because there was no other.

It may seem strange that a mighty province like Goa should have been so short of soldiers and ships of war, but it must be remembered that Portugal had hitherto had no enemies here, though many farther to the east, that church and army were always at logger-heads and the former was by far the stronger in these parts and that, finally, the dreaded jungle fever took heavy toll of the garrison at this time of the year.

The caravel, though speedy and handy, was scarce larger than a coastal hoy, and my small command packed it to bursting point. Clear of the harbor, I went round with Pereira and inspected our armory of six guns. They were but small twelve-pounders but I was glad enough to have them and I told Pereira that before arriving at our destination I should want four of them loaded with grape and two double-shotted. Then I sent for the native officer and with him I inspected the men. The Marathas are a fierce and warlike race who live in the mountains to the immediate east of Goa. They had little liking for trade or the husbandry of the soil, their only real interest lying in the art of war. When none raged on the frontiers of their own kingdom they would hire themselves and their swords to others. They were high caste Hindus and, as such, hated the Mekranis and other Mohammedans from the north.

I was pleased with the native officer, or *subadar* as they were called. He was an old man, but his steady step, upright carriage and clear eye gave the lie to the gray that streaked his fierce moustaches, and it was evident that his men respected him greatly. His name was Subram Rao and he was a veteran of many battles in a part of the country he referred to as the Deccan, the open stony plateaus beyond his mountains. I asked him about the Road, but he was a man of the south and although he had of course heard of it, he had never been as far afield as that and could tell me nothing.

Lobo read the landmarks along the beach as one would a printed page, and he told me that close-hauled as we were, in the gentle but steady offshore breeze we would arrive at Aligarh at sunset on the second day from the morning of our departure. But that did not fit the plan I had in mind, so, well short of our destination, I ordered him to pole inshore into the mouth of a creek and there, safe from observation from the open sea, we anchored. Since there was little space and less comfort for the men in the caravel, I told the subadar to take them ashore and to let them rest in the shade of the jungle, bidding him to ensure that they kept silent and did not expose themselves to view, and there we stayed until the sun had set and night descended swiftly upon us—then we set off again.

Short of Aligarh by some five miles, and hidden by a bend in the coast, we anchored once more, and I landed with the subadar and two of his best men. We set out along the beach in the darkness, and moving swiftly with swords and muskets muffled against clanking, we reached the river in little over an hour. We turned inland and then swam and waded until we had gained the side on which the fort stood, and I moved up onto an eminence from which I could survey the whole scene with eyes which had now become accustomed to the starlight.

The anchorage was empty and the fort a dark and silent bulk against the sky, while from the village there came not a sound nor a gleam of firelight. I was in a quandary. It might well be that the attack had taken place and the sorry story had repeated itself, in which case the fort would even now be full of watchful Mekranis waiting to ambush an unsuspecting relieving force. On the other hand we might have been fortunate enough to have forestalled them. Whichever it was, my first requirement was intelligence of the situation—and that had to be gained without disclosing my presence to the enemy, if indeed they were here. I discussed this in a low undertone with the subadar.

"Let us then enter the village by stealth, sahib," he suggested. "If it is deserted we may safely assume that the Mekranis have already been here. If it is not, we will be able to secure what news there is."

I commended him upon his ready wits and started to creep towards the village, but he restrained me and advised that we first remove our clothes, except for a piece of cloth secured about our loins. Then he produced a small metal box and took from it a greasy substance that stank to high heaven of death and corruption.

"Cheetah fat, sahib," he explained. "It serves a treble purpose. The faintest scent of it terrifies dogs so much that they cower and refrain from barking. Secondly, it keeps off mosquitoes and other troublesome insects. Thirdly, greased from head to foot it is extremely difficult for an attacker to grasp one."

Although my stomach was turning I saw the sense of this, and allowed myself to be anointed with the others. Then we crept through the grass to the first hut.

I saw with great relief that it was not deserted, as the villagers, in the custom of those parts, were sleeping in the open on string beds, muffled in white sheets. The subadar put his hand upon my arm and jerked his head at the two sepoys. They stole off into the gloom like two evil-smelling shadows, and I realized the efficacy of the cheetah fat when a dog flew snarling from under one of the beds, only to stop dead in his tracks, whine softly and then grovel, terrified, flat-bellied on the ground. There was a slight stir in the darkness ahead of us and I fancied I heard a muffled groan, then the two sepoys returned bearing between them a sagging bundle. We retreated round the fort to the river bank, and the subadar splashed water into the face of the bundle and I saw the whites of eyes in a dark face and heard a whimper of terror.

The subadar said, "We are friends, though lies could make us enemies. Tell us the truth, O my brother, and keep your throat uncut. Are the Mekranis here?"

"No, brave one, I swear it," chattered the villager, "though hourly we expect them."

"Then why have you not decamped into the jungle, as is your cowardly custom?" demanded the subadar.

"Because word came to us from the Terrible Ones that we were to stay in our village and so not give the sahibs in the fort cause to suspect that they were to be attacked," answered the other.

"And therefore you are prepared to betray your salt," spat the subadar.

"What can we do?" wailed the villager. "We are poor people, troubling none and asking only to live and toil in peace. If we had run to the jungle we would have been hunted down after the Mekranis had slain all in the fort."

"Why did you at least not warn the Captain sahib at the fort?" The subadar clamped his hand over the frightened man's mouth as the wail became louder and shriller. "A little seemly quiet, my friend," he hissed, "unless you want to feel the edge of my knife across your gullet."

"Because we were warned of the consequences by the Terrible Ones if we did that. We are poor people and—"

"When is the attack to take place?" went on the subadar inexorably.

"I do not know. I swear on the heads of my children—"

The subadar's knife gently pricked the skin at the angle of the villager's jaw, and the two sepoys moved forward grimly. The wretched villager was on the point of collapse through sheer terror, and I was convinced he was speaking the truth. For a moment I thought of intervening; then I realized that these people were of the same race and that I was as yet still ignorant of their ways and customs. I sat back on my haunches and left it to one who knew.

"They wait for the Portuguese to send another ship from Goa," gabbled the man. "Take away your knife, O brave one—I tell the truth—I swear it. They are in the jungle around us now. When the ship comes they will wait until she is being unloaded, as they did last time. Their dhow is hidden down the coast nearby, but she is damaged and they want another—"

I felt the hair at the base of my scalp prickling. So—we had almost walked into their trap. I nudged the subadar and drew him aside.

"Let us withdraw from here and return to the caravel," I told him. "But bring this man also in case he betrays us."

Stealthily, hardly daring to breathe, we moved to the ford and gained the other side and made our way back along the beach, my scalp still prickling because I felt in my imagination a thousand eyes upon us from the silent jungle.

Back on board the caravel, we questioned the villager with even greater intensity, and he was now more responsive with the increased distance between himself and the dreaded Mekranis. There was the one large dhow, he told us, and it bore nearly three hundred tight-packed men, but it had been demasted in a storm and now they had to row her like a galley, but even so she was still swift and maneuverable, though no longer fitted for lengthy journeys. Hence their desperate need of another ship.

I pondered for a long hour over this. The obvious thing for me to do, outnumbered as I was and with the enemy already in position ashore, was to return with all speed to Goa for reinforcements. But this troubled me greatly, and I could not help but think of the fate of the men in the fort—only some dozen or so now fit, according to the villager—should the Mekranis attack in the meantime. I questioned him about the galleon, but of her he knew nothing except that she had sailed south. These people were of a different crew, he assured me, and if anything more terrible than the others.

Then, after wrestling with the problem until I was near distraught, an idea occurred to me. It was a desperate expedient but given a modicum of good fortune it *might* have a chance of succeeding. *Might*. I called the shipmaster, subadar and master gunner into a council of war and put the plan to them, more than half hoping that they would endeavor to dissuade me from it, but all three, even the drink-sodden gunner, were loud in their praises of my stratagem.

We ran the caravel hard up onto the beach and unshipped three of the brass cannon, and by main force fifty men manhandled them up into the jungle under the direction of the subadar to whom I had given most careful instructions. Then we arranged the remaining

three guns so that two bore astern from the short poop deck, and the
remaining one was set on the starboard side of the forecastle, and all
were carefully covered and disguised under canvas. The fifty men I
had left I made lie flat in the waist of the ship out of sight, leaving
only a handful of sailors on deck under the command of the shipmaster, who then took the helm.

When dawn streaked the eastern sky we sailed boldly down the
coast and into the river, and the prickling of my scalp returned and
was only partially relieved by the sight of three bamboos stuck
carelessly in the sand opposite the anchorage. We hove to in the
exact spot I had indicated to the shipmaster, and he let go an anchor
at both the bow and the stern, thereby holding the craft straight, so
that she would not swing with the tide, and well to one side of the
channel so that another vessel attempting to lay her aboard could
only do so to starboard. We made no attempt to disembark, Lobo
pottering about the deck in the manner of one preoccupied with the
affairs of his ship rather than those of the shore, and soon the men
in the fort grew impatient and two of them came down to the
water's edge and hailed the caravel.

Lobo shouted, "I cannot come ashore, good sirs. I have holed my
longboat badly. Can you send out to me?"

"A pox on you!" bellowed one of the others. "Six of us left on
our feet and you ask for boats! Where are the reinforcements you
were to bring?"

"Alas, there are naught available. The fever has stricken Goa
badly. I bring you stores only," Lobo shouted.

The man ashore flew into a towering rage, cursing and reviling
poor Lobo as only soldiers can when dealing with sailors or vice
versa; then they went back to the fort to bear the unwelcome news
to their officer.

We waited a long crawling hour, myself and my fifty sepoys
crouching beneath the bulwarks. Two men from the fort rowed out
to us sulkily, and as Lobo lowered them a small keg of wine I told
them quietly but urgently through a gun port to make their way
back to the fort with all speed and to secure the gate upon themselves. They gaped and gawped a little at first but Lobo supplemented my instructions in language that rivaled their own and
promised that the lash of the garrison commander would be heavy

upon their backs if they did not obey me, or worse, warned our watchers by their demeanor. They went swiftly.

Then we saw the dhow.

She came round the point under oars, rowed fast and expertly, cleaving the yellow waters like a dart, and from her crowded decks came a loud baying like that of a hellish hound-pack when it sights prey. My palms were sweating in like manner to my sun-scorched back as I crouched, and I wiped them on my shirt, loosened my sword in its scabbard and looked to the priming of my pistol. Above me on the poop Lobo was behaving perfectly, wringing his hands and twittering with panic, and his sailors acting in like manner. And then the helmsman on the dhow observed for the first time that we were hard over on the western side of the channel and he had perforce to carry out the maneuver we intended him to, and go hard a starboard at the last instant and cross our stern. I sprang to the poop ladder and applied a smoking linstock to the first gun, and Lobo did the same to the other, and two heavy charges of grape raked the dhow from stem to stern at point-blank range, cutting hideous red swathes in the close-banked rowers and the clustered group of boarders waiting on their low forecastle to rush us as they grappled. Then I ran to the solitary broadside gun and added to the carnage—and my fifty sepoys were lining the side and firing their heavy muskets into what was left of them. The dhow swung side on to the current, and her wake was stained red from the blood that cascaded from her scuppers, and as a second musket volley blasted them she grounded hard on the bank. It was over in less time than it has taken to set it down here, and from her deck came no movement except that of some wounded wretches screaming in the waist, and a boarding party on the poop who appeared unscathed. But that was remedied before my sepoys had time to reload their muskets. Fire seemed to find powder somewhere amidships, and a sheet of orange flame leapt skyward a second ahead of the booming blast that near to split our eardrums, and it tore the side out of her, breaking her stern off like the end of a carrot and precipitating the dead and dying from the poop into the current.

Lobo was cheering like a madman and wringing my hand, and the sepoys were capering in a grotesque dance of victory, but we had little time to contemplate our handiwork, because at that moment from the jungle at the edge of the clearing swept a line of white-clad men, yelling and screaming like demons in a fury, making for the side of the caravel that was nearest to the shore, where a few short feet separated us from the bank. Again we dissembled, and I pretended to beat the sepoys into loading their muskets faster, and they in turn from jubilation fell into what seemed panic at this fresh threat, so not a shot was fired at the newcomers until they had all emerged into the open and were charging in a tight-packed mass which would have called for floggings all round from any commander who knew his trade, but which suited our fell purpose to perfection.

They reached the center of the clearing, and the three guns hidden to their flank at the spot marked by the three bamboos, spewed noisily into their midst, cutting the line down like a scythe through corn, and then the second fifty under the subadar were charging with flailing swords into what few of them were left standing.

We swarmed over the side of the caravel and joined our comrades, and for a moment I was minded to call them off because I wanted prisoners to take back to Goa, but I soon realized that I might as well have tried to halt a hurricane in its path, for my hitherto docile and disciplined sepoys were now berserk and were hacking to pieces dead and dying alike.

I walked across the clearing to the fort, and the gates through which I had crawled more dead than alive those long months previously were thrown open, and the Captain, a sick but very relieved man, received me most civilly even before I presented him my letter of authority from the Governor.

We remained there some days, driving the timid villagers to the task of gathering up and burying the dead, which numbered near to four hundred, for fear of pestilence breeding in the rotting corpses, and we found among them in the freakish chance of the battlefield some dozen unhurt or slightly wounded. These the Captain hanged with due ceremony on a gallows he caused to be erected at the edge of the clearing, looping strips of pigskin round their necks and throwing the guts of the slaughtered animals into the common grave of their comrades. This I deemed rather pettish spite, but he explained to me that for Mohammedans this place would hereafter be accursed and would be one to be avoided like the plague, for, he went on, word of this would travel the length and breadth of that coast in far less time than it would take a swift ship to sail it, in the mysterious manner known only to the natives themselves.

I spent some time trying to find the leper again, not from any feeling of sympathy or compassion I had for the loathely creature, but because I thought I might hear from him something of the fate of the galleon his ex-shipmate Weaver had stolen, but the natives evaded my questioning and denied all knowledge of him, and neither threats nor cajoling could get them to depart from this stance.

So, after embarking the sick from the fort and replacing them with the gallant Maratha sepoys, we sailed back to Goa on a fair wind, arriving there two days later.

The Governor received me with the greatest honor, causing flags and bunting to be displayed when we disembarked, and we rode together from the jetty to his palace in the richly carved and gilded howdah of an elephant which was caparisoned from trunk to tail in cloth of gold, our route bestrewn with flowers thrown by the shrilly acclaiming natives. A magnificent reception was held for me that night which began with a sumptuous banquet and went on into the early hours of the morning, and we were entertained by jugglers, tumblers and acrobats, and, after various high Jesuit dignitaries had left, by dancing girls from the palace of a nearby maharaja, as the princes of these parts are termed. It was my first experience of this type of diversion, and although I understood nothing of the elaborate symbolism of the Hindu dances at this time, I was vastly enthralled by it.

I was sitting in my place of honor at the right hand of the Governor when he caught my eye and signed to me that he wished to speak with me in private. I arose and followed him out of the banqueting-hall to the study in which he had first received me. He set me down in a chair and brought forth a decanter of exquisite wine of Oporto.

"We have word, dom Gil," he said, "of the arrival on the coast of the galleon that will take you back to Europe—the *Santa Marisa*."

This news would a few short weeks ago have sent me into transports of delight, but now after the events of the last weeks I experienced a slight chill of melancholy, and this must have shown in my face, because he said quietly, "You do not wish to go?"

"I have trespassed enough on your kind hospitality, Excellency,"

I answered. "But all things must end, and I shall take from here the warmest feelings of gratitude for all you have done for me."

"You are reversing the obligation, dom Gil," he said gently. "It is rather we who should feel gratitude to you. Had it not been for your bravery and fortitude in the first place in bringing us a true account of the attack upon the fort, we should not have been fore-warned of the dastards' second attempt. Then, to put us still further in your debt, to command so brilliantly the operation against this other attack, and to rout a foe who outnumbered you four to one—" He shrugged expressively. "But that is not what I have called you here to discuss. It is your future which interests me. What do you intend to do on arrival in Portugal?"

I was silent for some minutes, then I said, "To proceed to the Lowlands, Excellency, and there to sell my services to any who will buy them."

"Not to England?" he asked in some surprise.

Again I was on the point of telling him my true story, but some inner caution held me back, and I had perforce to lie again.

"There is naught in my own country to call me, Excellency," I told him. "As a younger son my patrimony is scant, and I had already left there to seek my fortune abroad."

"Could a larger fortune be found in the Lowlands than here?" he asked.

I felt my spirits rising. "I know little of the conditions here," I said, "other than that it is a preserve of Portugal and that I should imagine that penniless adventurers from England would receive scant welcome."

"That is where you make a mistake—in your own case, at least," he said earnestly. "Dom Gil, you have proved yourself a true friend of my country and a skilled and resourceful commander in the field. I offer you service with us—a commission from the hand of our king himself to bear arms against all our enemies in this realm, but to be freed of the oath of allegiance in the unhappy, and I hope un-likely, event of your own country ever falling into that category. You shall command a thousand native sepoys, a hundred mariners and a fleet of five fast caravels, be granted an estate commensurate with your dignity and an honorarium of one thousand gold mohurs per annum, and have a twelfth share of all booty seized by you in

the name of our realm from all who trade on this coast without the
authority of Portugal. I do not ask you to decide immediately but I
do commend it to your earnest consideration."

I had made up my mind before he had finished speaking, and I
stood and held my hand out to him.

"Your Excellency," I said. "My hand and my sword—and may I
never give you cause to regret the honor you have done me."

✧✧ 11

AND so I became a Commander of Portugal, with an army
and a fleet at my command and a thousand miles of coast my realm,
and for two years I harried the Mekranis, sinking and burning their
dhows and hanging the crews in pigskin and finally making an expedition to the Mekran coast itself, far to the north, where I set fire
to their villages and shipyards, so bringing to a well-merited end five
hundred years of cruel murder, robbery and rapine.

My success was due largely to the wisdom with which I chose my
lieutenants. I was a strict taskmaster and a hard disciplinarian, but I
endeavored always to be just, and although I never neglected to
punish when I deemed it necessary, I was equally scrupulous to
reward when it was deserved—in praise and honor and, even more
important with these people, in gold and silver, and I felt therefore
that I could always count upon the loyalty of my own command,
from Lobo, Pereira and Subadar Subram Rao down to the lowliest
sepoy.

The magnificent estate the Governor bestowed upon me consisted
of a thousand acres of well-established coconut palms and rice paddies on the island of Panjim, just across the harbor from the main
city of Goa itself, with a great house surrounded by gardens of
breathtaking beauty set on the shore and looking west across the Sea
of Araby. It had belonged to one dom Bothelo, a high official in the
government of Goa who had fallen foul of both church and state,
been attainted of treason and sent home to the mother country to

face trial. Found guilty and condemned to the block, his estate had been escheated, and I sometimes reflected wryly on the irony of Fate and wondered to whom my own estates in Yorkshire had been given, although, truth to tell, it worried me not in the least. A man can live only in one house at a time, and this gracious one here compared most favorably with that gloomy manor on the edge of the cold moors. And here I was doing useful work, putting down a cruel and barbarous tribe and allowing a gentle and harmless people to live in safety—protecting the peaceful merchantmen using the coastal seaways and generally bringing law and order to the wild places. There I had been, at best, a hired mercenary—at worst, a political cat's-paw for craftier men than myself. Here the issues were clear-cut and a man could live without subtlety and deceit dictating his every action. Or so I thought in those two halcyon years.

I was high in the councils of the Governor now, taking my seat as a matter of course whenever he summoned his committee of advisors on matters of state. At first there had been oblique and sidelong glances from the more conservative of his councilors at this stranger who spoke Portuguese with such a strong English accent, but as they saw that I had no political ambitions whatsoever, and wanted nothing other than to do my duty and enjoy my estates, even these ceased. At least they ceased in so far as the secular members were concerned, but I still felt I was regarded with suspicion by the Jesuits. With my rise in the official life of the colony came also the parallel one in society, and now I entertained and was entertained in a style befitting royalty, at routs and balls and masques and other diversions of an agreeable nature, and I met for the first time the wives and daughters of the nobility—fully chaperoned and with every discretion because the Portuguese were as careful of their women as were the local Mohammedans of their harems. By the very nature of things there was a great dearth of European ladies in the colony, the men greatly outnumbering them, but this seemed in no way to incommode the latter, as most had set up establishments very similar to the harems I have mentioned, and in Goa was already being founded that vast race of mixed blood which eventually spread beyond the confines of the colony and supplied the rest of India with its clerks, teachers and higher artisans—the Goanese.

I could have maintained such an establishment myself, and I have no doubt that most of my friends assumed that I did, but the fact remained that I did not. Moral scruples as such did not come into the matter at all. It was purely that bought women had no appeal for me whatsoever—and that is what a native mistress amounted to, however beautiful, gazelle-eyed and faithful she might be. One bargained with father or agent as one would for a bolt of silk in the bazaar, the physical points of the poor little chattel being lauded and expatiated upon by the seller and denigrated by the buyer, until a price was struck and she became just another possession.

No, I decided, such sordid trafficking killed romance. I could wait. But I was young and lusty and man cannot live overlong by bread alone, so there were dalliances from time to time. None made much impact upon me, and I hope little upon the other protagonists. Certainly none lasted, but at least their short and torrid spans were free of the blight of commercialism. There was the Persian princess taken by Mekrani pirates and held for ransom until rescued by us on one of our northern raids. Before God, all I wanted from her on that long run down the coast of Goa was some instruction in the art of astronomy in which I had been foolish enough to believe all Persians were per se extremely proficient. But the only stars I learned about were those in the lady's deep and luminous eyes, and I felt a varlet when I handed her over to the Persian ambassador and received from him in gratitude for her safe delivery the Order of the Thousand and One White Roses of Purity. Then there was the sprightly young Goanese widow who had inherited her elderly spouse's provender business and victualed my troops and ships. But she was jealous and demanding and made scenes if I went one single night without whistling softly beneath her window for the ladder to be let down. I suffered severe belly cramps when I started gently to extricate myself from this affair, usually after partaking of one of the excellent curries which she used to prepare with her own fair hands. Then I heard that it was the colic that had carried off her husband, so I departed north to inspect our forts. When I returned, I found to my relief that she had married a factor in the East India Company—who also eventually died of colic.

After that came a devidass, or Hindu temple prostitute. Technically *she* was a bought woman, but she was one so high in her craft—so diabolically skilled in the arts of love, that she had earned the privilege of choice and rejection, and her waiting list of postulants was long indeed. She danced—for a fee that would have re-roofed every farm on my Yorkshire estate—at a banquet given by the Governor for his senior officers and councilors. It was a banquet in the Oriental style and we lolled on cushions round a circular table raised but a few inches from the ground, and serving the dual purpose of festive board and stage—and the company was entirely male. It was the Dance of the Seven Goddesses of the Godaveri, a quivering undulation of limbs beneath a diaphany and an exquisite fluttering of hands in which even the most unimaginative could see the butterflies' courtship and mating above a breeze-ruffled cornfield, and in turn each of the other six dancers sank in the semblance of sated passion to the floor, leaving only this woman still moving above them.

She was not beautiful as I would have defined beauty before coming to this country, being rather heavier than our European women. Moreover, her face was painted grotesquely with a white pigment, her eyes ringed with kohl, and the palms of her hands stained with henna—but she was withal desire incarnate. She finished her dance before me and dropped a silk scarf as delicate as a spider's web over my head and eyes, and then ran from the room. I did not know the significance of this in those days, and I sat gawping like a landed fish, clapping my hands as one would when pleased in an English playhouse. The others did, though—and they congratulated me and pledged me in wine, then when I made no move they seized me and raised me shoulder high and bore me, shouting and cheering, through the palace and out into the bazaar to a shuttered native house of some grandeur behind the Temple of Shiva. There they left me as soft questing hands came out of the darkness and drew me down into the depths so sublime that I wished never to rise again.

I crept from that place three days later, and since the prime function and lifelong training of the devidass is to drain all desire and attendant unholiness from the faithful before entry to the temple, I lived the life of a Spartan for some months thereafter.

Then came Jeanne . . .

The Governor was a widower, having lost his wife of the fever long before my arrival, and being a man of great, almost austere, moral stature, he did not have recourse to the usual arrangement, throwing himself instead more and more into his work but, at the same time, not chiding his weaker brethren who had not his powers of continence. Then midway in my second year in Goa he himself fell ill and returned to Portugal to recuperate in its more temperate climate.

I well remember going aboard the galleon on his return to welcome him back. The Deputy Governor, the Council, high church dignitaries and myself—the city bedecked with flags and bunting under the blazing sun, and guns booming in a mighty salute. He received us on the high poop and we were delighted to see that the color had come back to his cheeks, the sparkle to his eye and erectness to his stooped shoulders and, after the stiff formalities of the official greetings, as we clustered round him to grasp his hand and offer our felicitations, he halted us and said merrily, "Yes, a cure gentlemen. Permit me to present you to that cure."

And Jeanne came through the door from the dark great-cabin into the sunlight.

The guns had just at that moment ceased their booming and in that silence all eternity seemed to hang upon a thread. Even the screaming gulls above us for some reason stilled their clamor, and there was the sound only of the gentle offshore breeze in the ringing, and the light tapping of her high French heels on the deck as she walked towards us.

"Gentlemen, my wife," said the Governor to us in Portuguese— and to her, in French, he added, "My dear, let me present first His Eminence the Cardinal Archbishop—my deputy M'sieur Furtado— the president of the Council, M'sieur Coelho—" And by the time it came to my turn to take and bend over her hand I had regained possession of myself.

It was no case of love at first sight; certainly not on her part, for she told me afterwards that she saw naught to distinguish me from any of the other officers then presented to her, save a certain skinniness and my execrable accent when I offered my greetings in French.

Her impact on me? None in those first few moments. I think I must have known a certain numbness—the shock, for example, that comes to a man struck by a musket ball. An absence of sensation.

Something so devastating has happened that the nerves and senses refuse for a time to register it. Then that of sight started slowly, almost painfully, to function, and I saw a girl who barely reached my shoulder, which made her the merest tithe below middle height when one allowed for the high French heels which had so prettily tapped across the deck. Her hair, high-piled and ringletted, was of deep lustrous bronze, her skin soft and creamy as the damask rose, eyes huge and of the deepest violet, the short straight-bridged nose that betokens breeding in a woman as surely as do certain points in a horse, mouth perhaps a trifle too full in contour to please a purist, but sensuous rather than sensual. Her figure beneath her magnificently gold-embroidered white silk gown was fairy slight when compared with the ampler charms of the Portuguese ladies to whom I had become accustomed, but it was exquisitely rounded and promised much.

A discreet cough behind me told me I had held her hand longer than protocol allowed, so I dropped it hastily and mumbled my apologies and drew back into the crowd.

I was her partner at the ball that night in a stately cotillon, but the tropical heat, on top of the fatigues of the official reception, was by now tiring her, so she asked me to conduct her to the balcony outside the ballroom. I did so with some little unease because this would have been unthinkable in the case of a Portuguese lady, but she was French and deliciously natural and although I was acutely conscious of scandalized eyes upon our backs as we crossed the wide marble floor between the bowing figures of the dancers, it bothered her not one whit.

We leaned upon the balustrade and she was entranced by the moon on the dark waters of the bay, and the fretted shapes of the palms against the night sky, and the stars that hung so low and luminous, and the scent of spices that was born on the hot still air, and she would fain have remained there much longer than the all too brief ten minutes I considered discretion dictated. But even in that short time I learned a little of this strange, disturbing woman. She was a distant kinswoman of the Governor, the daughter of a French branch of the family. She was much younger than her husband—I judged her to be little more than twenty, while he, I knew, could not be less than fifty, even allowing for the toll that years in a torrid clime had taken of him.

I sailed with the dawn next morning on a periodic patrol of the
southern forts, and was away some few weeks, and on my return I
dined with the Governor. He was, I was sorry to observe, pale and
tired, and the promise of improved health we had noted on his
return, had not been fulfilled. This was not a social occasion, but
merely one on which I presented my report on matters that had
occurred during his absence, and consequently his wife was not
present. Our dinner and business completed, I sat awaiting his dis-
missal, but he showed no sign of wanting me to withdraw. He
talked on many things—the state of politics in Europe—the increased threat of Dutch competition in trade with the Indies—some
friction between the church and the secular authorities out here,
and finally of his own domestic affairs.

"I fear my wife finds life dull in Goa, dom Gil," he said. "She
droops."

"She is young, Excellency," I answered, "and the period of accli-
matization is bound to sap her vitality in her first year."

He nodded but without great conviction.

"I dare say. But I am beginning to doubt my wisdom in bringing
her out here. Five years is a long time—and that is the term I have
remaining before returning to my estates in Portugal."

"I have been here nearly half that period, Excellency," I reminded
him, "and the time has sped like the wind."

"For you, yes—for all us men. We have our work. For a woman
immured here without much to occupy her it is different. For a
Frenchwoman who has had a greater measure of freedom than those
of my own country it can be even more tedious."

"Her Excellency keeps good health, I trust," I said.

"Health, yes—but ennui can undermine that of the most robust.
Dom Gil, I am worried about her."

"I wish I could help, Excellency," I said, knowing full well that
there was nothing I could do, but merely as a politeness, and I was
surprised at his instantly taking me up on it.

"I think you can," he said quickly. "This is a thing I would find
difficult to ask a countryman, bound as we are by our archaic code
of etiquette, but with you, my dear friend, I feel more at ease. Take
the matter of the language, for instance. She shows little interest in
studying it at present. The good Father Julian despairs of her and
she says the very presence of the munshi, who tries to teach her a

little of the local vernacular, nauseates her." He shook his head gloomily.

"I would be happy to assist Her Excellency in her studies," I said doubtfully, "although I feel I am so imperfect in the language myself—"

"Splendid, my dear fellow," he said gratefully. "And there is one other thing. Our Portuguese ladies take little or no exercise and dread going out in the sun even in the cool of the mornings and evenings—whereas she has ridden and hunted and falconed with her brothers in France—and sailed boats, and generally comported herself like a hoyden. I know that this would not be practical or desirable in this country, but at the same time I am sure a great deal of her malaise would be dispelled if she were able to go out more. I would gladly attend to these things myself, but as you know, my time is so greatly taken up with affairs of state—and I must confess that my own energy is not what it was when first I came out to these parts. Could you, do you think, devise some little outdoor diversion for her? I could arrange for a chaperon from among the younger wives or daughters of some of the officials."

"I will do all in my power, Excellency," I said sincerely. "It will be a little enough return for all the kindness I have received at your hands." And from the bottom of my heart I meant it.

We began the following day in that blessed hour of coolness that comes with the going down of the sun. I took my books round to the palace and we sat in a pavilion overlooking the sea, with the stout wife of a palace secretary sleepily embroidering a piece of cloth nearby. But Her Excellency was anything but an apt pupil— not from any lack of intelligence but more because she was just not interested in Portuguese, and she made no secret of this right from the start. I left at the end of an hour, depressed by a sense of failure, but she herself seemed delighted at what poor progress we had made, and she was good enough to tell me that she eagerly awaited our next period of study.

We met in this manner two or three times a week, and soon I found myself awaiting our meetings with the feeling of liveliest anticipation even though I soon gave up all attempts at teaching her anything but the most elementary conversational phrases. The Governor, however, was most pleased and gracious about my efforts, and he told me that he noticed a marked rise in her spirits.

Greatly encouraged by this I set about looking for a couple of horses for herself and the chaperon, as my own stable was a little too highly spirited for ladies, and with the help of Subram Rao I secured two good Kathiawar geldings which I trained to sidesaddle by dint of swathing myself in folds of cloth to resemble skirts, and schooling them thoroughly in the manège of our barracks, to the wonder and amusement of the sepoys who saw in this activity just another example of the madness that afflicts all white men.

But all did not go smoothly with the first excursion I had planned by horseback. Dona Ena, the chaperon, was terrified of horses, and when lifted to the saddle she sat as one petrified, emitting a long shrill wail of terror which did not cease until she had thankfully regained *terra firma* once more. Her Excellency, however, was an accomplished horsewoman and her only complaint was that she found her mount too tame.

"I wish to feel the wind in my face," she cried. "This horse must fly—fly!"

"I fear that that would greatly incommode the chaperon, Madame," I explained.

"Oh, Devil take the fat sow!" she exclaimed impatiently, and I was thankful that the good Dona Ena did not understand French. "Let her cling on—or break her stupid neck!" And with that she clapped her dainty silver spur to the flank of her horse and set off along the hard sand at the edge of the surf in a flat gallop. I grabbed the bridle of the chaperon's horse before it could follow, and struggled to control both it and my own nag while I slipped from the saddle and helped the frightened woman to the ground.

I was in a quandary. Although not far from Goa, this was a lonely part of the beach and not one on which it was advisable for a solitary woman to ride alone. At the same time the chaperon undoubtedly would, as Her Excellency had so lightly suggested, break her neck if her animal bolted with her. I therefore helped her to the shade of the palm trees, tied her horse and promised to return in just so many minutes as it took me to catch our joint charge and bring her back. Then I swung to the saddle again and set off furiously in the wake of that infuriating girl, with rage in my heart.

And I had to ride like the hammers of Hades to catch her, because she could handle a horse like no other woman I had ever met, and her weight was nothing to that powerful animal. I came up with her only when she herself chose to draw rein—and that was a good two miles or more up the beach and round the headland. I had been most careful and circumspect in my manner towards her until this, but now I was boiling.

"God damn you for a feckless slut!" I roared at her. "You might well have killed yourself, to say nothing of that poor wretch back there." But she merely threw her head back and laughed merrily and I could no longer be angry with her, because never had she been more beautiful than at that minute. Her jaunty feathered hat had fallen from her head and hung at the end of its ribands, her glorious red hair was flying free, there was a flush of color in her peerless cheeks, and her violet eyes sparkled with twin devils of mischief.

"Wonderful!" she cried. "Oh—wonderful—wonderful—wonderful!"

I quickly averted my eyes, not daring to look at her longer.

"We must return," I mumbled. "It grows dark quickly here and that woman will near die of terror."

She appeared to see the sense of this because she made hasty reparations to her ruffled state and then we turned and jogged sedately back.

Dona Ena was so upset that it took the combined efforts of us both to get her back into the saddle, but Her Excellency was both kind and penitent towards her, promising her a beautiful gown from Paris that she had never yet worn if she would but keep the secret of her waywardness from all at the palace in case the Governor forbade her to ride again. And she kept her promise, and added to the gown a purse of gold mohurs so I learned later, which the good woman was pleased to accept because her husband was not highly paid.

But that was the end of our language lessons. Thereafter she demanded to ride on all evenings that I was not engaged upon my duties. Dona Ena's fear of horses we considerately overcame by proceeding at a gentle walk from the stables to a ruined marble pavilion some distance up the beach, where I used privily to station a young Goanese under-officer of mine to protect her and bear her company while we others enjoyed a gallop farther afield—a suggestion of Her Excellency's which I deemed did her credit for a kind and thoughtful woman.

I think it was on our third such excursion that both our horses took it into their heads to curvet at one and the same time just as I was making some small adjustment to her bridle, bringing my knee hard up under hers. It was the first time I had had the slightest physical contact with her other than the most formal one of kissing her hand on official occasions, and I remember even now the tingling sensation it engendered, that was akin to touching hot metal on a cold day. Confused, I reined back sharply, but the spark was already akindle. She leaned towards me in the saddle, her eyes closed, her lips parted.

I slid to the ground and led both horses into the shelter of the palms, secured them by their reins and then lifted her down. Blindly we walked through the undergrowth to a stream that plashed over rocks through the cool greenery.

Then suddenly she was mistress of herself and of the situation. Firmly she checked my ploughboy fumbling at her riding habit, and she turned and walked from me, and for a moment I knew relief that this ultimate betrayal of one who had befriended me was put aside, but then came rage and I stumbled after her. She eluded me in the thick greenery and I heard her silvery laugh. I swore lewdly and crashed through the undergrowth with the lack of grace but the same inexorable purpose as a rutting elephant. My sword swung between my legs and brought me down heavily, mired and sweating, and I rolled down the bank towards a tiny embowered pool.

She smiled down at me mockingly, then, with a twist and a sinuous wriggle, she was quit of her riding habit and was standing before me, naked—slim—cool—maddening—

✧✧ 12

It was August, and the promise of the blessed relief of the monsoon was in the heavy air. The drooping leaves of the neem trees stirred almost imperceptibly about the hour of sundown, and on the southern horizon low banks of cloud built up at dawn, holding out against the brazen sky for a little longer each day, and there was a growing hint of thunder that was as yet more a feeling than a sound.

I remember that particular evening. We rode slowly along the beach on our way back from the waterfall, and I am afraid that my thoughts were not with my lovely companion. She was aware of this and, woman-like, was piqued and petulant because of it and she chided me angrily, saying that usage was beginning to dull the keen edge of earlier ecstasy. I stoutly denied this, knowing in my heart that she was right, but try as I would I could not dispel the sense of guilt that hung over me. It had been increasing lately—a compound of the consciousness of my treachery towards my friend and superior, perhaps a presentiment of impending disaster and, truth to tell, a certain weariness engendered by her persistent demands.

I cursed the time of the year. Any day now the rains would break, confining us all to the garrison because the jungle paths became well-nigh impassable, the streams swelled to raging torrents and sudden storms would soon make putting to sea a perilous business. The monsoon was, in short, equivalent in this country to the winter in Europe, and its effect on military movement was the same. We would be pent up in this place, and this woman, without even the temporary relief of our evening excursions, could in her frenetic desire be dangerous. Let me not sound too hypocritical, but I swear that at this time my concern was at least as much for her and her wronged husband as for myself. At any other season of the year I would have mounted an expedition to some far corner of the realm and protracted it to a point which would have given us both time to break the affair off without undue hurt to either.

"Damn you!" she said suddenly with heat, and I realized that she must have been speaking without my hearing her. I started to mumble my apologies but she clapped spurs to her horse and galloped furiously forward along the water's edge and I, glad to be alone, let her go and continued at a walk. I came up with her eventually at the ruined pavilion and I knew something was wrong immediately, because she was sitting on her sweating mount looking round her in deep mystification.

Dona Ena and Diaz, the Goanese under-officer, were nowhere to be seen, nor were their horses. We sat and looked at each other in dismay.

"What can have happened?" she breathed.

I shook my head in deep perplexity and then rode some distance into the jungle calling their names, but receiving no reply. Troubled and with a sense of foreboding, we rode swiftly back along the beach towards the town, convinced that they had been set upon and carried off for ransom by a band of dacoits, as the jungle brigands were called, my brain turning over furiously in an effort to think of a story to cover this absurd contingency, Jeanne pale with terror.

I said, "Let us say that we wished to gallop but that Dona Ena was nervous so we left her to follow at her own pace, but then, on our returning a few short minutes later round the headland, she was nowhere to be seen. I shall accompany you to the palace and then return here with some of my men to make a search for her."

"Who will believe us?" she asked fearfully.

"How do I know?" I snapped. "That is the sorriest best I can think of in the circumstances." And I must admit that even in my anxiety I experienced some slight raising of hope that this might yet be our deliverance in that she would be in no mind to carry on this affair even should we emerge from it unscathed.

I saw the lone horseman in the gathering gloom while we were still some two miles short of the city, and I spurred forward to inquire from him if he had seen the missing pair. Then, as I drew near him, I realized it was Pereira, the master gunner. He doffed his hat and shot me a swift glance, indicating that he had something to impart to me alone. I drew aside with him.

"Dom Gil," he said urgently, "forgive me this liberty but I must warn you, at the risk of incurring your displeasure, that you are in great danger, to saying nothing of"—his eyes slid sideways to Jeanne —"er—other persons."

"What is it, Pereira?" I asked.

"Subram Rao brought me word but an hour ago that Diaz, the Goanese jemadar, had been lodged in the House of Detention together with one Dona Ena—"

"On what charge?" I demanded, my heart turning right over.

"It would appear that they had been taken red-handed in—in— highly compromising circumstances, Sir, in a pavilion on the beach—"

I needed to hear no more. Two codes of law operated in Goa —civil and canon—and the latter was immeasurably the more severe, its administration resting as it did in the hands of the Inquisition. Adultery was a heinous offense under both.

"How did it happen?" I groaned.

"There has long been gossip in the bazaars about their association. I think it at last reached the ears of her husband, who accordingly watched her with two of his friends and an officer of the Inquisition."

"I see," I said slowly. "Regrettable, no doubt, but how does this spell danger for me—or Her Excellency?"

He looked at me with some reproach. "Dom Gil," he begged, "please forgive me if I seem impertinent, but matters of this sort cannot be long kept secret in Goa. The reason for their daily excursions has been a subject of speculation this last three months—and your name and that of this lady have been drawn into it. There have been stories told by the natives who had spied upon them there, and on—on you—" He trailed off, too diffident to continue. But I had heard all that was necessary. Fool that I was to imagine that our guilty liaison could have escaped notice, to have forgotten that the bazaar and the jungle had a thousand secret eyes. I felt a crimson tide creeping up my neck and face as I thought of what they might have heard and seen at the waterfall.

He went on: "Dom Gil—if these two are put to the question by the Inquisition—"

I said, "Wait," and reined my horse across to Jeanne and told her in an undertone what had happened. She swayed and near swooned in the saddle.

"Mon Dieu!" she gasped. "In a penitent's robe and hood—the fire—"

And she spoke no more than the truth, for that was the punishment. The stake for the woman—in the square before the cathedral, with the mob scoffing and jeering. For the man—garroting on the gallows. Prince or peasant, rank was no protection.

I grasped her hands.

"Trust me, Jeanne," I entreated. "Whatever may befall, I will not let the weight of this descend upon *you*."

"How can you prevent it now?" she demanded hysterically. "What can you do to protect me? Oh God, I wish I had never met you. It was all your fault—yours—yours—*yours!*" She ended on a scream.

Behind us I heard Pereira stirring uncomfortably. He came forward.

"Don Gil," he said. "We have a boat ready in the harbor—Lobo, Subram Rao and I. There is yet time. The Council does not assemble until morning, so even if they have babbled already no official cognizance can be taken of it until then. Their statements must be recorded before the Lord President."

This I knew to be true. That august body, the Inquisition, held to legal protocol above all things, and therein lay its strength.

"Go back down the beach," he went on. "Wait in the jungle by the Pahram headland until we come for you."

I said gently, "I appreciate your friendship, Pereira, but I cannot take base advantage of it. We would be outcasts without a harbor or a refuge open to us—".

"Portugal does not rule *all* the Indies, Sir," he said quickly. "There is always a market for a sword—and a good arm to wield it—and a hand and eye that can train a gun. With a man such as you to lead us we'll not lack bite, sup nor shelter for long."

I shook my head.

"I cannot lead you others into a morass of my own making," I said firmly.

"What else is there for it, you fool?" Jeanne asked bitterly. "Wallow in your nobility if you wish— but *I'll* not burn to purge your filthy lechery." She turned to Pereira. "We shall wait as you suggest. See my ayah before you leave, and get privily from her a few necessities for my comfort on your wretched boat—some changes of clothing, the large net from my bed, a mattress, my toilet requisites, oils and unguents to protect my skin from the sun, and lastly, and most importantly, my jewel case from the carved chest in my dressing closet."

I saw the stark amazement in Pereira's face turn to grudging admiration at her quick and shrewd recovery, but for myself I knew only disgust at the brazen creature's selfishness and greed. And another thought was worrying me.

"Who guards at the House of Detention tonight?" I asked Pereira.

"Subram Rao's company, Sir," he told me.

"Then it should be an easy matter for him to liberate Diaz and the woman," I said. "Have that done and bring them with you."

"Have they not caused enough trouble already?" Jeanne asked shrewishly.

"Be quiet," I told her sharply. Then I turned to Pereira and grasped his hand. "Do this," I begged. "I cannot allow them to suffer for that for which we are largely responsible."

Pereira nodded and I think I detected in his manner a covert satisfaction, even an eagerness, because he was a man who throve upon adventure, resorting to the bottle only when inactivity hung heavily upon him.

"The Pahram headland, Sir," he said. "We should make it five hours or less after darkness." And he wheeled his horse and galloped up the beach.

Then I heard from Jeanne a stream of such language in the French tongue as would have earned a trooper in a company of irregular horse the lash in any well conducted army.

"The sluttish bitch," she swore. "It is always the same with the lower orders. Treat them kindly and they behave like animals to repay you." Then she shrugged in her Gallic manner. "Oh well—at least I shall have a maid to attend me."

I said hotly, "Have you no thought of what we are doing to that good man, your husband?"

"No more than *you* have had this last three months," she retorted, and to that I had no answer.

We rode down the beach in the darkness, hour after hour, Jeanne complaining pettishly at intervals of the mosquitoes that afflicted us, the soreness of her rump and finally of her hunger, and I groaned inwardly at the burden I had inflicted upon myself, and wondered where and when it would all end, and the bitterness of all my fugitive days was returning to me. We rested, and I hacked open some coconuts with my dagger, but she turned up her dainty nose at them, and I thought of Cloda and her earthy sturdiness when last I was fleeing through the night, and I compared her in my mind with this shallow and worthless creature.

We arrived at last at the headland and I was relieved to see a dim light beating back and forth in the darkness a short distance offshore. I rode into the gentle surf up to my horse's belly and hailed. The light turned in towards us and the boat grounded gently on the sand. It was a small country dhow, no more than forty feet in length, but fast and seaworthy under her huge triangular sail, decked over fore and aft and providing a tiny cabin in the stern. Subram Rao, Pereira, and a sheepish Diaz formed the crew under Lobo's skillful command, while Dona Ena sat amidships, her head swathed in a cloak, wailing pitiably of her wickedness and its dire consequences.

"Be silent, you trollop," Jeanne raged at her. "It is all your fault, you fat Jezebel. You deserve to burn in a yellow robe and hood. Zut! You disgust me."

Poor Dona Ena lapsed into fresh transports of grief and shame.

I took both Lobo and Subram Rao to one side and bade them earnestly to consider their respective positions before leaving everything and following me into an uncertain future, but both steadfastly averred that they asked nothing better. Lobo stated that with a boat such as this we could soon get another and bigger one and that we could recruit and train a crew that would bring terror to the coast and proportionate profit to ourselves, but I sternly put aside all suggestions of piracy. Subram Rao, on the other hand, waxed lyrical over the beauties of the Deccan and told of the opportunities that awaited fighting men there.

"I was about to terminate my services here, sahib," he assured me. "There is much fighting in the land of the Marathas now. Some Mohammedans have come from the north—subjects of the Great Mogul—and they have had the insolence to set up camps and start to build forts. It would be an act of merit to help dislodge them. And the pay is good."

But I was too weary to think more that night. Lobo, in the haste of his departure had been unable to take on drinking water in quantity, and there was a leaky seam that worried him, so, since this was a deserted stretch of coast, he suggested that we stay until morning before deciding on our next move, and thereby give him the opportunity of attending to both matters.

Jeanne had by now lapsed into a sulky silence for which I was greatly thankful. I lugged her mattress and mosquito net to the edge of the jungle, and received scant thanks from her. Dona Ena crept away into the shelter of the undergrowth like a whipped dog, and I set Diaz, who had been seasick on the way down, to watch over the women, while I went with Pereira and Subram Rao to help Lobo with the repairs.

We worked far into the night, and then, exhausted, we all dropped where we stood and slept until the sun was well up over the fringe of the palm trees.

I was leaning against the side of the beached boat moodily breaking my fast on a banana when I heard the excited clamor of Subram Rao and Pereira, and on looking across to the edge of the jungle I saw them waving furiously to me. I went across to them and looked down at that which was exercising them.

Diaz lay as one asleep, as undoubtedly he had been when this thing happened, a look of slight surprise on his face, one arm upthrown as though to shield his eyes from the sun—and his own knife buried to the shaft in his throat. A thick gout of clotted blood stained the sand beside him, and heavy engorged flies rose in a swarm as I approached. I looked at Subram Rao in bewilderment, and then suddenly thought of Jeanne whose white mosquito net I could see some distance away above the undergrowth. I ploughed swiftly through the sand towards it.

She was not there—but Dona Ena was, lying face downwards— my own dagger, which I had left with Jeanne the night before for her comfort and protection, buried between her shoulder blades.

We searched the jungle for an hour before I stumbled upon that which I should have noticed in the very first instance. Both our horses were gone, and two sets of hoofprints led away from the spot where we had tethered them, skirting the jungle for some two or three hundred yards and then crossing the beach to the hard sand at the water's edge where they continued into the distance—back towards Goa.

I turned and looked at the others, open-mouthed.

"She is a devil, that one," said Pereira, and there was once more admiration rather than reproof in his tone. "But why back to Goa? Isn't her behind hot enough without wanting the holy fire to scorch it?"

I said grimly, "Get the boat heaved off into the water—we're going after her."

But the tide had dropped now and we had to fell coconut trunks to use as rollers to launch her again, and then toil like Trojans because a forty-foot boat is no child's plaything for even four strong men to move over a hundred yards of heavy beach.

She must have had a good three hours' start on us because we never caught up with her even though we did once raise a shout when we saw far in the distance a solitary horse. But on landing we found that it was mine, its reins knotted on its neck and obviously cast loose. One single set of hoofprints continued on without checking.

We were not far from Goa now, and the others were getting restive so I called a council of war.

"She has gone back, without doubt," Pereira averred.

"But why, why—*why?*" I puzzled.

"To atone," grinned Lobo.

"That one atone?" scoffed Pereira. "She's got the mark of Lucifer upon her. Besides, why add to the account two murders?"

But the question was purely rhetorical and only put into words what was mystifying us all.

Then Subram Rao had the only sensible idea that had come our way that entire day.

"Sahib," he said. "At the pace of a horse, she will already be in Goa, and that which is to befall *will* have befallen. Let me go in on foot through the jungle, by a short path that I know, and find out the tidings. It is nearly dark now and I will be back long before dawn."

But I demurred at that on the ground of possible peril to himself. He shook his head.

"Have no fear, sahib," he said. "In turban, loincloth and a coating of dust I will be no more recognizable than one grain of sand upon this beach from another." And I saw the force of his contention.

So he went off, melting into the darkness, and we lay at anchor a few yards offshore until the eastern sky was lightening and we heard his soft hail from the beach. He waded out to us and we pulled him over the gunwale.

"It is as Pereira says," chuckled Subram Rao. "She is the Devil, that one. Sahib, I regret to say that yours is the most reviled name in all Goa this day."

"Tell me, subadar," I said urgently.

"She came to the city as dusk was falling, sahib," he said. "Her clothes were torn and she was near exhaustion. She told the following story. . . . She was riding with the sahib, but her horse went lame so the sahib attended to it near the ruined pavilion. Dona Ena had meanwhile sought the shade and disappeared, so the gracious lady went in search of her—only to find her in the arms of Diaz. Horrified and disgusted, she turned and ran from the place, but they were so engrossed in their activities that they were unaware of her. She went back to the sahib and told him indignantly of what she had seen, but he laughed coarsely and made light of it. Angered, she demanded to be brought back to the palace forthwith, but the sahib, whom she now realized to her horror had been drinking heavily, laid violent and lascivious hands upon her—hotly declaring his love for her and demanding his payment for so many lessons in the art of horse-riding.

"The lady naturally spurned him. Maddened, he seized her. He bore her off into the jungle and there held her captive, making many proposals of an improper nature to her. She held him off and protected her honor throughout, until in the end the sahib tied her to a tree and threatened to keep her there indefinitely until she yielded to his desires. She remained there all night, praying for either death or deliverance. In the morning I came, and with me Lobo and Pereira. She heard us all talking. We have been, it appears, a band of brigands for these last three years, with Diaz and Dona Ena our accomplices. We upbraided the sahib for so compromising our beautifully organized schemes. The sahib was unrepentant. He ordered Lobo to steal a boat and to scuttle all others in the harbor, saying that he was tired of Goa and all therein and was going back to join the pirates with whom he had been before coming to our city. He then gave orders to me that I was to effect the escape of Dona Ena and Diaz, but that I was then to cut their throats in the jungle as they knew too much about us all. Having settled that, we then drunk much strong liquor and fell into a tipsy slumber, during which the lady managed to free herself, mount her horse and escape. The whole city acclaims her valor and deplores your villainy, sahib. Search parties will be dispatched for you with daylight."

He sat back and grinned with delight.

Pereira said, "And they *believe* all that?"

"They believe it, Pereira," Subram Rao answered, "because it is a very beautiful story. A story such as one pays good money to hear from the minstrels in the bazaar. A very prince of stories. The Governor sahib is delighted with it, I am told. Who would want willingly to wear horns when the alternative is the possession of a woman such as this? A woman who *successfully*, mind you, defended her virtue all night against such talent as the sahib, you, Lobo and myself." He wagged his head admiringly. "Yes, the very prince, the *king* of stories."

I sat reflecting savagely for some time, obsessed by a sense of complete helplessness. Once again I was a leaf at the mercy of any perverse wind that chanced to blow. The coast would now be closed to me. The Dutch I hated—the Portuguese were now my enemies. All hope of a ship to Europe was thus gone. There remained now only the Road . . .

I said, "Subadar, how do we reach this Deccan of yours?"

He grinned merrily.

"Put yourself in my hands, sahib. Only sail but a short distance down the coast—and then we march. Lobo, take your last look for many a long day at this horrible sea. *Deccan ki Jai!* Sahib, tomorrow we start to *live*."

✣ 13

THE air was still and heavy at sunrise, and the surface of the lagoon showed not the faintest catspaw of a riffle. It worried me a great deal because we were close to Goa here and if search parties were out they could scarcely fail to stumble upon us. I mentioned my fears to Lobo and suggested that we take to the oars and at least make good some distance offshore. He agreed with me but at the same time pointed to the northwest. I followed his finger and saw a huge black cloud over the horizon, the lower edge funneling to a point which seemed to be resting on the surface of the sea, giving the whole thing the semblance of a great misshapen tree growing on a slender trunk. Even as I looked, the mass grew perceptibly, rolling and billowing towards us menacingly, and one did not have to be a sailor to realize that a storm of no mean proportions was imminent.

"I do not like that," muttered Lobo. "Dirty weather from the south is to be expected with the monsoon—but only once have I ever seen it veer round to that quarter at this time of the year. That was when everything that floated in Goa harbor dragged its anchor and finished among the coconut palms."

"We cannot stay here," I insisted.

"Nor would I want to," Lobo assured me. "Sea room is what I crave in this sort of tamasha, but I have to warn you of what we are in for. To oars then, gentlemen."

We ran out the heavy sweeps and sweated and strained at them for half an hour before making a gap in the reef and gaining the open sea. The surface was still oily but now a heavy swell was making itself felt from the direction of the storm. The cloud had spread until it blanketed the whole sky, blotting out the rising sun and casting a sickly pallid gloom over sea and shore, that could be likened to neither day nor night. Lobo's face set grimly as he urged us to fresh efforts at the oars in order to claw the leeway that we would require so desperately when the hurricane broke with all its violence.

A few fitful gusts struck us, precursors of the shrieking fury to come, and Lobo drove us to the halyards and we hauled the heavy curving lateen yard halfway up its run and then reefed the foot of the huge sail in double brails. Close-hauled on the starboard tack we bore swiftly away from the shore, and we breathed a little easier. Then, when we were some three miles out, the gusts died completely and we wallowed in the swell, the masthead making a wide and sickening arc against the livid sky, now without control of any sort because we were rolling too much even to use the oars. Lobo broke out some fruit and coarse native bread and urged us to eat and drink our fill while we still had the opportunity, and it was while we were thus engaged that the high whining sound came to us from the northwest.

Lobo went to the helm and lashed himself to a cross-strake, instructing us to do likewise amidships, and we waited, the sound growing in volume and intensity until with a shriek of a thousand devils it burst upon us. The first shock had us right over on our beam ends, and a solid green wall of water surged over us, and I thought in that agonized moment that we were swamped and sinking, but Lobo, with the helm hard over and the close-reefed sail swelling to bursting point, now had steerage way again and her stern into the eye of the wind and sea. Like a hind from the coverts when the hounds are in full cry on her heels, the stout little vessel bore away to the south.

Hour after hour we ran, literally at the speed of the wind, our thankfulness for the seaworthiness of our craft now tempered by the knowledge that we were sailing in the opposite direction to that which we wished to go. Twice Lobo tried to ease her in a wide circle and so bring her up head to wind but, with all his skill, he near broached to each time and we begged him to desist. Then he started to lower the sail in the hope that she would travel the slower under her bare mast, but robbed of her steerage way she wallowed badly in the troughs, and the huge seas, now traveling faster than the boat, threatened to poop her. So we finally accepted what Fate was doing to us, and settled down to make the best of what we could not cure.

Then, as suddenly as it had struck us, the storm ceased and the air was still again although the waves abated not one whit. But they were in different mood now—coming from any and every direction and tossing and bouncing us like a cork, their crests breaking above us and threatening again to swamp us. Lobo explained to us that these storms blew in a circle like a gigantic wheel, and at the hub occurred this area of false calm which would soon pass over us, however, and we would once more be back in the thick of the fury.

And his words were more than borne out, because even as he spoke, we were struck by the wind again with such force that the weather shrouds, weakened by the strain of the previous few hours, snapped under the sudden shock like fiddle strings, and the mast came crashing down in a tangle of tattered sail and thrashing rigging. In the hands of anybody else but Lobo I feel that this would have been the end of our passage, but he kept his head and leapt for the wreckage with his heavy seaman's knife flailing. Pushing aside those of us who hamfistedly tried to help him, he slashed through the tangle at the side of the boat and let the huge spar and sail stream away before us on the surface, making fast the mainsheet to the stern. This brought our bows round into the wind and although we rode heavily and pounded badly, at least we did not broach to.

Mercifully this second ordeal did not last as long as the first, although its fury was even greater while it did, but once again, with dramatic suddenness, the full force of it passed on, leaving us water-logged and wallowing in the heavy seas. Night had fallen now and the scudding clouds hid the stars so we had no means of ascertaining our bearings. Dazed, bemused and altogether more dead than alive we clustered miserably amidships and waited for the dawn.

Exhausted, we must have slept because I remember nothing immediately prior to that grinding crash and the pother of white water which broke over us. Hands from below seemed to be clutching me and drawing me down into the black depths and there was a hellish drumming in my ears, and my lungs were bursting, and then, when I had accepted my fate and ceased to struggle, my head broke the surface and I snatched and held a blessed breath before sinking again. But this time I felt hard sand beneath my feet and I kicked desperately and shot to the surface before being forced down once more under the crushing weight of a curling breaker. I was flat on my face now, my fingers clawing at the shifting sand under me, fighting against the backwash that was dragging me into deep water again. Then another breaker rolled me forward and I managed to stagger to my feet and gain a yard up the shelving beach before being knocked flat by the next wave and rolling once more. I crawled on hands and knees over dry sand, and with the last ebbing remnants of my strength I rose and ran forward before collapsing in a heap in sheer exhaustion.

Dawn was streaking the sky when I came to. I sat up stiffly and peered around me, sore and battered all over, my eyes, nostrils and mouth tight-gummed with salt and sand. It was the same interminable beach that had bounded the western edge of my world for well-nigh three years—sand, lagoon and reef on the one hand—

coconut palms on the other—though which part of its cursed
thousand-mile stretch I had no means of telling. Groaning, retching
and spewing salt water I hauled myself to my feet and saw a man
lying face downwards, half-buried in the sand between myself and
the edge of the water. I went forward and turned him over.

It was Pereira. There was a deep gash across his forehead and his
eyes stared sightlessly up at me and I knew with a crushing sense of
personal loss, before I felt for his heartbeat, that he had laid his last
gun and cracked his last bottle.

I turned sadly away and gazed out to sea. There was nothing to
be seen there except the cruel coral fangs of the reef on which we
had struck, and beyond them the subsiding white horses of the now
abated storm. The tide was receding and leaving on the sands a few
sorry splintered planks, which was all that remained of the boat.
Consumed with a raging thirst, I walked back towards the jungle in
search of a coconut, and with a surge of thankfulness that had me
near to tears I saw Lobo coming towards me out of the shade. He
was naked except for the remains of his shirt which he wore round
his waist in loincloth fashion, but his knife had hung round his neck
on a lanyard and he was now using it to open a coconut. He came
up and handed it to me and then looked sorrowfully down toward
Pereira and crossed himself.

"Subram Rao?" I said hopefully, but he shook his head and
sighed.

"I've searched the beach a mile each way. I fear the old man
drowned," he said.

I drank from the coconut and felt immediately refreshed and
stronger, albeit sad and oppressed.

"What part of the coast do you think this?" I asked.

"We are a hundred miles to the south of Goa," he answered
unhesitatingly, "and about twice that distance to the north of Calicut."

"Between two fires," I mused, because Calicut was another Portuguese post, second only in importance to Goa itself.

He nodded. "An unenviable position, dom Gil," he said. "Of all the
coast this is the last part I would have chosen on which to be cast
away. The Moplahs—"

He needed to say no more. The Moplahs were even more dreaded than the Mekranis. Mohammedans like the latter, the Moplahs had immigrated to these parts from Arabia over the last two hundred years, and they were the implacable enemies of both Portuguese and Dutch; enemies of everybody except Moplahs, perhaps it would be safe to say. Bigoted and fanatical, they cruelly put to death any not of their religion unfortunate enough to find himself alone and unprotected on this coast, with the sole exception of the timid fisherfolk whom they graciously permitted to remain here in return for the greater part of their catch and also for information on passing ships. Unlike the Mekranis, with whom they lived in uneasy alliance providing the former did not set up permanent settlements within their domain, they were not a seagoing people, but their knowledge of the jungle was unsurpassed. The Portuguese, under dom Afonso de Albuquerque, had mounted many expeditions against them in the past, but always with disastrous consequences so that now for fifty years they had chosen to ignore them, contenting themselves with maintaining a strong garrison at Calicut and avoiding this particular stretch of the coast like the plague.

I said, "It will behoove us to leave here as quickly as possible, Lobo."

"And that will be easier said than done," he agreed gloomily. "The jungle has a thousand eyes. If any land here and are not reported to them with dispatch, they visit their displeasure on the fisherfolk, slaying them and burning their villages. We would be well advised to hide in the jungle by day and walk by night— between high- and low-water mark so that our footprints will be washed away by the tide before dawn each day."

"An excellent idea," I said drily, "if we could but be clear as to where we are going."

"You spoke of the Deccan with Subram Rao," he reminded me. "Had it not been for that cursed storm we should have sailed north from Goa for some two hundred and fifty miles to a small fort on the Gujerat—"

"Bombay?" I asked.

He nodded. "That is the best way to the interior. There is a trade road from there up through the mountains to the Maratha fort of Mahableshwar. Is it still your intention to go there?"

I shrugged hopelessly. "I do not know," I said. "Lobo, I am bereft of all plans for the future. I am a man undone by my own foolish-ness—and I have caused the death of four people, Pereira, Subram Rao, Diaz and that unfortunate woman—and I have robbed you of your livelihood. I wish to God I, also, had drowned out there last night, and the Devil take the Road."

"You didn't drown," he said quietly. "Nor did I. Don't reproach yourself for those deaths, dom Gil. I have been in these lands long enough to accept the workings of Fate—*kismet* as they call it here. We are alive. We are men. Are we to lie down and die here like animals? What is this Road you talk of?"

I rose and grasped his hand. "Thank you, my friend," I said sincerely. "No—we shall not lie down and die. The Road? I don't know. Probably an old wives' tale, but I must admit that it has captured my imagination. It's the road they say links China with the lands of the Turks—Constantinople. From there on I can speak with more certainty because there *is* a route to Europe. I had a mind to travel it. That is all."

"And I shall travel it with you," he said. "I am a sailor—but this coast palls upon me now. I am more familiar with sea charts than those of the land, but as I remember my globes, if a road runs from China to Constantinople it must skirt the north of this continent of India. To reach the north we would have first to traverse the Deccan. A man must have steering points or he *is* indeed an animal. Good—let our first one then be that Deccan. Heigh-ho—Bombay it is. The plan remains unchanged."

And my gloom and despair started to lift from me at that moment.

"Bombay it is," I agreed. "Three hundred and fifty miles up this beach, you say?—and a wide detour round Goa. Lobo, my friend, this coast is going to pall on you even more by the time we strike inland."

"Maybe," he grinned cheerfully, "but I have a better plan than walking."

"Flying?" I asked in jest.

"The next best thing to it," he said. "Let us make our way to the first fishing village and there steal a boat."

I looked at him with a new respect.

He then carried Pereira's body back into the jungle where, with

Lobo's heavy knife, we scratched a shallow grave and laid him in it, and Lobo took from round his own neck a small gold cross on a thin chain and twined it round the fingers of his friend's right hand before we gently placed the warm earth back on him. Then we moved a mile up the beach and sought the shelter of the jungle and slept like the weary men we were until sundown.

We walked right through that first night, my thoughts going back constantly to my previous journey, and just as daylight was breaking we saw ahead of us in the distance the fires of a village.

We turned from the water's edge across the beach, smoothing out behind us with a stalk of seaweed the footprints we left in the dry sand, and we crept through the undergrowth in a wide circle to a spot from which we deemed we could study the lie of the land and so make our plans for the night. But it was impossible to get close enough to see the village without ourselves being seen by its inhabitants, so we put a healthy distance between it and us and then climbed into the thick foliage of a giant neem tree where we possessed our souls in patience until nightfall. We came down then and drank our fill at a stream and ate bananas and wild green figs, then crept like thieves in the night, as indeed we were, to the place where their boats were drawn up on the sand.

They were all of a size—some fifteen feet in length and a bare three in breadth—hollowed from two logs laid side by side and bound together with tough fibrous creepers, and steadied by a third log set out from one side on outriggers. Short masts were already stepped in most of them, and in some were spars on which sails woven from coconut husks were furled. We selected one which was still damp from the sea, and equipped it with paddles, sail and lengths of woven cordage, then to hamper possible pursuit we collected up all other sails and paddles and made a bundle of them which we bound with rope and tied to the stern of our stolen boat.

Inch by inch, the hair prickling on the napes of our necks at the least sound, we strained and heaved to get the craft through the deep sand down into the water, then, not daring to splash with the unaccustomed paddles, we waded waist-deep a good half-mile up the beach, towing the craft between us, until we judged it safe to scramble in and make our way out to deeper water.

We paddled for miles through the calm lagoon, just in the lee of the reef, until we found passage through it, then we gained sufficient searoom for Lobo to try the sail. He was unfamiliar with this primitive rig, but he was a sailor to his fingertips, and dark though it was, he soon had it set and we were scudding briskly along in the light breeze, the dark line of the coast on our right hands. We towed the bundle of paddles, spars and sails for a couple of miles or so and then cut them free to float away on the ebbing tide.

We came inshore at dawn and worked like galley slaves to get the boat across the beach and into the shelter of the jungle, then after slaking our thirst and partially satisfying the gnawing hunger in our bellies with coconuts and bananas, we slept the sleep of exhaustion. Lobo, with his magnificent knowledge of the coast and his even surer instinct, judged that we had made over thirty miles that night and should, with an earlier start, be able to make forty each night thereafter, providing the monsoon storms held off. This, he reckoned, should bring us up to Bombay in some six days.

But the storms did not hold off, and it was on the third day that we were struck by a sudden squall that all but demasted us and, unable to shorten sail, we scudded like the wind itself along the reef which was now a boiling maelstrom of white water, looking for a break in it through which to seek the shelter of the lagoon. We found one at last, much wider than the normal break—perhaps some hundred yards across—and Lobo yelped with delight and shouted to me over the wind that it was the entrance to the Kalabagh River and that there was a safe haven inside—and mangroves growing down to the water which meant that we should not have the backbreaking task of hauling the boat into shelter.

We sailed in through the break, gunwales awash and outrigger lifted clear; Lobo, who had now mastered the art of handling this primitive craft like the natives themselves, steered her unerringly through the white water and into the yellow-stained stream of the main river. This place was a miniature, though uninhabited, Goa, in that it was formed by a small island standing square in the mouth of a river, so dividing its flow into a two-armed delta.

The rain was coming down in sheets now and it reduced our sight to a mere boat's length—so we didn't see the ship anchored on the shoreward side of the island until we brought up hard against her side. Too late, Lobo tried to luff and go about, but although he might have managed it in a conventional craft, the very design of this one forbade the maneuver, and we scraped along the side and round the bows, our outrigger fouling the taut anchor cable, then snapping off short and so rendering us completely helpless. Above us, from the deck, we could hear the pounding of feet and swearing in a variety of tongues, then a musket was fired point-blank down into us, and why neither of us was mangled by the widespread charge I cannot to this day say—but the fact remains that though it shot the bottom out of the boat between us, we ourselves were unscathed.

Then round the bows from the other side came the ship's long-boat in which were sailors who had evidently been tarring the planking. I stood poised to dive deep from our sinking boat, but something hard thrown from the deck above caught me on the top of the head and all was blackness.

✢ 14

A FOOT stirred my aching ribs ungently and I rolled over on the deck planking and sat up.

"This one is alive also," said a voice in bad Portuguese. "Cut their throats and drop them over the side."

There were two of them leaning on the poop rail and looking down on me in the waist so that at first I saw them only in silhouette against the sky, and in any case I was preoccupied with the third man, a pock-marked Mekrani who stood over me with the air of one who enjoyed kicking.

"But they might be sailors," said the other in the same vile patois.

"Sailors we have aplenty," the first man said. "It's a damned sailing *master* we lack. *Achmet—usko maro, jaldi.*" Against the sky I saw the speaker's hand go out, fist clenched, thumb pointing downward, and the Mekrani grunted and drew a long knife from his belt, his other hand grabbing my hair and jerking my head back.

I shrieked, "Hold! We *are* sailors—and one of us is a master."

There was an instant of surprised silence, then the first speaker grunted, "European. Just as I said. Bastard Portuguese spies. Over the side with the whoresons."

"Wait a minute," said the other, and came down the ladder to the waist. I tried to rise but the Mekrani twisted my hair and jerked my head back again, throwing me off balance onto my haunches. The man came forward, then I heard a bellow of laughter and he shouted, "By my stole, cassock and bloody surplice! Bardock, you gette!"

He pushed the Mekrani to one side and I struggled to my feet. He stood regarding me, feet apart, fists on hips, clad in gaudy voluminous pantaloons held up by a silk sash in which were thrust a long jeweled knife and a brace of pistols. He was bare from the waist up except for some strings of barbaric jewels around his neck, and his powerful torso was burned black. His sun-bleached hair was hacked off at neck length and he now affected gold earrings, a slight beard and curling moustaches—but he was still unmistakably the Angel.

"Where in the name of hell have *you* come from, you citizen of no mean Sodom?" he demanded. "And what's this about being a sailor? You were the worst carpenter who ever swung an adz when last we met."

But I was in no fit state to attempt to gabble my story at that moment so I countered his question.

"I thought I was the only one who survived that massacre," I said.

"The Devil looks after his own," he grinned. "Weaver liked my face, so I went with the ship." He gestured round with his hand and I saw that, filthy and neglected though she now appeared, we were in very fact on the same galleon that had brought us here. I glanced up at the other man but the Angel shook his head.

"No, that's not Weaver," he told me. "I cut the bastard's throat in the Celebes. He fancied himself on the recorder, and when he was drunk he used to play hymns out of tune. I could have borne with that if only he'd known more than two hymns and had been sober *some* of the time. Come." He turned and led back to the poop ladder.

I said, "My companion?" then I saw Lobo lying nearby in the scuppers.

"A pox on him," said the Angel. "Portygooser, isn't he? He's got some popish idolatry tattooed on his chest."

"He's a good man," I insisted.

"Then a double pox on him. He'd die of loneliness on this ship. Come and meet the nominal captain—and keep your mouth closed. I'll have a hard enough row to hoe keeping *you* alive. He thinks you're spies."

"But you said you needed a sailing master," I insisted frantically. "That man is the best on the coast."

He stopped short and turned and cocked an eye at me, stroking his beard. "Is he now?" he said softly. "Is he now? Well, I'd ask you to keep that to yourself for the moment. There are wheels within wheels on this craft. Don't worry about your friend."

We gained the poop, and the other man turned his head slowly and regarded me, without favor. He was broad, thick-set and bullet-headed, with little light blue eyes rimmed with sandy lashes that gave him an almost comically porcine look when taken together with his broad, upturned wide-nostriled nose.

"Captain Schmirke," said the Angel. "This is one Bardock—an Englishman and a good ship's carpenter. In fact he was on this very craft when we were laid aboard by the Mekranis—and he tells me he has been badly used by the 'goosers ever since."

"He said 'master,'" grunted Schmirke accusingly.

The Angel shook his head. "No, t'other's the master. Best on the coast, so Bardock says."

"We'll see," answered Schmirk noncommittally, and added, "He'll require to be more than the best to ballast the fact that he's Portuguese."

I started to say something but caught the Angel's eye and held my peace. Schmirke spat over the side and strolled forward along the deck to berate in Hindustani, which was considerably better than his Dutch-Portuguese, a group of Mekranis who were splicing some worn shrouds.

The Angel said quietly, "I'll give you some counsel which may help to keep you alive, young Bardock. Keep out of that man's sight in the forenoon. The afternoons do not matter because he's always drunk then and remembers nothing next day. Keep your friend out of his sight *always* because Schmirke hates the Portuguese with the hate of hell itself—and we're going to need a sailing master. Now come with me quickly."

He led me down into the waist again and we picked up Lobo and bore him through into the great-cabin which, like the rest of the ship, I noticed was foul, disordered and stinking to high heaven, with mildew and verdigris in great discolored patches on its once brightly painted bulkheads, and refuse ankle-deep on the deck. The Angel led us to a cabin opening off on the starboard side. It was small and cramped, having space enough only for a fixed cot and a table hinged to the inner wall—and these in turn were dwarfed by the breech of a twenty-four–pounder on a wheeled carriage which backed through the square port that formed the fourth wall of the cabin. He squeezed past this and raised a trap in the deck which led down to a lazaretto where I suspected gunpowder was normally kept, because the place reeked sulphurously. We dropped down into this and I took the opportunity of examining Lobo, whom I was relieved to see had suffered a blow on the head only a little heavier than my own, and was now showing signs of returning consciousness. The Angel sat on the deck in the semidarkness and regarded me with a wry grin.

"Well now," he said. "Tell us your story. But make it as short as you like because I have much to tell *you*."

I summarized in as brief terms as I could the events of the last three years, glossing over, it must be confessed, those which I found embarrassing—telling him, in short, that I had been found by the Portuguese, given employment by them, had been kindly treated by them but had recently fallen foul of the Inquisition and was, when we stumbled upon this ill-starred ship again, in flight with Lobo who was in like predicament with the ecclesiastical authorities. The Angel nodded from time to time but made no comment, seeming to accept my story without question. When I came to a halt he said, "Well, as for me, I had just come back aboard ship that day when the attack struck. We saw you people butchered but could give no assistance, as soon we were fighting for our lives against some more of the villains who boarded us from a dhow. We were overpowered and these damned Mekranis started to put the survivors to the sword, but their captain appeared to be an Englishman and I called out to him in desperation to spare my life. He did,

not from any kindness of his black heart, but purely because the
bastard was sick of talking Portuguese and Hindustani, a mixture of
both being, as you may have heard, together with a bit of brothel
Dutch, the language of the Middle Passage on this coast. It was
Weaver, a scoundrel marooned here many years ago. He was one of
the finest seamen I have ever met—and the biggest rogue. He had
succeeded in putting the fear of God into his Mekrani crew, but he
pined for the Spanish Main and wanted a ship to get him there. This
one was to be it. In addition to his Mekranis, he had gathered a
polyglot collection of Europeans around him—deserters from the
East Indiamen mostly—couple of Portuguese, couple of Dutchmen,
a German, a Frenchman and now myself.

"We set off from the coast intending to go back to the Main the
way Drake originally came. Through the Spice and Pearl Islands,
across the Pacifico and round Tierra del Fuego—three-quarters of
the way round the whole bloody world itself. And we'd have done
it had it not been for those same damned Spice Islands."

He closed his eyes and was silent for a time, and then when he
spoke again his voice had in it a dreamy quality.

"Small, but not *too* small—slim but not skinny—breasts like velvet sugar melons, eyes like the pools of night, voices that soothe like
the call of doves over a country vicarage in August—docile as
fawns—but they walk like princesses."

He sighed heavily. "But these dirty-fingered bastards of ours
spoiled it all, and we had trouble with their fathers and husbands—
trouble among ourselves, and sickness. There's a variety of the pox
there that can make a man fall into pieces quicker than leprosy.
Inside a year we had less than half a crew left, and most of those
mad with liquor they make from the sap of the palm trees. But
worst of all, Weaver had lost his star."

"His star?" I asked, puzzled.

"Yes, his star," the Angel said heavily. "Men like us must have
either our own beacon or that of another man who can command
us. Without that we drift and rot. Mine had once been God, but He
had abandoned me and I had cursed His name. Now I had hitched
onto Weaver's star—the Spanish Main. The place itself meant
nothing—it was the effort of getting there that counted." His face
contorted with pain. "Who wants to sit on a cloud and play a harp

of gold?—but who doesn't suffer the agonies of the damned when he is set aside from achieving it?"

Again he was silent, and I thought of Lobo's words, "a man must have steering points or indeed he *is* an animal."

The Angel went on, "Soon Weaver was as sodden and poxed as the rest, and he said to hell with the Main; it had nothing more than this place had to offer; so I killed him in a drunken quarrel one night and I tried to get this fellow Schmirke, the mate, to take over and go on. But the star had gone. Schmirke is a good enough seaman before the mast, but he cannot navigate, and anyhow the ship was in no condition to attempt the passage now. Her gear is rotten and her sails in tatters and the weed is two feet long on her foul hull. So we came back here to careen and fit out—and now Schmirke is fast going the way of Weaver." He leaned forward and took my hands in his. "Listen, Bardock, tell me the truth and you'll not regret it. *Is* this fellow a sailing master?" He jerked his head at Lobo.

"He is," I assured him.

"Then by God we'll do it yet," breathed the Angel. "Listen: this is what we must have, and the order in which we must procure it." He counted off on his fingers. "One, sailcloth for a complete set and one to spare. Two, five hundred running feet of planking. Three, tar and pitch. Four, fifty barrels of salt pork and beef and the same of cornmeal. Five, a renewal of all our running gear."

I said, "You'd need the resources of a European shipyard for that."

"I need one bloody ship the size of this," he snarled. "Either to take over as she stands or to strip down and use to patch this one up. An Indiaman—Dutch or Portuguese—and then finally a place along this coast where we could careen in safety without the fear of Moplahs or Mekranis—or Dutch or Portuguese coming upon us while we were helpless."

Behind me I heard Lobo stirring, and then he said weakly in Portuguese, "What has happened? Where are we?"

"What manner of shipmaster are you?" the Angel asked quickly in the same language.

"Qualified in the Institute di Vasco da Gama, Lisbon," answered Lobo. "Why? Who are you?"

"Have you the knowledge and the working of the globes, the astrolabe and the celestial tables?" asked the Angel urgently.

"Well, naturally," Lobo said impatiently. "But what is this? The Inquisition? If it is not, give a man a drink in the name of Jesus."

"And of shipwrighting?" demanded the Angel inexorably. "Can you beach and careen? Can you cut and stitch a suit of sails?"

"With your bloody guts if you harass me further," roared Lobo, recovering quickly. "A drink, you poxy lout!"

"Get him a drink," I begged.

"Ah, you, is it, dom Gil?" said Lobo rolling over on one elbow and peering at me in the gloom. "Who is this fellow?"

"The mate of this galleon," I told him. "He tests your qualifications for the berth of sailing master upon her."

"Did he have to recruit me with a snatch block over the head?" demanded Lobo querulously, feeling his wound and wincing. "Yes, yes, yes I can do all those things, master mate. But get me a drink before I answer further."

The Angel went quickly up the ladder. I said quietly, "These are Gentlemen of the Middle Passage, Lobo—but neither Captain nor mate navigate and they have the idea to sail across the ocean to the Spanish Main in the path of Francis Drake."

"By God, have they?" breathed Lobo. "I'd have kept a more civil tongue in my head had I known that. What manner of craft is this? I saw little or nothing of her before I was cracked across the head."

"She is a tall galleon," I told him. "I sailed in her from the Cape of Good Hope to this coast. The *Santa Elena*."

"I know her well—swift, but a little too scant in the beam for her great length," he mused. "But she'll do—aye, she'll do." He looked around him. "But what manner of place is this in which they keep us—if they bear us no ill will?"

"I cannot answer for their will—ill or otherwise," I replied. "But I know them to be murderous blackguards who would have slit our throats without compunction had they not thought they could use us. Even now it is a doubtful issue. This man pretends friendship only because he appears to be at daggers drawn with the Captain and I think he wishes to enlist me to his aid simply because I am an Englishman like himself. You they want for your skill, but even there the Captain, a Dutchman, hates the Portuguese and I have been warned to keep you out of sight when he is drunk."

"A pretty crew," he chuckled. "But not different from the rest of the Middle Passage. I sailed with them before and can do so again."

My heart sank, because of all my lieutenants in the Goa service, Lobo was the one I would have put my greatest trust in.

"You've sailed with them before?" I asked bleakly.

"Aye," he nodded. "It was none of my seeking. I was an apprentice master on a barque in the African trade and we were laid aboard by the Gentlemen off the Cape Verde Islands. They, also, lacked a navigator, and I had no wish to walk the plank with the others, so I shipped with them when they gave me the offer. There again Captain and mate were at loggerheads, and between them they piled us up on this coast. And I walked naked to Goa, even as you did, and told much the same tale, but not to such lucky purpose as yourself. *I* only became a coast pilot on a miserable pittance. So now we know the best and worst of each other, dom Gil."

"*I* told the truth," I said loftily.

"But you know *this* hearty well enough," he said quickly. "I have sufficient English to have got the gist of what you were saying together. Still, what does it matter? We're friends. Again this is none of my seeking nor, if it comes to that, of yours. Kismet, dom Gil. Let's see what it has to offer this time."

"This man is a link with much I would forget," I said. "Believe what you wish, but I have never sailed the Middle Passage, as you call it, and have no intention of doing so now."

"What choice have we—other than the plank?" he retorted.

"Over the side tonight," I answered, "and let us continue on our way to Bombay."

"Have you thought of—?" he began, but at that moment we saw the legs of the Angel coming down the ladder again.

He brought a puncheon of evil smelling, villainously strong palm toddy, a jar of water, and some cold rice and fish.

"All we have," he said. "We've been living like pigs for these months past—but if all goes well it will be best Oporto and fresh victuals before you can say Spice Islands." He put the food and drink down on the deck between us and then thumped us both on our chests in high good humor, winked and added, "The Middle Passage—"

"Gentlemen all and Merry Companions," supplied Lobo, and the Angel stared at him.

"So you've planked it with the rest of us, have you?" he roared. "You bloody rogue. Excellent, excellent. Fall to, gentlemen—I'll be down for you before long."

He went back up the ladder and swung the hatch down into place and I heard with heavy heart the wedges go home. I sighed and felt for the food and drink in the pitchy darkness.

"A hearty one, that," chuckled Lobo. "I could sail with him. It's the Dutchman I worry about."

"I'll sail with neither," I raged. "It's Bombay I'm making for." "Why?"

"Haven't we already discussed that?"

"Of course, but back there on the beach you weren't so certain. It was just a steering point. We had to go somewhere."

"What's your steering point now?" I asked bitterly.

"I don't need one. We go where we are commanded now."

It was strange how these two had, within minutes, each confirmed the creed of the other. Men had either to have their own star or be commanded by others. That had been the case with me as long as I could remember. Even in possession of a proud name and a competence to support it, I had never had my own star. I had placed myself under the orders of mercenary commanders in the Lowlands—and futile plotters in England, and had lost everything. Out here I had been commanded again—first by my Portuguese masters—then by a worthless woman—and once more I had lost. Now it looked as if I was tamely to become the creature of a murderous scoundrel and was to follow *his* star.

"No, by God I won't," I swore aloud. "*I* have a star—a steering point. The Road. I'll find it or die."

"Most likely the latter," Lobo said drily. "This toddy stinks, dom Gil, but it's heartening stuff. Drink deep."

But I pushed it away and paced restlessly to and fro in that confined space. Yes, the Road—that would be it. Not for where it led, but as a means in itself. Something *I* wanted to achieve and to hell with all who tried to deter me. I would escape from this ship and gain the shore—walk the coast again—I had done it before alone and unaided and ignorant—how much better equipped I was now. I needed none to help me—certainly not this broken reed here. He traveled fastest who traveled alone.

Tentatively I tried the hatch at the top of the ladder, but it was immovable. Below me I heard Lobo chuckle again.

"You can't belch against the tempest, dom Gil," he said, and there was now a hiccup in his voice. "Give it up. Kismet. Not a bad life—*if* you live. The Spice Islands, he said? The women are lovely, and the toddy is better than this." Then there was a gentle snore.

I sat in the darkness with my back against the bulkhead, and I think I must have slept also, because I do not remember any sounds from above that would have betokened preparations to move, but soon I was aware of a rolling motion and I could hear the creaking of the ship's timbers.

"Sail where you wish, you bastards," I thought. "I shall elude you—and find the Road."

It is hard to gauge the passage of time in complete darkness. It may have been two hours or twenty when next the hatch opened.

"Come up," bellowed the Angel.

We climbed the ladder into the cabin and he jerked his head and led off quickly to the companionway and we followed him up onto the poop. The sun was shining brightly, and I blinked painfuly after the darkness. The galleon was under an untidy and lubberly press of canvas which even my inexpert eye could see was spilling more wind than it retained, and she was heading down the coast—which was some miles away on our port beam, which meant we were sailing south—away from the direction in which I wanted to go. There was a Mekrani at the helm and a few others lounged in the waist, but of Schmirke I could see no sign—at first. Then the Angel grinned and pointed aloft—and I saw five figures leaping grotesquely at the end of the main topsail yard, spinning and unspinning, jostling each other in that dance of death, their limbs jerking like those of marionettes.

"From outboard inwards, gentlemen," said the Angel. "Captain Schmirke, Second Mate Johan Jaarsfeldt, then the gunner and his mate whose names I never could pronounce, and finally a useless gentleman who drew a supercargo's share for doing nothing but corrupt the cook. Bardock—I hereby appoint you mate in my place. Introduce the sailing master if you please."

"Lobo," I said, trying to keep the disgust and horror out of my voice and expression.

"Dom Lobo," said the Angel, "what would you say was wrong with the set of these sails?".

"Everything," answered Lobo. "What crew have we?"

"Only Mekranis," the Angel told him.

Lobo bowed and turned to the poop rail. *"Tum log soor ka bacha hain,"* he bellowed. *"Uncha jao—sab—aur yeh capra pukkha jumakaro."*

Lean brown men leapt for the rigging and climbed aloft and soon all sails were drawing sweetly under the direction of Lobo.

The Angel smiled contentedly. "Bardock, my dear friend," he said. "It was a lucky day that brought you floundering to the side of this ship."

✧ 15

AFTER some few hours we altered course a few points to starboard, bearing away southwesterly from the coast into the open sea. Because I was too heartsick to want to talk to either of them, I kept well away from the Angel and Lobo, who now seemed to have got their heads together and were not long in becoming the best of boon companions. At the same time I had wit enough not to antagonize the former, in whose hands my fate now rested, by any show of unwillingness or disapproval, so I busied myself with tasks around the decks and rigging, and heaven knows that there were many which cried out for attention. The ship was as foul aloft as below, and her running and standing gear alike were rotten. I shuddered inwardly at our certain fate should we be taken suddenly in a tempest such as the last we had run through.

It did not appear to worry Lobo, however, and my heart sank within me as I saw the lightning disintegration of the man, now he had thrown in his lot with the Angel. He went below and took over the cabin of the late Schmirke, to emerge on deck again later clad in the same sort of gaudy raiment as that worn by the Angel—silken breeches, turned down galligaskins, sash and sidearms—and I noticed something that must have eluded me before—his ears had obviously long ago been pierced and had semihealed over, because now he sported a ring in one and a gold coin in the other. Yes, Lobo had reverted to type and was now a Gentleman of the Middle Passage to the very life.

Under pretext of examining the braces, I climbed the mainmast and went out on the footropes of the topsail yard until I came to the point from which dangled the five hanged men, and I slashed each one of them free in turn, to drop with a splash into the creaming side wave. Looking down, my stomach turned as I saw the Angel, foreshortened on the poop, doff his feathered hat and assume a flippantly mournful stance, intoning an obscene parody of the burial service.

My acquaintance with the Mekranis hitherto had been in the role of savage enemies or sullen prisoners awaiting execution. I was therefore amazed to find them in my new relationship as mate, willing and docile seamen—and not at all unskillful if they understood what was required of them. It was indeed fortunate for the plans of the foul Angel that this was so, because he, Lobo and I were now the only Europeans aboard the galleon, against some two hundred of the others. But these people were accustomed to being commanded and apparently it mattered little who held the whip hand provided that hand was firm—or so it appeared.

I stayed aloft for some time busying myself on various tasks and instructing the native boatswain, or *serang*, in the replacing of the worst of the running gear, gaining strength and a certain clearness of head in the clean breeze, high above the stenches of the deck. My mind was now made up. Sooner or later we would have to put ashore somewhere, and when we did I would quietly slip away and hide in the jungle until this foul hulk had sailed again. In the meantime I must give this precious pair no cause for suspicion, appearing to fall in, if not with the wholehearted enthusiasm of Lobo, at least with some show of fatalism, with the schemes of the Angel. So resolved, I came down on deck again and went up onto the poop.

The Angel and Lobo were sitting on the cabin skylight sharing between them a large puncheon of palm toddy, the latter talking in an undertone and the Angel chuckling slyly. As I came up with them, Lobo broke off, looking a little confused, the usage of my long command over him not having yet completely sloughed from him. The Angel took another deep swig at the puncheon, passed it to Lobo, wiped his hand across his mouth and roared at me in high good humor.

"You hot-arsed young bastard! Laying 'em aboard as pretty as you please, eh? The High Don's bit of blanket-warmer no less, eh? As handy with the horny knight Sir Stiffly Standforth as you are with your other weapons, eh? You saucy young sod, cuckolding the chief Portygooser in his own bed! You who turned up your dainty nose at the bit of black velvet I cozen'd for you at Good Hope. Likes his meat dainty, does he?" And many more such coarse witticisms until I could have brained him, and probably might have tried had it not been for the brace of pistols in his sash. Instead, I made shift to smile sourly and told him that we'd better get some good cordage and canvas aboard her soon unless he wanted the yards down around our ears in the next hard blow. That sobered him, and brought Lobo's professional zeal to the surface.

"That I know full well," growled the Angel. "Isn't that what I've been telling you? Isn't that what I tried to tell the late Captain Schmirke, God rot him?"

"That's as maybe," I agreed. "But aren't you tempting Fate sailing out into the blue so ill-found, right at the height of the monsoon storms?"

"Tell him," commanded the Angel, applying himself once more to the puncheon.

"A risk we must take, dom Gil," explained Lobo. "At anchor in a creek we could never hope to obtain the supplies we so sorely need, so we must go and look for them—and where else better than in the westerly trades? That's a belt of wind, you see, a bare ten leagues across, blowing constantly from the Cape of Good Hope to the coast of Ind. All ships seek it, Dutch and Portuguese."

"So?" I prompted.

"So we accept what Providence sends us," put in the Angel. "Hollander or don, we're not proud. We lay 'em aboard and sail back lee-to-weather to some snug creek where we can refit and refurbish—then heigh-ho for the Spanish Main, or any other bloody main that takes our fancy. What say you to that, young Sir Randy Hotcrutch?"

"That you're mad," I retorted. "If you think that this scurvy sieve with her rotten gear and two feet of weed on her hull can outfight and outmaneuver a well-found Indiaman, Dutch or Portuguese—"

"Pish—squit," snorted the Angel. "There are two hundred black crows aboard here who'd liefer die on a blood-soaked deck than in a conventful of virgins. It's their religion to fall in battle against the Infidels. What crew does an Indiaman carry—Hollander or Portygoose? We know, all of us! Eighty to a hundred, the scumscourings of half the ports of Europe, with no stomach for a fight."

"Splendid," I agreed sourly. "All right, they won't fight. But how do you expect to lay them aboard? One sight of this coffinful of black sinners and they'll be off with a bone in their teeth to spread the news on the coast that there's pirates abroad. Then you'll have a squadron of galleons loaded to the scuppers with soldiers who *will* fight, out here to hunt us down."

I was only testing and pumping him for his intentions, and I expected an angry outburst at this, but he contented himself with winking broadly and clapping me on the shoulder.

"Take the watch, young mattress brigand," he commanded, "while the sailing master and I get a bite and sup."

"Sou'west by west, quarter-west—close-hauled as she'll take it into the eye of the wind," Lobo told me, and it was at that moment I realized that mate though I was, this was now the man who stood higher in the Angel's counsel.

They went below, and through the skylight I could hear the Angel's rumbling bellow and Lobo's braying laugh, and the latter was the harder to bear. I cursed myself for being so deceived by a man for nearly four years, and I sorrowed afresh for the loss of Pereira and Subram Rao. Would they, I wondered, have so willingly sold to this blackguard their allegiance to me? I shrugged to myself, for there was no answer to this, but I swore that never again would I put my trust in any man, for no man was to be trusted— myself least of all. Had *I* not betrayed the one man who had used me kindly in all these years?

I leaned on the poop rail and ran my eye over the ship again, noticing that there were now lookouts at each masthead, fore, main and mizzen, and one right out on the towering uptilted bowsprit, and yet another perched monkey-like on the gilded roof of the enormous stern lanthorn. I noticed another thing also. Every Mekrani had a knife, as every sailor must, but all these had had their points removed, leaving only a bare two or three inches of cutting edge, and so useless as a weapon of offense; and if that were not enough, as an added precaution, each knife was secured round its owner's neck by a riveted chain which allowed just enough slack to cut a piece of cordage or canvas at waist height, and no more. Weaver, the late Captain Schmirke, and now the Angel, apparently took no chances of mutiny. Lobo, I had seen, was also armed like the Angel, but I, as yet, had been given no weapon.

It was now fast getting dark and I was wondering how long my watch would last, when I heard a faint hail from the foremasthead, "Bigli hai—bigli! A light—a light!"

I answered his hail and asked where-away, and the man told me it was hull down on the weather horizon. There had been silence hitherto among the Mekranis, but now I could feel their excitement mounting. I strained my eyes out over the darkening sea but could make out not the faintest twinkling from the level of the deck, so I mounted the shrouds and went aloft.

Yes, there it was, the veriest pinpoint in that soft velvet expanse, abeam and to the south of us, and, as I checked her bearings over the next five minutes, obviously going the other way, towards the coast we had quitted.

I was joined in the rigging by Lobo then, who studied her for some further minutes. He sighed.

"She's got the legs of us," he said regretfully. "If I put this craft about we'd lose much time, and no doubt the light would drop below the horizon before we were sailing steadily on the wind. No, that's one that gets away and lives to sail another day, dom Gil."

The Angel was on the poop when I came down, and he was in a towering rage.

"Master Bardock, I'm a tolerant and easygoing man, God wot," he swore, "but there are limits to my patience. Neglect to inform me on the instant, by day or by night, whenever you are holding the watch, of sail or light when it is first reported and I'll slit the wedding tackle from you, and keelhaul what's left. Get below, eat, rest, and take over again from Lobo at midnight. Where's that bloody serang?"

In the faint light of the binnacle lanthorn I saw the old Mekrani come forward and salaam respectfully. In addition to his knife he wore his badge of office round his neck on another, lighter chain. It was a silver boatswain's pipe. The Angel jerked it from him, snapping the chain, then as I went down the companionway to the cabin, I heard the boom of a heavy pistol and the thud of a body on the deck. That, then, was the secret of the discipline on this foul ship. For an instant I once more knew nausea in my vitals.

I tried to force down a few mouthfuls of the mess of fish and rice which stood in a dirty kit on the cabin table, then tasted with suspicion a tentative draft of palm toddy, which made me gag and retch. A silent bawarchi, who appeared also to be the steward, appeared from the shadows and indicated the cubbyhole that apparently was my cabin. It was the gun-filled space that we had entered earlier, lighted now by a guttering tallow dip that floated in a keg of water on a piece of cork bark. Some gaudy clothes similar to those worn by the Angel, and now Lobo, had been thrown on the filthy cot, the property no doubt of one of the hanged five, and though I would fain have thrust them all through the gun port, I realized that I had no choice but to wear them or go naked, for my own now hung upon me in shreds. Wearily I threw myself down on the cot and, tired near to death, I appeared to sleep but for some few seconds before I felt a hand shaking my ankle. I sat up and gaped at a Mekrani.

"*Chaubis ghanta, sahib,*" he said, and I realized that my midnight watch was about to begin. I struggled unwillingly into the horrible garments, noting that still no weapons were yet being offered to me, and as the ship's bell sounded the hour I came out on deck.

"We're on the other tack," the sailing master told me. "West-nor'west and, as before, close to the wind as she will bear. Watch for lights, and remember the Captain's warning. Call me on the sixth turn of that," pointing to the large hourglass which stood beside the binnacle, "or before, should the wind or weather change."

There was a new authority in his voice and I felt my nerves tauten and temper rise, but I kept rein upon myself and merely grunted an acknowledgment. He hesitated for a moment or so as if he wished to say more, but then thought better of it, turned away and went below.

Nothing of import occurred during my watch and I was thankful that I saw no lights. I had privily determined not to report any had I seen them, unless I was certain that the other ship had the legs of us, but on reflection I had reluctantly abandoned this as it was clear that it was the duty of all who saw light or sail to inform the foul Angel and, unarmed as I was, I could not hope to prevail if he indeed did turn the vials of his wrath upon me, as he had upon the wretched serang. Thankfully I sent a sailor below to call Lobo just as I turned the hourglass for the last time, and dawn was streaking the eastern horizon.

And so it went on for fifteen wearying days; Lobo and I relieving each other in six-hour watches, our course a little to the north or to the south of due west, according to tack. The Angel stood no watch himself, spending his time either up in the rigging keeping the look-outs upon their mettle or, when sleeping, locked in the stern-cabin behind a stout oaken door. Lobo now seemed to be completely in his trust and had tacitly taken over the duties of mate from me in addition to his own as sailing master. The Angel still indulged in bouts of roistering good-fellowship, but they were of shorter duration and less frequent than at the beginning of the passage, and I noticed that neither he nor Lobo applied themselves so often to the palm-toddy puncheon. In fact there was now over the whole ship an air of coiled watchfulness that I understood the better when I learned that he had promised an extra share of the booty to the sailor who first raised a sail or light that would lead eventually to a successful action, and second choice should there be any women aboard. A sail or a light. Nothing else mattered.

And then it happened. Halfway through the forenoon watch on the sixteenth day.

The ship was hull-down on the southern horizon, and the wind had changed so that it was dead on our starboard beam, and so behind us when we changed course towards her. Lobo sent aloft every stitch of sail our rigging could carry, and he made rapid calculations of windage and the run of the following sea, then changed course again so that ours would cross hers on a converging line.

The Angel called me to him and for the first time told me of the plan he and Lobo had made between them.

"All Mekranis will be below the bulwarks and out of sight," he explained, "except for twenty of the lighter colored crows who will be dressed in Christian breeches and Flemish caps, or kerchiefs round their heads, according to whether she's Hollander or Porty-goose. We run her as close abeam as she'll let us, keeping to wind'ard and showing whatever colors she herself is showing. If she's Hollander I shall be captain here, because I can speak enough of their poxy tongue to deceive them over the sound of wind and water. If she's Portygoose, Lobo will be captain, and do the parley-ing. You will be yet another supernumerary officer and will take command here on the poop while Lobo goes about the business of handling her from the waist, and I in charge of other matters."

Suddenly I saw in all this a possible way out of the intolerable trap in which I now found myself. Unarmed, I was helpless against the Angel; with as much as one pistol or sword I might accomplish his undoing. Of Lobo I was now uncertain, but my relations with him over the past years had been cordial, so there was still a chance that I might yet win him back to my side if I could negotiate from a position of strength. Yes, if I were armed, I could topple the Angel from his malodorous dunghill and perhaps save an Indiaman from pillage, murder and destruction. Of the Mekranis I had no fears or doubts. They obeyed whoever commanded strongly enough.

All this sped through my mind while the Angel was still speaking. I nodded profoundly, pursed my lips and endeavored to give the impression of one who heard, considered deeply and finally ap-proved that which was being said to him.

"A seemingly sound plan," I averred.

"I'm glad it finds favor with you, young Sir Randy Breeks," he cried, clapping me on the shoulder, "because that is what will come about—unless every man dog of you wants bloody keelhauling."

The rigging was now black with chattering Mekranis, with Lobo high above them at the very truck of the mainmast, armed with a magnificent Genoese spyglass. He hailed us faintly from his eyrie.

"Her mainmast is lower than her fore or mizzen," he shouted, "and she carries only courses and heads'ls. She's been through dirty weather and is jury-rigged."

And that threw the Angel into transports of delight, because it explained why we, who were foul and rottenly found, were so fast overhauling her. He ordered down from the rigging all except Lobo and the new serang, for he never trusted one man alone on a duty of import, and had the twenty-four guns we carried each side run back on their carriages and loaded, charged and double-shotted alternately with grape and heavy ball. And then he brought into play a devilish device of the late unlamented Weaver, who had caused the shutters of the gun-ports to be reversed on their hinges, so that they swung inboard instead of out, and the yawning ports themselves were closed by flimsy black canvas screens that simulated solid wood. This meant that the guns could be fired without warning the victims by first raising the ports on the outboard tackles.

This done, he broke out a motley collection of garments from some sea-chests in the great-cabin, many torn, foul and blood-stained, which he distributed to twenty of the lighter-skinned Mekranis. He himself assumed more sober raiment than his gaudy pantaloons and sash, and topped them with half-armor and casque. At me he threw a russet coat and breeches and also a monk's habit and cowl.

"If she's a Portygoose you'll take Holy Orders of the Romish persuasion," he told me in explanation. "If she's a Hollander you'll be a bleak-faced Frisian master's mate."

Then he had both the Dutch and the Portuguese colors laid handy by the helm ready to be run up at his order. After that he unlocked the armory which had ingress only through his own cabin, and had laid out ready for instant issue an assortment of cutlasses, pikes, calivers and boarding pistols, and he set over them a guard of four Mekranis whom he threatened with instant death if they permitted any but himself to approach them without his order. At this I endeavored to venture with as casual an air as possible, an inquiry as to what arms I was to carry.

"Monk or mate," he grinned, "you'll be either too holy or too busy to require any." I shrugged and gave him permission to dispose of his weapons lewdly, whereupon he grinned the broader and winked, and I knew then with certainty that he was still suspicious of me and that I would have therefore to be doubly careful.

The gap between the two ships had now closed considerably, and we were able, even with the naked eye from deck level, to discern more of the cut of her jib. There was naught remarkable about her;

about our size or perhaps a shade lighter, deep-laden under cargo, high poop and forecastle, square-rigged on fore and main, lateen on mizzen, twelve gun-ports on the port side which we could see—which meant twenty-four guns altogether, with perhaps, as we had, two sternchasers on the poop and a swivel carronade at the break of the beak. And her gun-ports were open, which meant she was prudently suspicious of us. She wallowed along slowly although the wind was fair on her port quarter, but we already knew the reason for this. A recent storm had apparently carried away her main topmast and weakened her other two sticks so that she carried, unhandily, only a minimum of canvas.

The Angel was now herding and arranging the Mekranis, other than the chosen twenty, into the waist below the level of the high bulwarks, and Lobo came down from aloft and joined me on the poop. He was a new Lobo, and one who repelled and sickened me. There was a lean and vulpine expression on his face and he trembled with a barely suppressed excitement, and I found myself likening him in my mind to the baser mercenaries I had commanded in the Lowlands, just before a raid upon a village—or ladies of gentle birth but sporting proclivities at a meet of the hounds before a stag hunt. The loot or quarry took but second place to the blood.

"Portuguese or Dutch?" I asked him.

"Could be either," he answered. "Build and lines of the big fellows differ little these days. Were she Portuguese and had on her best dress, her sails would be emblazoned with crosses and holy emblems, but that is storm canvas she is bearing—plain and unadorned, as is ours. We can but sniff each other's sterns like questing hounds for the nonce."

His hand went out to the palm-toddy puncheon he had brought on deck with him, but a booted foot shot between us and kicked it into the scuppers.

"Clear heads it is for this ploy, sailing master," chided the Angel. "You can swill with the best when we've taken 'em."

Lobo grinned and accepted the rebuke with the best of good humor, and my heart sank a little further as I realized how much a creature of this foul ruffian the weak Lobo had become.

And now but a scant two miles separated us and we were fast closing the gap, coming up apace on her weather beam, and Lobo, quizzing through the glass, told us that her decks were crowded with people, but of what kind or manner he could not as yet tell, but that there was a flash from time to time as the sun glinted on arms and armor of those on the poop.

"Damn them," fumed the Angel. "Why don't they signal us?"

Then, even as he spoke, there was a puff of white smoke from her poop, and Lobo held up his hand for silence and started to count aloud, then there was a splash midway between us as the ball took the water and ricocheted twice on the crests before sinking, and finally the boom of the cannon itself reached us against the wind.

"Two miles plus a quarter of that away," muttered Lobo after a mental calculation. "That's the bitch's snap at the questing hound— not meant entirely to discourage, just to warn. Now she should show her colors."

She did, at that very instant. A black ball ran up to her mizzen peak, and broke into the Portuguese colors.

"A bloody 'goose," said the Angel. "She'll fight fiercer but not so sustained as the mynheers. Up with the colors and into your black nightshirt, young Randy Breeks. Stand by the helm, tell your beads and 'pax vobiscum' like a mother superior in a bawdy-house."

In retrospect I swear that at this point, had I possessed the means, I would have cut him down weltering, and if necessary Lobo also, and taken my chance with the Mekranis, had I thought I could save those souls on the other ship. But I had not the means. Both the Angel and Lobo were armed to the teeth with a brace of pistols apiece, cutlasses unsheathed and ready to hand, and also daggers, while I was as bare of steel as a badger's rump. There was naught for it, therefore, but to appear to be as eager as they for this piece of villainy and to fall in with them to the full, waiting my opportunity in the excitement of the action to strike down and disarm one of the Mekranis. Quickly I slipped into habit and cowl.

The serang now ran up the Portuguese colors to our own mizzen peak, and we fired an answering gun—upward into the air and unshotted, as a salute.

We waited with bated breath to see how our duplicity was being received by them, then sorrowfully I heard over the water a ragged cheer from the other, and gaily-hued flags were run up to every point of her rigging at which they had halyards to attach them, and the poor fools fired many more guns in salute, which meant that they were, in their obvious joy at this encounter, weakening their defense. And then finally, as is the courtesy of the sea when suspicion is allayed, her gun-ports closed and she backed her mainsail and lateen and hove to. To leeward of us, robbed of way, with half her guns unshotted and all her ports closed, she was now at our mercy.

Swiftly we bore down upon her.

❖❖ 16

OUR first broadside raked her from the distance of a bare fifty yards, cutting bloody swathes through the poor tight-packed wretches who crowded her bulwarks, while yet the Angel and Lobo were mockingly doffing their hats and bowing, and I was standing deafened beside our helmsman. Then we went about, and about again in the perfect maneuver dictated by Lobo in high-pitched Hindustani, our Mekranis moving like well-drilled monkeys aloft and at the braces. This brought us up on her other side from astern, and we were thus able to blast her again before they had the wit to swing her larboard gun-ports open and bring fire to bear upon us—and in those few sickening moments her undoing was complete. And now the Mekranis were aloft in our rigging and were pouring small-arms fire down upon her decks.

On her poop, I saw a man crawl to the mizzen shrouds and cast loose her ensign halyards, running down her colors in token of surrender, but that did not stop the Angel from raking her again and again with our stern chasers as we crossed her bows, went about, and came up once more under her lee.

Grappling irons snaked out from our sides and in a twinkling we were fast held to her, and a shrieking horde of Mekranis swarmed over her bulwarks and descended upon the bemused survivors. I followed the bellowing Angel in his leap from poop rail to poop rail, my habit brailed up around my waist like a farm-wife's petticoats, seeking frantically for a cutlass wherewith to cleave his skull. But then I saw that he was wading into the Mekranis like a huntsman bringing the hounds to heel after the kill, and since he was well equipped to do this I let him continue, and even helped him, because they were now blood-maddened and were butchering fiendishly any who seemed still to have life left in them. I seized a boarding pike and rammed it through the vitals of our serang as he was in the act of hacking off the head of a Portuguese seaman, achieving a moment's savage satisfaction from it, but nothing more, because other Mekranis turned their enraged gaze upon me, then two others set about me with cutlasses, and I received a slash across my right shoulder which would have had my arm off had it not been for my stout hair habit and folded cowl. As it was, the pike fell from my hands and I was at their mercy until I was rescued by Lobo who blasted both with his pistols.

The Angel had the devils back under control in a matter of minutes, killing without compunction a further two who threatened in their blind fury to turn upon him. Then he and Lobo herded them into line, while they gathered up all fallen weapons and then surrendered their own quite meekly. This, I learned later, was the usual method adopted with Mekranis. Their arms were issued to them like the steel spurs of the gamecock for the fight only—then as quickly withdrawn. Only when every pistol, caliver, pike, cutlass or dagger except those of Lobo and himself were safely back under lock and key on our own ship did the Angel draw breath. He came up onto the poop of our prize and regarded me with amused contempt as I sat shivering on the cabin skylight, my arm hanging uselessly beside me and my habit soaked in blood.

"Not so handy in fighting as fornicating, eh, young Friar Frigmonger?" he chuckled. "Ah well, ne'er fret. Which of the Portygoosers did this to you? I'll have him slow-fried for your edification."

"Our own crows," Lobo explained. "Dom Gil was trying to call 'em off like you but he hadn't the knack."

"Take 'em from behind," advised the Angel. "With your boot—up and between—right in the seat of their connubial bliss. While they're standing on one foot calling upon Allah, you swipe 'em sideways with the blunt edge of your cutlass. Got to be quick though."

Then he was off again like a demon, darting here and there, routing out the few survivors of the cannonade and the butchery that followed, and forming them up in a straggling line, sound and less severely wounded alike, and putting all to the question.

"Shipwrights, sailmakers and those skilled in blacksmithing," he roared. "Any for the Middle Passage, Gentlemen all and Merry Companions? Speak up, any that are—or by God, tread the bloody plank."

None moved at first, being all dazed with the horror that had so suddenly befallen them. The Angel cursed filthily and roared to the Mekranis to ship the plank. Nothing loath, they sought a long grating from amidships and ran it out from the sally port at the head of the gangway, weighing down the inboard end with a gun-carriage. The Angel turned to the first man in line and inquired in his vile Portuguese what his calling might be, if any, other than tosspot brothel lackey. The poor wretch, not understanding aright, mumbled something which did not seem to satisfy the Angel.

"Plank the bastard!" ordered the Angel, and to my horror I saw the man pushed forward onto the grating and, screaming and begging for mercy, forced along its length at the ends of boarding pikes by two Mekranis until he was at the outer extremity poised above the water. He stood there for a moment or so, his face convulsed with terror, then he turned and desperately tried to force his way back inboard against the pikes. The Mekranis were playing with him now, like two cats with a single mouse. They would desist in their efforts and turn away as if tired of this sport, then wheel suddenly and force him outboard again. Then finally other Mekranis, laughing and yelling with the sheer enjoyment of this ghastly game, started to pelt him with chunks of wood and broken gear, until half a snatch block caught him fair in the midriff and he fell into the sea.

Yet other Mekranis had meanwhile been heaving the dead and sorely wounded overboard, and already the telltale triangular fins of shoals of sharks were darting hither and thither. Horrified but unable to drag my eyes away, I saw the poor wretch in the act of trying to swim back towards the side of the ship, suddenly jerk to a stop and disappear below the reddening surface. I sought Lobo who was leaning on the poop rail watching the shambles.

"Lobo," I implored. "Do something, anything. Join me in pulling this fiend down."

"There's naught to be done, dom Gil," he said without looking at me. "The die is cast and the Devil has claimed his own. I've seen all this happen before. If we overthrow him, what happens? The Mekranis would tear us to pieces."

"I'll answer for that," I said hotly. "They'll follow a strong leader. *You* know that."

"And who's the strong leader?" he asked drily. "You? You're sore wounded. A man needs both hands and both feet to command Mekranis."

"*You*," I pleaded. "Let us kill this man and I swear I will place myself under you thereafter."

"And go where? And do what? The brand is on us now, dom Gil."

"Let us sail back to the coast, burn this vile ship and seek our fortunes inland—as we were going to do when we fell in with her." I was shaking, as if in the grip of a fever, because now the second man was on the plank.

Sadly he shook his head. "As we *were* going to do. You had a star then. I was content to follow it—but another star, maybe an evil one, but still a star and a sailing mark, has arisen and eclipsed yours, for better or worse. Kismet, dom Gil. A man cannot fight his kismet." He gestured to the waist of the ship. "This may not be pleasant until one's stomach becomes accustomed to it, but it is the law of the Middle Passage. For us or against us, and the plank for the latter. There—" he said quickly. "There's one who has found his tongue and will live to walk another day—and another—and the next."

And it was even as he said. One man had understood what was being asked of him, and was on his knees babbling to the Angel that he was skilled in sail-making, and the others, all of the remaining five, were likewise claiming similar trades—one a carpenter, another a gunsmith, yet another was the boatswain.

"Aboard my ship with you then, you idle scum!" roared the Angel. "By God, there'll be a covey of examiners shrewder than the dons of Oxford to test your words tomorrow. Then it will be a gay life or a short one according to how well you served your apprenticeships, you lying bastards."

He came up and joined us then, and ran his eye aloft. "Is there aught we need up there?" he asked Lobo.

"All the yards, sails, running and standing gear," the sailing master answered. "What is left of it appears new and of good condition—replaced since the storm." He stamped with his heel on the planks of the deck. "For the rest, she is old but sound—slower, I should say, than our own craft and not so handy to leeward, even allowing for her jury rig. Tear a few hundred ells of planking out of her and load it aboard us, take whatever else you want from below, and set fire to the rest. We'd sail the faster back to the coast for refitting if we hadn't got her to shepherd."

"By God, there's more in that head of yours than bilge water and tar slush," said the Angel approvingly. "Right, that's the way of it then. Set the crows to work getting all gear and cargo opened up to let us see what the Lord has sent us. We've lost four of 'em, but gained six white men of sorts. How many of them remain unplanked by this time tomorrow is a matter to be seen." He turned to me. "How now, Friar Fart? You look a little milky round the jib."

He shot out his hand and dragged me closer by my blood-stained habit, and then slid the rough cloth off my shoulder. He inspected the cut closely, and I turned my eyes round to see to what extent I had been wounded. The cut was deep but since there was some slight movement in my lower arm it appeared to have stopped short of any major muscle although I could not lift it of itself. The blood had flowed copiously and I was greatly weakened thereby. He turned to Lobo and demanded his white shirt, and when the other had removed it, he tore it into strips which he soaked in the drinking-water barrel lashed to the foot of the mizzen mast. "Tell Achmet to bring the slush," he told Lobo.

"The slush" turned out to be a small cauldron of molten pitch which was always set upon the galley firehearth before an action, to cope with such contingencies as this. When it was brought, the Angel summoned two Mekranis to throw me to the deck and sit upon me, and the wound was anointed liberally. I did my best to hold myself from swooning, but only partially succeeded, then with surprising skill and dexterity, the Angel bound my shoulder tightly with the wet rags.

"There," he said heartily. "That will keep the weevils out of it. A Gentleman of the Middle Passage without a sword-arm is as useful as a whore without buttocks. Let that lot set hard and you'll still be able to put your hand where it oughtn't to be when we strike the Portygoose coast again."

By this time the Mekranis had got the hatches off and were dragging up the cargo into the light. The Angel cursed as he saw the bulk of it, which comprised, for the greater part, ploughs, harrows and other implements of husbandry, and sacks of millet and barley seed, and I remembered with a fresh pang of remorse how my friend and benefactor, the Governor, had ordered all this gear to be sent out from Portugal in an effort to improve the lot of the native farmers of the territory. All was dumped unceremoniously over the side, but the Angel brightened considerably when they brought up several casks of gunpowder, shot, both heavy and light, and many nets of solid cannon balls of a caliber suitable to our twenty-four-pounders. There were some bales of sailcloth also, and hundreds of fathoms of stout cordage that made Lobo's eyes gleam. In the lazaretto was an abundance of salt pork and beef, all of which the Angel loudly pronounced to be mutton in order to still the religious prejudices of the Mekranis. And there were dried peas and good corn meal and hard ship's biscuits also, while the cabin yielded much food of a durable but daintier nature, with some barrels of good wine of Oporto. There was a heavy treasure chest and a stand of small arms and Toledo swords, but these the Angel had conveyed quickly to his own quarters upon our ship. For the rest, he let the Mekranis have their head and their pick for a mad hour, and they swarmed like ants backward and forward over the rails between the two vessels, conveying that which took their fancy—clothes, bedding, china, fine glass and silver from the cabins, and the pitiful sea-chests and dunnage bags of the murdered officers and sailors, fighting like wolves among themselves over that which they deemed the more desirable.

And while this was going on, Lobo had a picked party of the higher skilled Mekranis adzing out long timbers from above the water line and stripping down the gear aloft before swaying it aboard the *Santa Elena* at the end of our yardarms, until our prize looked like the vulture-picked skeleton of some dead sea monster.

Then, as I sat drooping on the rim of consciousness on our own poop, to which they had conveyed me, I heard above the din of these activities the piercing scream of a woman. I sat up, galvanized.

There were three of them. One, from her manner and bearing rather than her now torn and disheveled clothing, evidently a lady of quality, though no longer young. The others were respectively her buxom but undeniably plain tirewoman, and a young and beautiful nun in black habit. The Mekranis had gone completely mad and were fighting and tearing at them, until the Angel, bellowing like a bull, once more sailed into them and restored order.

The Angel stood before them, rubbing his chin ruminatively and running his eye over them in the manner of a yeoman at a cattle fair. The older woman stood proudly before him returning his scrutiny with disdain, her arm about the shoulders of the terrified servant. The nun stood a little apart, her eyes downcast and her hands crossed on her white wimple. Across the breadth of two decks and the intervening gap, and over the excited buzz of the slavering Mekranis, I could not hear the Angel's words, but speak he did, and he made a gesture with his hands. There was a howl from the Mekranis that sounded like the baying of the hounds of hell itself and they surged forward and seized the lady and her servant, and then, fighting like furies bore them out of sight below decks. I saw the nun look upwards and make the sign of the cross on her bosom, then the Angel swept off his hat, bowed with mock gallantry and called to Lobo, pointing to our deck and then to the lifting tackle they had been using to sway the pillaged stores across to us. The whole scene, though in dumb show as far as I was concerned, needed no explanation. The young nun was the Angel's prize, the others had been tossed to the wolves.

Lobo was by his very nationality a papist, though I had never known him to assume any of the obligations of his religion, and I heard myself praying in a babble to whatever God looked down upon us, Catholic or Protestant, for some forgotten and forsworn remnant of his faith to return to him at that moment and to give him the stomach to strike the Angel dead before this final blasphemy.

But no sign came, and I stood clinging to the mizzen shrouds, too weak to stand upright alone, the tears streaming down my cheeks, as Lobo came slowly forward to the gentle creature and, after bowing slightly, fastened the bight of a bowline round her under her arms. He then took the running end of the line and hauled her aloft, and she started to come the way of the casks and dunnage that had preceded her.

Then the miracle happened, though it was not apparent as such to me at that moment. The line appeared to snarl up in its passage through the yardarm block, and the nun halted in her travel over the gap between the ships, swaying in a sickening arc. Lobo shook and twitched at the running end, and I heard the Angel bellow at him above the uproar, then the line seemed to jerk loose from his hands and the nun plummeted down out of the bowline into the water between us. I tried to climb the bulwarks, not so much in an effort to save her as because of a great weariness that was upon me and the knowledge that I had my life to live with this scene graven upon my consciousness, and I had stood by then as much as I could bear. But I was unable to make even that feeble gesture. I just collapsed in a heap and lay staring up at the sky, more dead than alive.

It was dark when I was next in a state to notice such things, and we were sailing steadily, fair before the wind. Lobo was bending over me holding a cup of wine to my lips. I summoned enough strength to knock it from his hand and to spit at him. He shrugged.

"Foolish, dom Gil," he said quietly. "Wine is life, and you have little enough of that left in your battered hulk of a carcass."

"Filthy blaspheming bastard," I said. "Yes, God knows I have little life in me at the moment, and that little I would fain have thrown away this day—but He also knows what is in my heart now, and that is the fervent prayer to live long enough to slit the throats of you and that Devil of a master of yours."

"And for myself I'll probably thank you when the time comes," said Lobo wearily.

"I doubt it," I snarled at him. "You'll whimper for a priest to shrive you into your Catholic heaven, you scurvy louse, but you'll whimper in vain. I know little enough of your religion, but you've done this day that for which not all the Jesuit College could give you absolution."

"I did what I could," he said heavily. "She could not have taken her own life, even in face of what she knew lay before her."

"Why did you not take *his*, you cowardly swine?" I demanded.

"That would have availed her nothing but an even worse fate at the hands of the Mekranis thereafter," he answered. "You saw what happened to the other women. No, dom Gil, that which I did, horrible though it seemed, would have been what she might have prayed for. A quick, clean death, not at her own hands." He crossed himself and bowed his head. "May she intercede for me with the sweet Mother of God, for what I did when I tied that slipping knot about her was the first dictation of true conscience I have followed in my rotten life."

He went back to a cask of wine which stood beside the binnacle and drew another cup, and this time I drank because I was knowing the tortures of the damned myself with the pain of my shoulder.

"Dom Gil," he said in a low voice. "Listen to me, I beg of you. This is for your sake more than mine. We are bound on the fair trade wind back for a quiet part of the palm coast, far to the south of the Portuguese settlements, there to refit. By the time the work is finished you will have regained some of your strength and can make your decisions at your own will. Until then, you are in the power of this man. If I killed him now it would be signing the death warrant of us both, yours and mine, at the hands of the Mekranis. You say that they will follow any strong leader. That is true, but only to a point. There is also an oath which binds them, the oath of the *namook hallal*—the oath to the salt, and every last mother's son of them has taken it to *him*, as they do to every captain."

"Then let them take it to us when he is dead," I retorted.

"You have lived long out here," he smiled sadly, "but not long enough, dom Gil, or you would know that no Mohammedan can swear an oath on the salt except in a mosque, before the mullah."

And that, at least, I knew to be true—and it explained fully and for the first time the real reason for the Angel's power of life and death over them.

"He has told me of it," Lobo went on, "for I am a brother of the Sign of the Gentlemen. He was able to overthrow Weaver only because they were all ashore at the time, in the Celebes. He cut Weaver's throat while he was in a drunken slumber, *after* he had bribed the mullah to swear the crew in afresh to him. You need a

long spoon to sup with this particular devil, dom Gil. Wait until
yours is longer, and you have the power to wield it, and I'll help
you hang him—and I'll so fix this ship that she'll never sail again to
harry honest seafarers. You have *my* oath, for what it's worth, on
that. Then I'll follow you to your Road, and to hell thereafter if
you wish it."

And such was the earnestness of his speech and demeanor that I
could not forbear to believe him and to see the reason in his contention. Slowly I nodded my agreement, though with some mental
reservation and inward equivocation. I would sail lee-to-windward
with him until my strength returned to me and we had settled with
this blackguard, but after that I wanted no further truck with Lobo.
We were heading back to the coast now. To the coast—and the
Road—I would this time travel alone.

Lobo gripped my sound hand, then with the help of one of the
watch he bore me below to my cabin and made me as comfortable
in my cot as my poor circumstances permitted.

I know not how long I lay there, for a burning fever set in almost
immediately, like unto that which afflicted me on my arrival on the
coast, made worse this time by my wound and my great loss of
blood. I dimly remember Lobo coming and going with wine and
other medicaments, and once or twice I half woke to see the Angel's
hateful face peering down at me.

I think I first returned to full consciousness by reason of the
terrific noise immediately about me—and at first I thought I had
gone insane, for Mekranis were feverishly working at the gun
which shared my cabin, laying, firing, running back, swabbing and
reloading, then firing again. And there were sounds of yet other
guns being fired, both far and near—until finally, when a round shot
came fair through the port and mashed half the gun-crew to a
bloody pulp, even I had the wit to realize that we were in the thick
of a sea battle, but I was too weak to do anything but lie there like a
babe in arms and listen to it.

How long it had been going on I do not know, but it certainly did
not last long after I became aware of it, because soon there was
cheering all around me, and the heavy pounding of feet and the
clash of steel overhead, and when I came to again all was silence. I
remember Lobo's face just once again as he stood above me, looking

down at me sadly, and there were others with him—fair men with stolid faces who were strangers to me.

My next memory is of a narrow bed with white sheets, and other similar beds in a row, and of cool vaulted stone arches above me, and this picture dims again into more heavy features poised above me.

I woke fully one hot morning and lay and watched the sun on the blue ocean through the embrasured window in front of my bed. A fly settled on my nose and I raised my hand to brush it away. It was my right hand and my shoulder hurt a little with the movement, and that brought things back to me. I struggled to sit up, and a man in one of the otherwise empty beds bellowed, "Apothecary!" I turned and stared at him. Another man came hurrying in through the arches and gently eased me down on the pillows again. I asked him, in English, where I was and how I came there. He answered me in Dutch and told me to lie quiet, then hurried away again.

He returned shortly with yet another man, a small shriveled clerkly fellow who addressed me civilly enough in very fair English albeit with a thick and heavy accent.

"You must remain quiet, Mynheer Bardock," he told me. "You have been near to the door of death for these many weeks."

"What is this place?" I asked.

"Der infirmary," he answered.

"And how came I here?"

"Carried on der hurdle."

"From whence?"

"From der schip. Der pirate schip."

"Please tell me more," I begged, my vitals chilling.

"Dere iss der fight. Our schip of war sights your schip as she is refitting in a creek, and bears in to speak her. Your schip makes what sail she can and tries to slip avay, but our schip has der legs of her and der iss der fight, and your schip is der losing vun. Den dere is der trial and der Burgomeester says that all must hang, because all bear der Sign."

"What sign?"

"Der Sign of der Chentlemen—der dead head and der bones tattooed on der ass—" He pointed to his skinny rump. "Black men and der two white men, dey all have it. So they haf to hang."

"Lobo—?" I started to ask, my heart standing still.

"Der Portygoose?" He nodded vigorously and with some satisfaction. "Yah, yah, *he* hang. Der odder schlim, der Captain—he cut a guard's t'roat one night and get avay in der jungle. But I don't think he vill get far." He grinned widely. "I think dey maybe hang you too if dey get you to stand up for it, but der Portygoose tell the trut'—"

"The truth?"

"Yah, yoost in time. He tell us dey take you off dat Portagoose schip dat dey fight some days early, dat you are an Englander taking passage in her, not a papist, and dat dey hope to get some ransom for you but you get wounded and sick in der fight. All right. We don't hang you. Now you stay quiet—get strong and we give you soon a passage upcoast to Goa, vere you vos going before der fight."

I lay back and digested, or tried to digest, this news. So once again I had been helped on this coast and by a man near death. What made Lobo do it, I wondered? He owed me little enough, in all conscience. I also wondered how much a Protestant prayer would mean to his Catholic God, and I asked in the deeper reaches of my heart for the young nun, if such things were indeed ordained, to intercede for him. Then I must have slept.

I slept until I saw Cloda come towards me through the arches.

✧ 17

OF course my reason told me it was not Cloda—that it could not possibly be—but there was no denying the resemblance. A cleaner Cloda than the pretty young trull who had walked those miles from London with me; cleaner in all truth, and tastefully dressed in cool white silk, her golden hair carefully tended, and bearing a basket of bright flowers on her arm. No, this was a lady of quality, and if further proof was needed of that, it was amply provided by the attitude of the apothecary and the clerk, who danced in obsequious attendance each side of her, bobbing and bowing like marionettes.

She came right up to my bed and stood looking down at me, then she addressed me in High Dutch, which I had difficulty in following, mine being that of the camp and shipboard. She asked me how I found myself this morning, and whether I had all I required, and if I was being well looked after, and the two Dutchmen fell over themselves to translate my answers—in their own favor. She told the clerk to bring her a pitcher of water, then she arranged the flowers in it prettily and had them placed on a table beside me, and while she was thus engaged she gave careful instructions for my future treatment, saying that all food and wine were to be brought from her own house each day, together with fresh linen and other comforts.

I lay back on my pillows as this went on, scarce able to withdraw my eyes from her, so remarkable was the likeness of this Dutch aristocrat to that poor little English doxy whom life had treated so ill, and I had been forced so basely to desert near Robertsbridge that dark night. Where was she now, I wondered, and what had befallen her?

The lady finished her agreeable task, smiled kindly on me and then left, promising to call and see me again in the near future, and after stammering my thanks in my uncouth soldier's Dutch I turned eagerly to the clerk and asked who she might be.

"She is the Mevrouw Nassau van der Buhl," he answered with awe. "A lady of high rank and wealth, wife of Mynheer van der Buhl, Chief Commissioner of the Netherlands East India Company."

I started to mend apace from that day, and soon was able to leave my bed for some hours, suffering, it appeared, little worse than a certain stiffness in my right arm and an intolerable weakness in my knees; but even these disabilities left me in time, and I found myself looking forward with the keenest anticipation to the visits of the Mevrouw van der Buhl, who almost daily brought me dainties and wine from her house, and watched over my well-being with the greatest kindness.

And I had other visits—from the Burgomaster, the Port Admiral, the predicant of the Dutch church and other officials, all of whom showed me the greatest courtesy, for, it appeared, between the Dutch and the English now existed a temporary peace. I found that

I had to exercise extreme care in my conversations with them in order not unwittingly to expose my own duplicity, because Lobo had told them that I was fresh out from England, bound as an envoy from the Lord Protector to Goa, and therefore it would naturally be expected that I would be *au fait* with all matters of current politics at home. I managed, however, to cover my grosser blunders by pretending a greater ignorance of the Dutch tongue than was really the case, and to hearken rather than to speak until such time as I had picked up the threads of European affairs once more.

My hosts were overjoyed at the capture of the pirate vessel, because under the command of the notorious Weaver she had played havoc with their trade up and down this coast. They were naturally angry at the escape of the Angel, and had solemnly hanged every member of the guard on duty the night he flew his prison, less the one whom he had dispatched himself, and now they had placed a price of one thousand gold mohurs upon his head.

I awakened one morning shortly after this to find the Burgomaster standing beside my bed, together with two Indian servants who bore between them a large and varied selection of garments for my inspection. They were considerably more sober than those I had been accustomed to wear in Goa, but were nevertheless of excellent quality, and he had been civil enough to include a fine German sword and, with delicacy, a purse of golden guilders, and I marveled afresh at the way history was repeating itself in so short a span. Twice I had now arrived on this coast well-nigh naked and completely penniless, and each time I had, like the cat thrown into the air, landed on my feet. But this time, I swore, I was not going through my own folly to allow Fate to make me its plaything, nor, if I could help it, to repay my hosts so scurvily for their kindness.

Clothed and armed once more in the habiliments of a gentleman, I left the infirmary and accompanied the kind Burgomaster back to his official residence, a magnificent house overlooking a bay so like that of Goa that I felt I had been here previously.

The Burgomaster, whose name was Hans van Hoogewerf, presented me to his stout and comfortable wife and solemn, flaxenhaired children, and then installed me in the guest-chamber, placing at my disposal an Indian servant, and I checked myself just in time before addressing this menial in his own tongue.

"Regard my house as your own, Mynheer Bardock," invited Van Hoogewerf. "Mynheer Nassau van der Buhl, who is at present on an inspection tour of our outlying forts, should return within the month and will, I am certain, be happy to arrange for your onward transportation to Goa. In the meantime rest and recoup your strength."

I thanked him, realizing with relief that I would therefore have some days yet in which to consider my next move—a return to Goa, of course, being the last thing I wanted. However, for the nonce, things were shaping not so badly. I was my own man again, my strength fast returning to me, decently clothed and housed, and with a purseful of money.

I professed, with truth, a great interest in this colony which was, I learned, that of Trivandrum, a large fortified town not far north of Cape Comorin, which is the southernmost tip of the subcontinent of India, overlooking the narrow straits which divide the mainland from the large island of Ceylon, a land rich in spices, ivory, gold and precious stones, which resources were now being exploited to the full by Holland. But I sighed when I studied the maps in Mynheer van Hoogewerf's study and found how much farther I would have to work myself up that cursed beach before I came to the island of Bombay and struck inland. Still, beggars cannot be choosers and it was now left to my native wit to take the best advantage of things as they were. And they could have been much worse. Much worse indeed.

I found life in this colony much different from that of Goa. Here the Europeans were a much tighter community, keeping themselves to themselves and having little or no social contacts with the Indians. Such diversion as there was took the form of formal Dutch dinners at which the fare was solid and abundant, but conversation slight, and ladies seldom if ever attended. Sunday was the one day when the solemn and assiduous pursuit of the golden guilder was forsworn, and on that day the good burghers went in solemn procession with their wives and children to the plain white church in the center of the town and listened to the heavy sermons of the predicant, before returning to their homes to partake of equally heavy midday dinners. Balls, masques and routs were unknown, and I shuddered to think what would have happened had a troupe of dancing girls suddenly decided to give a performance in the central market place, as had been the almost daily custom at sundown in Goa. Still, it was peaceful—and I found myself enjoying my stay there for that reason alone.

It was on my seventh day in the house of the Burgomaster that I saw the Mevrouw van der Buhl again. I had strolled down to the harbor to watch idly a huge Dutch Indiaman loading spice and ivory for the return voyage to Amsterdam. She was the only ship of size in port at that time, save for a long, lean, heavily-gunned dhow anchored at the harbor mouth, which was manned by a native crew and a heavy complement of Dutch soldiers, and was, in fact, the ship which had dealt so justly with the pirate vessel. Like the Portuguese, the Dutch inclined to the use of indigenous shipping for use in these treacherous coastal waters in preference to the more unhandy galleon. I was not, however, much interested in either of these ships, my eye being cocked privily at the fishing vessels which packed the inner harbor and lay drawn up on the beaches either side. That was my way, I decided; a good stout offshore fisherman, with perhaps a crew of three, who would, for a price, bear me a hundred miles or so up the coast and land me one dark night on the beach. A couple of golden guilders should do it, with perhaps a couple more to ensure their silence thereafter. It would be as much as they would make, even with the best of good fortune, in six voyages to the fishing grounds. I had, indeed, selected the man I would approach —a merry little Konkanese who crewed a thirty-foot sailing outrigger with his two sons, and, making sure that no Dutch ears were listening, I engaged him in conversation in his own tongue, talking of the sea in its many moods and listening in turn to the trials and travails of a fisherman's lot. It was while thus employed that I heard a soft step behind me. The fisherman salaamed respectfully and withdrew. I turned and saw her standing behind me.

She was dressed, as was her invariable custom, in cool white silk, and I marveled afresh at her resemblance to Cloda. I wondered if she had heard me speaking in the native tongue, but it did not worry me unduly, and I prepared to explain that I had already started to study it in preparation for my duties in Goa. I swept off my hat.

"I am glad to see you so recovered, Mynheer," she said in

her faultless High Dutch. "You find much to interest you in our harbor?"

"I do indeed, Mevrouw," I assured her. "In everything in this strange new land."

She said, "*I* find it excessively fatiguing. Tell me, Mynheer, how came you to select service in the East Indies?"

"To seek my fortune, Mevrouw," I told her. "Opportunity is circumscribed for a younger son of not rich parents in England."

"And yours are not rich?"

"On the contrary. Mine is an old family, but practically estateless. Fortunately we still have influential friends who were able to procure this preferment for me."

"Is this your first employment?"

"It is, Mevrouw, except for some slight military service on the continent of Europe."

"Is that where you learned to speak Dutch? Low Dutch—but still adequate."

I bowed. She regarded me shrewdly for a moment, and I began to feel uncomfortable under her scrutiny, then at that instant, high on the battlements of the landguard fort, a gun boomed, and, turning, we saw the white puffs of answering guns on the armed dhow and a trumpet sounded faintly over the water. Around the point of the harbor headland came another dhow, heeling under full-drawing lateen sail, and almost immediately we were surrounded by the clatter of the guard as they turned out under presented arms and flying colors, and somewhere a drum was rolling in salute. I looked at my companion questioningly.

"The Commissioner, my husband," she explained. "Word came by runner an hour ago that he was arriving. I was on my way to the jetty to receive him. Come, he will be interested in meeting you."

Officials had already gathered when we arrived at the jetty, and the dhow had been brought smartly to anchor some little distance offshore. A longboat, rowed by eight oarsmen, shot out to her and I saw a tall figure step over the dhow's gangway and drop into the sternsheets. Mevrouw van der Buhl went forward to the steps, and in a few minutes she was greeting her husband as he stepped ashore.

He was, as I have remarked, tall. I saw now that he was heavy as well—heavily paunched and heavily jowled—so that it came as a shock of surprise when I heard him answering the greetings of the officials in a high and squeaking treble. Had I been asked, I should have said, without malice, that some thirty years separated him from his wife—this man being in his mid-fifties at least. Did all high East Indian officers invite trouble by acquiring late in life young and beautiful wives, I wondered?

They greeted each other, I noticed, with a solemn handshake and I heard him make some perfunctory inquiry before turning away to engage in matters of evidently more moment with his deputy. I was about to slip away when Mynheer van Hoogewerf caught sight of me. He came forward and took me by the arm and presented me to the Commissioner.

"Mynheer Bardock, Mynheer Commissioner," he said, "of whom I wrote in my dispatches."

"Ah, yes, yes," said Van der Buhl, shooting me a swift glance. "Yes, I would like to talk with the gentleman. Bring him to dinner tonight." He nodded affably and the crowd closed round him.

I wended my way slowly back to my quarters, marveling again at how history was repeating itself. But this time I was forewarned. This cold and austere lady, beautiful though she was, was no Jeanne. And even had she been inclined to dalliance, I would have hurled myself into the shark-infested ocean rather than put myself into the same sort of jeopardy as that from which I had so recently escaped. No, if Mynheer Commissioner was to be cuckolded in his own castle it would not be by me, that I swore.

Dinner that night was at six, and I sighed when I arrived with the Burgomaster and saw that it was to be preceded by a *reistoffel*. This was a gargantuan repast in itself, consisting of rich rice pilau fried in butter, and anything up to fifty side dishes of meat, fish, chicken, fruit, all hotly and exotically spiced. One sat at the table, and one servant per guest then served the dishes in rotation. It was polite usage to protest feebly from time to time at this superabundance, but if a good Dutch host saw a guest's plate anything but over-flowing, he snapped his fingers at the native majordomo, and the unfortunate servant concerned was soundly beaten for a breach of his master's hospitality. The service of the reistoffel, washed down by quantities of heavy Dutch ale, usually went on for two hours or more—after which, dinner proper was served. A man who would dine with the mynheers must needs be of stout constitution, and it was the custom, then unknown to me, to take purges and potions to cause vomiting before attending one of these functions. This night my position was doubly parlous because I had been placed next to the Commissioner and on his right hand.

Every burgher of standing was there—some two hundred in all, and, well served with schnapps before our arrival, the majority of the guests were in high fettle. For this I was grateful at first because I thought that escape from this torment would be the easier as the night wore on and the tide of liquor rose higher, but to my dismay the Commissioner summoned me to his side immediately we made our appearance, and pledged me in a huge goblet of schnapps, and then made an interminable speech in his shrill voice, of which I understood no more than one word in six, but I gathered that (and why, God alone knew) I was a gentleman who had found much favor in the eyes of this community, had been the instrument by which the pirates had been undone, was a credit to my great and glorious country, and one who could not help but improve relations, and thereby trade, between the Dutch and Portuguese colonies. He regretted that my stay was not to be longer, but trusted that I would return to visit them when my duties permitted. In the meantime he was generously speeding me on my way with all dispatch and was, in fact, taking me upcoast to Goa in his dhow that following morning. This brought loud and rousing cheers from the guests and more pledges, but it succeeded in taking away completely what little appetite I had. This was serious. This meant that I had to get away from this place now—tonight.

How I sat through that ghastly marathon of trenchermanship I know not to this day, except that I embarked upon a system of subterfuge which helped not a little. The napery which covered the table in the Dutch style, as distinct from our own bare boards, was of the finest white linen inset with Brussels' lace panels, and I managed to slit one of these latter with the point of my knife, and privily from time to time to shovel large spoonsful of food through it and onto the rich Persian carpets which covered the marble floor. The enormous tankards of ale also assisted, for nature having its limits, even among wassailing Dutchmen, frequent trips to the decent darkness of the garden outside were necessary, so there was a constant coming and going through the high jalousied windows, and an increasing tendency to sit in the nearest and most convenient vacant seat on return, so that the original seating order of the guests soon became confused.

I made my plans accordingly, and as my host became more engaged upon discussions of trade with other officials, I slipped out into the garden and away into the shadows.

I knew I would have to return to the house of the good Burgomaster, because my purse of money and my sword were there, and to leave without either was unthinkable, but since I was near to the harbor here, I decided it expedient to go down there first to make my arrangements

But I searched in vain for my friendly little Konkanese. His boat was not there, although several others were. I pondered hard and decided that I would have to risk trying another fisherman, so I made my way to their huts which lay above the beach to one side of the jetty, back among the eternal palms.

As was the custom of the natives upon retiring for the night, all doors and windows were tight-shut against the evil spirits of the darkness, and I got no response to my hammering at the first hut other than a frightened twittering and the crying of children. In vain I whispered my plea for a boat to the occupants, but they either would not or could not understand me, and begged me to go away. I tried the next and the next with like result, and to make a desperate situation worse, I was assailed by a pack of mongrel curs, and their clamor, added to the growing outcry of the fishermen and their families, attracted the attention of the Watch, and I was hard put to it to make my escape among the palms and eventually to wend my dispirited way back to the Burgomaster's house.

There was nothing for it now. I would have to secure my money and my sword and then return to the beach and steal one of the smaller boats, and then endeavor to make as much distance up the coast as I could, singlehanded, in the few remaining hours of darkness; then run for the beach, cast the boat loose if I were unable to find a suitable hiding place for it, and lie low myself until the next night, when I might hope perhaps to make a bargain in one of the outlying fishing villages. It was a plan full of pitfalls at best, but I saw naught else for it. The prospect appalled me.

Silently I crept through the Burgomaster's garden and climbed through the window into my darkened room. I drew the curtains and fumbled for my tinderbox, and struck a light and set it to the candles.

Then I near collapsed through the floor, for Mevrouw Nassau van der Buhl sat in a chair regarding me with a mocking smile, and she said, "How now, my Lord bloody Bemforth?"

And she said it in English, in the ripe accent of Cockaigne, and followed it with a string of oaths that could only have had their origin in Alsatia.

❖ 18

I WAS conscious of my mouth opening and shutting loosely, but of no word issuing therefrom, a manifestation which appeared to offer her some contemptuous amusement because she remarked upon it coarsely, likening it to a bull's vent in fly-time, and the rest of my person and demeanor to that of a ploughboy taken in adultery with the farmer's wife, and my manners and honor, or lack of them, to those of a brothel pot-washer, and similar lewdnesses which she poured out upon me in an unbroken stream until she had perforce to pause for breath.

I said, and meant it, "Cloda—thank God you are safe and well," and I knew an overwhelming relief that this was indeed so, but my words only served to open the floodgates of her spleen the wider.

"Liar, poltroon, tailor's pricklouse!" she spat at me. "You dare to say that? You, who left me in the mire of a Sussex lane when you thought you had no further need of my help? You, who basely deserted me when—"

"Cloda," I begged, "whatever it may have appeared to you at that time, hear me now. Yes, I left you, but what in heaven's name was I to do? I was running for my life and there was fair chance that I should be caught, and had that happened, all who were with me would have paid the penalty too. I did the sorry best I could at the time. In point of fact I *was* caught, at the Flimwell Crossroads within the hour of leaving you."

"As was inevitable," she stormed at me. "You hadn't the wit of a gadfly in April. Wasn't that the proof of it? Had you stayed with me I would have got you to safety. As it was, I shared your fate."

"Tell me what happened," I implored.

"What will undoubtedly happen again this very night if you stand there like a cowardly fool, whimpering lying excuses," she answered. "What does it matter what happened? The thing that concerns us now is to get away from this place."

"*Us?*" I echoed, aghast. "*Us?*"

"Yes, *us*," she mimicked. "You don't think you're creeping away again, to leave me to face the fiddlers, do you?"

My wits returned to me at that moment. I strode forward and gripped her by the arms and shook her mightily.

"Listen to me," I told her through set teeth. "All that you think of me, and more, may be the veriest truth, but if you imagine that I'm going to repay these good people for their kindness to me by despoiling one of them of his wife, then—"

"Pish! Squit!" she broke in. "You did that very thing in Goa, did you not? You weren't so high-stomached about bedding the Governor's wife *there*, were you, you wicked, lascivious mattress-gallant."

Once again I was reduced to gaping. "How—how—?" I gulped, and then broke off impotently, unable to formulate my words further.

"How do I know what went on up in Goa, with you coxcombing it with that French Jezebel?" she asked. "You poor fool, the whole coast knows it—Portuguese and Dutch. We may be at each others' throats in the matters of trade and religion, but gossip is a common currency to both. The story is told in a hundred different versions and sniggered over wherever white men gather and swill their pots."

"I don't believe you," I said hotly. "These people here have received me with kindness and honor. Your husband is taking me to Goa in his own dhow—"

"Where you will have your arse singed by the Inquisition fires—and serve you right," she shot at me. "Yes, that is right. He is going to hand you over to them. There's a price upon your head, and that pasty-faced eunuch could no more resist a quick-earned golden mohur than a shark could turn away from pork."

"If that was his intention why would he go to such lengths of subterfuge?" I demanded. "He would have but to clap me into irons and convey me there by force."

"Because he is not sure of the real facts of it," she said. "There are some who say that the 'Goose Governor was tiring of the baggage anyhow, and misses your services with fleet and army, so might be disposed to pardon you. Taking you in irons could in that case be embarrassing for both sides. If, on the other hand, you go as my lord and master's honored guest, he is covered on either count. That is a little-held version, however—but my husband never wagers on Mistress Chance when Dame Certain is running."

"The poxy varlet!" I thundered indignantly, and she threw her head back and rocked with laughter until the tears came.

"Oh, dearie me, you'll be the death of me," she gasped. "They were all 'kind and good people' a moment since. I'll warrant, nonetheless, that you had little intention of going to Goa tomorrow. Which brings us to the real point. Where *are* you going, my flash cull?"

"Never mind," I answered gloomily. "But wherever it is, I shall go alone."

"You won't," she said firmly, and I groaned afresh. "You're not casting me adrift so easily *this* time."

"Cloda," I said earnestly, "let us finish with this childish bickering and face the facts as they are. I don't know *where* I'm going, except that it manifestly must be away from this place without delay. I possess, through your husband's bounty, that which I stand up in and little else. You yourself have made it clear that all men's hands are against me. But you have an honored position here. With your experience of life hitherto, can you be so mad as to contemplate, even for a moment, wantonly throwing everything away and becoming once more an outcast?"

"Yes," answered the wicked creature without turning a hair. "I have had a bellyful and to spare of that canting half-man, so don't flatter yourself I'm tossing my cap over the windmill for love of *you*. That might have been the case last time, but five years and much water have gone through the sluice since then, my bonny buck. This time *I'm* using *you*."

"But how—? Where—?" I asked. "Cloda, I don't know the answer to that myself."

"I do," she answered, and threw her cloak about her shoulders. "What do you think I've been doing this last week? Come, you fool, before that toad of a husband reaches the point where all go out to the bawdy houses."

And indeed there seemed little time to be lost, because from the Commissioner's house, lower down the slope towards the harbor, came the noise of revelry reaching its zenith, and drawing back the curtains I could see the flaring of link torches as sedan chairs filed up to the front entrance.

What was there to do except to follow the baggage?

We slipped out of the window and across the garden into a narrow lane which led up to the landguard wall which encircled the town. There was a gate here, and a vaulted arch which spanned it, and to one side a guardroom in which a dim lanthorn burned. We halted and drew into the deeper shadows, and I heard the clink of arms against armor as a sentinel moved slowly along the battlements above. We waited until his footsteps had died away to a flank, then Cloda drew a large key from under her cloak, and we crept forward to a small wicket gate beside the larger one. I found the keyhole by touch and gently eased the lock back, and then we were through it, and Cloda whispered to me to lock it again.

We were on a road now, a road which was cut sheer through the close-packed jungle and led directly inland away from the coast. We set out swiftly, our feet making no noise in the ankle-deep dust, I knowing not where we were going and this wayward creature not in any way disposed to tell me. I did, in fact, venture the question after we had been walking some ten minutes or so, but received scant courtesy in reply.

"You go to keep your rump unbroiled, you tavern blanket-twitcher," she answered. "I to escape a canting hypocrite and his pointless fumblings. How we accomplish this is my business, so have done with your puling questions." And that was the way of it.

We walked for over an hour until at last we heard the yapping of curs in the jungle to one side of us, and then there was the dull gleam of a smouldering fire beside the road, and muffled figures sleeping around it. Cloda strode boldly up to the nearest of these and applied her dainty foot to the ribs of it with unlady-like vigor.

She addressed him in a tongue of which, though I had heard it spoken sometimes in the bazaars of Goa, I understood not one word. The man unrolled himself from his sheet and I saw the whites of his eyes glint in the darkness, and he answered in the same twittering language. He arose, clad only in the merest string around his loins, salaamed and gestured to us to follow him. We pushed through the jungle screen to one side of the road, and came after some short distance to the banks of a small stream.

"Take off your clothes," Cloda commanded.

"Why?" I asked, surprised at this peremptory command and not in any way prepared to obey.

"Because I tell you," she answered, and started forthwith to remove her own.

"To the black pit of hell with you," I swore. "Tell me what is afoot or I leave you here and now and take my chances, such as they are, in the jungle."

"As you wish, you fool," she answered coolly, climbing out of her shift and standing gleaming palely in the darkness. "Those chances will be small enough unless you accept guidance from one who knows better than yourself. When it is found in the morning that both you and I are missing, two things will happen. The armed dhows will be dispatched north and south up and down the coast, calling at every fishing village for a hundred miles each way in search of us. If any have seen us, they will inform of it, for the Dutch have quick means of extracting information. There is no seaward escape from Trivandrum, I assure you. Others have found that out to their cost."

"So?" I asked.

"Apace with that," she went on, "the landward search is put afoot. Parties of soldiers with bloodhounds will come down this road, the only one that leads inland, and these dogs will pick up our scent as easily as an eagle espies a white crow in a flock of black ones. Therefore our clothes will be burnt by these people, and we

will wade naked along the course of this stream for some miles,
before assuming other clothes and going our way when the search
has abated."

"Who *are* these people?" I demanded.

"Friends of mine," she answered succinctly. "And now mind
your own cursed business."

There being naught else for it, seemingly, I stripped bare and
stepped into the warm stream after her. Behind us, the native collected our garments into a bundle and melted into the shadows.

I followed the white smudge of her back for what seemed hours,
stumbling over fallen tree trunks, wading through fetid mud and
stubbing my toes on rocks, reflecting bitterly that in something less
than thirty years I had spent a good third of them running from
some pursuer or other, and that once more I was the sport of malign
Fate.

As the first rays of dawn started to pierce the green roof that met
over the stream, she stopped and seemed to cast around her as if in
search of something, then went on. The stream that had seemed so
warm in the hours of darkness was now striking chill, and I was,
momently, becoming more weary and dispirited. Then she stopped
again, this time at a spot where the stream came down towards us in
a waterfall over what seemed a solid rock face. Motioning me to
halt, she went forward and pulled a shaft of bamboo from a bank-
side thicket and commenced to probe into the white curtain of
water, I gazing at her the while in amazement. Then, seemingly
satisfied, she turned and beckoned to me, took me by the hand when
I came forward, and led me under and through the cascade of water
into a cave the other side.

It was about six feet wide and perhaps as many high, and it went
back into the solid rock some twelve feet, and unless one had known
where to look, as Cloda had, one might have passed that way a
hundred times or more and never have suspected its existence, so
perfect a screen made the roaring torrent over its portal. It was
evident that our arrival had been expected, because the floor had
been stewn with rushes and there was a shallow gourd of fruit
standing on a ledge; mangoes, papayas and bananas, a pineapple.

The sun was now above the rim of the trees and it shone through
the water onto us in a translucent green shimmer that was both
pleasant and restful. I sank down onto the rushes thankfully.

"Don't your friends provide clothes also, you shameless baggage?" I asked.

"Not at this point," she answered. "Not until the soldiers have withdrawn. If they passed this way the hounds might scent us even through the curtain of water. Clothes give off a stronger trail than naked skin."

I turned my eyes upon her, and, angry though I was, I had grudgingly to admit that the passing years had taken no toll of her, but rather the contrary. Nourishing food and gentle living had given her a grace that had not been there before. Beautiful she had always been, but now she was superb. Her eyes caught mine, and for the first time since our encounter the previous night, she smiled at me. Typically, she was no more self-conscious at her mother-naked state than she was at mine.

"Poor Bemforth," she said. "You burst with questions, don't you? Ask what you will, but I shall answer only at my discretion."

"Who in the name of the Devil are these blackamoors you seem so familiar with?" I growled.

"The Bhils," she answered. "They are a shy and gentle race, living in the deeper reaches of the jungle. Few Europeans know their language."

"How came you to?"

"A simple story. I was out riding one day when I came upon a young girl injured by the fall of a rotten tree at the side of the road. I caused my servants to have her conveyed to the Commissioner's house, and there I nursed her back to health. She became my maid. That was two years ago. I have often gone with her back into the jungle to meet with her people. When one earns their gratitude they are the firmest of steadfast friends. They will escort us through the jungle with safety when it is expedient to go on."

"That is the nub," I retorted. "Escort us to where?"

"That is for you to decide," she laughed. "I provide the means—you the destination."

"Cloda," I entreated her earnestly. "Why have you come with me? What can the future hold for you now? Why, why, *why* have you wilfully thrown away a life of ease, comfort, respect?"

"Fiddlesticks," she retorted brusquely. "It stifled me. God's teeth! I had rather be back in Alsatia. Had you not come along when you did I would have cut and run with the first likely man who had shown himself of spirit, though heaven alone knows that they were scarce enough in that gaggle of fat-bellied money-grubbers."

But how on earth did you fetch up here?" I insisted.

"Willy-nilly we will have to go back to that night outside Robertsbridge for the truth of that," she answered, and lay back on the rushes, staring up at the roof of the cave.

"I had come back," she told me, "having found a drunken wagoner asleep in the back of his cart, and having no further use seemingly for a loaf of bread and a heel of bacon and a quartern of ale which lay beside him. I bore them back to the barn—to find you gone, and your guineas in a piece of rag telling me their tale. I sat and wept for a time, then rage assailed me and I bethought me of your intentions. You had not gone on towards Romney or I would have passed you on the road, so you must needs have retraced your steps towards London. I set out after you, not from any love of you, but to give you a piece of my mind. But when I got to Flimwell I learned at the tinkers' camp that you had been thief-taken by the parish constable and his bullies—so I went on to Tonbridge to see if I could get news of you. I got little enough except that you had been lodged in the bridewell and were like to be hanged as a footpad."

She was silent for some time, then she continued in a flat expressionless voice which told me that she drew no joy from this narrative.

"I was near to frantic and I assailed the constable with tears and entreaties to allow me to see you, but he drove me away with his staff round my rump. Then the Lord of the Manor, Sir Robert Manforth, happened along. He was kindly and of sympathy and took me to his house while he sought some way to help me in my distress. I spent the next few days chained in an upper chamber, as naked as I am now, and used by him in a fouler way than that of any ten drunken sailors I had ever met in Alsatia—the gentry is always the worst—until I managed to break a pot and put a mark upon his face which he was still wearing when last I saw him.

"And when was that?" I asked, my fury choking me.

She laughed. "Chained with five others, going aboard an Arab slave dhow at the Cape of Good Hope," she said. "He gave continual trouble to his Dutch master, so he sold him. But let me tell this my own way. Sir Poxy Robert, his face like a bull's rump after a baiting, made great outcry and the servants came and hammered down the door. I was flogged near to death and there was some talk of hanging me, but Sir Robert was never a man to throw away a guinea or two, so he arranged to bond me to the Dutch. I was taken down the Medway one dark night and put aboard a brigantine—and it so happened that he had outstanding business with the shipmaster over a payment not made for some previous transaction, so he came with us, which was not wise as it turned out, because he, the constable and the whole boat's crew were promptly knocked on the head by the jolly Hollanders, and bonded to the last man of 'em when we arrived in Amsterdam.

"As for me, I was taken low with the ship fever, and as they did not want it to spread among the other bonders, they shifted me to the lazar house where I lay near to death for some time. There was a predicant—that's a parson—who used to visit there with his wife to do what they could for the sick." Her voice softened. "I think they were the only truly good people I have ever met, though I did not realize it at first. They had compassion for me, and I, quick to seize upon the advantage of this, told them a sorry tale of a young girl of poor but honest family left an orphan and cruelly used by the son of my employer, a master cutler, and then bonded. They were vastly indignant, and having much influence in Amsterdam, they secured the discharge of my bond and took me into their own house.

"In not much longer than it takes to tell, I was like a daughter to them, they being childless since the early death of their only one, making myself useful in their heavenly clean home and being schooled by the old gentleman." She laughed again. "It's funny—I, who speak like a gutter brat and scarce read or write in my own tongue, can pass as a lady in Dutch. Clean, well fed and comely clothed, I should have been safe and happy there, but you, you worthless lout, kept clouding my thoughts and troubling me. I made such privy enquiries as I could, round the bonding wharf for you in the name of Bemforth, but none had heard of you, so at last, repenting of my evil intentions towards these good old people whom I thought at first to rob and go my way, I settled down to be a dutiful ward to them—and I was for nigh on two years, until the old gentleman caught a foul fever in the lazar house and died of it in a short time, quickly followed by his wife.

"Once again I was left to my own devices, though not in such poor shape this time. They had made me their heir, and while theirs, good souls, was not a large fortune, giving so much as they did to charity, it was at least as good a dowry as most young ladies of Amsterdam could hope to bring to their husbands, so I had no lack of pudding-faced, square-headed suitors.

"The old people had laid down in their will that should they die before I married, or was of full age to manage my own affairs, I should be placed under the guardianship of their lawyer, Advokaat Piet van der Buhl. This yellow-faced, dried-up old rascal told me many tales of his young and handsome son, who was fast rising to high places in the service of the East India Company, and he would read me long passages from his letters telling me of the wonders of this country. Soon the son was sending me tender little messages through his father, and I was sending others back to him—then, to his father's vast content, he made suit for my hand, and I blushed and stammered prettily and lisped my consent, and settled down primly to collect together my linen and delph and silver for our grand house out here, and to wait his return on leave to claim me.

"I could have slit the weasands of both of them when Nassau arrived. I had pictured him as young and comely, and here was this paunchy oaf of fifty and more, as precious as a hen-pigeon with a voice as shrill as that of a pig at sticking-time.

"But what was I to do? 'Twas to be a big wedding, high in the social events of Amsterdam, and to have drawn back then would have been to cause much gossip and clatter. Added to that, old parchment-face had the handling of my money, and devilish awkward he could have made my circumstances until control passed to me. So I put as good a face upon it as I was able, and resolved, believe me when I tell you this, to make Nassau as good a wife as lay in me."

For a long time she was silent again, then she sighed.

"I've done that, although it wasn't a wife he wanted, not while there are boys upon this coast; it was merely a hostess to grace his table and to entertain his official guests—and my dowry, small though it was, had its attractions also. Oh, he hasn't used me ill—he hasn't used me at all, and I suppose for that alone I should be grateful—but I do not feel that I owe him aught. I've been out here three years now, going no farther from the Commissioner's house than a horse can take me in the course of a cool morning, meeting nobody but stolid trade burghers and their fat pale cows of wives, until there have been times when I thought I should go mad. I've been living only for his next leave to Holland. Oh God! Still another seven years off. Then I should leave him as soon as my feet touched Christian shores again, even though I were as penniless as the night they shipped me down the Medway."

I lay considering all she had told me until she nudged me impatiently and said, "That is all, and it's the truth as I'm a living woman. Now tell me of yourself—as truthfully."

And I did, right from that selfsame night outside Robertsbridge, hurrying and glossing over in part, but omitting nothing important. She heard me through to the end without once interrupting.

"You are a great liar," she remarked when I had finished, "but at least you appear to have told me the truth now, because of course I had heard tales of this Englishman, Gil Bardock, who served the Portuguese. There have been times when I was convinced that it was indeed you, because the name was familiar, but then I told myself it couldn't be, and that it was the Romney smuggler to whom we were journeying when we separated. Why did you choose his name?"

"Why not?" I asked. "It just so happened to be the first that came to my tongue when I was put to the question."

"This Angel seems a deep-dyed blackguard," she reflected.

"He is," I agreed. "And one whose throat I shall take the highest pleasure in cutting one day, if he still lives."

"Unless he cuts yours first," she retorted tartly. "You seem to have been underdog up till now."

There was truth in that, but I liked it none the more because of it, and we lay in the rushes wrangling and reviling each other until the sun was well up to its zenith—and then, seemingly nearby, we heard the baying of hounds.

They came upstream in the path we ourselves had come; six Dutch troopers, leather-booted to the hip, and carrying muskets, and from their demeanor and language not in love with their task. The hounds, six couple of them, half swum and half waded, and they looked as weary as their masters, but one brute, more sagacious than the others, seemed to get our scent even through the curtain of water, and we lay close-pressed together scarce daring to breathe as it gave tongue and strained at its leash towards the cascade.

Pulled forward by the excited beast, the trooper lumbered heavily in its wake until the hound's head almost thrust through the curtain, and discovery seemed inevitable, then, at the last heart-halting instant when all seemed lost, the man stumbled on a submerged rock and fell his length in the bawling stream, his arm nigh pulled out of its socket at the end of the leash which, thank God, remained fast to his wrist.

He rose spluttering and cursing, to an accompaniment of guffaws from his comrades, and vented his spleen upon the hound, hauling it in short and kicking it mightily in the ribs, and falling yet again in his efforts—and bedlam was let loose as the other hounds joined in the plaints of the offender.

Then the troopers turned to the corporal in joint and noisy persuasion to call the hunt off and return to the town, as it was plain to any man of sense that if we were in the jungle at all we were, they fervently hoped, safe couched in the belly of a tiger. He gave way after some halfhearted pretense of authority, and they made off in the direction they had come. Beside me I could feel Cloda quivering convulsively, and seeking to comfort her I put my arm about her bare shoulders, only to find that the baggage was laughing fit to split her sides.

"You've talked your way out of many a parlous situation, you randy mattress-gallant," she gasped, "but I warrant *that* would have taxed your powers of invention. Stark naked with the Commissioner's lady in a cave. What would you have said we were discussing? Last Sunday's sermon?"

I drew my dignity around me, having naught else wherewith to cover myself, and ignored the baggage, but she kept up her lewd baiting of me until I lost my temper completely and threatened to strike her. But this was a different Cloda to the one I had known previously. The laughter left her and her eyes narrowed.

"Just try, my flash cull," she spat at me shrewishly, "and I'll put a scar across your ugly mug that will outshine that upon your shoulder."

And this seemed as good a moment as any to discuss our future ploy. Armed with my anger, I said, "I don't know where I'm bound

or what I'm going to do, but of this I am certain; not one step of the
way do you come with me. Find your savage friends, get decent
covering from them and return to your husband."

"To be branded with the scarlet letter, shorn and sent back to
Holland to the House of Correction?" she scoffed. "Not for you or
a thousand like you. We stay together for as long as I need your
company—and it's not for the regard I bear you, either. I hate the
mortal sight of you, you craven louse."

"That need not come about if you keep your wits about you," I
said. "Tell them that I carried you off, as I did that other trollop.
She gained renown and acclamation from it."

"She's welcome to it. From what you say, she was well content
with her lot, and wanted but a little extra lechery the wrong side of
the blanket. I don't. I want only escape from him, from you and
from every male and half-male who ever drew breath. You're the
means of that escape—a sorry means, God wot, but the best that
offers at the moment. We stay together until I give you quittance."
She threw herself down upon the rushes and turned her back upon
me, drawing as far away as the confines of the cave permitted.

I realized that my whole approach and attitude had been wrong,
and I made shift to amend them speedily. I rolled towards her and
put my arm about her tenderly.

"Cloda," I said softly, "believe me when I tell you that I have
only your safety and well-being at heart when I say—"

But there was a pineapple amongst that damned fruit, and she
grasped it and turned upon me like a coiled viper. I shrieked in
agony and she dived through the curtain of water, and as I lay and
writhed over this dastardly assault upon my manhood, I could hear
her taunting me from the pool below.

Verily, I reflected sourly, I was once more off the griddle and
into the fire.

❖ 19

THE Bhils came to us when night had fallen. They brought with them a loose shirt for me and a cotton dhoti, or loincloth, and a turban and stout leather sandals. For Cloda there was a similar shirt and loose pantaloons and a sari, with the end of which she could, when required, cover her golden hair and all but her eyes, in the manner of a native woman. They also brought us heavy *chhuris*, or jungle knives, and a bundle of small necessaries such as a cooking pot, light sleeping mats and other articles normally carried by the Indian traveler, so that when equipped we were unremarkable, I, as I have already explained, being so burned by the sun that I could haved passed in any company as a light-skinned native, albeit of larger stature than most.

We fed upon a mess of meat and rice that they provided, then after some colloquy with Cloda, they led us out of the course of the stream onto a faintly defined path through the jungle.

We walked all that night, four almost naked little brown men before us in single file, and two behind, the path leading steadily upward, until, when dawn broke, we found ourselves high upon a mountain ridge, with the sea but a glimmer in the distance.

Without a word they spread our sleeping mats in the shade of a giant *peepul* tree, and Cloda and I sank down upon them gratefully and slept for some hours. When we awoke they had green pigeons cooking in the pot, shot with the ridiculous toylike bows and arrows they carried. They stayed with us until sundown, then other Bhils, as like the first as peas in a pod, replaced them and led us onward, still traveling east-by-north, as I could see from the pole-star, but this time downhill into a valley where we came to a large and slowly flowing river. Here we camped again until morning, then yet other Bhils appeared from out the jungle bearing upon their heads a long but light canoe. Once more we fed and then embarked—two Bhils paddling in the bows, two more astern, with Cloda and I sitting amidships. The other little men melted away into the jungle without a word, and those still with us pushed out into the stream and paddled away northward.

Still upon my dignity, I had had little or no converse with my companion since we had set out from the cave, but now I could not forbear to ask her where in the name of the Devil we were going.

"Out of my sweet spouse's realm in the first instance," she told me. "There are a string of Dutch trading posts and forts along this river, and the paths are much used by the factors and soldiers. We shall not really be safe until we are a good hundred miles and more to the northward."

"And what then?" I asked.

"Mind your own cursed business," she answered, but there was uncertainty in her voice and I realized that she knew no more than I.

I swore at her in language that she would readily understand, and lay back against the thwarts. It was pleasant thus traveling, even when one knew not the destination. We were moving against the current, but the river was slow and the paddlers expert so that it made little difference to our light craft, and we traveled at excellent speed. The sun was hot, but not unbearably so, tempered as it was by the shade of the giant trees that almost met overhead, and there was much to divert one upon the banks either side—now a troupe of monkeys swinging through the branches, chattering at us angrily for the intruders we were—then a sullen splash as a crocodile slid from a mudbank into the brown water at our approach. And there was ever and anon the sudden flash of the beautiful blue kingfisher, and the brilliant flame-of-the-forest tree, and the silver streaks of fish breaking the surface. The river seemed like a road that wound endlessly through the jungle and—

I sat bolt upright with a start that caused Cloda to turn her head and look at me in surprise, and something in my face must have told her of my inner excitement, because she looked at me suspiciously and asked sourly if I sought to upset the canoe. But I did not answer her, and, woman-like, her curiosity was piqued and she turned and faced me, and thereafter all peace was gone. But I minded not, for now once again I had my star and my steering mark. The Road. The Road was before me, and I was headed for it—and this time I would brook no turning aside before I reached it.

"Plotting with yourself, are you?" she probed shrewishly, but again I made no reply, which seemed to provoke her rage.

"Don't think you'll leave me in the lurch again, you poltroon," she railed at me. "I've a specific against *that* ploy this time."

"And what's that, O pearl of price?" I bantered to cover my sudden unease, for the witch had come uncomfortably close to my line of thinking.

"Just this," she answered. "We're not out of danger for many a long mile yet. Here there are the Dutch, and ahead of us the Moplahs; then the Portuguese; then the Moguls of the Deccan." She laughed shortly as she saw my amazed face. "Yes, gawp if you will, but I know what I'm talking about. There was little enough to do back there in the Commissioner's house but read, and I got quite a taste for it. Great Dutch tomes of travel, and maps and charts, and a huge terrestrial globe. Yes, many's the hour I have spent in that cool library, traveling in spirit away from that cursed place, making long voyages in my fancy. Merciful God, the worlds that open to one when one has the gift of reading. Of all the many kindnesses I have to be thankful to that good old man for, that is the greatest. He taught a nameless brothel-brat to read."

She was silent for a time, as was I, because now I was seeing this strange girl in yet another light.

She went on, "Yes, I have a specific against your cowardly deceit this time, if running away is in your mind. Try it, my bonny buck, and see where it will land you, except in the Inquisition fire, or with your head adorning some Shah's gateway, or on the rowing benches of the Dutch galleys. There's nowhere to run to. No place to hide. The specific? Simple. Only the Bhils can get us through this jungle and over the mountains to the north—and they are my sworn friends, and I speak their tongue. Leave me some dark night before I say you might go, and it will be your last. You wouldn't even know what had the killing of you. See those childish little bows and ar- rows of theirs? Some arrows they keep for pigeons; others, no bigger, for men—but those are tipped with poison. One scratch and you'd die screaming within the hour. And they'd use them, never fear. Because I've told them to, if you should slip away some time —or if aught should happen to me while I sleep."

"Why are you at such pains to keep me with you since you hate me so much?" I asked her.

"I've told you," she answered. "Because I might need your help —and for no other reason."

"No other reason at all?" I asked teasingly, hoping to blandish her and so allay her suspicions. I put out my hand and smoothed her hair. She drew my hand down gently, her eyes wide upon me, and she stroked it down her cheek to her lips—then suddenly she sank her sharp little teeth in it, and I yelled and jumped and near had the canoe over. The Bhils twittered angrily.

"Don't try your false cozening on *me*," she blazed. "Not again. Keep it for your French doxy—if you could get near enough to her again without having your rump spitted on a 'Goose halberd."

"So that's the way of it?" I taunted. "Jealous."

"Of *you?*" she demanded indignantly. "God's teeth! I'd rather lie with an Arab leper."

"You should be the judge," I retorted. "You no doubt know."

Only the skill of the Bhils prevented our frail craft from capsizing as she turned upon me in a fury. We shot into the bank and re- mained there for the night, and there was blessed silence between us through the dark hours and all next day as we once more paddled swiftly northward against the current.

The river was narrowing now and there were signs that we were approaching its headwaters, and indeed the next night we came to a rocky gorge that marked its source. The Bhils landed us, fed us again on pigeon and rice, salaamed and turned away downstream, and I thought that this would be the last of our silent escorts, but next morning another six were on hand, squatting in a silent circle around us.

They led us up through the gorge to the top of the ridge in front of us. To the south, looking back the way we had come, stretched like a green blanket the countless square miles of the jungle, with the river shining like a golden sword through it in the rays of the rising sun. Before us was more jungle, but this rose in serried ridges to a range of high mountains, blue and remote in the far distance.

"The Western Ghats," said Cloda, breaking her two-day sulks, but whether to inform me or to parade her own knowledge, I know not. But she was right, and I marveled afresh at her erudition, be- cause she could only have known this from her studies in the library of the Commissioner's house, whereas I had seen their length, from the land of the Mekranis, far to the north, to where they finally tailed away to flatness in this very jungle, as I sailed the coasts the last four years. Yes, these were the Ghats, whose blue bastions heaved themselves upwards from the coastal jungle to the Deccan Plateau that had been our immediate goal when we left Goa—Lobo, Pereira, Subram Rao and I. And now I, the only one left, was approaching it from another angle. The sailing marks were plain again.

I said, "Cloda, cannot we call a truce to this childishness?"

"Whose fault has it been, with your taunting and your base affronts?" she demanded.

"All right, mine then," I said wearily. "But let us at least be reasonably civil to each other, since God knows how much longer we have to bear each other company."

"That and no more then," she agreed. "No man has touched me since the bold Sir Robert had his way of me, and I would fain let it rest at that. He marked the end of a road that was never of my choosing. My skinny child's carcass was the property of any filthy oaf who had the price to rut upon it. But ne'er again. I have some wit and learning now, and strength to repel lechers and mattress-knights."

"Cloda!" I began indignantly. "I had no such intent—"

"Shut your mouth and let me finish," she cried passionately. "Whatever your intent was then, keep your hands to yourself for the future, do you hear? For I'd as lief stick a knife in your belly as blink my eyes—"

And then the stupid creature did blink her eyes, and she turned and walked rapidly ahead. But this time I had the wit not to intrude upon her. She halted after a while and waited until I had caught up with her.

"All right," she said. "A truce then—but play fair this time, my Lord Bemforth."

My own name sounded strange after these years. "Men call me Gil now," I told her.

"Play fair," she repeated, and there was entreaty in her voice. "I'll not bother you once we have reached some place where I can have time to consider my next step."

"You have my word," I said quietly. "Upon my honor—or what tattered remnants are left of it."

"Good," she answered, and she sounded more cheerful. "And you have my word that I'll try and keep a more mannerly tongue in my head, and my teeth to myself, and"—she grinned impishly—"pine-apples will be but for the eating so long as you keep your distance."

For the first time we walked together, side by side, she striding out tirelessly in her loose and untrammeling clothing, the upland breeze playing in her golden hair. And a right diverting companion she was. Her reading might have been untutored by donnish standards, but none could cavil at its scope, and she had acquired a knowledge and a gift of discourse that was far in advance of any woman I had ever met. She talked of the voyages of Vasco da Gama, and that of Drake—of the policies of the Dutch and the Portuguese out here—of the power of the Jesuits, and this last objectively and without bigotry, which was strange amongst us Protestants. She knew of manners and customs of which I had never heard among the natives, both the local ones and those about whom she had only read—and not a little botany of this jungle, and the ways of its strange fauna. And on the malleable tablets of her clear and excellent memory she seemed to have etched a knowledge of the geography of this vast land that amazed me and roused my admiration.

And all this she had acquired in a tongue which I, in spite of my residence in the Lowlands, could speak only uncouthly, and could not read at all. Her English, perhaps by the very necessity of having mentally to translate from the store of her knowledge, took on a clarity and a refinement that was far removed from the alleys of Alsatia, now that she was no longer spitting abuse at me—and I found myself cursing once again the system that could breed minds like this only to stifle and kill them in the lower morasses of what we had the effrontery to call a free and enlightened country.

I mentioned the Road, tentatively to test her knowledge—and she responded immediately.

"The Silk Road, they called it once," she told me, and I felt her interest quicken. "It goes back many hundreds of years. From Peking in far China, skirting the hot deserts of the Gobi and crossing the highest mountains in the world, along the rooftree of this land of India, through Persia and Araby and up to Constantinople, across

the Caucasus to the shores of the Inland Sea—the Mediterranean as
the Romans called it—over the Alps, through the Savoy and finally
into France on the one hand, and the Lowlands on the other. Oh
yes, it exists—though few since Marco Polo have trodden its whole
length, and indeed many travel along it in short spans and do not
know it. Why do you ask me of it?"

"I had a mind to walk it sometime," I answered as carelessly as I
could. " 'Tis but a dream, and one that will haply come to nothing."

But already I had said too much, and I knew with dread certainty
that my words had awakened a wild longing within her. It was as if
our minds had come together like flint and steel, and sparks had
flown from the contact. It would be hard indeed to earn my quittance now.

I expected her to follow the subject, but she let it drop and picked
a flower from the branch of a tree that we call "dead man's bones,"
and which is beautiful in spite of its grisly name, and she plucked
the petals apart and showed me the wonder and delicacy of its calyx
and stamen, and expounded upon it most learnedly, until I rallied
her and asked her if she had an ambition to be the first lady don.

"I could not be the first," she told me gravely. "There are many
learned nuns in the Catholic church who teach in schools. There are
two in this very land, at the court of the Great Mogul."

"In his harem?" I jested coarsely.

"In it, but not of it," she informed me. "He is an enlightened
monarch and has decreed that those of his wives and concubines
who can benefit from it may have instruction in foreign tongues—
English, Dutch, Portuguese and French. The nuns have all those
languages between them, but are placed under difficulty because
they do not yet speak Hindustani." She paused. "I am not under
that difficulty, as I speak it fluently—"

"*Mujhko bolo yih zabani men,*" I tested her. "Speak to me then in
this language."

"*Mera zabani, tumhara se behta hain,*" she answered promptly.
"My speech is clearer than yours." Then she went on in English,
"That is my plan, if plan it can be called at this stage. To go to the
court of the Great Mogul or some other high officer of state, and

there try to find employment as a tutor to the ladies of the harem, where no men can go."

"And where is this court?" I asked.

"In Delhi, far to the north and on the way to your Road," she told me.

I clutched at this straw and waxed enthusiastic over her plan, telling her it was the very pearl of ideas, and one that could only have occurred to a clever and educated woman. But her interest seemed to have waned now, and her answers were distrait. In her eyes was a faraway look, and I felt jealous of my Road and kicked myself for so incontinently betraying myself.

My thoughts go back often to that part of our journey. Day after day we marched, now alone, for the little Bhils had left us at the edge of their country, and we climbed the Ghats without their guidance. The air up here was clean and cool and we did not lack for food, for they had left me a tiny bow and a quiverful of arrows, and since archery had always been a sport of mine, I found that although I had not their consummate skill with this weapon, I was at least adequate when the pigeons were sleepy at high noon. And there was an abundance of wild fruit along our path—the bananas and papayas with which I was familiar from the coast, and many others I had not seen before but which Cloda named unerringly, readily telling which were wholesome and which best left alone.

And so we marched for near twenty days, until we came to the first signs of habitation. It was but a small clearing in the jungle—a rice paddy or two and some brinjals, a large gourdlike vegetable, growing on a rough stone terrace. The farmer and his timid wife and children ran into the shelter of the undergrowth when they saw us approach. It took us a long time to coax them forth, Cloda speaking softly to them in a mixture of Bhil and Hindustani, though the latter proved so much Greek to them, as it was, she told me later, a language of new origin, brought in by the Moguls—a bastard mixture of Persian, Arabic and the native Sanskrit—and it had not penetrated thus far inland, or south, as yet, though it was the common tongue of the parts we were seeking.

They spread a mat for us before their mean hut and served us liberally with such fare as they had—rice and curried brinjal, and eggs and fresh milk—I sitting cross-legged on the mat itself, with Cloda on the bare earth behind me, hair covered and face all but enshrouded by the end of her sari, meekly receiving that which her lord and master tossed over his shoulder to her, as the custom decreed. They accepted our story, these gentle people, without question. I was a man of the south, a devout Hindu but of lowly caste, and Cloda was my Bhil wife, and we journeyed to the north because of famine in our country. My halting, broken accents far from arousing their suspicions, served to help our guise because the languages of India are many and varied. I sought to bestow a small golden coin upon them from the purse which I still carried, but a sharp kick in the small of my back from Cloda halted me. She was closer to these people than I, and knew that an offer of payment for hospitality was a deep affront to a peasant, however poor he might be.

Greatly strengthened and refreshed, we went upon our way, thanking our kind hosts and receiving their blessing in return, hands pressed together as if in an attitude of prayer, grave bows and murmured rituals of farewell, I watching Cloda closely and following her example in all things. Verily this girl was not only of quick intelligence, but she was possessed of an inner sensibility that made her aware and appreciative of the exquisite courtesy of these people. It had been a good test of our guise and story, at least as far as these simple countryfolk were concerned, and it heightened our confidence accordingly. That should be our story from now on, we decided, until we had left the Hindu part of this land and come upon the Mohammedans of the north.

And now habitations were becoming more frequent. First isolated huts like the one we had visited, then collections of two or three together, then villages—all alike in pattern; an open space surrounded by a straggle of huts, a temple in the center, a palisaded compound to one side to protect the cattle at night from the depredations of tigers and leopards.

The narrow path we had been treading had now become a road of sorts and there was open cultivation on both hands; rice in green paddies, sugar cane and groves of mango trees. There was wheeled traffic here, too—huge ungainly carts with monstrous solid wooden wheels, drawn by patient oxen.

On we went, day after day, seeing and hearing much to interest and instruct us, now falling in with a party making for the market in the next village, the men riding small donkeys and discoursing wisely in front, the women trudging in the dust behind them, bearing mighty burdens on their heads, and small brown naked children gamboling happily like puppies; now overtaking a wedding, the bridegroom, a splendid figure in brightly-hued clothes always riding a caparisoned horse, the tiny bride—for child-marriage is their custom for girls—a pathetic figure smothered under swathes of heavy silk and cotton on another and usually sorrier nag, bringing up the dusty rear surrounded by the quietly weeping women of her family.

Then there were the funerals, the first I had seen, because the Portuguese abominated this custom and would have none of it within sight and hearing of their settlements. The dead man would be placed upon a bier, clad in his best garments, garlanded with bright flowers, and his brow painted with the marks of his caste, then the procession would set out for the nearest stream, the bier carried shoulder-high by his friends, the family mourners, headed by the eldest son, following behind the bearers. A band of native instruments would precede the party, playing airs which fell strange upon European ears, but of a lively and cheerful tempo. In fact the whole party would appear cheerful, and always about them would be an atmosphere of suppressed excitement. Finally, walking alone, far behind the cortege, would come a lonely figure dressed in white robes, eyes cast down and hands crossed meekly upon her bosom. The widow.

On the bank of the stream would already be erected a funeral pyre. For a poor man it would be of ordinary firewood hewn from the jungle, for a rich one it would be of sweet-scented sandalwood logs. The bier would be placed upon the pyre, and a shaven Brahmin priest would then anoint the dead man with ghee, the clarified butter of India, and place around him small gourds of milk from the sacred temple cows. Then, amid eulogies and panegyrics from his family and friends, fire would be set to the pile.

It was an uncanny and unnerving sight, for invariably, at a certain stage of heat from the blazing pyre, the backbone of the dead man would shrink, causing him slowly to sit up amid the flames. At that, the eldest son, standing as near to the head of the pyre as the heat would allow, would come forward with a large stone in his hands. Leaping through the flames he would dash the stone down upon the head of the corpse, splitting it and, according to their beliefs, allowing the soul to escape from the body. At this there would be a deep sigh from the crowd, and a murmur of approval. Then would come the most horrible moment of all. It would begin at the back of the crowd—a faint whisper at first, then it would gain in volume until the whole concourse shrieked in unison.

"*Aurat ané do!* Let the woman come!"

The crowd would open up, making a path to the blazing pyre, and the lonely figure in white would appear. Eyes fixed upon the corpse, she would walk slowly forward, pausing briefly as the priest anointed her with ghee, then, with a wild cry she would dash the last few steps and throw herself into the flames, to be burnt alive and so accompany her husband to paradise. That was the horrible custom of suttee, or the suicide of widows, which was at such variance with the other aspects of this kind and gentle race.

✧✧ 20

AND so we came at last to Mahableshwar, a frowning fort which perched high on the crags of the Western Ghats and looked down upon the distant ocean to the west, where lay Goa, and to the east across the mighty Deccan Plateau.

This was the stronghold of the Marathas, the race of warriors from whom Subram Rao had descended, and it was plain that the old man had not lied when he told me of their soldierly proclivities. Few men walked here, and those who did were the lowliest. Never had I seen such a plenitude of magnificent horses, for the most part Arab stock from the north. My soldier's instinct told me that preparations of a warlike nature were afoot, there being much bustle and coming and going between the fortress and the town which nestled in the shadows of its walls. Warriors in both chain mail and beautifully damascened plate rode hither and thither, singly and in groups, and the usual gait was a stretched gallop, and on the open plain, or maidan, were squadrons of cavalry at drill, the standard of which would have done credit to any horsed regiments I had ever seen in Europe, regular or mercenary.

Yes, something was afoot here, and since Hindustani was freely spoken in the bazaar, together with their own Marathi, of which I had learned a little from Subram Rao, we were not long in learning what it was. Shah Jahan, the Mogul Emperor, who ruled in the north of India, from the grim mountains of Turkestan and Persia down to the magnificent city of Delhi, where his grandfather Akbar the Great had long ago established his court, had over the years been assiduously spreading his empire farther and farther to the south until now he had reached the banks of the River Godavari, which, rising in the Western Ghats but a few miles from the coast, differed from other rivers of the region which rushed rapidly into the Indian Ocean, by turning east and flowing the full distance across the subcontinent to the Bay of Bengal. Its source, said Hindu legend, was at a spot where an ancient god had shot an arrow into the air which had landed in a mango grove, and at once a spring had miraculously appeared. The resultant river, therefore, was sacred throughout its entire length to all castes of Hindu, and was second only in holiness and magical properties to the mighty Ganges. But now the tyrant Shah Jahan was building a fort right on the pilgrim route to the tomb and shrine of a Brahmin holy man, and had had the effrontery to name it Ahmednagar after a *Mohammedan* holy man. This was too much, and the Maratha King, Sivaji Peshwa, was now mounting an expedition to drive the intruders back to the north.

We learned that Ahmednagar was some hundred miles to the northeast of Mahableshwar and that the fort that was being built there was under the generalship of Salahbar Khan, a name that was used by Maratha mothers to frighten naughty children. It lay, apparently, right on the route to Delhi, which would have boded ill for our plans but for the fact that the Moguls' policy had always been one of tolerance towards other religions, and they still allowed the pilgrims to go through to the river.

Cloda and I wandered through the bazaars, ears acock but lips tight shut, for, as I was at pains to make clear to her, I had always found that too great an interest in current matters in a city as close as this to a proposed field of battle could oft land the unwary or indiscreet in dire trouble.

Along the path hitherto we had camped at night under the stars, with a fire lit to keep away the unwelcome attentions of wild animals, but now, once more in a settled area, this was manifestly unwise, so as night fell we sought shelter. There were native inns aplenty, but these we shunned because most were for definite castes, and while we could pass well enough in the thick of the crowd, to claim the religion of people of whose customs we knew little would be to invite trouble.

With an ancient rogue of a moneylender near the city gate I changed two of my gold pieces into silver coins less likely to attract attention to us, and we ate at a stall in the bazaar. Strengthened by this, but deadly weary after our long march, which that day had been of greater length than most and for the main uphill, we continued our search for shelter, for night was now descending and the air struck chill at these heights.

We found it at last in a pilgrim serai, which was merely an open yard surrounded by high walls, with at one end a low shed with a rush-thatched roof. It was already full to overflowing with men, women, children, sheep and goats, which latter the pilgrims invariably drove for the milk they yielded on their long journey, and sometimes to sacrifice at the shrine. Caste, we discovered, mattered not in such a serai as this, as the pilgrimage conferred much merit upon those undertaking it, and the greater the degree of discomfort endured by the faithful thereon, the greater the *izzat*, or prestige claimed at its completion.

We pushed through the crowd, finding scarcely space to put our feet, let alone our bodies, until at last, giving up hope of getting beneath the thatched roof, we satisfied ourselves with a corner in the open, which pleased Cloda more than it did me, because out here in the dark she was able to dispense with her head and face covering without exciting attention.

The pilgrims were in the main simple countryfolk, as poor for the most part as church mice, but with here and there a more prosperous family trying desperately to temper their disdain with increased piety. I was struck by the similarity of these people to other pilgrims I had seen, for Goa was a port from which Indian Mohammedans left by the dhowload for the holy Islamic city of Mecca. Indeed, they had many points in common with bands I had met with in Europe, patiently plodding to various shrines and grottoes, and they aroused in me the same pity. All were actuated by the same spirit of faith, and all were being exploited by the same type of loathsome rogue. In Europe one heard of swarms of bogus priests and charlatan "saints" selling pardons, indulgences and relics to the credulous; in Goa were the hadjis and mullahs vending hairs from the Prophet's beard; here were Brahmins on the same lay with charms, amulets and vials of Ganges water which came, no doubt, from the nearest well.

From our vantage point in the darkness we could see into the rush-lighted covered portion, as a theater audience looked upon a stage. There were a dozen or more of these gentry, shaven-headed and clothed in white robes which left the right shoulder and arm bare and so exposed the sacred thread which all Brahmins wear across their chests. They were lighter skinned than the peasantry, a fact which in itself seemed to give them a certain self-assumed ascendancy, and their arrogance was unbelievable. They battened upon these people but quite obviously held them in the greatest contempt. Each was accompanied by a chela, usually a man of lower caste who combined the functions of disciple, servant and bodyguard, and desperate gallowsflowers most of them appeared. They moved through the crowd, the Brahmins disdaining even to speak to the pilgrims, but at great pains to keep their robes gathered tightly to them to avoid the pollution that the touch of those of lower caste would convey, the chelas preceding them and clearing a path, and holding aloft and extolling the merits of the rubbish they were purveying. Here was a prayer from the Vedas, written by the hand of a holy saddhu of Benares, and a sure specific against the fever; here a pebble from the shrine of the Madura Shiva, a guaranteed cure for barrenness in women; here a twig from the holy neem tree of Harwah which could not fail to cure blindness in newborn infants if laid across the eyes at the first full moon after birth. With a purchase went a curt blessing from the Brahmin; to the penurious or unconvinced, a malignant curse. But there were far fewer curses than blessings, for such is the superstitious sway the Brahmins hold over the lower castes, that few dared hold out against the chelas' mixture of cajoling and threats, and in the end most parted with yet another tithe from their pitiably slim purses.

Repelled but fascinated, we watched this scene for a long time. After the Brahmins came lesser jackals in the form of tumblers, clowns and jugglers and the ubiquitous storytellers, these last being of great skill and talent, telling with both word and mime vastly entertaining and exciting stories of the ancient Hindu heroes, but stopping ever and anon at most crucial points, with their audiences adrool and agog, and steadfastly refusing to go on until yet another collection of suitable proportions was taken up.

And simultaneously with this we listened to the talk around us and learned that this particular party of pilgrims had been held here for several days because Sivaji Peshwa could not guarantee its safety if it went forward into the country that lay between here and Ahmednagar. But now word had come through privily that Salahbar Khan had promised not to molest them, so they marched tomorrow at daybreak. I pondered this deeply.

"It would seem to be the way for us," I said to Cloda. "Let us join this band."

"Agreed," she replied. "But let us seek a barber tonight. No Hindu ever sported a beard such as the one you are wearing."

She was right, as ever, for I was by now as whiskered as any Gentleman of the Middle Passage and was attracting some attention thereby, as I could easily have passed for a Mohammedan or a Sikh, neither of which race shaved. Greatly rested, we left our corner in the serai and returned to the bazaar. The barbers of India, who are also its doctors and tooth-pullers, work in the open, squatting on mats with their customers before them, and since space in the bazaars is always at a great premium, they rarely leave their pitches, preferring to sleep upon them than to have them stolen in their absence.

We found a row of these still at work by the light of flaring torches, as this restless city seemed never to sleep, and I waited until some warriors had been shaved and had their moustaches curled and primped, before submitting myself to the shears and razor. Beside me an ancient coxcomb was having his scanty white locks dyed black in preparation, he declared angrily, to taking arms against the Mohammedans, but an interested ring of onlookers ribaldly suggested it was for an encounter of a tenderer nature while some young husband was away fighting, and I was vastly amused thereby.

Shorn to the skin and feeling freer and cleaner than I had for many days, I rewound my turban and joined Cloda, who had been waiting for me in the shadows. She bore a jar and seemed greatly excited, but she would tell me nothing until we had quit the bazaar, then she revealed that she had bought some of the black dye from another barber and could scarce wait for daylight before trying it upon her own hair.

In the dawn, at the side of a stream which crossed the road which led out of Mahableshwar, I applied the dye to her tresses by the simple expedient of pouring the contents of the jar over her head and rubbing it in vigorously, both of us standing naked and shivering waist-deep in the icy water to avoid fouling our clothes. The result was satisfactory beyond our expectations, the dye remaining fast upon the hair without staining the skin, and since the sun had already imparted to her a beautiful olive tan, she was now able to dispense with the hated trammel of her veil.

From the city gates came the sound of gongs and the wailing of conches, and the head of the procession of pilgrims emerged and set out upon the road, some thousand souls I estimated. We joined them as they passed us, and thus began the second stage of our journey together.

The pace of the march was of necessity that of the slowest, oldest and feeblest, but even so it was by no means uniform throughout the column, the lustier striding out ahead and allowing the others to follow in their own gait, though there was a compassion among them and the march never recommenced from the resting places until all stragglers had caught up. The resting places themselves were a matter of interest, and my soldier's eye approved the forethought of those who had set them along the routes. They occurred at regular intervals of about ten miles and were invariably in the form of a symmetrical grove of mango trees set close together so that their interlocking branches and dense foliage formed an adequate shelter against both sun and rain, and their delicious fruit a refreshment for the weary travelers. There was always a well in the center, and dead branches, twigs and the dried dung of the sacred cows that frequented these places provided an amplitude of fuel for the cooking fires.

The country was here, in striking contrast to that of the coastal plain, open and barren—a bare, almost treeless plateau, broken by fantastic outcroppings of rock—and by day the sun beat down in a blinding glare, but it was not unbearable because the altitude tempered the heat. After sunset it struck cold, and we bought a *chaddar*, a heavy cotton blanket, at a village through which we passed, and we were glad enough to huddle together under it at night. With my shorn head and face, and Cloda's black hair, with the weather-beating the elements were giving us and the constant coating of dust we wore, we were now a part of the column, as indistinguishable from our fellows as two grains of sand upon a beach. And our language progressed apace, because we listened to the storytellers at night and to the conversation of our fellows on the march, and we made it a rule always to talk to each other in the Hindustani tongue and to correct each other's mistakes. We watched the customs and manners of those around us also, and took pains to follow them— removing sandals and washing hands and feet before taking food, rinsing out the mouth noisily after it, eating always with the right hand, being careful never to allow our shadows to fall across, and thus defile, the cooking pots of another, and above all, though loathing the Brahmin priests who still haunted the column, remembering always to murmur, "*Main apke paon bosa.* I kiss your feet," when passing one, and receiving his mechanical "*Prahnam.* Blessing," in return.

It was an exciting and profitable time, and each day's march, though of but a short ten miles in duration, taught us something fresh, and since it is manners rather than appearance that make the man or woman, we felt ourselves accepted by our fellows without question or equivocation.

In only one particular did we make a slip, and that could have been a bad one for us. It was on the evening of the third day, and we had arrived at the camping ground and there happened here to be a dearth of small twigs wherewith to make a fire, and not yet having the skill to make one of cow dung, I ventured further afield until I came to a large fallen branch. I took my knife from under my shirt and started to hack it down into suitable billets, and I became aware of curious and reproachful eyes upon me, and men around me drew away and murmured among themselves. Then an old woman started to berate me angrily, calling me a rogue and a brigand and a betrayer of trusts and a bringer of trouble upon poor people. I was at a loss to understand her at first, feeling the greatest embarrassment as others took up her cry. Then Cloda came quickly through the gathering crowd and whispered to me urgently that it was an abomination for pilgrims to carry knives or other weapons of offense. She then made show of being greatly enraged with me, snatching the knife and hurling it away into the undergrowth, asking pardon of the crowd and explaining that I was of weak intelligence rather than evil intent. She drove me back to the camp, upbraiding me loudly in more than fluent Hindustani, calling me an owl, an ox and the droppings of a sow, and, I swear, enjoying this play-acting no little—as did the crowd.

But, as we discovered jointly a little later, I was by no means the only offender in this respect. The clear and bracing air, my now fully restored strength, Cloda's splendid health and, above all, the excitement that was within us, lent wings to our feet, and it became our custom to stride out to the head of the column and so avoid the dust sent up by its passage. On this day we pressed even faster than usual and reached the next resting place far in advance of the main body, only to find that there were people there already, some two or three hundred of them, dressed in the simple travel-stained garments of the pilgrims, but somehow of a different air and appearance. These were silent and purposeful, and they eyed us suspiciously and returned our greetings curtly and showed no signs of wanting any converse with us other than a demand to know who and what we were.

I salaamed respectfully and told their leader that I was but a poor pilgrim with my wife, and that we had walked ahead of the column, and I pointed back into the distance to the telltale haze of dust that was now becoming visible. That seemed to satisfy them, because they left us in peace to find a resting place at the far end of the grove. We busied ourselves with the simple tasks of camp-making—collecting firewood, drawing water and preparing to cook our evening meal. But I watched them sidelong, and I could see that all of them were armed beneath their loose robes with curved tulwars and heavy knives, and some were quite openly cleaning short bell-mouthed flintlocks which they appeared to carry in cloth-wrapped bundles. I feared for the safety of the poor people who followed us, and I spoke in a low voice to Cloda.

"It would not need as heavily armed a band as this to deal with pilgrims," she said shrewdly. "Besides, who would go to the trouble with such? They have naught worth stealing."

There was sense in this, and since these people, whom I now realized were all men, even those who wore women's clothing, seemed not to bear us any immediate ill intent, I waited, albeit with some apprehension, until the leaders of the column arrived. It was fast getting dark now, and in the clatter and confusion of a thousand people, and their bleating animals, making camp and preparing food, the newcomers appeared to escape undue notice.

Next morning, they were still with us, and they merged into the column with the others, but still seemed unremarked by the real pilgrims. And at the next resting place I found that there were more awaiting the column—and at the next and the next—until it was obvious even to the meanest intelligence that our numbers were now swelled threefold by these grim, silent men, all bearing concealed arms, who were with us but not of us.

A nervousness had now settled upon the pilgrims, and gone was the chatter of the earlier stages of the march, and there was a tendency among some of them to drop out of the column or to remain behind at the morning start. But the newcomers herded them forward like sheepdogs handling a flock, seldom with words, but with gestures that left no doubt as to their meaning.

Then it became clear to me what was happening. This was the spearhead of an army, marching under the guise of pilgrims to the site of the fort at Ahmednagar, and I could not forbear to admire the stratagem. But Cloda was of another mind.

"A curse upon them," she said bitterly. "Yes, no doubt they will fall upon the Mogul's troops by stealth, and there will be a great battle, and one side or the other will triumph, or both will withdraw to lick their wounds, to fight another day. But what will happen to these harmless folk? They will be crushed between two millstones, and their bones will bleach on this barren plain. For what?"

I tried to reassure her, but it was not an easy task, and we were looking at the plot from widely opposed standpoints. She left me several times during the march that day, and I could see her moving among the women and engaging them in murmured converse, and I was greatly afraid because it was clear that she was trying to organize them into resistance to this plot by halting and going no farther, and I knew within me that she would receive short shrift from the strangers if they should realize what was afoot.

But she received scant response from the pilgrims, who were now all in the grip of deadly fear and who marched on like driven beasts, because they had not the will to do else.

We talked far into the night at the next resting place, I trying to persuade her to drop out of the column with me and to steal away into the darkness, since there appeared naught else that we could do, she railing at me for a poltroon.

"That was ever your solution, my Lord Bemforth," she said with icy contempt. "Steal away in the night. A pox on you for a creeping craven. To the black pit of hell with you—our truce is over and you have your quittance. Go, and be damned to you, but you go alone."

She flung out from under our *chaddar* and stalked off in a dudgeon, and I deemed it best to leave her alone until she found her temper again, or the cold of the night made her seek warmth beside me once more. I turned over and went to sleep.

But when I awoke at dawn she was not beside me.

✧✧ 21

FRANTICALLY I searched the camping ground from one end of the grove to the other, inquiring of the pilgrims if any had seen her. But if they had they were not disposed to tell me, because of the fear that was now upon them, and the fact, no doubt, that I myself was suspect because of the incident with the knife. I started to range out into the open plain, but I was speedily driven back and threatened with the muskets of the newcomers. I tried to remain behind when the march began, but in that, also, I was foiled and I was finally placed in the center of a group of armed men at the head of the column and obliged to accompany them, it being made abundantly clear that I could expect short shrift if I attempted to escape. I think they put me down as a harmless idiot, and I was careful once I had had time to reflect fully, not to let them know that Cloda was missing, in case they searched for her and did her harm.

I stumbled along that dreadful day, downcast and sick at heart as the full bitterness of it all came home to me. I would fain have shaken loose from her in the earlier days, but now I would have given my right arm to find her again. I resolved that as soon as I could escape these people I would go back along the road and search until I found her.

We were now on the last stages of our journey. Ahmednagar lay straight ahead, but here the pilgrim route turned off at a tangent to the Godavari, for the site of the fort and that of the shrine were some dozen miles apart. There was a small camp at the crossroads, and it was here that I first saw Mogul troops, and, dolorous though I was, I could not forbear to admire their military stature and deportment.

There were about a hundred of them, tall men, fiercely bearded in the Moslem fashion, clad uniformly in crimson tunics with half-armor over, and beneath their high-piled turbans I could see steel caps rising to a point through the folded silk. They were armed with long curved scimitars, a multiplicity of knives thrust into their sashes and, when mounted, short bell-mouthed muskets and matched horse pistols. Their horses were magnificent, and I learned later that they were the direct descendants of those brought to India by Alexander the Great centuries before, which were originally a cross between Arab stallions and Flanders mares, combining the grace and speed of their sires with the strength and endurance of their dams. These Mogul troops were, in fact, the finest mounted and best equipped cavalry I had ever seen in any part of the world. Well led, I reflected, they could be invincible.

But this detachment, at least, did not appear to be well led or commanded. These soldiers seemed sunk in Oriental indolence, and they made no attempt to examine our column closely as we shuffled

past in the dust, and so three thousand Marathas passed the guardpost, fully armed and barely disguised, and in full daylight at that,
and it came home to me again that guile so often can prevail over
skill and valor.

I wondered, as we marched, what our leader's plan was. It would,
of course, depend upon the strength of the Ahmednagar garrison,
and of that I had no idea, although it was to be assumed that the
Marathas had. Three thousand armed infantrymen with the advantage of surprise? They could do much, even if the Moguls far outnumbered them, because the latter would be strung out in a cordon,
no doubt, guarding the builders of the fort—and there might indeed
be other columns such as ours. It could be that the Moguls, at this
far southern extremity of their sweep through India, were due for a
crushing defeat.

On and on we trudged that last day, not stopping to rest in the
heat of high noon as was our normal custom, because now the river
was in sight, a thin silver thread far away in the distance winding its
way across the scorched plain, seen from above as we gained the
summit of a line of low hills and commenced our downward march
through a narrow rocky defile. The pilgrims raised a great shout and
new life seemed to enter into them, and their feet appeared to grow
lighter, and even I, heartsick as I was, was gripped by their exalta-
tion. Soon we would be there, soon I would be free to go back and
search for Cloda, and then, our quarrel mended, we would go on
through the Mogul country. Go on to the Road.

The attack broke upon us as the tail of the column entered the
top of the defile, but before the head had emerged onto the plain
from the bottom of it. Perfectly timed, faultless in execution came
that first withering blast of what must have been at least a thousand
muskets, followed by flight after flight of crossbow shafts, and from
the tops of the cliffs above us on either side rose a tremendous battle
cry, "Ullah—Al—lah—ul Akbar!"

Around me several of the men among whom I had been marching
lay twitching and writhing in their death throes, but I, by very
reason of their protective phalanx, was unscathed. I flung myself flat
among the dead and dying and from that position had little opportunity of watching the progress of this short and dreadful battle, but
the sounds of it were plain enough to read. After the deadly fusil-

lade of shot and arrows came the charge of the ambuscade down the rocky slopes, hacking and hewing at all who stirred—then there was a trumpet call which had for an instant the effect of freezing the whole scene into silence. A mighty voice bellowed from the slopes in Hindustani and then bad Marathi, that no harm was intended to true pilgrims, provided they bore no arms and stood their ground without moving.

Raising my head I saw a curious sight. The main body of the pilgrims had been marching between the advance and rear guard of the disguised Maratha warriors, and they now stood more or less intact in a shivering group, while the head and tail of the column was a broken and bloody shambles. Yes, their pantheon of strange gods seemed to have protected these simple people, and had at the same time put down the mighty from their seats. But I, unfortunate wretch, was among the mighty.

The Mogul troops came on, reloaded now and with muskets primed and ready and arrows fitted to tautened strings, calling upon the surviving Marathas to lay down their arms and yield. Most did, though I saw a few die bravely and futilely under the swords and axes of the victors rather than surrender. The whole thing took but a scant five minutes, but the debacle was complete and absolute.

With such of the others who were still enabled to do so, I rose to my feet and stood with my hands held aloft in token of submission. Mogul soldiers herded us to one side and we waited while the survivors from the tail of the column were driven down to join us. I looked around me and judged in a quick count that there were perhaps some two hundred of us left.

Other Mogul soldiers had now approached the pilgrims and, although I could hear no words from where I stood, they seemed to be examining and questioning them and, when satisfied, passing them forward through the heaps of dead to the foot of the defile. I spoke to one of the Moguls guarding us and explained that I too was a pilgrim but had by chance been marching with the warriors. He listened to me civilly enough, then called to a group of pilgrms who happened at that moment to be passing, inviting them to confirm my good faith or otherwise, but as ill fortune would have it one of them happened to be the old woman who had seen my jungle knife at the resting place. She chattered shrilly and angrily and denounced me as a wolf in sheep's clothing and one who brought trouble upon the poor and defenseless, and the soldier sneered and pronounced me a coward as well as an enemy and smote me across the shoulders with the flat of his sword when I attempted to plead further.

The pilgrims having gone upon their way, escorted by a score or so of Mogul troops, we captives were then taken back along the route we had come, until we arrived once more at the guardpost at the crossroads, and there we found waiting a dolorous and forbidding heap of gyves and chains and fetters, and a score of blacksmiths to rivet them upon us.

It was night when this grim task was completed, and we were then left under the stars in the courtyard, without food or water, until dawn stained the eastern sky.

We marched that day to Ahmednagar, chained together in groups of twelve. We were not treated with undue cruelty by our guards, most of whom tended to ignore us as human beings and to stand towards us in much the same relationship as drovers to their cattle. They had a duty to transport us from one point to another, and this they did, dispassionately and without spleen, allowing us to halt upon the way once or twice to drink, like cattle, from streams that crossed our path. But, again like cattle, they dealt promptly and stringently with all who tended to stray or to falter, slashing at us from their saddles with long riding whips.

But if there was an absence of spleen in the treatment of the guards, it was abundantly made up for by that of my fellow prisoners on the chain. I was a stranger, one who spoke little or no Marathi but, at the same time, better Hindustani than they, and was therefore suspect as a spy put amongst them to listen to their converse and subsequently report it to our captors. They therefore would have none of me, talking but little, and then in whispers, as far from me as the tolerance of our connecting chain would allow, and when at midday greasy wheaten cakes called chapatties were tossed among us, I was deprived of my miserable share, and attacked and clawed and bitten when I attempted to enforce my claim.

We arrived at Ahmednagar before darkness fell. It was a mighty fortress, not then quite completed. It stood crowning rising land some miles from the main stream of the Godavari, upon a tributary of it. It was constructed in the star shape which I later learned was typical of all Mogul military architecture—eight long bastions jutting out from a central keep, the whole surrounded by a thirty-foot high wall and a wide and deep stone-faced moat.

Footsore, weary, dust and sweat begrimed, we filed across the drawbridge and through the tunnel-like sally port into the enormous courtyard, in which could have been accommodated without cramping a fair-sized village. Many hundreds of stonemasons still worked upon it although the hour was now far advanced, but one could see that their labors were not yet to cease because even then torches and tar-barrels were being lighted along the line of battlements to illumine the scene, and strings of bullock carts were still filing across the plain, nose to tail in an unbroken line, each bearing huge shaped blocks of red sandstone.

Arrived in the courtyard, we were herded into a long, low dungeon slightly below ground level and still damp from the fresh mortar that bound the walls, fed again, and left in the darkness. I was one of perhaps two hundred, but I do not think I ever before or after felt such a dreadful weight of oppression and loneliness as during the hours of that night as, drawn as far away from the other eleven as possible, I tried vainly to sleep.

When morning came we were brought out again into the courtyard, where a magnificent figure came forth on a horse and addressed us in most kindly tones, telling us that he, Salahbar Khan, commander of the Emperor Shah Jahan's fort of Ahmednagar and Viceroy of the Deccan and all Southern India, bore us no ill will even in view of our dastardly attempt to attack him by stealth in the guise of poor harmless peasants. The Emperor, he continued, wished to live in peace with all people, even the foreign dogs of Portuguese and Dutch and treacherous Marathas. Shah Jahan brought protection and prosperity to all realms which came under his suzerainty. Shah Jahan was our father, be we Moslem or Hindu. Shah Jahan wished us well and now gave us the opportunity of sharing in the building of this outpost of his Indian empire. He, Salahbar, also wished us well, and hoped we would be happy in our task and work hard—and not put him to the painful necessity of pegging us out on the plains, faces upward into the sun, with our eyelids removed, and partially disembowelled for the kites and vultures to complete the task. Salahbar hoped that he had made himself clear.

If he had not, his overseers demonstrated his meaning with the utmost clarity. Whips cracked and curled about our shoulders and we were driven out through the sally port and over the drawbridge, with the whole populace of soldiers, artisans, and their woman and children deriding us and pelting us with filth. We marched along the beaten track of the bullock carts some ten miles, choking and gasping in the heat and dust, until we reached some huge quarries in the hillside. Here other wretches like ourselves were working on cutting the huge blocks from which the fort was being built, and loading them on to the carts. We were partially released from our chains and driven to the rock face. I say partially, because the method by which we were chained was by a clumsy anklet of iron upon one foot. Set into this anklet was an eyelet through which, until now, a chain had run, tight-locked at either end, so holding us in groups of twelve. The chain was of such length that it allowed us an interval of some two or three yards between men, and we had been enabled to march by holding the slack of the chain between us in one hand. Since we could not work on the rock face without a certain measure of freedom, we had so to be released, but the anklet itself weighed at least twenty pounds so all thought of making a dash for freedom, even had the opportunity presented itself, was thus nipped in the bud.

We worked all that first day, two men to a block, cutting them out of the living rock with hammers and chisels and then rolling them to the floor of the quarry for loading onto the carts. It was woe betide the man who ceased in his labors for as long as it took to wipe the sweat from his eyes, for then the lashes of the hawk-eyed overseers descended upon him without pity, and it was their custom to beat both men impartially, thus ensuring that each prisoner kept his partner diligently at his task, in the interests of his own hide.

When night was falling we were driven once again to the floor of the quarry and there counted into our parties of twelve, and the chains were served to us and we had the melancholy task of threading ourselves upon them once again like strings of living beads, then the overseers came and locked the ends with huge iron padlocks, and we were marched to a rough stone compound, open to the skies, some mile or so away, and food was thrown down among us like husks among swine, and we were allowed to slake our thirst in parties at water butts set at each angle of the wall, but for other needs and purposes we were constrained to remain where we were and were not allowed even to approach the walls, so that the place, from long usage, was a foul cesspit and stank to high heaven.

I could not, that first night, force myself to fight for the scraps of food upon that filthy ground, but I had to suffer being dragged and rolled in the wild scrimmage by those of stronger stomach than myself. But the next night, and the next after that, I found myself fighting with the same silent ferocity as the rest for the sorry sustenance thus served to us, kicking, biting and clawing like some feral beast of the jungle.

With the first morning light we were aroused by the lashes and marched back to the quarries, and then once more released for our tasks, and again we labored through the livelong day save for a break of half an hour at high noon, when we were herded to a nearby stream to drink and also gnaw such food as the provident had managed to save and secrete from the night before.

I cannot recall for how many days this misery went on because all now is compounded in my memory to a searing hell of beatings, bestial fights for food, unremitting toil and the constant lash. It was long enough, however, for two on my chain, and certainly many more in other parties, to find surcease from this torment in death. In all cases, if I remember aright, it was due to the ghastly suppurating ulcers on their ankles caused by the clumsy iron anklets, which quickly became putrescent in that climate, and brought on a short but agonizing fever which killed as quickly as the plague. And now I also had such a sore upon my leg.

I tore a strip of tattered cloth from the remnants of my loincloth, and sacrificed twice a day a few moments of my rest to soak it in drinking water and lay it upon the wound, if only to keep it protected from the bites of bloated green and gold flies that battened upon all of us. It was that pitiful strip of rag that first gave me the desperate glimmering of a hope of escape.

As I have recounted, when our labors ceased for the day we were driven into our parties of twelve and our chains were handed to the first man of each group. He then threaded the end through the eyelet on his leg-iron and passed it to the man behind, who did the same thing, and so on to the next until it reached the last man. Then the overseer would walk along the lines padlocking the end links so that the chain could not be drawn back through the eyelets, so freeing the men again.

If only, I thought, I could contrive not to be so locked upon the chain one day . . . but I put the thought away. We were counted and inspected as we left the quarry, marching between two stationary overseers.

It was, as I say, my pathetic bandage that proved to be my deliverance.

All day I pondered upon it, weighing the pros and cons of the devilish dilemma. I had scant chance of success, so chancey was my plan and, if caught, I would die a lingering death pegged out upon the plain, for this was no idle threat, as we had cause to know when one demented wretch had turned upon an overseer one day at the rock face. On the other hand, if I only made a brief dash for freedom, death might conceivably be quick and relatively clean under the muskets of the guards. I *might* gain my freedom, and God knows I had little enough to lose if I failed.

We left the rock-face and slithered wearily down to the quarry floor, the dust rising in clouds at our passage, and the whips of the overseers cracking like a forest fire because they, even as much as we, were glad to be quit of this sun-scorched pit of Hades at the end of the day. Our chains were dragged to us and flung at our feet. I had straggled to a position in the center of our party, which had now been reduced to ten, and when the chain was passed to me by the man in front I pretended to be in even greater misery than I indeed was. I sank down into the dust and took the chain, pulling it to its full length and handing the end back, but without letting the man behind see that I had not in fact, passed it through the eyelet of my leg-iron. Instead, under guise of rewrapping my pus-dripping ankle, I tied the chain to the eyelet with a strip of my bandage and then covertly covered the whole thing with dust.

Inwardly praying that the frail rag would hold until we passed the overseers at the entrance to the quarry, I marched in the strict military tempo we had perforce to keep if we were not to fall headlong through some poor fool missing the step. Nearer, nearer we came, I thankful for the first time for the clouds of dust our feet sent up. And now we were level with them and I could feel the rag breaking under the weight of the chain, and I knew that the man behind me would betray me if he noticed, if only to curry favor with the overseers.

But now we were past, and trudging along the trail to the compound, and the short tropical twilight was fast merging into night. The rag had finally broken away, but that did not matter so much now because I carried the slack of the chain in my hand in the customary manner and none was likely to inspect it closely here.

In the compound itself I had to exercise care and guile, and run and scramble and fall over with my party in the nightly fight for food, in case it was noticed by a guard on the walls that I was free. But at last, the filthy struggle over, and the strong gnawing ravenously at their food and the weaker whimpering piteously, we settled down to sleep the sleep of the near dead in our own ordure.

I waited perhaps an hour before I commenced my crawl away from my companions. Inch by inch I slithered through the serried lines of sleep-drugged men until I had reached the outskirts of the mass. There was an interval then which had to be kept clear—some twenty feet between the sleepers and the ten-foot high wall of loose unmortared stone. This was the really dangerous part, because guards sat on platforms outside, and although they did not seem to keep a very strict watch, relying on our chains and the impossibility of twelve men escaping in unison without noise, they certainly did not sleep, because one could often hear them in converse during the night, and the rattle of arms and the challenges and answers as they were relieved and replaced.

Scarce daring to breathe—indeed, scarce wanting to, so foul was that ground within an inch of my nose—I crept across into the shadow of the wall. I climbed upon it, my heart near stopping when once or twice I dislodged a stone and it clattered noisily to the ground. Then I was up on the coping, lying flat on my belly and fighting to recapture my wind.

Slowly I lowered myself down the other side, and then commenced to crawl in like manner until I had put a hundred yards between myself and the wall, then I dared to rise and make off in a silent shambling run, the anklet giving my sorry ankle the pains of all hell. I skirted the barracks of the guards and overseers and made for the open plain, having no direction in mind save that in the opposite direction to that in which the quarry lay, but as a matter of instinct I saw before long from the polestar over my left shoulder that I was going due east.

But now, the excitement of the actual escape over, came the reaction and it was fast brought home to me in what poor shape I was. The cursed anklet was weighing a ton and my chest heaved and panted like a broken bellows, and in spite of the heat of that torrid night a cold sweat was upon me and I shivered until I feared my very bones would fall apart. Then the cold ague gave place to a burning fever that sapped the strength from me. I was tortured with thirst and there was not even dew on that parched plain that I could lick from the rocks.

As dawn came I found that I was nearing a river, but it gave me no comfort at first because I had been having tantalizing visions throughout the night and I thought that this was but another. But this was real enough, as I found when I had fallen headlong down the bank and into its brown waters. I lay and drank and drank and drank until I near ripped the shrunken guts from myself by vomiting. Then I drank again, and finally I climbed up onto the bank, found a clump of bushes and crawled into the cover of it and knew no more.

✢✢ 22

I AWOKE when the sun was high in the sky, somewhat refreshed though very weak and famished by hunger. I crawled out of my hiding place and sought higher ground from which I could survey the surrounding plain. Nothing moved upon it except the dancing heat-haze, and there appeared no sign of any pursuit or search. Indeed, now that I had time to reflect, I did not greatly fear any, as I realized that we were only nameless faces to our captors, and our numbers were already being depleted by death.

I searched in vain for sustenance of any sort along the river bank and thought with regret of the abundance of fruit and shellfish in the coastal areas. Here were only sparse and bare thorn trees, and if there were fish in the river I had no means of catching them. However, there was no profit in remaining here to perish of starvation, so, in spite of the encumbrance of my anklet and the pain it caused me, I started to plod my way, still eastward, along the river bank.

I had been walking an hour or more when I saw the man. He sat under a tree on a small square of frayed matting, naked as the day he was born, lank and filthy hair falling around his shoulders, smeared from head to foot with grey ashes and daubed with cow dung. I recognized him for what he was immediately. A saddhu, or holy man. I had seen many such before and I knew that although some were harmless enough, they numbered among them some very great rogues who battened upon the superstitious fears of the simple peasants. Their normal mode of life was to take up a position such as this, either close to a village or at least near a path that was frequently used, and sit all day contemplating infinity, with a begging bowl before them into which gifts of food were dropped by the pious or the frightened.

There was such a bowl before this man, and I regarded it hungrily, and then approached him and made a deep and respectful salaam and murmured the salutation normally given to a Brahmin. He made no sign of having heard me, but continued to gaze out across the river, so I pointed to his bowl and then to my open mouth, at which he made the slightest inclination of his head which I hopefully took to be one of assent. Greatly daring, I squatted native fashion before the bowl and tentatively reached out my hand towards it. Hindus though they are, the restrictions of caste seldom concerned the saddhus, but it is always a dangerous thing in India to touch another man's eating utensils without permission. This one, however, made no sign to stop me so I plunged my right hand into the bowl and soon was eating ravenously of the cold rice and curried vegetables it contained. It was a large bowl and there was much food within it, but I stopped long before I was satisfied as, starving though I was, I had no wish to leave him bereft. But he made another gesture to me to continue, so I gorged until I could hold no more. Replete, I stood up and once more salaamed, but this time the salutation was sincere because I was filled with gratitude as well as rice. He made no acknowledgment of my salaam, but I saw a flicker of interest in his deep-set eyes as he caught sight of my anklet. He leaned forward and inspected it closely, putting up his hand to restrain me when I started to back away. He shook his head as he saw the horrible sore which was now spreading above and below the circlet of iron, and murmured some words in a language I did not understand, then he pointed to a patch of shade behind him and bade me in sign language to sit down. I was glad enough to do so, because combined with my former weariness and now the effects of my full belly, a great desire for sleep was upon me. Nothing loath, therefore, I sank down and soon was once more deep in slumber.

I awoke as the shadows were lengthening. The saddhu seemed not to have moved from his former cross-legged posture on the mat. As I sat up he raised his hand to bid me be still, then, approaching along the river bank I heard women's voices.

There were three of them; shy and timid village women with the ends of their saris modestly covering their faces. Two of them bore baskets, and the other a small naked baby. They came up to a spot before the begging bowl and placed food in it, and laid a votive offering of faded marigold flowers around it, then, after a deep obeisance they drew back and stood waiting. The saddhu sat on for a long time, making no sign of his awareness of them, until suddenly he raised his hand and beckoned the woman carrying the baby to come forward. She advanced a few paces then sank down on her knees, holding the child up in both her hands. It could not have been more than a few weeks old, tiny and shriveled and ill-nourished, bearing round its neck the usual strings of amulets these people put upon their children to ward off evil spirits, and I saw that it was stricken with the eye-sickness that is the scourge of so many native infants and which so often led to total blindness. The eyes were closed, the lids gummed shut with running rheum, and it mewed faintly like a small sick animal, and clenched and unclenched its tiny fists convulsively. The mother's eyes were wide and stricken to their dark depths with the agony of her silent pleading.

The saddhu made no sign towards her, but fumbled under the edge of his mat and produced some dried leaves. He put them in his mouth and chewed upon them for some time before spitting them out into the palm of his hand, then he motioned the mother to come closer. She did so, shuffling forward on her knees until the baby was in reach of his hands. He picked from his daubed hide a few particles of dried dung, and ground them between finger and thumb into the already revolting mess in the palm of his other hand, then he liberally anointed the baby's eyes with this foul ointment. The mother swaddled the child in the end of her sari, bent forward and laid her brow on the edge of his mat, then rose to her feet, salaamed and made quickly off, followed by her companions. The saddhu called once, softly, and they paused and turned. They bowed their understanding and hurried upon their way.

I deemed it high time to go mine also, for while I could not approve his filthy alchemy or his cozening of these poor people, I could not dispute his kindness, and had no will to abuse it further. I accordingly rose and salaamed to him and tried by signs to convey my gratitude, but he shook his head and motioned to me to sit down again, pointing to the food bowl and gesturing to me to eat. Since I knew not when such bounty would come my way again, I did so, though with rather more delicacy this time.

An hour passed by, and now, full fed once more, I was again thinking of taking leave of my gracious host when again I heard voices approaching—but this time they were in the deeper tones of men. My first thoughts were ones of treachery, and I sprang to my feet and prepared to make off into the gathering gloom, but they were already with us. The saddhu motioned me once again to sit down, then I saw that the two newcomers were but peasants, and one of them bore upon his brow the caste mark of the *Lohar,* or blacksmith, and that they carried between them a small anvil and a pouch of hammers and chisels. They treated the saddhu with the same deference as had their women, then, without further direction from him they knelt before me and inspected my leg-iron.

They were as gentle and considerate as the case permitted, but I suffered the agonies of the damned as they hammered the rivets out of that cursed thing. Finally they got it off, then one of them bore it to the bank of the river, spat upon it and seemed to mumble a curse upon it before casting it far out into the dark waters. The saddhu signed to me to advance my maltreated leg for his inspection, then to my horror and disgust, he produced some more leaves and anointed the sore with the same panacea as he had used for the

THE ROAD AND THE STAR

baby's eyes. This time I needed no invitation to rest further, indeed it would have been difficult to put one foot before the other in the state I was then. I lay down in my old place and went to sleep again.

He was sitting, unmoved from his former position, gazing into the rising sun when I awoke, singing in a muted undertone some hymn, no doubt to his strange gods. I lay listening to him, conscious of a feeling of well-being I had not known for many a long day, but being unable to account for it until I realized that it was due to no positive thing, but rather the contrary. It was the absence of the throbbing, searing pain in my leg. Amazed, I sat up and looked at it. It was still ugly, but the angry inflamed area that had been around it was greatly reduced, and the pain, as I have said, was gone. I waited until he appeared to have completed his devotions, then I all but prostrated myself before him in my gratitude. But he disregarded my thanks and signed to me to be quiet. Then he took from the still well-filled bowl several handfuls of the cooked rice which he kneaded into small balls, and he set these round himself in a half-circle. A chipmunk, the shyest and most timid of all Indian animals, scuttled down the trunk of the tree behind us, approached the rice without fear and sat back, squirrel-like, on its haunches, holding a ball between its small forepaws, nibbling daintily. Then there was another, and another, and many birds—mynahs, hoopoes and even crows, and finally a slinking she-jackal with her cubs, and even a mongoose or two, all eating without fear.

I sat there fascinated and delighted as he presided over this animal banquet, encouraging the shyer and gently chiding the greedy, until the food was finished and the small beasts had departed. Then he signed for me to eat again, and once more he examined my wound and seemed satisfied with what he saw. He anointed it again and gave me a small quantity of the salve which he instructed me to place upon it at morn and night, indicating this by pointing to the east and west. He lapsed then into his customary posture, and I deemed that I had his leave to depart. I tried to thank him again but received no answering sign, but when I had walked some distance I turned and raised my hand in farewell. He bowed his head gravely and I saw him smile for the first and only time as he made the graceful Hindu sign of the blessing. Strangely moved and near to

tears, I went on my way, heartened and strengthened by this encounter with a true saint.

I came upon a village after some miles, and I was about to make a
detour, because I was now a wild and terrifying sight, my hair and
beard matted and unkempt, my skin burned almost black by the
sun, and the merest wisp of tattered rag about my loins barely
preserving decency, when I passed a woman who bore a baby on
her hip. It was the one who had come to the saddhu. Instead of
drawing away in fear, she smiled and turned and called back into the
distance, and other people came out from their huts and I could see
that they accepted me as one who bore them no ill-will just from
the fact that I had been in the old man's presence.

On I went some further miles, still without guiding marks except
for the river on my left hand and a desire to put as much distance
between myself and that cursed quarry as I could, until I came to a
dusty road which approached the river over the plain and crossed it
by a ford, winding away in the distance the other side. I turned onto it purely because it led to the north.

I crossed the ford and took some time to bathe and to scrub at
myself with handfuls of sand until I felt again some measure of
cleanliness. And now I found myself thinking clearly again, and I
was able once more for the first time since the day of the ambush to
reflect upon the fate of Cloda. Enraged at what she thought, perhaps
rightly, was my cowardice, I felt that she must have turned back
upon our path that last night rather than accompany me another
step forward, although where she could have gone, except perhaps
back to her friends the Bhils, I could not conceive.

But I knew beyond the merest flicker of a doubt that I would
never find peace again until I knew what had befallen her.

I threw myself down under a tree and cudgeled my brains for the
best course to pursue. Every instinct drew me north—except that of
my heart, and that chancy compass chided me for a poltroon. Yes,
I would have to go back to seek her.

I tried to determine my present position, drawing in the dust with
a twig a rough plan of my wanderings as far as I could reckon them.
Here we were attacked, some ten miles south of Ahmednagar; then
we were taken back *here*, to the crossroads; then on again to
Ahmednagar by *this* debouching road; then, as far as I could reckon

on that terrible march, ten miles to the east, to the quarries; a night and a day's march from *there*—still to the east, along the line of the river. That should put me about *here* . . . say thirty miles east of Ahmednagar. A road, I believed, led due north from Ahmednagar to the empire of the Moguls, to the city of Agra, some hundreds of miles away. It must be a road of some size. If I went to the west, inclining just a little to the north, I would of necessity come to that road. If I were decently covered in the habiliments of any except a Maratha, I might approach the fort from the north, openly and without fear, and then from there retrace my steps along our trail, seeking tidings of her. Yes, I decided, that was it. But first things first. I possessed in this wide world a small strip of tattered cotton, and nothing more. I must obtain clothes and get my hair and beard shorn if I was not to attract too much attention nearer to civilization. Having arrived at this conclusion I rose and continued on my way up the road in search of some human habitation.

After about a further hour I overtook a sturdy old farmer and his wrinkled wife driving a herd of water-buffalo calves, and the beasts, in the manner of their kind, were balky and willful, straying from the road, scattering and pausing ever and anon to graze on the parched herbage of the plain. The old man hailed me and eyed my wild appearance askance, then held muttered converse with his wife. I could not understand their Marathi, but its purport was clear enough. They were asking me for my assistance, and the farmer produced some small copper coins from his pouch and showed them to me enticingly. Overjoyed, I nodded vigorously and seized a stick from the side of the road and set about the laggard cattle with gusto, shouting, leaping and running to and fro behind them as I had often seen the natives doing, and soon I had them in some semblance of order moving along the road, much to the content of their owners.

Soon we arrived at a large village where there was a bustling market in progress. I stood sweating and panting, awaiting my quittance, but the farmer seemed favorably disposed to my prowess as a cowherd because he produced two silver rupees and held them up to me in obvious offer to continue in his service longer, to which I willingly agreed, so I tended his herd on the outskirts of the village while he went upon his business within it. He came and went throughout the rest of the day with buyers, and finally, after much voluble chaffering, had disposed of all his beasts and was seemingly well satisfied with his transactions, because he paid me off with my two rupees and added another to them as an honorarium. Almost stunned at my good fortune, for in my present near-naked state, fortune indeed it was, I went on into the market and purchased after haggling mightily at many stalls, a loose shirt, a decent dhoti, or loincloth, and a turban, and also a brass drinking vessel without which no respectable Hindu traveler is ever seen abroad. Then I sought an itinerant barber and was once more shorn and shaved. Donning my garments and wrapping the turban round my head in the loose untidy folds of the *zamindar*, or small farmer, I was once more a figure as like those around me as one sheep in a flock; caste high enough to be respectable, but still sufficiently humble to be a person of no importance. As a zamindar I was not vegetarian as are the more elevated of the Hindus, so I went to a booth from which came the appetizing scent of curried mutton and saffron rice, and since here came all manner of men, both Hindu and Moslem, and a variety of tongues were spoken, I was able to engage in converse with many of them without arousing suspicion.

I was, it appeared, in the village of Vizapur, and the road running through it continued but a few miles until it joined that which connected Ahmednagar with Agra, so the map I had cogitated in the dust was not so very far at fault. There were serais and resting places along the length of the road, but they were widely spaced, and the wilderness which lay between them was dangerous even for large and well-armed parties. In addition to the perils of nature— wild beasts, serpents and desert areas where neither food nor water might be found in the length of a three-day march—there were also those of both man and devils: wandering bands of dacoits who would slit a throat for the sake of a traveler's drinking vessel; dreaded thugs who strangled at the behest of their foul gods; also creatures who appeared as beautiful and enticing women by day but who turned into bats by night and sucked the blood from those incontinent enough to lie with them; and many such other ter- rifying monsters, ghouls and evil spirits—afrits, djinn and bhuts as they were called.

I listened intently to all this, privily discounting that which I ascribed solely to ignorant superstition, but mentally noting all that would be of use in the future, because, although I intended immediately to go in search of Cloda, my will to turn back towards the Road when once I had done so was unshaken.

I rested that night in the village serai, and next morning, as the sun rose, armed with a stout staff, a small amount of food in a bundle with my brass lota and my remaining silver rupee, I set off across country to the Ahmednagar road which lay, I was told, some ten miles due west.

My leg, with the second application of this wondrous balm, was now healing apace, and rest and good food had put new life into me, and, even more important, I had once more a definite purpose in view, so I made little of those ten miles over the open plain.

Fortune was smiling upon me that day, because I struck the road at the place where the first serai north of Ahmednagar was situated, so I rested there and ate my food and found myself sharing the shade of a tree with a man of the north, of a race I had not met with before—a Sikh. These people, though Hindus, differ from the rest of that religion in that they grow their beards long and wear their hair, which they are forbidden by custom to cut, coiled high inside their tightly wound turbans. They are fierce and warlike and had long been a thorn in the side of the Moguls, but now, apparently, they were about to come to terms. This man, who told me his name was Bagwant Singh, was not, however, a warrior. He was a guru, a religious teacher, and he had been on a visit to some holy Hindu shrines in the south. He was a learned and widely traveled man and he spoke in beautifully clear and cultured Hindustani which I found easy to understand, and he seemed in no wise put out at my own uncouth speech.

We had long and most interesting converse, and he courteously offered me some of his food, which was prepared for him at a small fire by two chelas who accompanied him and who treated him with the greatest deference. He was now returning to his own country, which lay far to the north of the Mogul capital of Delhi. For my part I told him I was of farming caste from the south, but that I also had traveled widely, having been to the coast and met with Dutch and Portuguese and even made some voyages with both. I mentioned this, not in the spirit of boastfulness nor yet for any love of unnecessary lies, but I wanted him to talk of the parts of this vast country through which I desired above all things to journey—and travelers talk best to travelers.

"A great and wonderful land," he told me, "though not without its dangers. The Moguls, enemies of my people until recently, are, it must be admitted, now pacifying the countryfolk, and although they deal cruelly with all who bear arms covertly against them, they are not unjust, and are tolerant and respectful of all religions."

That surprised me, for I had heard the contrary in Goa. The guru shook his head. "Shah Jahan, like his father Jehangir and grandsire Akbar," he pronounced, "is a great seeker after the truth, and despises no road which might genuinely lead to it. At his court may be found Brahmins, Sikhs such as myself, Chinese sages who preach the way of Confucius, Buddists and now, I am told, he has invited Goa to send some Jesuit priests to expound their faith to him."

"An enlightened ruler indeed," I said.

The guru shook his head again thoughtfully. "Enlightened, yes," he agreed. "But many think he advances too fast along the road of progress. His own Moslem mullahs plot against him. His sons and brothers are held only by their fear of him. Should he ever show the slightest sign of weakness they will drag him down—unless he can organize the women."

"The women?"

"Aye, the women," answered the Sikh. "In that I am doubtful. Whoever heard of women being taught to read and write? Aren't they plotters enough with their tongues? But that is what he intends to do—to give them learning, and even, in time, to let them sit in council with the men. Already he permits them to leave the harem and to wander abroad without so much as a wisp of veil to cover their faces, like whores and others of low caste. We Sikhs are less strict with our womenfolk than most, but even to me that is near blasphemy. The effect on the orthodox and pious can be imagined."

We sat on long into the afternoon, I enthralled with his stories, and he no doubt flattered by my attention. I wished with all my heart that I could have gone north with this learned man, and he indeed did suggest that.

"I travel as all the wise and prudent do up the Agra road," he told me. "I wait for a party of Mogul troops returning to their homes in the north at the end of their duty down here. That is another thing we have to thank the Moguls for; their soldiers are under the strictest orders to help and protect peaceful travelers, so military parties quickly become caravans, people waiting at these serais for days until one comes through. Come with us, young man, for I greatly enjoy your discourse. Had you the advantage of booklearning such as I, you would be an educated man."

I thanked him but explained that I had business to the south of Ahmednagar that had to be attended to first, though I promised that it would not be long before I turned my face to the polestar again. Then I bade him farewell and expressed the hope that we might meet again in the not far distant future.

I set off down the road towards the fort, thinking to walk through the cool of the night and arrive there with the dawn, but I had not gone many miles when I saw a vast cloud of dust in front of me which, as the intervening distance between us decreased, I made out to be a column of cavalry moving at a smart trot, the sun glinting on their half-armor; superbly mounted Mogul troops. I stepped off the road and prepared to salaam to their captain, as seemed to be the custom among the peasantry.

On they came, lances aloft and pennants fluttering, a sight which set me tingling, as trotting cavalry always was wont to do. Some fifty passed me, in files of four, then there was a break in the column to allow the dust of their passage to subside, then I saw a cavalcade of Mogul officers, and in their midst were ladies, veiled and hooded against the sun, and riding sidesaddle, then in the distance behind them were the sumpter beasts, and finally another squadron bringing up the rear. But this I realized later. At that moment all else was struck from my mind. Cloda rode among the ladies.

✦✦ 23

THERE was no mistaking her, even in her rich silk brocades, because, unlike the others, she was unveiled and unhooded, and the sun glinted on her hair. She rode superbly, straight-backed as to the manner born, whereas the harem ladies around her bobbed and joggled woefully. I thought for one fleeting moment that she was a captive, but that manifestly was not so, because of her magnificent costume and the fact that she was engaged in lively and obviously amiable converse with the Mogul officers who rode near her, and I knew a swift pang of jealousy.

Then she was gone, whirling swiftly by, and the rearward squadron swept past, and I, a faceless peasant, was standing bowing in their dust.

Without conscious volition, I turned and followed in their wake.

My thoughts and feelings were in a mad turmoil. First I knew overwhelming joy and relief because she was safe and well—but then came black doubts. How came her fortunes to be repaired so quickly? Had she already sold herself into some noble's harem? Was she a concubine or even a courtesan? But I forced them from me. Sufficient for the moment that she was alive, and that once more I was facing towards the Road, and our paths, if not together, were at least in the same direction. There was *some* explanation—there *must* be. Tonight they would tarry at the serai I had so recently left, and I would contrive to speak with her . . .

I forced my feet back along the road as if the Devil himself were behind me, breaking ever and anon into a run, and I covered the return journey in a tithe of the time it had taken me in the opposite direction. But even so, my heart sank when I came once more in sight of the serai, for there was no sign of the cavalcade. My friend the guru was still there, however, and he told me of their passage. They had but paused to water their horses and then gone swiftly on.

"A party of nobles and important officials," he explained. "Traveling too fast for humble wayfarers on foot to keep up with them. They will stage and obtain fresh mounts at the military stations, completing the near thousand miles to Agra in a third of the time it takes the ordinary column of foot soldiers."

"What will be their first halt then?" I asked, seeking to sound but idly curious.

"Daulatabad, undoubtedly," he told me. "A wondrous fort in the sky, perched on top of a towering needle of rock that rises sheer from the plain. It was the southernmost point of Akbar's advance until now his grandson builds the fort of Ahmednagar."

"How far is this Daulatabad?"

"A three-day march on foot," he answered. "But change your mind, young man, and come north with me. I heard from the cavalcade that a military foot-party comes through from Ahmednagar in some ten days' time. I intend to put myself under their protection."

I pretended to give this some thought, but already my mind was made up. To wait ten days in my present seething state was unthinkable. No, I decided, I would go on that very night. I therefore privily bought chapatties from the serai-keeper—large flat leathery cakes that rolled into a bundle which I tied to my back, and I filled my drinking vessel with water and slung it about my neck, and when all were asleep I stole forth and set foot firmly to the north. Ladies, I bethought me, could not possibly be expected to ride a thousand miles without long halts. Somewhere I would overtake them.

All that night I marched at a swift military pace, pausing only to rest briefly at long intervals before pressing on. I was unshod, but this I found to be of little hindrance, but rather the contrary, for by now my feet were as hardened as the toughest leather. When dawn came I sought the shelter of a clump of bushes clear of the road, and slept well into the day. Awakened, I ate and drank sparingly and then set off again.

But, fast as I marched, cutting the three-day journey to two, they had gone on by many hours when I reached Daulatabad, and, exhausted, I was fain to rest there for a full day before continuing. It was, as the guru had told me, a wondrous place. The rock on which it was built was a perfectly symmetrical natural column, a bare quarter-mile in girth, but soaring sheer to its needle-pointed summit a clear four hundred feet, its sides bare and weather-polished granite. The fort which surmounted it was perforce tiny and insignificant, and there was no exterior way up to it, but I knew from the guru that there was a winding passage inside the column, hewn from the living rock, and many chambers and gun emplacements led off it, with embrasures from which large-calibered cannon could sweep the surrounding plain. From the lower chambers a well had been dug sheer down into the bowels of the earth, for use in case of prolonged siege. The upward-winding passage bristled with secret traps and pitfalls for the undoing of attackers, and there were said to be hidden loopholes from which sections of it could be covered by musket and arrow. There were also chutes in the roof from which boiling oil and molten lead could be poured down. But these inner precautions were seldom likely to be called upon, because the base of the column was surrounded by three high battlemented walls, one within the other, and two wide moats fed by natural springs and accordingly never dry in the most torrid weather, and the only way in was across closely guarded drawbridges and through the stoutest gates.

The thriving, bustling village was set outside these three walls, and only Mogul troops, officials and their families were permitted to cross the drawbridges.

This, I bethought me as I regarded it, must be the most impregnable fort in the world.

On again I went that night, deeming it better to travel in the cool of the dark hours and to rest in the heat of the day. The country was now changing in character, as here the road was leading down from the high and barren Deccan Plateau to the lower plain of Central India. The jungle was becoming more dense and there were more streams, for which I was thankful, albeit most of these were now reduced to the merest trickle, but I could tell from their deep-scoured banks that they must have been raging torrents in the monsoon season.

Twice during that night I heard the coughing growl of a panther, and once the distant roar of a tiger, and I would have given much to have had the means of making fire, for a lighted torch of tinder-like kikar wood, I had been told, was the surest means of keeping wild animals at bay.

I was thankful indeed when dawn broke the next morning, the more so when I found myself close to a small village. Boys were driving goats and cattle out to graze from a thorn-surrounded compound, and I was relieved to see that my appearance caused them neither alarm nor surprise. They returned my salaam gravely and politely, as is the wont of Indian children, and went their way chattering among themselves in Hindustani I understood perfectly, so I boldly entered the village and asked of an old man if I could buy food with the few remaining copper coins I had left. He seemed greatly put out at my request and led me at once to his hut where, at a fire in front of it, his wife was preparing their simple morning meal, but he would have none of my coins, begging me to eat my fill and pressing me to great drafts of sweet and fresh milk.

Let me at this point of my chronicle repeat once more with all the earnestness at my command, that the simple Indian villager is the most courteous and generous host I have ever encountered in the length and breadth of my travels, and his welcome is as warm for pauper as for prince. My heart warms within me as I think back upon them.

As we ate we talked, and I, not having the stomach to lie to this old man, merely told him that I had business to the north and was walking to Agra. He was far too polite to question me upon this, but he seemed greatly concerned for my safety, telling me that no prudent man traveled this road alone, and especially at night. He begged of me to rest with them until a party of Mogul troops came through, as was the custom, but I assured him that I was too poor for any self-respecting dacoit to bother with me, and that my business brooked no delay. I asked him then about the cavalcade and learned that they were now but one march ahead of me, having rested at this village at this time the day before. Thanking these kind and gentle people as graciously as lay in my power, I took my leave and went on, promising at least to heed his words about marching alone at night.

I saw nor heard no other soul that morning, but when the sun was high in the sky behind me, I overtook a strange and motley gathering.

They were Indian gypsies, not greatly differing from any I had seen in Europe except that they were somewhat darker in complexion and wore fewer garments, though those they did were just as garishly hued. The men wore kerchiefs over their neck-long hair, and voluminous pantaloons held in place with brilliant sashes. The women were arrayed in wide-belling skirts over a multiplicity of petticoats, with beaded bodices above bare midriffs, and they carried a fearsome load of barbaric silver necklaces, and wore ornaments in their ears, and silver anklets with bells attached on their feet, which tinkled musically as they walked straight-backed and proudly. Many naked brown children played and gamboled in the dust of the road, and they had a host of animals with them—ponies and donkeys carrying their chattels, goats and sheep, two muzzled bears being led in chains, and a score or more of scabrous yellow dogs which set up a great outcry and bid fair to tear me to pieces as I approached.

They viewed me with some curiosity but were civil enough when they saw my lowly state. There were some thirty of them, if one counted the children, strolling entertainers—tumblers, clowns, jugglers and musicians—such as I had often seen before, though they had been discouraged by the church authorities in Goa. They moved at a pace slower than that at which I had been marching, but I was glad of their company and I asked their leader, a huge man with the muscles of an acrobat, if I might fall in with them for some part of their journey. This he readily agreed to, and I walked beside him for many miles, vastly diverted by his stories and by the antics of his band who seemed at all times to behave as if the eyes of an audience were upon them, playing on native lutes and dug-duggi drums, singing songs that were bawdy and lewd in the extreme but withal very amusing, turning cartwheels and handsprings, climbing trees and pretending to scratch like monkeys, and cutting similar capers which I thought at first were for their own and my entertainment, until I saw their leader's stern and critical eye upon them and realized that this was but practice of their arts.

We rested that night at a village, and the troupe erected their tattered tents on the outskirts and sent boys through the market place beating drums and extolling the wonders of the spectacle that would be unfolded before the eyes of the populace later. Everyone, down to the smallest children, worked with diligence and feverish energy, and to me fell the task of collecting bundles of neem-wood from the jungle and setting them in a circle round an open space that was to be the stage, then these were lighted so that they cast their illumination over the scene.

I had seen circuses, routs, masques, plays and divers other diversions in many parts of the world, but never before one like this. Every man, woman and child of the village was there to witness it, and a wondrous enthusiastic audience they were. I warrant Will Shakespeare himself could not have asked for a better at the Globe. They started with a wild dance by the women, which made up in graceful abandon what it sadly lacked in modesty, for the

handsome hussies were all but naked, much to the noisy content of
the male beholders; then came fire-eaters and men who balanced in
blood-chilling manner upon the points of sharp swords, and one
who wrestled with the unmuzzled bears. Then there was a break in
the performance while the leader, who was named Gahan, ha-
rangued the audience about the next part of the performance, of
which what they had already seen was but a tithe. While this pro-
ceeded, all others, including myself, went round with gourds ex-
horting the audience to contribute lavishly to the collection. After
that came jugglers and tumblers and clowns, then another break and
a collection—and so it continued far into the night.

While all this was afoot, the older women of the troupe were
preparing a vast repast of baked meats, and when the torches had
burned down and the villagers had sought their huts, we repaired to
the camp and sat in a circle round a fire. We, the collectors, went
before Gahan and rendered to him our harvest of small coins, and he
was amazed at the weight of mine, cursing his own people for
thieves and rogues who secreted part of their collection in their
mouths and other privy parts, and avowing that I, a stranger, was
the only honest one among them. Even so I was greatly surprised by
the large amount of money that Gahan locked away in a stout iron
box from which he was seldom far distant, and I calculated on this
basis that poor as was their appearance, and rough their manner of
living, they must have been very rich indeed.

Gahan invited me to sit at his right hand and he saw that my
platter and drinking vessel were kept brimful, and he invited me to
stay with them at least until they reached Agra, where they intended joining with other gypsy bands to form a vast circus to
perform in that great city for the wild celebrations that followed
the Moslem fast of Mohorram, which is akin to the Christian one of
Lent, but is marked by even greater austerities. I was a strong and
lusty man and withal honest, he told me, and one whose services he
could use, and when I took my quittance it would be with my fair
share of the contents of the iron box. I gladly accepted his offer,
for although I knew I might no doubt travel faster alone, this way I
was assured of my daily bread, earned rather than begged, and
would have a competence in my pouch at the end of the journey.
Gahan loudly announced this to the troupe, and those friendly and

generous souls welcomed me right royally to their midst, pledging me again and again in the palm toddy to which they were very much addicted, until I was even tipsier than they.

I awoke next morning as the sun rose, feeling that goblins within my skull were beating upon my brain with sledge hammers, to find that I was lying beneath a gaudy patchwork quilt with a sleeping woman. I was greatly troubled for I feared that I had thus spoiled my promising start with the troupe, but she awoke as I tried to creep from under the quilt, and sat up and looked at me. She was a comely wench, raven-haired and flashing-eyed and most lissome of form, who had danced and sung ballads the night before most pleasingly. I mumbled that I had no doubt strayed by mistake in the night, and begged her forgiveness. She threw back her head and laughed, showing me a flash of dazzling white teeth.

"A likely story," she scoffed. "You stray in the night? You were too drunk even to crawl. I had to drag you here by main force."

At this I was even more troubled and I asked where her husband might have been.

She shrugged. "The Dutchmen hanged him on the coast six months ago and more," she said carelessly. "The fool tried to steal a bolt of silk in the bazaar in broad daylight."

I expressed my sympathy but she merely laughed again.

"It saved me the trouble of knifing him myself one night," she said. "He drank too much, beat me too often, and was no use under the quilt." She looked at me appraisingly. "I hope I have not chosen unwisely again."

Never before or since had I felt at such a loss. I started to mouth and stammer my excuses, but she would have none of them. She rose from the ground, sinuous and graceful as a she-leopard, so scantily clad that she would have been cloaked in a yellow smock and haled before the Inquisition in Goa, took me by the hand and led me to the tent of Gahan, who was just awakening and bellowing for something wherewith to slake his burning thirst. He glared up at us through bloodshot eyes.

"This one will do," said the girl coolly.

"And high time, you masterless trollop," grunted Gahan. He turned to me. "Your name?"

"Gil," I answered. "But please hear my plea——"

But he cut me short. "The baggage is yours," he said.

In vain I pleaded that I was not a free man, but he seemed not to hear me.

"As a widow, she has the choosing from among all unattached men within the troupe," he told me. "Our laws are simple, but very binding while you remain with us. For your part, you may not make advances to another woman within the tribe; for hers, she stops making eyes at all other men. She will do as you tell her, and half of her share from the iron box is yours. If you beat her after the hour of sunset, it must not be in such a place or position from whence her outcries might disturb the rest of others. Her late husband's tent now belongs to you. Take her away. We start the march when the rim of the sun clears the top of yonder tree."

Dazed and bewildered I suffered myself to be led away by this shameless hussy.

I said, "Since the halter is already around my neck, it would be seemly if I at least knew your name."

"Parvani," she told me. "And now let us get the tent struck and ready to be loaded on the pack donkey. Gahan is always short-tempered after a carouse, and hates to be delayed."

I marched all that day in a state of great confusion. Yesterday I had stumbled casually upon this tribe; today I was married into it.

"But the Devil take it," I muttered to myself. "It is not yet consummated, and I know of no law to keep me here while I still have the use of my feet."

I accordingly started to stride out longer and faster until I had passed the head of the troupe and was eventually round a bend of the road from them and out of sight. Had we then been marching through jungle I would, without hesitation, have taken to the undergrowth and lain hidden until this worrisome crew had passed on, but here, as luck would have it, was only a line of stunted trees each side of the road, with bare open plain thereafter, so my escape, if I was to make it, would have to depend upon my legs alone.

But it was not to be. I had not gone very far when I heard a clatter of hooves behind me, and she arrived in a cloud of dust astride a swift pony, grinning impishly. Thereafter she kept me in sight.

There was no village, and consequently no performance that night, but we camped on the banks of a large river, and the tired gypsies went quietly and soberly to their tents as darkness descended upon us. Once again I harbored thoughts of escape, this time by swimming downriver and hiding until the troupe had marched on, but I must confess that after I had eaten I felt a great weariness upon me and a consequent disinclination to drive my tired limbs farther. I accordingly bathed in the stream and then sought privacy under a tree well outside the circle of firelight.

But I might just as profitably have bid the sun rise in the west. I was dropping into slumber when she arrived with her quilt, and like me she was fresh bathed from the stream and had combed her wondrous hair out into a cloud, and perfumed herself with sandalwood and jasmine. And she was very beautiful.

And I was but human . . .

That was the pattern of the march thereafter. Gahan knew the road and planned accordingly. One day a short march and a performance; the next and perhaps the next, a long march and a quiet camp in the wilderness. I came to know this man and greatly to admire him, for he kept tight discipline over this unruly band. He punished, when it was necessary, swiftly and rigorously, usually in the form of a hearty beating with a split bamboo, but he was scrupulously just and, I was told by Parvani, he paid from the box fair and square to the last copper pice. The performance never became dull and irksome, for he was always dreaming up and trying new acts and capers—sometimes a show in mime, sometimes a short play skillfully performed by the troupe without one word being written, but told to them line by line by Gahan as we marched, heard back, corrected, trimmed and polished until, had the work been in English, it could have held its own on any stage in London.

I was always in demand for parts because he delighted to use Dutch and Portuguese characters, and he considered that I had seen enough of them to simulate their ways to perfection. And I must confess that I greatly enjoyed this foolery and, more important, drew profit from it because I was not only perfecting my Hindustani while I was doing this, but also picking up rather more than a smattering of other native languages also, including their own "gypsy bolee," which, Gahan informed me, was spoken by his people throughout India and right across Asia into Europe, where it formed the basis of that which we called Romany. Gahan, like the rest of them, could not read or write, but never have I met a more widely informed man.

But if I enjoyed the company of Gahan, Parvani fast proved another matter altogether. She was perverse, impudent, arrogant and sometimes downright evil-tempered. This last I welcomed at first because it gave me reason to avoid her during the day and even on occasion to drive her off with a stick and reviling. With the night, however, always came reconciliation, try as I would to fend it off, because she could be sweet, tender and very penitent when it suited the minx, and I found it increasingly difficult to hold out against her. She could be generous too, as I had cause to reflect upon with a cold shudder one night.

We had had a longer march than usual that day and it happened to coincide with a village and a performance. We were dusty and sweat-begrimed, and the gypsies all bathed in a stream, as did I, before proceeding to the market place, for they were most fastidious when they appeared before an audience. But whereas they were enabled to change their clothes after their bathe, I was not because I possessed only those in which I stood up. Parvani, however, produced a wondrous soft white shirt and pantaloons and a gaily-hued turban which she pressed upon me, and when, arrayed more smartly than I had been for many days, I preened myself in them at the performance, she told me casually that they were the garments in which her late husband had been hanged, he being a man of great conceit whenever appearing at a public function.

✧✧ 24

AND now we were approaching Agra, and the winter being well upon us the days were crisp, clear and bracing, and the nights struck cold so that all were well content to seek the tents rather than sleep in the open as had been usual heretofore. Never did a prisoner look forward to his release with greater longing than I, for Parvani was making my life intolerable. She was a lustful woman, insatiable in her demands, with a temper like a fiend if they were in any way gainsaid, and withal she was very jealous. If I were out of her sight for more than a few minutes she came to seek me, and if I dared but to return the polite greeting of another woman, her wrath knew no bounds. The normal remedy for this would, of course, have been to take a split bamboo to the baggage and beat her soundly as the occasion warranted, but this I could not bring myself to do, and she knew it and took full advantage of it.

In vain the other men of the troupe counseled me to take a strong hand to her, but I resolved to bear things as best I could until Gahan paid me my quittance, and then to put as much distance between myself and this virago as possible as soon as we arrived in Agra.

I shall long remember my first sight of that magnificent city. It is built on the banks of the mighty River Jumna, which sweeps across the breadth of India to join, far to the east, with the sacred River Ganges. The fort that Akbar had built here dwarfed those of both Ahmednagar and Daulatabad, being a city within itself, containing many great palaces and mosques whose marble domes and minarets soared high above the massive surrounding walls, and to one side of it was then in process of being built the most beautiful edifice I have ever seen before or since. It was a wondrous temple of white marble, inlaid with precious stones—agates, jaspers, jade, bloodstones and amethysts—in designs of exquisite intricacy, the whole being surrounded by marble lakes, fountains and terraced gardens. Gahan told me that it had been built by Shah Jahan, ostensibly to the glory of Allah but in reality as the tomb of his favorite wife, Muntaz. This was the Crown Palace, or, in the native language, the Taj Mahal.

We fell in with other gypsy bands on the outskirts of the city and made a huge combined camp, and there was much wassailing and singing throughout that first night, while Gahan conferred with the other leaders on the form the circus should take. I would fain have left them there and then but Gahan begged me stay with them until they broke up at the end of the fair some four days later, and I could not forbear to do so in view of his great kindness to me this last month. I did, however, beg one day's grace from him to go about my private business in the city, and to this he readily agreed.

Rejoicing in my freedom I set off towards the fort, but I had not gone far when I heard the baggage call shrilly after me, and her feet pattered along the road behind me. In vain I pleaded, promised and cursed her, but she attached herself to me and refused to leave me until, in desperation, I belabored her mightily with my staff and left her lying at the side of the road shrieking and spitting vile insults after me, much to the amusement of the passers-by. Greatly relieved at this temporary surcease I went on over the drawbridge into the city.

It was a wondrous sight that met my eyes as I emerged from the sally port. The walls must have greatly exceeded a mile in circuit, and were surmounted at frequent intervals by soaring towers. The roadway round the parapet was wide enough to allow four horsemen to gallop abreast, and they were protected on the outer side by high crenelated battlements which dropped sheer to the wide moat which was really a swiftly flowing branch of the main river, thus making the fort and city an island. The whole mighty structure was of a rich red sandstone, from paving stones to battlements, but the palaces and mosques within were of white and pink marble. The streets were wide and all led to an immense central square, and in the spaces between the houses were fountains and small beautiful gardens. The shops and stalls which lined the streets were stocked with a variety of goods, the like of which I had never seen in such abundance before—silks of every color, carved ivory, gold and silver ornaments, jewels, damascened armor, swords that Toledo itself could not match, and boots and sandals of beautifully tanned leather. There were spices there which scented the air heavily but agreeably, and mounds of strange and exotic fruits, and over all the heavy perfume of roses, for Agra was a center for the manufacture of rose water and attar.

I walked round entranced, not only at the riches displayed in the bazaars, but also at the many and varied types who made up the population of this fascinating place. There were swaggering Mogul troops, Afghans and Sikhs, delicately featured Rajputs, Kashmirians and divers others to whom I could not at that time put a name. Yes, this, the southernmost of the Moguls' cities, as distinct from their purely military stations, was a place to quicken the interest and set fire to the imagination of the most cold-blooded.

I entered mosque after mosque and none gainsaid me, though my guise was that of a Hindu, and when I had explored them and marveled at the beauty of their architecture, I mounted from the central square towards the battlements which were reached by flights of marble steps leading up between high-walled gardens. The absence of townspeople should have told me that these were privy parts, but so bemused was I at the grandeur of the place that I did not pause to think.

It was quiet here, the silence broken only by the musical plash of fountains playing unseen behind the high walls on either side; so quiet that the voice came to me quite clearly.

"Thee cart sart on thee mart," intoned a female.

"No, no," said another woman's voice. "Listen again, Naira: the cat sat on the mat—not 'cart—sart—mart,' " and much giggling ensued.

And so I, who had been walking the streets like a ploughboy in London for the first time, wondering where first to begin my search, had come by the veriest chance right to her. I did not hesitate. I walked back from the wall and then turned and took a run and a spring at it, and my fingers found the top. I drew myself up onto the parapet and looked down into the garden, but could see naught of humans although it was clear that the women were in a tiny marble pavilion the other side. I lowered myself down and eagerly crossed towards it. I quickly ran round in search of door or window for there was no opening in the wall facing me.

Her back was towards me but there was no mistaking that arrow-straight figure even in the richly embroidered sari that enfolded it, nor the golden glory of hair that surmounted it, for now the black stain was all removed.

I said, "Cloda!" and all my heart was in my voice.

But that was all I said for a very long time thereafter, for sitting cross-legged facing her was a beautiful young Indian girl, scantily clad and unveiled. She looked up at me past Cloda, her eyes widening with terror, and I saw her mouth opening long before her piercing shriek transfixed me. Cloda whirled on me.

"Go, you fool—GO!" she shouted. But it was already too late. I barely saw the huge bearded figure that bounded from a divan in the shadows at the back of the pavilion, but I heard the swish of his scimitar as it clove the air a bare hairsbreadth in the rear of my rump as I raced back for the wall. I leapt like a stag for the parapet but felt my pantaloons catch in the thorns of a rose bush that clung to it, and my frantically clawing fingers missed the top by inches. I fell backwards and heard again the swish as the sword passed my head in a sweep that would have had it off my shoulders like a turnip off a hop-pole had the wielder not been so blinded with rage. Flat on my back I kicked upwards, and both my road-hardened feet took him 'twixt the legs like twin battering-rams, and since there is naught else even the strongest man can do when so foully attacked in that particular region, he howled in agony, dropped his sword and rolled on the ground clutching at his connubials convulsively. Had he been my only adversary the day would have been mine, but others were bounding into the garden—big fat blubbery men as black as sea coals, who twittered in high birdlike voices, and they fell upon me before I could once more leap for the wall. I fought like a wildcat but it was hopeless before it ever started, and I believe that they would have hewn me limb from limb with the miscellany of weapons that they carried had it not been for the bearded one, who paused in his dolorous bellowing long enough to tell them not to kill me now and thereby spoil his satisfaction later. I was thereupon picked up bodily by the black men and borne rapidly from the garden through various lanes and passages, and hurled into a dungeon in the shadow of the high perimeter wall.

The black men stood in a half-circle and regarded me quite kindly, giggling and twittering in their peculiar voices in a language that I understood far too well for my peace of mind. What the "Great One" would undoubtedly cause to be done to me when recovered from the outrage to his privy parts, would be, they were certain, an entertaining diversion at the fair the next day. They themselves appeared to bear me no ill will whatsoever, but rather the contrary, as it appeared from their conversation that they took a malicious delight in the "Great One's" discomfort, they being unencumbered since early boyhood with such impedimenta themselves. They informed me that I had offended twice in matters which called only for the death penalty, in that I had kicked a prince of the royal house of Akbar in the cods, and had gazed upon his youngest, fairest and favorite wife in the harem garden while she was unveiled. I was thus the very Devil of a fellow in their eyes and they seemed quite regretful at the horrible death I was to meet in the central square tomorrow, though this did not prevent their going into the minutest details of it, much to my grave discontent. I tried to divert them from this subject by asking after Cloda, but they seemed both ignorant of and uninterested in her. She was a foreign woman, they told me, and hence a whore, and she had been brought from the south to teach the ladies of the harem various foreign languages—another of the mad whims of Shah Jahan and one which was most distasteful to the more orthodox of the nobles, though none dare disobey him. This but confirmed what I had guessed previously and did not add to the sum of my knowledge. I tried to persuade them to take a message to her but they recoiled in horror from the very suggestion. Eunuchs they might be, they informed me haughtily, but they were also men of honor with a duty to their master, and besides, I had naught wherewith to bribe them.

I lay the rest of that day in the dungeon reflecting bitterly on my fate and seeing no escape from it, and nightfall brought no surcease except for an uneasy slumber which came to me through sheer exhaustion in the early hours.

I woke as something fell onto my face, then something more, and I was aware of small pebbles striking me, and an urgent whispered voice coming to me from the grille above my head.

"Gil! Gil! Wake up, you great lout!" the voice said. I fumbled my way to the wall and strained upwards but could not reach the hands she thrust to me through the bars. Eagerly I called her name, but received only a torrent of abuse back from her, though I detected a sob in her voice.

"You fool!" she berated me. "What ill star led you back across my path?"

"To see if you were alive, you ungrateful bitch," I answered. "And much good it has done me."

"But to invade a harem garden!" she cried. "Haven't you been long enough in this country to know the danger of that?"

"If I hadn't, it has been brought home to me now," I said dolefully. "Unless you can help me I am to be publicly castrated and then flayed alive."

"A pity the former had not been done to your father," she said spitefully. "As for helping you, what do you think I have been trying to do these past hours—without profit? I have besought the gentleman you so foully assaulted, with tears and entreaties, but he has driven me away."

"Then at least smuggle me a pistol or a knife," I begged, "so that I may make some bid for escape or, if that fails, make an end to myself with what dignity I can still muster."

"Fie upon you, Gil Bardock," she answered, "even to think of that coward's way out while there is yet life in that hulking carcass of yours. No, I have still one hope left, and on that I pin everything."

"What is that?" I asked, though with little faith.

"There is a Jesuit Father here with a small mission of attendant priests, though unfortunately he has been on a journey to Sikandra and returns only in the morning," she said. "I shall have audience with him and beg his intercession."

"And the Devil's chance there'll be of his according it," I answered moodily. "Why should he help *me*—a heretic?"

"The Jesuits have great influence with the Moguls," she told me, "and few nobles would disregard a plea for clemency, for fear of bringing the Emperor's wrath down upon themselves. This particular priest is a man of gentleness and great learning. He had long discourse with me on my arrival here, and supervises my teaching of the harem ladies. I know he would help me if I asked him. I shall wait upon his arrival and—" she broke off suddenly. "I must go," she whispered urgently. "I hear the guards stirring."

I remained for the rest of the hours of darkness a prey to alternating fits of wild hope and deep despondency, with the latter gaining fast over the former until, with the morning light, I was convinced nothing now could save me from my dreadful fate.

Giggling shrilly in the manner of their kind, the eunuchs came for me eventually and bound me fast with ropes, allowing only my feet to be free, and then they led me from the prison and down to the central square.

How different that enchanted place looked to me now. A huge concourse was already gathered, and they set up a wild baying as our sorry party arrived and threaded through to the high wooden stage erected in the middle of the open space. I was pushed up the steps and then came face to face with the horrible creature who was to be my executioner. He was a huge coal-black Nubian, also a eunuch, naked except for an abbreviated loincloth, shaven of head and wearing a ghastly red mask, and in his hand he held a knife similar to that with which pigs were gelded on my estates in Yorkshire. My legs buckling beneath me with terror, I sought to bolster what remnants of courage were left to me by one last act of defiance, and I cleared my almost dry mouth and made shift to spit in his face as he approached me, which pitiful act seemed to meet with the loud approval of the crowd. He spun me round and stood me with my back to a post and bound me to it, then pulled my feet apart until I was standing wide astride, and tied them to two smaller posts.

In the forefront of the multitude I could see Gahan and many other of the gypsies looking up at me compassionately, and two of them were holding the shrieking Parvani who was trying to break away from them and fight her way to the scaffold. Then an officer mounted the ladder, bearing a scroll, and he held up his hand for silence, though the gesture availed him nothing, and he read in sonorous Hindustani the catalogue of my wrongdoings, which took an unconscionable time, thank God, for it was while he was still reading, that a second officer came hurrying through the crowd, clearing his way with the flat of his sword, and he called up to those on the scaffold to hold, because it appeared a short respite had been ordered. Half the crowd, led by the gypsies, yelled their acclamation at this, but the other half, disappointed of the promised spectacle, were equally loud in their disapproval.

Near dead, I was untied and lowered to the ground and delivered to the eunuchs who had brought me hence, and escorted back to my former prison, and there I was left for the remainder of that day, once more torn between hope and despair, until I was near mad.

That night they came for me again, but this time I was not bound. They led me from the prison and conveyed me quickly up toward the main palace and through a door into the lower portions of it, and it seemed to me that the eunuchs were doing it privily and with a desire not to attract attention, and I wondered what further foul torments were before me.

They hurried me along dark passages past doors which were unbolted for our ingress and bolted again by unseen hands after we had passed, and there was much hurried whispering of countersigns, and all seemed to be done with the greatest caution and secrecy. Then finally they admitted me to a bare stone chamber which was dimly lighted by a single guttering tallow dip, and I stared at it agape—for it burned in front of a small altar that was surmounted by a crucifix. Protestant though I was, I sank down on my knees and near sobbed with relief and gratitude, and I was in this posture when a small door beside the altar opened, and Cloda came through.

I rose to my feet and went towards her impulsively but she held me off with outstretched hand.

She said, "Save your bleating for later, you oaf. You are not through the forest yet—and I have brought peril upon many good men in my efforts to save you."

"Have you brought danger to yourself?" I asked, troubled. But she told me to hold my peace and added many epithets which should not have been uttered in that sacred place.

"Listen to me," she commanded. "Sher Safaraz, the high officer you attacked, has not pardoned you. He lies sick of a grave rupture and none dare approach him for the signing of the warrant which Shah Jahan insists upon before sentences of death are carried out, but you may take it from me that you'll be dealt with as he intends just as soon as he can take his hands from the pit of his belly long enough to hold a quill and make his mark upon the scroll. In the meantime you have been brought here by much bribery and a forged release warrant which cannot but be discovered in the morning."

"Turn me loose," I begged, "before I bring trouble upon any more."

"To be caught again with daylight?" she snapped. "I know you, Master Wily Bardock-Bemforth. You cannot keep free of trouble for long, and when it finds you, you bring it on all around you. No, this time you go far from this place, and far from me—and once having put you upon your road, may I never set eyes on you again."

But with my deliverance my manhood was returning to me, and in spite of my gratitude to her I was stung by her injustice.

"The Devil take you, you baggage," I swore at her. "Twice I have delivered you from positions you were not in love with—and without prosy lectures—"

"And twice you've left me in the lurch and run off when danger threatened," she flashed.

"That's a lie," I shouted. "I left you the first time because that seemed the wisest counsel. The second time *you* left me."

"But I came back for you," she answered. "You wanted to run away and leave those poor people to perish when the Marathas and Moguls met. I went on through the night towards Ahmednagar, and I came to a guardpost and I warned the soldiers there of what was about to befall, and they conveyed me swiftly to Salahbar Khan, who gave me his promise that when they struck they would spare all pilgrims, and deal only with the soldiers. And he kept his promise because not one pilgrim was hurt in the ambush. But when I came among them to look for you they told me you had already thrown in your lot with the fighting men."

"Another lie," I raged at her. "I was marching with them by force because I had tried to remain behind to search for *you.*"

"I don't believe you," she told me icily. "It was ever thus with you. When danger threatens, drop all and run, and Devil take those who can't run with you. If that fails, throw in your lot with the stronger side—"

"Cloda, listen to me," I pleaded, but she cut me short again.

"This is the way of it now," she said impatiently, "and if you value your hide—which God knows you do—you'll listen to what I say carefully. Father John, the Jesuit, is a true Christian and a saint, and he is on his way to Delhi to the court of Shah Jahan at the head of a small mission. He has consented, in answer to my pleading, though sorely in conflict with his conscience, to your going with him—in the guise of one of his priests."

The nobility of this good man near took my breath away, the more so since I had been bred to a hatred and distrust of papists in general and of this particular order more especially. Cloda seemed to follow my thoughts, though she misinterpreted them.

"And don't look down your hypocritical nose, either," she snapped. "Most of the troubles that afflict the world today have their roots in such bigotry as yours."

In vain I swore that my emotions were ones of gratitude only, but she cut me short again and carefully instructed me in my behavior while traveling with this party, for, as she pointed out, although the priests would be aware of my false colors, the others with us would not, and any untoward move on my part would arouse suspicion and thus imperil people who were helping me at the greatest danger to themselves—then she left me as abruptly as she had arrived.

I sat on in that tiny chapel for some hours, shaken to the very depths of my being by the narrowness of my escape from that horrible fate, and wondering what lay before me, and how I could clear the doubts which now existed between this strange girl and myself, and I was not aware of the arrival of the priest until he stood over me.

He was clad in a long black cassock, and a cowl covered his head, but I could sense that he was an Indian, probably a dark Goanese. Without a word he held out towards me a bundle of garments which he signed to me to put on, and when I had done so I found I was arrayed as he—cassock and cowl and stout leather sandals, with cords and beads and a crucifix about my waist. He signed to me to sit before him in the light of the tallow dip, and he produced shears and a razor with which he clipped and shaved a tonsure on my head, then, bundling up my discarded native clothes he signed to me to follow him.

We emerged into a courtyard in the pale light of early dawn, and there the party awaited us—three other priests in addition to the one who escorted me, mounted upon sturdy mules. My mentor signed to me to mount another mule and we set out through the city to the main drawbridge where we were joined by a group of mounted Mogul soldiers and native bearers leading pack animals. Led by the tallest and most imposing of the priests, we crossed the bridge, receiving a most civil salute from the guard, and turned north along the high road. Once more I was progressing towards the Road—but once more I was leaving Cloda behind me, and my spirits sank accordingly.

I fell in with my clerical brethren, all of whom sat drooped in their saddles, their cowls over their heads, obviously deep in meditation, so I deemed it wise to follow their example, but, when well clear of the city, the priest who led us signaled me to trot up the short column and join him. I did so, and drew rein a respectful half-mule's length behind. He turned and looked at me.

"How now, you randy young bastard?" he greeted me. "So that troublesome organ has been leading you into peril again, eh? And you near lost it this time. If ever a blanket-tiger needed a Guardian Angel, it's you."

✧✧ 25

I NEAR fell from my saddle in shocked dismay. He grinned wickedly at my widened eyes and sagging jaw.

"It was ever thus," I said bitterly when I was able to control my voice. "From the cursed griddle into the blistering fire."

"You ungrateful young whelp!" he cried. "Saved from a fate worse than death—literally—and you croak like a Puritan gospel-spouter. What ails you?"

"You," I told him. "I'd rather meet the Devil himself."

"Me that's looked after you like a mother?" he said indignantly. "Shame upon you, Gil Bardock. Tell me when I have ever done you ill."

"Your very presence does ill to whoever crosses your path," I told him. "You're a murderous, blaspheming ruffian."

Far from rousing his ire, my denunciation seemed to afford him the acutest merriment, and he bellowed with laughter. I turned in my saddle to see what effect this unseemliness was having on his fellow priests, but I need not have concerned myself. They all now had their cowls thrown back and were grinning broadly.

"So your companions also are bogus?" I remarked.

" 'Also' be damned," he retorted. "They may have false colors at their jack staffs, but I'm genuine. I've never been unfrocked, my lad. I beat the bishop who was coming to do it by the skin of my backside. I'm still licensed to put a pox on you by bell, book and candle—so keep a civil tongue in your head."

"You're not a Jesuit," I answered. "You're not even a Catholic."

"All things to all men," he laughed. "Judge not a wine by the daub upon the cask. But *you're* a bright one to be taking the poor old Angel to task, ain't you? Rigged out like a crow yourself, prior to that a blackamoor, running with the Portygooses, flirting with the Dutchmen, and a trail of cuckolded husbands behind you. *You* to talk about being bogus!"

And having no suitable answer for that, I had perforce to keep silence.

"Tell me what has befallen you since the Hollanders laid us aboard," he went on.

I told him curtly that I misliked the Dutch so had taken the first opportunity of escaping from them, and had wandered north, but that through ignorance I had trespassed into a harem garden in Agra and had so found myself in my present predicament.

He turned and gazed at me in mock admiration.

"How well such modesty becomes the very young," he said. "As *I* heard, you skipped with the chief Hollander's wife—just as you did from Goa, whereas for the harem junket, I am informed that you raged through that garden like a barley-fed cockerel through a barnyard, kicking in the conjugals all who sought to gainsay you."

In my mind I cursed Cloda for telling this blackguard so much that could redound to my disadvantage, but then reason told me that she was not to know, and that she had taken him at his face value when she pleaded with him to help me. In order to avoid further embarrassing questions I asked him for his own story, and he was nothing loath to tell it.

"Like yourself, I mislike the Dutch," he chuckled, "particularly when they're so poxily ill-mannered as to start building a bloody great gallows outside a man's cell window. I accordingly left them one dark night after feigning illness and cozening the guard inside to see what ailed me. His own knife through his gullet ailed *him*, and I departed for the jungle clad in his clothes and boots. My plan was to make for the north and to join up with the Mekranis once more, so I padded along the beach by night, lying up in the trees by day, and a pestilential time I had of it too, what with damned soldiers with dogs hunting for me by land, and their patrol ship skimming up and down by sea, and their threats of death and maiming to all fisherfolk who helped me or failed to report me." He sighed lugubriously.

"An Ishmaelite. Everybody's hand against me—and that jungle fruit purging the guts out of me. But Providence came to my aid in the form of these crows." He jerked his thumb over his shoulder at the other "priests." "Felons from the Portygoose prison at Marmagoa. They were clearing an area of jungle for a new trading post, over two hundred of them, but lightly guarded because they were shackled in groups. There was an armed dhow anchored offshore, and my mouth drooled as I regarded her from the shelter of the undergrowth. With her and a crew my troubles would be over. I could beat upcoast to the Mekrani country, doing a little profitable Middle Passaging on the way, and so arrive as a man of substance and not as one upon whom Fortune had been frowning—a very important point when dealing with the superstitious Mahounds.

"Well, I sat and pondered it for a whole day and a night, then I made my plan. I settled upon a party of six Goanese who looked stronger and of more spirit than the rest, for a pretty miserable crowd they were on the whole, and I made parley with them when they were in the jungle, and put my plan to them. Four were with me and two were timorous, but were soon prevailed upon to reconsider. With their levers and machetes we managed to sunder the chain that bound them together and we made off farther into the jungle and laid low until night. Then we heard commotion from the barracoons when the guards missed them, and the fools started to scour the undergrowth with torches and bloodhounds—but by this time we were swimming silently out through the dark lagoon to the dhow. There were only four men aboard her as an anchor watch, and these we dispatched before they even awoke, then we cut the cable and ghosted out on the ebbing tide before hoisting sail and making due west out to deep water."

He was silent for a long time, head bowed on his chest, swaying forward and backward in the saddle in unison with the clopping of his mule's hooves.

"I should have stuck to my original plan," he said at length. "Sailed in a wide arc through that empty ocean until I reached the Mekrani coast, and there set myself up again properly. But there were some casks of Oporto wine on that damned dhow—and me without a sup of strong drink for many a long day. Pot-valiant, I plumped for the shorter passage and stood inshore—and ran in with a Portygoose man-o-war—the *Santa Paola*, damn her blasted keel and keelson. She had the legs of us and obviously knew us for what we were, because she bore down upon us, all sails drawing and guns run out. I did the only thing possible and ran helter-skelter for the beach and hard up on the sand. She, being of greater draft, had to heave to a quarter of a mile offshore and lower boatloads of soldiers —so we made it for the deep jungle with the howling devils on our tails, and we kept running until we had outstripped them, they being encumbered with heavy armor.

"Well, there I was back where I started—or perhaps not quite, for at least I now had a crew even if I didn't have a ship, and we were clothed and armed, and with a modicum of fortune a man can Middle Passage it as well on land as on the briny. So that is what we settled upon.

"Fortunately I had fixed my position on the dhow's charts and I knew roughly where we were: on a portion of the coast near the island of Salsette, or Bombay as the natives call it. I remembered Lobo telling me that that was where you and he were making for when the storm overtook you and blew you south, and he said there was a high road leading to the interior. That seemed to answer my bill of requirements, so we sought this road and started upon it—and a poxy difficult one it was too, rising sheer up over the Western Ghats in a very short distance, which made the climb murderous.

"We came at last, after a march of ten days, to a small serai just short of the village of Nasik, and it was there that Amardo, that's that wicked swivel-eyed bastard tricked out as a lay-brother behind you, had his idea. The serai was in the keeping of an old Goanese, and there was nobody resting there at the time. Amardo said it might be a good plan to relieve the old man of his onerous duty and take it over ourselves—one of us acting as serai-keeper and the others laying up in the jungle, disguised as dacoits, so that when a pigeon worth the plucking came along we could descend on him and rob him—robbing the serai-keeper at the same time to avoid suspicion attaching to him. And a good ploy it seemed, and one that worked well for a time, for many fat Parsi and Hindu merchants tread that path, protected for the most part by chowkidars or armed watchmen, who would fire their pieces wildly into the air when attacked, and then run like frightened hares, leaving us to strip their masters at our ease.

"But we reckoned without those stinking, treacherous Porty-gooses. A caravan of merchants came through one day, guarded by the usual chowkidars, but when we came out of the jungle that night and called upon all to stand and deliver, by God they did. They delivered the contents of their muskets in amongst us and followed it up with a charge of swords and halberds that had *us* running like hares. Soldiers they were, disguised as bearers, chowki-dars and mule drivers. We got away by superior knowledge of the country thereabouts, but unfortunately we had to leave the booty we had collected, so there we were again, just as we had started."

"In short you were following the usual pattern of your ill-begotten ways," I said. "But tell me, what brought you to Agra in your present guise?"

"Devil take you for a spoiler of good stories," he swore. "Let me tell this my own way. We continued our march into the interior purely because we deemed it unhealthy to go back towards the 'Goosers. None of these crows had been up this way before, so they knew as little about it as I. Soon we were in parlous plight because the villages were few and far between, and the people of harder fiber than those with whom we had truck heretofore. At night they retired behind wooden palisades, and a man was like to get a charge of lead slugs in his guts if he ventured near in the hours of darkness. The serais were dangerous too, as we discovered at the very first one we visited. The keeper made us welcome, but Amardo overheard him dispatching a boy to summon soldiers from a nearby fort, because we answer to the description that had been put about by the 'Gooses, the long-nosed, interfering bastards. We got away in time, but we were nigh to starvation since all places of rest and refreshment were closed to us and we knew we were now being hunted. My crew was reduced to the three you now see, by this time. One had gone mad and tried to do for me, and I had to do for him. Another was bitten by a poisonous serpent and yet another gave up the ghost and refused to march another step. However, Providence came to our aid once again, just as I was thinking of lying down at the side of the road and doing likewise."

I said, "I am not a religious man, but your references to Providence frighten me. I wonder that this party is not struck by lightning at your blasphemy."

But he only smirked and winked. "Me and Providence is old friends," he said. "But you are interrupting again. As I was saying, I was near to throwing my hand in when we fell in with this clerical party, and what was that but the Divine Hand? The numbers were just right too—three priests and a lay-brother on mules, traveling in advance of their bearers and baggage by a couple of leagues or more. We presented a pitiful sight—and told an even more pitiful story—three devout Goanese and me, a good English Catholic, beset by bandits and left to die, and the good fathers took us at face value and befriended us. They were bound from Goa to Delhi, calling first at Agra, a mission sent at the request of Shah Jahan himself to explain the Gospels to him and his court—Father John, a Swiss, Father Francisco, Father Paolo and Brother Sancho—all Goanese. A white man and three crows in other words—and you question the hand of Providence!

"We made camp at the side of the road and waited for the bearers and baggage to arrive—a party of six with their pack animals, guarded, save the word, by four chowkidars. But as ill luck would have it, one of the chowkidars was a crow who had cause to remember us, seeing how we had shot him in the rump in a little foray earlier on at Nasik. He made great outcry, and Amardo pistoled him, whereupon the others betook themselves off after throwing down their muskets, which was lucky because we snatched them up and were able to drop them before they reached the cover of the jungle. That left only the priests and the bearers—the former busy praying, the latter kowtowing and wailing."

He beamed at me. "Surprise, young Randyblade. You often wearied me in the old days with your military discourses, but that much I remember—and commend. Well, after that it was plain sailing. We shaved our scalps and donned the habits—"

I felt sickness and horror churning at the bottom of my belly. "What had you done to the priests?" I asked.

"Don't interrupt," he snapped. "At the next serai we told the keepers that we had been attacked by dacoits and that our rascally chowkidars and bearers had run off." He choked with laughter.

"They were deeply grieved because word had been sent to all serais from Agra to afford us every aid and comfort on the road, so they provided us with fresh servants and a bloody cavalry escort. Now, let me make myself clear—our only thought at taking the cowl was to cover our identities until we reached a more hospitable region, but, as we progressed and met more and more high Mogul officers at the serais and forts, and realized how much the Mogols' protection meant, fresh ideas came to me. Why not? I said to myself. Better parsons than I had done it. Why, damn me, since Harry the Ram's time they've been backing and forthing between the two pastorates like battledore and shuttlecocks. So I applied myself diligently to Father John's books and parchments, and found my Latin none so bad for all its lack of use in latter years—and I engaged my clerical brothers in much argument and implanted in them some good if slightly unorthodox theology. And that was it. We arrived in Agra and were made most welcome, and even the fact that the Porty-goose ambassador to Agra was on the point of departure to Goa did not trouble me. I declared a holy retreat for myself and my brothers in thanksgiving for our safe journey, and I wrote a heart-warming letter to my superior in Goa, penned in my best Latin and sealed with Father John's seal in such a fashion that would defy detection —stroke for stroke copied from the good man's own diary—and I excused myself to the ambassador in case he should have known the real Father John previously, and sent him the letter for delivery when he arrived on the coast."

"How long do you think you will remain undiscovered, you foul blackguard?" I demanded hotly.

He tapped his forehead and winked. "As long as I continue to use this," he said smugly. "What could go amiss? I am in regular corre-spondence with my superior, whose good opinion of me grows apace. It would appear that the real Father John was little known in Goa, having but recently arrived there by the last galleon out from Europe. It would also appear that my alter ego was a scholar in German and English as well as Latin and Greek. So am I. As a matter of truth I am not unlike him in appearance—same stature and coloring—and blast my buttons and hide if I wouldn't chance my arm in a year or so by going to Goa, and I warrant nobody would know the difference. This climate changes one's appearance—

people die and faces are forgotten—and a name is but a name. No, I stepped into that saintly man's sandals at the direct intervention of Providence—and very comfortable they are."

"You besotted fool!" I cried. "You could not wear the easier yoke of the English church. Hypocrite and lying villain though you are, you could not hope to present to the world the austere exterior of a Jesuit for long before all the wickedness that is within you bursts forth and betrays you."

"If you had aught to wager, my young friend, I would accommodate you at the longest odds you care to name on that," he answered calmly. "I have no other priests to spy upon me here—real priests, that is." He jerked his head back at the others. "Those crows know which side their bread is buttered, and if they ever should forget they know damn well they'd be reminded—with a foot of cold steel atwixt their ribs one dark night."

"If they send up other priests from Goa—" I began.

"They won't," he said. "Not until I tell my superior that the time is ripe, and that time will be one of my own choosing—if it ever comes. You see, I know the whole ploy up here now, and what the Jesuits are after, so I tell 'em just what they want to hear."

"What are they after?" I demanded.

"The soul of Shah Jahan," he chuckled. "But the old fox has put a high price upon it."

"But Shah Jahan is a Moslem," I said.

"And the Devil was once an angel," he retorted. "It's all a matter of politics—on Shah Jahan's side, at least. Yes, he's a circumcised Moslem all right, though it rests lightly enough upon him. He drinks wine, which is forbidden by the Prophet, and it has been said that when hungry on campaign and there was little else to eat, he didn't turn up his nose at a well-roasted slice of pork on occasion. He is tolerant of all religions—scornful, if you like—though he realizes the necessity of them. Here, in this vast subcontinent, he rules over millions of Hindus, Buddhists, Jains, animists, who, combined, outnumber his Moslems many times over. He allows freedom to all, and hangs out of hand any of his soldiers who desecrate a temple or offer violence to a priest of any religion. You would think that that would endear him to all races and sects—but it doesn't. If he pats a Hindu on the head, his own Moslems join with the Buddhists and the other crows in murmuring. If he condescends to nod to a Buddhist, the Jains and the Hindus take umbrage and start stirring unrest. If he cried a pox upon the lot and professed atheism that would go up the noses of all of 'em. So what he wants is a comfortable neutral religion whose adherents are not numerous enough to be dangerous to the others, and who don't mind particularly if one or two of 'em are martyred from time to time. What better than Christianity? He knows that the Portygooses wield it very well on the coast. He knows that they are rich and that they have a knowledge of the sea and its ways, which he would dearly love his own people to master. Hindus and Moslems lose caste if they venture upon the *kala pani*, as they call the ocean. No, Christianity is the faith for Shah Jahan—and it's my task to lead, explain and mentor him. Once *he's* over, the nobles will follow. Once the nobles are in, the whole of the army will be baptized. After that it would be but a matter of time for the whole of the teeming millions out here. So you see the size of the task—and the prize." He chuckled. "I could be wearing a red hat in Rome yet."

"God forbid," I breathed fervently. "But what *is* your aim? Or are you merely living by the day?"

He rubbed his chin at that and appeared genuinely puzzled. "I don't know," he said. "And that is the truth. At first it *was* that—to live by the day, I mean—but then the very immensity of the thing took hold upon me. A man who could effect the conversion of millions would leave his name upon the tablets of time itself. And it *can* be done. From Father John's letters, and my correspondence with the superior, it would appear that Shah Jahan is more than halfway over already—just as his grandfather Akbar was once. Two things fret him—open avowal of the infallibility of the Pope, and the eschewing of multiple marriage. He says he wouldn't object to kowtowing to a *dead* Pope, but he'd lose face if he did it to a live one. The Dutch heard about this and sent a Protestant pastor up hellfor-leather to say that they could accommodate him and gladly—but he was a joyless and long-faced Puritan and his brand of religion lacked the color that these people out here demand, so he was sent packing. And anyhow, the question of polygamy remains. You can't expect a man who has had a thousand to settle down with one. Ah well, let's see what I can offer him when I meet him."

"You have not met him yet?"

"Not yet. He remains more and more in Delhi these days."

"What happens if this foul plot of yours fails?" I asked.

"Feather my nest and pass on to other things, I expect," he answered. "But it needn't fail now that I have a helper."

"A helper?" I queried, staring at him.

"Of course," he laughed, clapping me on the shoulder. "Why do you think I've been explaining all this to you, young Gil?"

❖ 26

"NEVER in a thousand years!" I cried. "Ungodly though I may be, and a Protestant to boot, I'll not be a party to *that* sort of blasphemy."

"Have you thought of the alternative?" he asked.

"I can guess," I muttered.

He showed his first sign of anger. "Don't try and becozen *me*, you bloody young cockchafer," he snarled. "*You're* not of the stuff of which martyrs are made. You have only one specific against danger or discomfort. You run. You've been running all your miserable life, leaving in the lurch those who have befriended you. Well now there's nowhere to run to. You've reached the end of your rope . . . and that end is round your neck and my hand is on the other. Look sideways just once or develop an itch in your feet, and by God I'll swing you as high as Haman, with a touch of Inquisitional fire at the soles of those same feet to speed you on your way to hell."

He cleared his throat noisily and spat. "*You'll* not be a party to it," he mimicked. "Who in the name of perdition are *you* to look down your damned nose, eh? Listen to me. You've puked and whined 'blasphemous' and 'ungodly' at me until my stomach has heaved. All right, that I accept, but this dream of mine is something which transcends the oaths and cursing that come so readily to my lips. This is something greater than ecclesiastical cant and claptrap.

Don't you realize what I am going to do? I'm going to change the whole course of history of a land twice the size of Europe. A conquest wider than that of Alexander the Great, a conquest of the mind rather than one of the sword. I've offered you a part in that conquest, damn you, and you have the effrontery to refuse it. I don't need your help. I don't need anybody's help, but every master can find use for a mate, every prophet for a disciple, to do his deviling and lickspittling for him while he is engaged on the greater issues. So that's what *you* are, a bloody disciple, see? And you'll tell your beads and look holy when I pass you the order, and you'll keep your eye on those crows back there just as they'll be keeping *their* eyes on *you*. You'll act as my secretary and amanuensis, and when the flock are not watching you, you can live high and soft. In short, behave yourself and do as I bid you, and you'll have everything to gain and nothing to lose but your hangman's knot. On the other hand look as if you are *thinking* of playing me false and by God you'll have cause to curse your mother for bearing you. Do you understand me?"

There was nothing to do except to nod, for now I knew that what I had long suspected was indeed the truth. This man was mad. Completely and utterly mad.

As if to confirm this, his mood underwent another lightning change, and once more he was all joviality and boisterous good humor.

"That's it, my flash cull!" he roared. "I knew you'd see things my way. Just you ride along lee-to-weather of the old Angel and you'll go not far wrong. This is my star."

"What about the Spanish Main?" I could not forbear to ask.

"Pish! Tush!" he said. "That *was* my star until this, my real star, was revealed to me. Same with you, same with everybody. A man will follow anything, like a newly hatched chicken the hen, until that moment of revelation. But when it comes he knows it. Like Paul on the road to Tarsus. Poor old Lobo's steering marks, remember?"

And so, heaven help me, I found myself once more an unwilling member of the crew of this vile creature, the circumstances differing but little from those on the galleon, because now, as then, he and the Goanese were armed under their cloaks, and I was not. I resolved to make my escape at the first opportunity, but none presented itself. Day after day I was obliged to ride beside him while he discoursed, sometimes with great skill and learning, on comparative religion. There were times, indeed, when his baser self seemed to slough away from him and he dropped his foul language and wanton blasphemy, when his entire personality and his very voice changed, and he became once more the scholar and the savant. Then, without warning, he would change again, and filth and ribaldry would pour from his lips in an unbroken stream. It was once when he was in this latter mood that I abandoned all thought of escape before we reached Delhi.

"What ailed you so lightly to throw aside that filly back there?" he demanded one day. "Have you taken to black velvet in preference to cloth of gold?"

"It was by ill chance," I explained. "There was a fight upon the road and we were separated."

"The Devil take that for a story," he retorted. "She had already left you, though she confessed that she was looking back over her shoulder when she did so, expecting you to follow. When you didn't she wrote you down as a poltroon and continued on her way alone."

"How could I follow when I was held fast in chains?" I raged. "I have already explained that to the stupid baggage."

"Baggage maybe," he answered, "but stupid, never. That girl has wit and intelligence, and a certain facile learning which she is improving fast by avid reading." He leered. "I have a mind to take her instruction in hand myself when she arrives in Delhi, in more branches of knowledge than one."

"Keep away from her, damn you!" I shouted.

"Hoity-toity!" he laughed. "What concern can it be of yours? I have already told you, she is finished with you. She begged of me to save your life, but that was only loyalty, not anything tenderer. Forget her, my dear Gil, as she no doubt has forgotten you. How and when did you fall in with her in the first place?"

"I had met her in England," I answered cagily.

"Under what circumstances?"

"What has that to do with you?" It had become a duel now, he probing with his questions, I not knowing how much he knew, and wishing not to betray anything that he didn't.

"Everything," he snapped. "So curb your ill temper, my fine young cockerel, or I'll wring your withers for you. She is like to become a power with the ladies of the court, and as such I can use her. The Emperor might even take her into his own harem, for his tastes range far and wide, and there I'd have a trump card indeed." He smacked his lips. "In the harem with her little ears wide open, but having to see me in private very frequently as her spiritual adviser. Come on now, her background, and let it be the truth. Was she one of your inept political plotters?"

"How could she be?" I temporized. "She was but a child when I met her."

"Where?"

"In a house in London . . . the house of a friend." I was sweating now. If this vile creature did not know her sordid story it was the last thing I wanted to tell him. But she trusted him as the priest she thought him. If she had not already told him, there was every chance that she might at some time in the future, unless I could warn her of his true identity. If he knew her as a reformed whore he would have a moral ascendancy over her, whereas on the other hand if he really thought her to be a woman of learning and culture by advantage of birth, he would be more circumspect in his dealings with her. *Did* he know already? Was he even now merely trying to trap me? I was cudgeling my brain over this when he fired his next question at me.

"And while we're on the subject, young Gil, I'd like to know a little more of *your* background," he said. "You were always a plaguy close customer in the old days, though you know everything that is to be known about *me* . . . the worst and the best. How about *you?* You have little enough real learning, God knows, yet you speak like a man of birth and breeding. In addition to English you speak French, Portuguese and a smattering of Dutch, not to mention a good command of the barbarous tongue out here. You are versed in the military arts, and that as an officer and a commander, yet I doubt if you have yet seen your thirtieth year. You can handle a ship and know the uses of the globes and astrolabe well enough to navigate in a rough sort of fashion. You are a man of parts, my Gil. Come on now, a little frankness. Where had you sprung from when first we met in that pesthole in Amsterdam?"

"I fell afoul of the law," I told him truly enough, "by reason of some golden crowns in my pocket which I could not account for when taken by the parish constable. For that I was bonded to the Dutch, as you were."

"I see," he nodded. "A gentleman fallen on evil times who took to the road as a highwayman. Is that it?"

"Near enough," I growled.

"No, not *quite* near enough," he answered. "Groombridge, that chawbacon who sailed with us to the Cape and then to the Coast, told me different. I mentioned political plotters just now and you all but acknowledged it. What's the story, Gil? If we are to work together I must know *all* of you, past and present. How came you by the name of Bardock?"

"The usual way . . . for those who are not bastards. It was my father's," I told him.

"Liar," he shot at me. "Bardock is a name common among the Sussex peasantry. You are not a peasant, and your voice in moments of stress has the roughness of the north in it. Lancaster? Yorkshire? Which is it?"

But I was saved from my predicament at that very moment by a chital deer which crossed the road before us in full flight, and the cavalry escort were after it with wild halloos, followed by the "priests." The Angel cursed the latter roundly for thus betraying themselves with unseemly conduct, and roared after them to come back, and when they had done so, sheepishly, he soundly berated them.

"Piety, modesty and gentleness I want from you bilge-scourings," he told them, "or by Christ I'll put some into you with the lash. Do you heed me, you brothel carrion? Sweetness and bloody light, damn and blast your poxy eyes. Now get on with telling your beads and not as if you were splicing rope yarn. Eyes down and mumble piously for the next hour or so, or I'll qualify you for harem eunuchs before we reach Delhi."

So what with that and the return of the guards with the dead chital, he forbore to interrogate me further, but I knew that this was but a temporary surcease. Whatever happened I must now remain with this foul party until we reached Delhi, and try by every means in my power to find Cloda and give her warning about this man. I resolved, therefore, to dissemble and to fall in more and more with his evil plans as if convinced in spite of myself of their scope and brilliance. Fortunately I was aided in this by the conceit of the fellow. He loved one thing more than the sound of his own boastful voice, and that was an intelligent audience to listen to it, and of that he had been deprived for many a long day, as his fellow "priests" were ignorant men whom he held in deep contempt. Therefore, whenever he showed signs of recommencing his interrogation of me, I skillfully steered him off into yet another flight of self-eulogy. But the danger was always there that he would catch me off my guard at some moment and worm from me something of my past, and whereas I cared not one whit what he found out about me, I was fearful that through it he would bring harm to Cloda. This thought tortured me, for now I was deluding myself no longer. I loved her. Her past meant nothing to me. It had been no fault of hers, and when the opportunity to escape from it had presented itself she had seized it eagerly with both hands. Only the future mattered, and if I could clear the morass of doubt and misunderstanding that lay between us, and persuade her to share that future with me, that was all I cared about. True, I had naught to offer her but a life of uncertainty and wandering, but that would mean little to one of her spirit and courage. Only let me find her again, and having found her, rid myself of this last obstacle to our safety and happiness: this fiend who would use her as a pawn in the furtherance of his mad ambitions, and incidentally, no doubt, as a plaything for his lasciviousness.

I pondered long, as we rode, on the advisability of accomplishing this latter aim first; of taking the earliest chance of killing him while we were still upon the road, and of reporting his death as due to fever when we arrived in Delhi. But I put it from me, not from any scruples on my part, but purely because of the presence of the guards. The "priests" worried me not at all. That carrion would follow any who commanded with a heavy enough hand, and I felt they hated the Angel as much as I. No, first I must find her; and in the meantime act the part of the diligent apprentice to this hateful creature.

And so in due course we came to Delhi, and if the magnificence of Agra had amazed me, that of this city took my breath away completely. It was said that it was five cities, each built upon the ruins of the one preceding it, and that I could well believe because there was an antiquity here that was missing in Agra and Ahmednagar, where the stones were fresh-hewn and the smell of new mortar was still heavy upon the air. This was the keystone of the mighty empire of Akbar, who had won it in the battle of Panipat from Adil Shah, the Afghan king, while still a youth fresh from the hills of the north, some eighty years previously. It rose sheer from the flat surrounding plain, enfolded in a wide sweep of the River Jumna. Ahmednagar was a fort enclosing a village; Agra a greater fort holding within its wall a small city. This place was a mighty city in itself, enclosing many forts, the whole then surrounded by a seemingly impregnable wall and series of moats and ditches to a total circumference of over ten miles. It was a marvel of architecture, a miracle of military engineering. The mind reeled in contemplation of its immensity.

The inhabitants of this teeming metropolis were even more colorful and varied than those of Agra, and here for the first time since my arrival in India I beheld Europeans in the streets and market places without their appearing strange or isolated among the natives. Here were Hindus and Moslems, Afghans and Sikhs, small black Dravidians from the south, fair skinned Kashmirians, and men of yellow hue with strange slit eyes, whose identity mystified me until the Angel told me they were Chinese, he having met with some of them in the Celebes; and there were Persians and Arabs and Dutch and Portuguese and some who would not have been out of place in the streets of London.

Our escort led us through the Southern, or Agra, Gate and then on through the center of the city, across a vast open space whereon were being conducted a diversity of activities. Soldiers exercised here, and there were many bazaars and open serais, and a market where cattle and fine horses were being bought and sold, and there were mighty caravans of laden camels which, so the captain of the escort told us, came over the passes from the very center of Asia, as far in some cases as China itself.

So here was the Road, I told myself, or at least an offshoot from it, and I felt my blood quicken. It should be simple enough to attach myself to one of these bands returning to the hills. All I had to do was to rid myself of this devil, acquire by some means or other some suitable clothes, and then march north from this city to one of the serais, and there offer my services to a caravan master as a guard or chowkidar or, if need be, even as a menial. The clothes might present some difficulties, but I did not doubt my ability to surmount them. I had, in all truth, been naked and penniless often enough before. There was the heavy iron treasury box that the Angel had taken over from the murdered priest. There was more in that than parchments and letters. If I could get my hands on the key that he constantly carried round his neck on a chain . . . But first of all I must see Cloda.

My train of thought was interrupted by our arrival at the gates of a huge redstone palace, from the magnificence of which, together with the richness of the apparel of the soldiers who guarded it, I guessed could only be that of the Emperor himself.

Here our escort handed us over to a functionary at the guardroom, and then left us with deep salaams and bows, and we were led through many gardens and courtyards to a beautiful marble pavilion detached from the main bulk of the palace and surrounded by lawns and beds of brilliantly hued and heavily scented flowers, among which splashed musically a myriad of fountains.

The functionary, a venerable old man in scarlet robes with a gold chain of office around his neck, told us that his name was Abdar Malik and that he was a scribe of the inner palace and had been put at our service by the Emperor himself, and that he was therefore ours to command in whatsoever we required. He spoke a beautifully classical Hindustani and a little Portuguese, in both of which I was more proficient than the Angel, so I was gratified to find myself accepted as interpreter, a position I determined to exploit to my own advantage.

"It would be better if these other minions of yours did not hold converse with palace officials," I told the Angel. "Their speech is that of ignorant felons, coarse and profane, and would be certain to arouse suspicion."

He agreed with me, and promptly clapped a vow of silence upon them, threatening to cut the tongue out of any whom he heard attempting to speak henceforward without his leave.

Abdar Malik told us that we were to have audience of the Emperor the next morning, and he begged us to take our ease and rest in the meantime, and he assigned to us a host of servants whose only desire seemed to be to anticipate our every wish before we even voiced it. Scented baths were prepared for us, and then a sumptuous meal was served, and it was while we were eating this that an idea occurred to me. We had only one cassock apiece and these were now dirty and travel-stained, so I suggested to the Angel that they should be taken away and washed and repaired in order that we should present a decent appearance at our audience the next day. To this he readily assented, so we were provided with clean and comfortable white cotton robes in the meantime. Thus arrayed, while the others sought their couches after eating, I set out on a tour of exploration of the palace environs.

The marble pavilion in which we were housed was, I discovered, the principal guesthouse. It was a huge building, comprising many halls and chambers and passages in which a stranger might easily lose himself at first. There were other guests there, but so huge was the place that none obtruded upon the other, and in my anonymous white garments I found I could wander at will without exciting curiosity. This rejoiced me, because I realized that Cloda's party, when it arrived, would almost certainly be housed here in the first instance, and so my task of finding her would be made the easier. It would appear, therefore, that all I had to do was to possess my soul in patience and await her arrival, which should not be long delayed, because the Angel had told me that she was following us but some few days behind. Cheered by these reflections, I sat in the courtyard and watched with great interest the throbbing life of this strange and wonderful place. Couriers on magnificent horses constantly arrived, and others as constantly departed, and there was a great and ceaseless coming and going of state officials, on horse and in palanquins—magnificent affairs of intricately carved wood inlaid with ivory and richly draped with silken brocades—and twice, to my vast entertainment, came rajas on elephants, the great beasts caparisoned in cloth of gold, with gem-encrusted tusks, and bearing on their backs great structures called howdahs.

How long I sat there observing all this I cannot say, but I was finally aroused from the reverie into which I had fallen by the arrival at the outer gates of a large party on horseback. They appeared to have traveled far that day, because their beasts were sweat-soaked and drooping, and their riders dust-begrimed. They had obviously been expected, for Abdar Malik was at the gate to receive them, which he did with great deference. They had a Mogul cavalry escort even as we had had, and my heart gave a leap because I thought at first that this might be Cloda's party, but then I saw that the four men who rode at the head of the column were Europeans who wore great feathered hats.

I watched them cross the vast courtyard towards the guesthouse, in front of which I was now sitting . . . and then I felt the hair on my scalp prickle, because their leader was none other than Mynheer Nassau van der Buhl, the Dutch Trade Commissioner.

✧ 27

HE strode past me into the guest-house, followed by his three companions, all of whom I recognized as burghers of Trivandrum, and I had just enough wit left not to try and avoid his glance, even though I thought I saw in it a sort of puzzled half-recognition, as one who asked himself where he had seen me before. I prayed inwardly that he would not run into the Angel inside the building, because that, I am sure, would have swept away all doubts from his mind. Even so, one of the others checked his pace and stared me full in the face. I felt my heart skip a beat, but I returned his look boldly, and after a moment he shrugged and followed on behind his master. Of course, they had last seen me in European clothes, pale from long illness, and wearing long hair, moustaches and short beard. Now I was shorn and shaven, dressed in white native garb, and burned near black from the sun.

But it was a near thing, and I knew that I dared not risk another encounter.

I walked round the courtyard in an agony of indecision. Left to myself I would once more have taken to my heels, for I felt I owed the Angel less than nothing. True, he had delivered me from my peril in Agra, but that was for his own ends alone, and he would have used me, betrayed me or even killed me himself without a moment's compunction if a tithe of advantage to himself lay that way. No, Devil take the Angel; he was well equipped to look after himself. On the other hand, if he were unmasked, he would undoubtedly betray me, if it were only from spleen. If I were taken I would be unable to warn Cloda, and she would walk blindly into a trap; and liberal though Shah Jahan was reputed to be, I did not think that he would have hesitated to hand an erring wife over to her lawful spouse.

There were two courses open to me. I should either warn the Angel of Van der Buhl's presence, thereby giving the former the chance to lie low until the Dutchman was quit of this place; or just slip away myself and go south down the Agra road until I met with her cavalcade. Warned, she could feign illness and remain safe within the women's quarters until the coast was clear again. In the former case I could demand of the Angel a mule, suitable habiliments and money to bribe my way past the cavalcade guards once I fell in with it. On foot and in nondescript garments I knew I would find it well-nigh impossible to get near her.

But what if the Angel had other ideas? What if he decided that it would be best in his own interests callously to stand aside and let Cloda be taken? I knew the answer to that. He would merely have his priests hold me in restraint, and there would be no way to help her. No, I could not take that risk. I quickly made my decision.

Without a backward glance, I walked out of the courtyard and found my way through the crowded bazaars to the Agra Gate.

The sundown gun boomed as I reached it, and I just had time to scurry through before the massive portals slammed shut behind me, for which I was thankful, because it now meant I was safe from pursuit even if the Angel missed me immediately, though in that event I felt sure he would assume I had gone north.

The short twilight descended like a curtain and, the year being well advanced, the evening chill struck keenly through my thin cotton garments, but at least, as far north as this, there were no mosquitoes to plague me. I walked throughout that night, and as the sun arose I came to the first serai. I entered and ranged through the stirring travelers, but they were for the most part poor countryfolk, and there was no sign of a military cavalcade. I drank my fill at the well, then moved outside and sat in the shade of a kikar tree, whence I could watch the road to the south; and since, penniless as I was once more, it was doubtful when I would eat again, I decided it was better to remain here and conserve my strength than to continue walking, for there was no other route by which she could come.

All that livelong day I sat there, my hopes rising thrice as I saw the dust of approaching caravans, only to be dashed when they turned out to be those of merchants; then, when night fell once more, I rolled myself in my cotton robe and tried to find escape from cold, hunger, and black depression in uneasy sleep.

They came in the morning. There was no mistake this time. The rising sun gilded their fluttering pennants and darted back in a myriad points of fire from their armor as they approached at a swift trot. I stood beneath the tree, a prey to a thousand fears. What if she was not with this cavalcade? But then, while they were yet a good two hundred paces short of the serai, my heart gave a great leap as I saw the familiar formation: first a half-squadron, then an interval to let the dust subside, then a party of ladies, then the rear guard with the baggage animals. And she was among the ladies, riding proud and erect, her sari thrown back to reveal the glory of her hair.

They swept up to and past my tree, then, to my horror I saw that they were not stopping. They passed the serai without drawing rein, and I realized that they must have camped short of it and, with fresh and rested horses, they were traveling on to complete the journey in one long, fast stage. I shrieked and ran after them through the choking clouds of dust that they threw up, but I might just as well have chased the whirlwind, although in my madness I kept running and calling until finally I fell flat on my face and watched miserably as they grew smaller in the distance.

But now at least I knew where she was, and there was the faint chance that they might halt for a short rest when the sun reached its zenith, so I regained my feet and set out grimly after them. But hope was fast fading by mid-afternoon when, famished and weary, I had to seek rest at the side of the road. I tried to comfort myself with the reflection that, at their pace, they would arrive at the city after nightfall, but, being a military party, the gates would be opened for them. The ladies, in that case, could only be expected to go straight to their quarters, and they would be too weary to rise early next morning. If I rested a little, then pressed on again through the night, I might still arrive before she was abroad, and I could then hope to send a warning message to her that would keep her hid until the cursed Van der Buhl had departed. Drawing what little comfort I could from this, I slept for perhaps an hour before being awakened by the sound of approaching voices.

I peered into the dust and saw a large caravan of donkeys and garishly dressed people, and two boys turning handsprings and another leading a chained bear, but it was a full misery-dulled minute before I realized that my old friends the gypsies had caught up with me, and never was man gladder to see the rogues. I sprang to my feet and ran towards them, my arms outstretched, scarce able to speak. Gahan, walking at their head, stared at me, then let out a great roar of welcome, in which the others joined in with a will when they recognized me. He was about to halt the caravan, but I begged him not to on my account as it was a matter of life or death for me to reach Delhi quickly. But he saw at a glance that I was footsore and near the end of my tether, so he sent for a donkey and insisted that I ride. Then he caused a goat to be milked and from somewhere produced a mass of chapatties and half a broiled guinea fowl, and, curious though he undoubtedly was, he would not let me speak until I had eaten my fill.

But then Parvani, who had been straggling some distance behind, must have got wind of my return, because she came running through the crowd, alternately shrieking abuse and heaping endearments upon me, and seeing my embarrassment, Gahan unbuckled his belt and called to her that if she did not keep a respectful distance while we were talking, he would put it around her rump. Glossing over that which I deemed expedient, I then gave him a brief account of my adventures since I last saw him, and my immediate problems. He walked beside me for some time in silence, deep in thought.

"Hm. First we must make sure that you are not recognized in Delhi," he said at last. "That will present no difficulties. As you know, the fools and clowns pigment their faces and wear motley. I suggest you join them in this. Next, you wish to get a message to this lady in the harem quarters of the Emperor himself. That will not be so easy, but I have no doubt that you will find a way somehow. But first, Gil, I must give you a warning. You are becoming a subject for song and legend in the serais along the road. A mysterious European, they say, who has cuckolded the Portuguese Governor, the Dutch Commissioner and penetrated the harem of a Mogul prince."

"That is not true!" I began angrily.

"True or not," he said soberly, "that is the story, and it loses nothing with each telling. You are the very Devil of a fellow, with three prices upon your head—Portuguese, Dutch and Mogul. You would be a valuable man to betray."

He caught my quick look of dismay, and held up his hand.

"Have no fear of *me*, or of any of my own band," he reassured me. "But I have been joined by many others in Agra and along the road since. Of these newcomers I could not be so certain. Fortunately they are half a day's march behind us, as they incline to keep to themselves. I shall pass the word among our own people that you are not to be discussed when they join us in camp tonight."

I breathed a heart-felt sigh of relief.

"Thank you, my dear friend," I said. "I fear I have been a trial to you."

"Think no more of it," he answered. "Only I beg you to behave with circumspection while you remain with us. These Moslems are even more jealous of their women than those of your own race, and if you should be caught interfering with them again, well . . ." He trailed off awkwardly, and I was appalled to realize that I had willy-nilly gained for myself an unwarranted reputation as a lecher and violator of other men's wives. And it was no use my trying indignantly to gainsay it, because he merely rubbed the side of his nose and smiled knowingly.

We arrived at the city gates late that night, and camped outside until morning. Before the new recruits to his troupe arrived, Gahan provided me with parti-colored pantaloons, a shirt of many hues, and painted my face in a fool's mask of red nose, blue circles round the eyes and the rest in deathly white, until I shuddered on beholding myself in a looking glass. But as a disguise it could not have been bettered, particularly since I was but one of half a dozen others thus bedizened. So effective was it, that when the importunate Parvani stormed into the presence of Gahan at daylight, loudly demanding my return to her, she passed me without knowing me, and my kind benefactor was enabled to assure her that I had left in the night and departed for a destination unknown, promising her the prince of all beatings and the confiscation of her share from the iron box if she continued to weary him with her clamor.

We filed through the bazaars to the central maidan, beating drums, playing upon shrill pipes and shouting lewd witticisms to the townspeople who thronged to see us, promising them that night the greatest show that had ever honored the Mogul's provinces with its presence. I capered and turned handsprings with my fellow fools like an imbecile afflicted of Allah, but with my eyes constantly searching the faces of the crowds for sign of anyone I knew. And it was not long before my vigilance was rewarded, because at the main serai where the caravans to and from the north had their lodging, I saw two of the "priests," no longer in their monks' habits but dressed as Hindu peasants, and it was plain from their manner that they were on the alert for someone, but to my great content they spared our noisy crew not a second glance. Later I saw yet another of them moving from one group of camel drivers to another, jingling with some ostentation a handful of small coins in the fashion of one who sought tidings and was willing to pay for them, and it needed little imagination on my part to realize that the Angel was indeed reacting as I had suspected he would, and that he assumed that I had either gone north with a caravan or was intending to do so when the opportunity presented itself. This, however, brought me no nearer to the information that I so desperately required. Did Van der Buhl yet know that the "Jesuit Father" at the Emperor's court was one with the rascally pirate he himself had recently sentenced to hang? And, even more important, had the Dutchman yet found out that his wife also was here? If only I could get word to her! But cudgel my wretched brains as I would, I was no nearer the solution by the time we had made camp on the maidan.

It was the custom of Gahan, when playing the larger towns and cities, to send out the troupe in groups of three and four to extol the wonders of the show he would give that night, and in this the fools and clowns played a large part. Accordingly, that afternoon I set

out with three of my companions, beating drums, striking at passers-
by with bladders of dried peas, and pretending to quarrel and fight
among ourselves until, when the inevitable following had swelled to
sufficient proportions, one of us would mount upon the shoulders of
another and we would sing our own eulogies, urging all and sundry
to attend the grand spectacle that night prepared to contribute generously to the collection. Having thus adjured the multitude, we
would pass on to another spot and repeat the process, our task
being made the easier by an ever increasing and very vociferous
following of small boys. In such circumstances it is usually he who
shouts the loudest who assumes the leadership. I shouted very loudly
indeed, and gradually edged towards the palace, and finally right to
their very gates which, with the privileged impudence of the clown,
I essayed to enter, promising the guard a show which would cost
them nothing but their good will. But while the soldiers themselves
viewed us with indulgence for thus enlivening their dreary vigil,
their officer did not. He appeared on the scene roaring his disapproval, whereupon we were driven forth with blows and reviling,
to the added hilarity of our audience, who deemed our cries of woe
to be designed especially for their amusement. We returned to the
camp, I now in a fever, and no nearer to the solution of my problem.

But Gahan was in the highest fettle, because an officer of the
Emperor's household had summoned him to the palace and had,
after the delicate preliminaries of the officer's bribe had been settled,
engaged the entire troupe on Shah Jahan's behalf to give a private
entertainment that evening, after the public one in the city; and this
was to be staged in the inner courtyard of the palace, for the edification of his court, his guests and the ladies of the harem.

"Fifty golden mohurs!" exulted Gahan. "More than we'd take in
twenty nights playing to the mob! *Fifty!* And after that the run of
our teeth on what is left over from his nightly banquet. Enough to
feed an army—and wine too, for although it is forbidden of the
Prophet, Shah Jahan never was a bigot. Gil, my friend, once more
you have brought me luck. But for the sake of all the gods of Ind,
keep your questing nose and other more privy parts out of the
harem this time, or we'll *all* suffer 'neath the gelder's knife."

This I promised to do though, it must be confessed with some equivocation and mental reservation. I was to gain admittance to the palace—but how I was to communicate with her was another matter.

I puzzled long over this, then, for want of a better plan, I begged from Gahan a few coins against my share from the box, which he let me have, and more, with the greatest heartiness. I went to a bazaar letter-writer and bought of him a sheet of rice paper, an ink-block and a quill stylus, and I retired to a quiet angle in the city wall, spat upon the ink-block, and settled to the task of composition. After several false starts I essayed the following:

> Cloda,
> Beware, Van der Buhl is at Shah Jahan's court. Beware also of Father John the Jesuit. He is a false priest and is in fact the Angel, the pirate your husband sentenced to hang in Trivandrum. He bodes ill to both of us. I shall go to the small garden opposite the palace gate when this performance ends. I pray you to try and meet me there, if only for a brief moment. Destroy this when you have read it.
>
> Gil

I wrapped the missive round a gold coin, inscribed her name upon it once more, and tucked it safely into my waistband. Then I tried to possess my soul in patience for the rest of that long afternoon and through the public performance, which I am afraid we were all inclined to skimp in anticipation of the greater one later.

Workmen were just finishing the erection of two richly draped platforms when we arrived in the courtyard. It was quite dark now, but a multitude of brass lanthorns were hung in the branches of the large peepul tree which grew beside a fountain in the center, and others were arranged in a circle round the space which was to be our stage. I rejoiced inwardly to see that this meant that we, the performers, would be in a pool of bright light while our audience would be in corresponding darkness. I had no plan as yet for getting my note to her, nor indeed had I any certainty that she would even attend the performance. I could only hope and sweat and pray.

The courtyard was deserted except for the workmen and occasional palace officials who came and went through the encircling shadows, and Gahan, whom I had never before seen nervous, took this last opportunty to gather us all around him and earnestly adjure us.

"This is no belly-scratching tumbling bout," he told us. "No howling of lewdities for the bazaar offal. Here we perform for the all highest, and they will throw gold pieces into the ring if we please, or set the guard to scourge us if we don't. Which will mean *two* scourgings for the whole crew of you, for I'll take the skin off the ill-conditioned rumps of any who fail to give of their best. Singers, warble like the velvet-throated bulbul. Jugglers, blind them with your skill and dexterity. Acrobats, leap higher and land lighter than the mahseer, and if you break your stupid necks in so doing, bow, smile and skip out of the light like young fawns before dying in the dark. Dancers, outdo the houris of paradise itself. Fools, make even *me* laugh but without unseemly bawdiness. Musicians, for the love of Ganesh the Amiable, try for once to play in tune."

Then the courtyard started to fill. First came the menials and off-duty soldiers, squatting under the marshaling of the guard in concentric rings on the ground; then came the minor officials, seated farther back on cushions that raised them a little higher than the lower orders . . . and finally, through a reverend hush, came the high officers, clustered in a tight phalanx round the person of Shah Jahan himself as a precaution against assassination, and with them I saw Van der Buhl and his companions. They ascended to the nearer of the platforms and settled themselves comfortably upon couches, and Gahan, with a final muttered prayer to some strange god, went forth into the light and prostrated himself, before rising, a magnificent figure in his garish travesty of a maharajah's costume, and clapping his hands sharply.

There was a clash of cymbals and a thud of drums and the high piping of the flutes and the outlandish plunking of the sitars, all of which totaled to my still unaccustomed ears the most excruciating of cacophony but which passed for music in the East, and the whole troupe came forward to bow and salaam before breaking into their individual acts. Tumbling, rolling and scratching like a monkey, I circled the patch of light, my eyes searching the other platform which I could only dimly discern in the outer gloom, and it was some time before I realized that it was now full of women in brilliant saris who for the most part were veiled.

And then, my eyes becoming accustomed to the tricks of the light, I saw her.

The women were seated in rows upon cushions, and she was in the center of the first one. I thought at first that it was the light upon a golden sari of an Indian woman, but then I realized that it was her hair, and hair like that belonged only to Cloda. She stood out in that assembly like a white dove in a flock of ravens, and I realized with a start of fear that even if Van der Buhl was not already aware of her presence, he could not fail to see her from the men's platform, a scant few yards in front, should he happen to turn his head, and I prayed that the show would prove sufficiently diverting to rivet his attention.

Then I sought some way to get near her without finding myself spitted on the spears of the guard, and it came to me in the form of one of my fellow fools who, in aiming a blow at me with his bladder of dried peas, let it fly from his hand out of the circle of light towards the women's platform. He stood slack-jawed for an instant, in genuine dismay, and I yelped like a dog and ran after it. He chased me and buffeted me on the ears to get it back—poor, clumsy, bucolic buffoonery—but it pleased those of the nearer audience mightily. Thereafter I concentrated on this man, herding him always towards this spot in front of the women's platform, wresting from him his bauble and throwing it ever and anon nearer to it, then running and capering with him and fighting to regain it, until finally, with a mighty throw, I hurled it under its very shadow, and I ran as I'd never run before, to get there ahead of him, hoping against hope that our ridiculous sideshow was not attracting the attention of the main audience away from more worthy things in the center of the stage.

I arrived right under her feet, babbling incoherent gibberish, then, risking everything, I cried in English, "Cloda . . . it is I . . . Gil. Read this." And I slipped the coin and note into the shadows near her outspread skirts, skipping nimbly away as my fellow clown tried to trip me up and running with a bear-gait back to the stage, just as the muttering guards came forward to drive us away.

I could not tell whether she had heard or understood me, but later, when I dared look that way again, I saw her place was vacant, and the sheer relief of it near caused me to be sick upon the spot.

The show, thank God, appeared to be pleasing our audience, and the beaming Gahan was sweating in his efforts to get even more from us. Never did tumblers tumble, singers sing or dancers dance as did the troupe that night, while I, in gratitude, near split my belly with my leaping and cavorting.

Then I saw the Angel and his hell-bred entourage. As priests it would, of course, have been unseemly for them to witness openly such a vulgar display as ours, so they stood discreetly in the shadows of a balcony overlooking the courtyard, and it appeared to me that he, like Cloda, had obviously been unaware of the presence of Van der Buhl, who was now an indistinct figure among the nobles around the couch of Shah Jahan.

The show came to its finale at last, and as Gahan had hopefully prophesied, there was a shower of gold coins from the high and mighty, with smaller silver ones from the lesser fry, and we scrambled and scrabbled for them in the dust as the audience withdrew. Then came a procession of menials laden with baskets and dishes of mutton and capons and rice and many exotic foods that I had not seen even in Goa. And there were flagons of very strong wine which soon had the troupe in even higher spirits than had been engendered by their success.

Gahan crooked his finger to me and motioned me to the seat of honor on his right, under the peepul tree, and he pressed upon me a small silk bag of gold pieces which he said I had earned by my performance and even more as the bringer of good luck.

"But Gil," he reproved me, "my heart leapt to my mouth when I saw you approaching ever closer to the harem ladies. We, as great artists, are allowed a certain indulgence in these matters, but by Ganesh, I could feel that gelder's knife round my privy regions. This is the Mogul capital, you scoundrel. I beg you to keep away from all such dangerous ground while we are here. Hasn't your lechering got you into enough boiling oil already?"

I assured him earnestly of my good behavior in the future. Then, as he turned to pledge the others in his third flagon, I silently withdrew into the shadows and made my way to the small garden opposite the palace gates.

✤ 28

THE garden was deserted when I arrived. The moon was near the full, and its light reflected back off the white marble walls, intensifying thereby the inky blackness of the shadows cast by the shrubbery, for which I was thankful, as the guard were but a few scant yards away at the gate opposite. I waited about half an hour, my doubts and anxieties increasing with each slowly dragging minute. Would she come? And if she did, what would it avail me? My way led to the north, and hers was now cast with these people. She would not come with me—that I knew with a doleful certainty—but I knew also that I could not drag myself away without seeing her once again, and perhaps trying, however vainly, my powers of persuasion in the matter of changing her determination.

And then at last she came. She had covered her bright sari with a dark cloak, and I did not see her until she emerged from a patch of shadow cast by the palace wall opposite. She came into the garden and stood looking round uncertainly, and she was not aware of me until I whispered her name. She looked at me for a long moment, then she laughed fit to burst, for with my sweat-streaked paint and dusty motley I must have looked every inch the fool I was supposed to represent.

"Oh, Gil, my poor stupid Gil!" she spluttered. "Had I but a looking glass at this moment . . ."

"Peace, you silly slut," I swore at her. "Do you want the guard around our ears?" But there was no anger in me, for in that instant my heart was as light as a bird on the wing at seeing her once again the gay Cloda of old.

"How came you to this pretty pass?" she asked, snatching my clown's bauble and buffeting me about the ears with it.

"Have done, woman," I begged of her. "Do you not realize the danger in which you stand?"

"Pish!" she retorted. "I had seen Mynheer Cheese-faced van der

Buhl long before you tossed me your note, though I'm none the less grateful for your efforts to warn me. It is but a matter of my keeping out of his way until the sprauncing ninny has gone."

"And of course you knew the real identity of the saintly Father John?" I asked sourly. "So there was no need for me to risk my neck in bringing you warning. Damn you for an ingrate."

"No," she admitted. "Father John cozened me, although now, on thinking back, I see the likeness to the hairy scamp who stood in the felons' dock in Trivandrum."

"He'll do more than cozen you should he get you alone one dark night," I warned her.

"Neither him nor any other man again," she spat. "Let him lay one filthy finger upon me and I'll betray him for what he is . . . a pirate whose neck is forfeit to both Dutch and Portuguese."

"Hoity-toity!" I scoffed. "You don't know the forces arrayed against you. Have done with this foolish venture and take the road again with me. *The* Road. Do you realize how close we are to it here? Come with me, Cloda," I begged. "Araby . . . the land of the Grand Turks . . . the shores of the inland sea. The Road goes through and beyond them, right across Europe to the Lowlands. Remember how we talked of it at nights? The things we shall do, the sights we shall see . . ."

I heard her catch her breath in what was almost a sob, but she shook her head firmly.

"What is there for us together?" she asked.

"I ask for nothing you are not inclined to give freely," I told her earnestly.

"And that is all I *can* give," she answered. "Nothing. All that was worth giving has already been taken from me. I am but half a woman, and that half bitterness and gall. You are all man, whatever I may have screeched at you in my fury. Go your way, Gil. You will never know real happiness until you have trodden the Road. Tread it, every mile of it back to Europe. They tell me the Protector and his son are gone now and the young Charles sits upon the throne. Return then and maybe claim your estates again."

"Not without you," I swore.

"Nor with her," said a shrill voice close to my side in the darkness. "Keep very still, Mynheer Gil Bardock, and you also, wife of my bosom. Two horse pistols would scatter you both to the winds."

How long they had been standing there, I did not at first realize, but his next words told me that they had heard most of our converse.

"The Devil's net spreads wide," he chuckled evilly. "We thought we only followed my errant wife as she crept through the shadows . . . but now we have Mynheer Gil, and also, if I caught the allusion correctly, the Angel. Father John, eh? You *were* right, Dirk. Your memory for faces has stood you in good stead. You shall have half the reward when we once more bring them to dock. Now move forward towards the gate, Mynheer Gil, and no tricks, please, unless . . ."

But that was as far as he got, except for a retching grunt as his knees gave way under him. He lurched towards me, then sprawled his length on the marble pavement. Cloda drew her breath in sharply. "Tipsy as a newt," I heard her mutter. "Damn all men to perdition."

I caught her wrist and started to draw her away while the man Dirk stared stupidly at his supine master, his pistol no longer pointed at my midriff, but then, at that moment, the same thing happened, and he buckled at the knees and started to collapse. The Angel and two of his priests stepped out of the shrubbery, and I saw the moonlight glint on the knives they all carried . . . knives that were red-stained from point to haft. I swung Cloda behind me and dived for the pistol that Van der Buhl had dropped in his death agony, but the Angel was quicker. He kicked it to one side and I heard him snarl to his followers, "*Us se maro . . . . . . Shor mat karo!* Kill them . . . without noise!" Then Dirk, in his last instant of life, must have squeezed the trigger of his pistol, because there was a shattering roar and an answering scream from one of the priests as he took the heavy charge in his carcass. I waited no longer. I grasped Cloda round the waist and jumped with her over the parapet of the garden, landing in a marble irrigation channel twelve feet below. The Angel and the unwounded priest were right upon our heels, but they, unhampered by a struggling woman as I was, jumped farther and landed dry-shod on the opposite bank of the channel . . . and it was that which saved us, because even as the echo of the pistol shot died, the guard came swarming from the palace gate-house and into the garden. I crouched neck-deep in the water, hold-ing Cloda, while the soldiers, in full cry like a pack of hounds, leapt the ditch in hot pursuit of the villains.

I waited until their cries faded in the distance, then, dragging Cloda, I half-waded and half-swam with the current until we came to a large cistern which served the many fountains round the edge of the main city square. Here we climbed out of the water and stood shivering in the chill night breeze, as bedraggled as two drowned rats, while that unreasonable woman started to berate me as though our present plight was all of my contriving.

"A pox upon you, you unhandy oaf," she swore. "Always, when circumstances seem set fair for me, *you* have to turn up like a bad groat and unset them. Why can't you go your way and allow me to go mine?"

"I wish to God I had done just that," I told her bitterly. "Had I not turned back along the road to warn you this time, I should by now have made my escape from this place and have been continuing on my way north."

"Do that now," she retorted. "And good riddance to you."

"And what will you do?" I asked.

"Mind my own affairs, as I commend you to do also," she an-swered pettishly.

"You mean to return to the palace?"

"Why not? I have naught to fear."

"They cut the noses of unfaithful wives under Moslem law."

"I never was an unfaithful wife, in spite of your hot-handed attempts at lechery."

"Try to convince the Mogul officers of that."

"Why should I have to? There is nothing to connect me with that which has just occurred in the garden. Van der Buhl, poor wretch, can no longer testify against me. Nor his man."

"There are others in the Dutch party," I said. "And if the Angel is taken he will talk, if only from spite."

That had no doubt already occurred to her, because she had no answer for it except another tirade of abuse. I quickly seized my advantage.

"All right," I said. "If you are determined to put your head within a noose, your way lies across this square to those steps. Up them and round to your right you will find the palace wall. Follow it left-handed until you come to the gate. If the guard look askance at you, tell them that you are tutoress to the ladies of the harem, and that you habitually bathe by moonlight . . . for preference in the city drains. They might believe you. Good night, my lady, and may good fortune attend you. You'll need it."

I turned on my heel and walked away, but I had not gone many steps before she was behind me, clutching at the wet sleeve of my motley. She was now near sobbing with rage.

"Curse you," she spat. "You have burned my bridges behind me. All right, I'll come with you—but upon my own terms."

"Which are?"

"As heretofore. I am not your chattel, and if you attempt to force yourself upon me, it will be more than a pineapple I'll use next time to cool your ardor. There is to be nothing between us, do you understand? *Nothing.*"

"Let there at least be civility," I suggested coldly, but within me my heart rose once more. "Right, let us begone. First we need repairs to our woeful appearance."

Keeping to the shadows, we found our way to the serai outside which the gypsies had made their camp, there to find them all abuzz with excitement not a little mixed with apprehension, because the turmoil at the palace had broken out just as they were leaving, and there were many rumors as to its cause. Leaving Cloda in the shelter of a clump of palms, I sought out Gahan. He blazed with anger when he saw me.

"Damn you," he raged. "You promised that for once you would stay clear of mischief."

"The mischief was not of my seeking or making," I defended.

"Camel dung!" he retorted. "Two dead Dutchman—and the guard clamoring about a fool and a woman running with a covey of black-robed priests! How long do you think it will be before we are all hauled before the high officers and put to the question?"

My jaw dropped, for if this was indeed the truth, the answer would not be long in forthcoming.

"I am sorry, my kind friend," I mumbled. "I had best put as much distance between myself and you as I can." I turned away, once more heavy hearted.

"How far do you think you would get in those clothes?" he asked sourly. "Keep your distance from the camp while I procure you others."

"There is also a woman . . ." I began.

"Did I not know it?" he growled. "Go, wait for me."

He joined us at the clump in a very short time, and he was no niggard in what he brought us. For me, once more, there were the nondescript habiliments of a peasant farmer, together with a warm quilted cloak, a knife and a stout staff, sandals, and a scrip of bread and meat. For Cloda was an all-enveloping *burqa*, which is the white cloak and headpiece in one which orthodox Moslem women wear, covering them completely and allowing them to see through a small piece of veiling sewn into the material at eye level. And to all this the good man added my share from the box—a further six golden pieces. I could scarce thank him, so constricted was my throat at this open-hearted generosity. His anger abated a little as I grasped his hand in farewell.

"Wait in hiding near the city gates," he advised. "North, south, east or west is a matter for your own choice, but join in with a caravan. Traveling just two together you might invite questioning. Fair kismet go with you, but for the sake of Ganesh the Amiable, keep clear of my troupe should you come across us again." And he went, bearing with him our discarded garments to burn in his camp fire.

We followed his excellent counsel and waited until dawn at the Northern, or Lahore, Gate, squatting with many other travelers in the dust which rose in clouds with the passage in and out of camels and donkeys, and which soon covered all of us in a gray uniformity that I for one found very comforting. That something was afoot became evident as the caravans formed up and filed under the archway of the towering gate. There were more soldiers there than usual, and all were subjected to more than the casual scrutiny I had become accustomed to at Mogul gates. Keen eyes searched every male face, while the veiled Moslem women were made to lift the hems of their burqas so that the size of their feet and the hairiness or otherwise of their legs could be examined, it being forbidden of the Prophet to gaze by force on the face of another man's wife. I feared for Cloda, for her feet, subject to the hard usage of long roads as they were, were still small and well-formed and of a greater degree of whiteness than those of the sturdy countrywomen who marched with us. But evidently they looked for a man in female guise, and Cloda, who had the wit to waddle rather than walk and who was as dusty as any of her coarser sisters, came through without question. In front of me, a Rajput with patrician features and better clothes than the rest of us, was pulled from the line for questioning, and in the indignant outcry that he made, I shuffled through quickly with only a cursory glance thrown in my direction.

And so we were through, once more upon the road—the road to the Road—and we marched through the crisp morning air towards the Great Plain of the Five Rivers, which Indians call Punjab, the land all around us flat as far as the eye could see, right to the rim of the horizon, and I thought I had never seen so arid and poor a country, but a man of Jullundur with whom I held converse told me that after the monsoon each year this dusty plateau that we traversed grew two grains of corn where one would be yielded in more salubrious parts of the great subcontinent, and therefore this place was pillaged and raped with grim regularity after the harvest had been gathered.

"By whom?" I asked, and he looked at me in amazement until I explained that I was an ignorant man of lower India, driven from my miserable farm by famine, and seeking my fortune to the north. Then he became loquacious in the manner of one who seldom has the opportunity to display his superior knowledge.

"The Pathans," he confided. "Fierce men of the Hills, proud, cruel and cunning. They are Moslems like ourselves, but far more rigid in their observances than we more humane people of the plains, and they regard us as infidels."

"Where is their country?" I asked him, and he swept his arm in a half-circle.

"Before us and to each side," he said. "We march into a narrowing valley. As each morning dawns you will see the distant hills faint blue against the sky, getting nearer and nearer, until they tower above one to the very stars themselves. That's where the Pathans live, like the eagles they so greatly resemble."

"Will they not attack this caravan?" I asked, pretending great fear, but he shook his head.

"No. We march under the Truce of the Road."

"What is that?"

"You are in truth a very ignorant man, my friend. The Truce of the Road is the system that has been brought in here by the Moguls. All caravans pay a tithe to the Pathans, in return for which they are given safe conduct while they travel upon it. The Moguls find it cheaper to do that than to send armies against them."

"Who but the Moguls would devise a scheme such as that?" I proclaimed piously.

"Camel dung," he scoffed. "They merely brought down here into India what has been done for centuries throughout Asia, ever since the days of the great Genghis Khan. It is a system which has its limitations."

"Such as?"

"Try going beyond the Khyber Pass in those clothes and you will see," he grunted, then he looked around cautiously and lowered his voice. "The Truce only applies while one is in one's own country. For Indians it extends to the Khyber. Beyond the Khyber only Afghans may travel without molestation, and they only to the land of Persia. After that, one must be a Turk to get as far as Constantinople. Beyond that, I do not know. They say it is a land of brigands and eaters of human flesh."

"But these merchants, and the camel drivers," I protested. "They are not Indians . . ."

"The merchants and camel drivers are free of the Road for all parts of it," he told me. "To Constantinople to the west, to Cathay itself in the east. It is they who pay the tithes." Then he seemed to weary of our converse, because he walked on quickly ahead and joined another group.

But I had learned much that first day, and I talked long with Cloda about it, and thereafter we gleaned more and more knowledge of the Road and its customs. We heard of the Powindahs, a race of camel breeders who had much skill with medicines; people who could take a train of camels across mountains and deserts, where others would suffer losses of their animals which would prevent their going farther. They came from near the great city of Samarkand, but they were a vanishing race, because of their custom of all the sons of one family sharing a single wife. This they did because of their great love of their camel herds, in order that they would not have to be split up between too many heirs in each generation. Sometimes a young Powindah would rebel against this vicious ruling, and take a wife unto himself but then he was cast out of the tribe and his claims to inheritance were abrogated. These men could always earn their bread, however, and even amass modest fortunes by joining caravans as camel doctors, and there was in fact one such with us, together with his veiled wife. He was a strange and quiet man, gentle almost to the point of timidity, a fact that was at variance with his appearance because he was of great stature, fairer than most people I had met since I came to this land, and strangest of all, he had blue eyes and reddish hair; but this, Cloda told me from her previous reading, was common among the Circassian races of Asia. I tried to engage him in converse on more than one occasion, but with scant success, for though he was always courteous, he was little disposed to make friends.

Then one day while he was at the head of the caravan doctoring a sick animal, his wife, riding a camel near us, withdrew from the column. There was little strange in this, but with the quick intuition of a woman in these cases, Cloda sensed something that was hidden to us men by the all-enveloping folds of the woman's burqa. She whispered to me quickly and went out to the Powindah woman, who had now clucked to her camel to kneel. I, not knowing what was afoot, followed on Cloda's heels.

The woman had slipped forward from her saddle and was lying prone beside the camel, shielded from the passing column by the bulk of its body. I had seen the miracle of birth before. With native women it is something quick and natural which incommodes but few of them. But this woman was little more than a child, and her delivery was not a simple one. Cloda, however, knew what to do, while I sat doltlike watching the tail of the caravan disappearing into the distance. By the time the Powindah came back on his magnificent trotting camel, the baby was new-swaddled and bawling lustily, and his father's joy and gratitude knew no bounds, for this caravan was not the warm and kindly band that the pilgrims had been in the Deccan. There were few women with it, and each man attended to his own affairs, and help such as Cloda had given was rare indeed. Even I, who had merely waited, was included in his good will.

We stayed there all through that night, clustered for warmth between the two camels, not daring to light a fire, because now, severed from the caravan, we no longer had the protection of the Truce, and we were within sight of the hills, and the dreaded Pathans had sharp eyes. It took us all the next day to catch up, because Cloda, who had taken complete charge, would not let the camels proceed at anything above a steady walk, in consideration of the young mother. There were tears in the eyes of the Powindah, who told us his name was Achmet Safaraz, when we eventually rejoined the main body at the next serai. He insisted on procuring for us two camels, and although we found their gait uncomfortable at first, we were glad of the rest from the stony track that had been sorely trying our feet. Thereafter we rode together, I with Achmet and Cloda behind with Aminah and the baby. They both spoke excellent Hindustani in addition to their own dialect, and he told me much of the strange customs of his tribe and of the lore of the camels, which they venerated as Indians of the south did their cattle. And soon I was helping him in his tasks, for now we were in the rising hills, and these strange beasts take unkindly to cold weather, and there was much to do with them until we reached the warmer climes the other side. Cloda and I were also suffering acutely from the cold now, and the gentle Achmet bought beautifully tanned sheepskin robes for us at one of the serais, robes which matched their own and indeed made us look very akin to them—so much so that men calling for aid for their sick beasts took to addressing me quite naturally as Powindah-ji, which is an honorific term. And I was quick to learn the various herbs and simples that he used, and how to tell what ailed the animals from the sounds they made, and how to ease a gall or a wounded pad—and even quicker to collect the fee after much vociferous arguing. This money Achmet insisted on my keeping, though I always rendered an account of it and indeed tried to press it upon him, for now the idea was taking shape, and I knew that I would shortly ask of him a favor far greater than the silver with which he was so generous.

And so we came at last to the grim Khyber, which is the northern gateway to all India, down which have swept the conquering hordes from Alexander the Great, through Tamerlane, Genghis Khan, to the Moguls themselves. And here, as Indians, our safe conduct should have ended, in fact we were the only travelers apart from the merchants and drivers still left with the caravan.

Achmet and his wife and child were going on to the east, towards Bokhara. We, with Europe on our far horizons, wished to go west, through Persia to the land of the Turks. Achmet looked grave when I broached the subject by the fire of the Khyber serai.

"My friend," he said gently, "you know that I would grant you any favor before you even put it into words . . . but this is too much for your own safety. You do not speak the dialect beyond the few words you have learned from me."

"How often have *you* spoken Powindah in the last few months?" I asked. "Hindustani is the patois all understand. I have heard it is spoken all through the caravans on the Road, from Cathay to Constantinople."

"That may be so," he assented doubtfully, "but what if you meet with other Powindahs?"

"I shall say I married at the age of three and was cast out," I grinned, "and so have forgotten my mother tongue."

He laughed at that, but still had his qualms on our behalf. Finally he gave in, and having done so, entered into the spirit of the adventure so far as to give me half his great stock of herbs, some of his instruments and a complete Powindah wardrobe, Aminah doing the same for Cloda.

We parted the next day with heavy hearts, for these were people we had come to love. When they went on eastward to Bokhara, we—Cloda and I—waited for a caravan whose way led to the north and the west.

❖❖ 29

WE waited three months in that serai. Two caravans for the north went through in that time, but each had with it a Powindah, so I deemed it discreet to remain hidden until they had gone on. I was not idle in that time, however, and I earned a comfortable competence physicking camels and cattle belonging to local Pathan tribesmen, and sometimes extending my services to their owners, cupping, purging, lancing boils and even drawing teeth, until my fame was spread afar. I bought there a small traveling tent, of the type used by the Asian nomads. These are made from black camel's hair felt which is then stretched over a framework of osiers, and they have an aperture in the top so that a fire may be kindled inside them; they are thus warm and comfortable even in the foulest weather those devilish mountains can brew.

I bought also two fine Bactrian camels, which have shorter legs than their Lowland cousins, and two humps, and are hardier in cold climates. These not only carried Cloda and me and our daily increasing impedimenta, but one of them, a female newly calved, even supplied us with milk which, though peculiar in flavor to our unaccustomed palates, was said to be nourishing and sustaining. We labored hard and long in those days, I with my doctoring of beast and man, Cloda in sewing warm garments against the rigors of the journey ahead of us, and in drying beef and parching barley which she then packed tight in raw leather bags in the manner of those parts, which kept it fresh for many months to come. She had dyed her hair again, not black as before, but with henna which turned it an exact Circassian red, and that, with the healthy tan of her skin, made her not remarkable from the other women of the serai, except in the matter of her beauty, which hardship always seemed to increase rather than ravage. She was able now to discard the trammeling burqa which custom decreed in lower India, and she wore garments of beautifully tanned soft leather which set off her figure to perfection, and a green silk scarf about her hair, which was the sign of the respectably married woman and was supposed to keep lascivious eyes from her, though this last I doubted. Her manner towards me changed, and once more she was the gay and helpful companion of our march from Trivandrum to the land of the Moguls, at least during the day. At night she withdrew from me as far as the confines of our small tent allowed, and I, fearful of a rift in our otherwise pleasant relationship, respected her privacy, though Lord knows I found the trial upon my manhood at times well nigh intolerable.

And then came the caravan we waited for, the last of the season,

for the early snows were closing the upper passes of the mighty
Pamirs and their neighbors of the Hindu Kush. I can see it now as
the advance guard arrived at the serai through the morning mist, six
thousand camels we reckoned them to be, snaking slowly down the
Road, so that it was nightfall before the inevitable stragglers arrived
and made camp. And the men who came with them, those also can I
see. Chinese, Mongols, Bokharans, men of Tashkent and Samarkand . . . all of whose features and costumes we could now read
like a printed page. But, to our great content and relief, we could find
not one high black Powindah turban among them, and as we moved
through the teeming camping ground, our eyes alert and watchful, I
was constantly hailed by merchants whose camels had become footsore and galled, so that even in that first day I amassed a goodly sum
and had to reject much more because of lack of time to attend to
all.

We marched with the rising sun next morning, due west to
Kabul, which is the seat of the Afghan kings, a place of great
fortification but little else save miserable hovels clustered about a
stinking bazaar, and we were glad to be quit of it and on the Road
once more to Herat, a hundred leagues away across the dreaded
Kohi Baba. Then came the hellish nightmare of the Dasht-i-Kharif
which is a great salt desert where many camels perished of their
hardships, and I was engaged each night on the distasteful task of
slitting the poor beasts' throats so that their owners might at least
profit by their blood and the pitiful remains of such water as was
still within their bellies, intoning as I did so the holy verses of the
Koran that Achmet had taught me, for only that way is the
slaughter of a camel lawful.

And so we came at last to Baghdad, the caravan the less by near
two hundred camels, but I the richer by six which their owners had
abandoned and which I had managed to nurse back to health. These
I sold in the market together with our first two, for here the camel
train ended and the Road went on by water up the mighty River
Tigris, right into the land of the Turks itself.

I was by now a man of quite substantial fortune, and I had
profited by much converse and greater listening to the discussions
of merchants during the journey. Cloda and I talked long into the
night, and next morning we repaired back to the market, where we

bought carpets of unbelievable richness of texture and color, then we entered into the company of ten Tashkent merchants, and together we chartered an Arab felucca to take us upstream on the next stage of the journey to Constantinople. The others tried to prevail upon me to buy five Nubian slaves also, as they were doing, because these could then be used to haul the felucca from the bank at the end of stout ropes when the wind failed, and Nubians, they assured me, fetched high prices in Constantinople at the end of the journey. This struck me as good sense, but Cloda would have none of it. In vain I argued that the poor creatures would be in no worse predicament in Constantinople than here in Baghdad. Slaves they were and slaves they would remain, and at least they would be assured of kindly treatment while within our brief ownership. But she railed against me and threatened to leave me that very day if I so much as gave it another thought, and I knew there was no moving her in this. I therefore went back to my associates and told them that I had already spent more on my carpets than I had intended, and so had no further funds for Nubians. They grumbled somewhat, but made no objection to our accompanying them in the felucca, providing I agreed to doctor the slaves when necessary in the same manner as I had ministered to the camels. This Cloda accepted, albeit with reluctance, but during the entire journey she scrambled onto the bank with the fifty Nubians each time it became necessary to haul, and added her puny strength to theirs on the rope, much to the amazement of the merchants. And since, if I wanted comparative peace, I could not suffer myself to be hauled in comfort while she toiled, I had perforce to follow her stupid example, and thereafter we tugged like barge horses for some hours each day, mocked and jeered at by the merchants, who deemed us mad and thereby afflicted of Allah.

Never was man gladder than I when this tiresome water journey came to an end a month later, and we left the felucca at the headwaters of the Tigris, near Lake Van, and continued onwards in ox carts until, on an evening obscured by driving rain, we came to Uskadar and across a narrow waterway which the merchants told us was the Bosporus we saw dimly the minarets of Constantinople.

We crossed next day and sold our carpets after much murderous haggling in the square before the Mosque of Suleiman—ten bales of them, as much as could be carried between twenty stout porters.

We rested that night at an inn kept by a Greek, and next day we bought European clothes, and much constrained we felt in them because it was almost two years to the day since either of us had worn such. But it had to be, for this was the end of the Road. True, it went on from here to the countries of the north, but it was divided and divided again into mere rivulets of dull trade, lacking the color and the zest it took unto itself in Asia. Here it began, and here it ended—a two way ant-track across the high places and the low, the snow-covered mountains and the burning deserts, and we who had trodden it knew that nothing again would hold such savor. We sat in a window that overlooked the Bosporus and watched the twinkling lights on that other darkening shore, and I clinked idly between my fingers the golden dinars we had amassed that day, two thousand of them; and they seemed so many pieces of dross.

"What now?" I asked her.

She did not answer, and when I looked at her I saw two tears slowly coursing down her cheeks. I crossed to her and tried to put my arms about her, but she fended me off firmly, though not, as in the past, with anger.

"We go our ways, Gil," she said. "You to England, I to . . ." She shrugged and left the words unsaid.

"To where?" I insisted. "Back down the Road? What is there for you there? You, a woman alone—?"

"What is there for me in England?" she asked. "Nurse to some rich man's brats? Keep a tavern or an alehouse? Go back, perhaps to that which I left? I'd rather die first."

"What need is there for any of those?" I demanded. "Marry me and let us face whatever the future holds together."

"My Lady Bemforth?" She smiled sadly and shook her head. "No, Gil. Too much that is evil and foul stands between us."

"That was before we met—and the fault was never yours," I told her. "And I have not been such a spotless lily myself."

"For a man it is different," she said, and I laughed scornfully.

"*You* to say that!" I scoffed. "You who have so often berated me on the subject of woman's inequality with man, and cursed the injustice of it."

"That is the way of it, nevertheless," she sighed. "How could I, who could not count the men I have lain with, bear your children?"

"Oh, be damned to that!" I raged. "As if it mattered a tinker's

oath. It never touched the real you. You are a different being now
—born again the instant you left the place. You are the woman I
love, have always loved, and always will. Cloda—listen to me, I beg
of you."

But she would have none of it, and in the end I kicked the neatly
stacked heaps of golden dinars all over the floor and stormed out. I
fell in with some of the merchants, who, Moslems though they
were, were celebrating the happy conclusion of their business with
much carousing, and I got as royally drunk as ever I had been in my
life.

When I returned with the dawn, she was gone. Her fine gowns
were neatly folded upon the bed, but of golden pieces there was no
sign.

I sat down and started to laugh. I laughed until I was sick and
empty of everything but the pain that was in me. That I could not
spew forth. Then, exhausted, I slept.

I found her note when I awoke some hours later. It was pinned to
my pillow, but in the blindness of my drunken fury I had overlooked it before. I carried it to the window and scanned it with
aching eyes.

"Follow your Road to the end," she had written. "I pray you
not to try and seek me, for in so doing you would but waste your
time and substance. I thank you for the happy days we have spent
together, and ask your forbearance in those which were spoiled
by my fickle temper and bridleless tongue, for you are withal a
good and kindly man and one I hope may still find happiness.

Cloda."

And then she had added, "Your gold, less two hundred dinars I have
purloined to my use, you will find in your valise beneath the mattress."

I searched that cursed city for three full days and nights, but
without avail, then I crossed back over the Bosporus and took the
Road south, retracing our former steps, but I knew that this was
fruitless even before I started, because the caravan season was now
ended and naught would pass this way for many months to come, so
after some days of it I returned to the city.

Heavy-hearted, grief-stricken and in despair, I could not quit

Constantinople, even though I knew that no hope of finding her now remained. So there I bided for six long months, setting forth each morning from my lodgings and returning footsore each nightfall, there to rest a short while before continuing to scour the streets, bazaars and alleys far into the night, until I became known among the denizens of those unlovely places as the Mad Englishman, ever questing and questioning, willing to pay good gold to the countless rogues and charlatans who dogged my footsteps with lying tales of a woman they were certain existed only in my imagination.

With the coming of spring, reason returned to me and I continued on my way through Greece, the Balkans and over the high Alps, by diligence, horseback and at times on foot. The journey was mechanical and for the life of me I could not have told the reason for it, unless it was the vague hope in the back of my mind that she might have returned to the Lowlands. But seeking tidings of her in Amsterdam was like searching for a needle in a haystack, so eventually I took ship for London, landing there seven years almost to the day on which I had set forth from it.

I put up at the sign of The Golden Cockerel, a modest but comfortable hostelry within sight of the Palace of Whitehall, calling myself plain John Smith, a merchant recently returned from travels in Europe, and for three days I perused the broadsheets and pamphlets which were on sale in the streets and which gave garbled accounts of the events of the day. We were now in the reign of Charles the Second and it would seem that many who were once outlaws were now enjoying the fruits of office under this merry monarch. I saw references to one Pengelly, now elevated to an earldom and sitting as chairman of His Majesty's Commission for the Furtherance of Trade with the Indies, so I waited upon him at his chambers in the palace.

It took three days of importuning, and finally a bribe of five golden guineas to a weasel-eyed secretary, before I gained admittance. I wondered how he would receive me, but all doubts were dispelled the moment I entered his office of state. He was dictating a letter, and he held up his hand importantly to check me as I stood within the door, bowing outwardly though grinning bitterly inside, for this was a different Pengelly from the nerve-racked conspirator

I had known—stouter, sleeker and very much assured of his new importance.

"Your indulgence for a moment, Master Smith," he said. "Ahem . . . pray continue, Taverner: and it would appear to His Majesty's Commissioners in the matter of trade with the Spice Islands . . ." And then he recognized me and his eyes bid fair to pop right out of his head.

"Bemforth!" he roared, and seized me by the shoulders. "Bemforth, you tardy blackguard! Where on earth have you been these last months? That rogue Faraday said you were hard upon his heels. Sit down, man, sit down and give an account of yourself."

He forced me into a chair, but when I attempted to open my mouth he overrode me.

"God's teeth, man, you've cut time short enough," he went on. "If you're to sail before the winter gales, that is. And I suppose you'll want time to visit your estates in Yorkshire although I can tell you that they're in excellent order. I appointed a steward on your behalf, not a week after Charles returned, and we got 'em out of escheat. No, you'll have naught to complain about on that account. But the ships and all that pertain to 'em—we're going to have our hands full to fit out in time. And then the . . ."

"Pengelly," I managed to get in, "what in the name of the Devil are you talking about?"

But at that moment a flunkey, in peacock trappings and bearing a long ivory wand, threw open the door and announced that the King would see my Lord Pengelly in his privy chamber immediately. Pengelly threw up his hands in despair, swore mightily, but again ignored my question.

"Always the same when I have business of importance afoot," he cried. "A pox on the feckless varlet. Wait, Bemforth, wait. I'll beg my leave as soon as I may." And he dashed out.

The scrivener sat pretending to continue with his task, but I could see that his fox's eyes were slewed covertly upon me.

"What talk is this of ships and sailing and fitting out and winter gales?" I demanded. "What is the fool babbling about, and how does it concern *me?*"

"My Lord Pengelly has been concerned at your non-arrival," he said primly. "Although he has a high regard for your partner, he would not have wished him to proceed without you."

"Partner?" I shook my head in despair. This was getting madder every minute.

"Master Faraday has repeatedly pressed his ability to navigate to the Indian coast," the scrivener said. "In fact he assured my Lord Pengelly that it was he who taught you the rudiments, but my Lord was rightly cautious and has insisted on awaiting your return."

Some instinct warned me then to pursue this mystery with caution.

"Quite right," I agreed. "But Master Faraday, where can I find him? I have but lately returned and have not seen him yet."

"He lodges with a Mistress Nixon in Fairbell Yard in Southwark," he told me. "It is quieter on the other side of the river, and since this business is of a privy nature . . ." He nodded knowingly and came as near to winking as his pursiness would permit, gathered up his papers and bowed himself out.

I sat on in that cursed office for near two hours, but Pengelly did not return, so in the end, being able to bear my thumb-twiddling no longer, I took my leave and repaired to Westminster steps where I engaged a waterman to ferry me over to Southwark.

I found Fairbell Yard without difficulty. It was a small court fronting onto the Thames, accommodating on its three inner sides some half-dozen modest but respectable dwelling houses. I inquired of a baker's boy the whereabouts of that of Mistress Nixon, and was directed to one from which came the sound of sweet treble voices raised in an evening hymn. I waited by the door to the house until they ended, then stood aside as it was thrown open and several children came bursting through, carrying scholars' satchels.

"Might I find one Master Faraday here?" I asked the last urchin. He jerked his thumb back over his shoulder and hurried on to join his companions. I went through and found myself in a hall which was furnished with benches, and at one end was a large blackboard which a man was just wiping clear of chalked lessons. He turned as he heard my step—and I found myself staring openmouthed at the Angel.

My hand flew to my sword and I had it half-drawn ready to run him through, so great was the revulsion within me at seeing him again. He raised his right arm as if to ward off my thrust, and I saw that his wrist ended in a stump from which the hand had been roughly severed, and it was that alone which saved him. He bowed his head and said sadly, "So you've come, my Lord. We expected you earlier."

"Then you've lived the longer, *Master Faraday*," I said grimly. "This time you won't slip your head from the hangman's noose. Walk before me to the Watch at London Bridge—and no tricks, unless you crave for a foot of steel through your liver."

"Master Faraday?" he repeated, and then smiled bitterly. "By that I take it you have already had audience of my Lord Pengelly." He sighed. "Oh well, it is the noose for certain now . . . and I'm not sure that I won't welcome it with outstretched neck. Anything is better than this life of harlotry I am leading."

"Harlotry?" I repeated in amazement, and then laughed sourly. "That is about the only sin I would not lay at your door, you blackguard. It's precious few clients *you'd* attract."

"There is no call for lewdness," he said with dignity. "I was referring to the prostitution of my intellect and great talents," He gestured round the room with his hideous stump. "I, Nathaniel Saunders, Doctor of Divinity and Fellow of All Souls, Oxford, reduced to instructing the snotty-nosed little bastards of the lower orders of tradesmen in writing, ciphering, the rudiments of Greek and Latin, plain song, descant and the lessons of the Scriptures, for bed, board and what small ale I can prig from the cask when Mistress Nixon's back is turned—which is seldom enough, damn and blast her bloody eyes."

"Do you teach them also navigation, you impudent scoundrel?" I demanded sarcastically.

"Forgive me for that," he begged. "I went to the Commissioner with a tale of misfortune which beset me in the East, in the hope of cozening a groat or two from him. He became interested, but wanted to know more of me, so the story grew, burgeoned and developed."

"I'll wager it did, you lying hound," I said grimly. "But how came *my* name into it?"

"By the merest fluke of fortune," he answered. "He asked me the

nature of my transactions in India and I told him I was in partner-
ship with one Lord Bemforth, having recently learned of your true
identity. His reaction was instant, tremendous and favorable. He
grew very excited and begged for news of you. I gave it straight
from the sleeve, saying naught but that which put you in the most
favorable light, of course." He sighed. "I entered his presence a
mendicant. I left with a commission from The Honorable East India
Company well-nigh in my pocket." Genuine tears came to his piggy
eyes. "And it might so easily have come to fruition," he finished
glumly. "My Lord Pengelly is a pigeon for the plucking if ever I
saw one."

"How came you back to England?" I asked, my curiosity getting
the better of me. "When last I saw you, you were running for your
worthless life before the Mogul guards."

He sighed again and reached for a chair and sat down, and now
that my eyes were becoming accustomed to the gloom of the hall I
saw that he was a vastly changed man from the coarse and ruddy
ruffian he had been but two short years before. He was thinner, and his
face was pale and drawn.

"A long story," he said sadly, "and one with which I will not
weary you except in the barest outline. As you say, I was running
for my life, but those cursed robes tripped me and I fell headlong,
and the pox-ridden soldiery was upon me. I was taken before the
Great Mogul, and there was a great outcry because they had found
two dead Hollanders in the garden. I lied like a hero—two heroes—
and such a tangled tale did I tell that they were confused and put at
naught as to the truth of things. I verily believe that I could have
got clear, but for one of Van der Buhl's entourage who reconized
me, or thought he did. Anyhow, the upshot of it all was that the
Great Mogul himself decided to send me back to Goa for the 'Goose
Governor to unravel matters. The fat was in the fire then, and so,
damn nearly, was I—literally. I had no chance to escape on the road
because I was fast chained between two soldiers, right until they
threw me into prison in Goa. I was brought before the Council of
the Inquisition, who took but a few minutes to expose me, and I was
sentenced to burn at the stake, but on what was to be my last night
in this vale of tears, a great monsoon storm arose. A huge peepul tree
outside the prison was uprooted and it breached the wall of my cell.

I tarried not, but set out with all speed for the waterfront, where I relieved a drowned Moslem of his robes and purse, and two days later, that pestiferous town being too hot to hold me longer, I joined a party of pilgrims who were setting sail for Mecca, which as you know is the holiest of holies to that peculiar faith.

"It took us many weeks to reach Medina, which is the entry-port for the country of Araby. I sat on my haunches saying nothing but observing much, until I could go through their ritual like the most learned hadji of them all, washing my mouth, hands and feet before praying five times a day, and mumbling to myself long passages from what might have sounded like the meditations of the Koran, and since the pilgrims came from all parts of the Indies and had more tongues than the Tower of Babel, none thought my halting Hindustani strange.

"I remained in Mecca but a few days, seeing naught in that poor city to hold a man of my talents, most of the pilgrims being as poor as mosque mice, so I attached myself to a band of Turkish Moslems who were returning to Constantinople—by ship to the head of the Red Sea, and thereafter by caravan across the neck of Asia Minor. It was on this journey that I, now running somewhat short of funds, attempted to recoup myself by lightening another hadji of his pouch. I was caught, and suffered the traditional penalty imposed by that barbarous race . . ." He lifted the stump of his right wrist.

"I landed in Constantinople more dead than alive, and in fact have never quite recovered my full health and vigor. I was reduced to begging at the city gate, and I was in that sad condition when I fell in with Mistress Cloda—"

He got no further than that, because I had him by his collar and was shaking him like a rat.

"What was she doing? Where was she going?" I shouted.

He cursed me lewdly and shook himself free. "Damn you, Gil, let me tell it my way, if you want to hear the rights of it," he spluttered. "What was she doing? Trying to leave the city. But there is an ordinance there which very wisely prevents women doing what they please, and only whores and widows may travel the roads unaccompanied by their lords and masters. She was loudly proclaiming her rights upon both scores, and she was lucky not to be thrown into the city pound, there to be auctioned off into concubinage as an ownerless wench. I recognized her with the greatest amazement, for she was in Powindah clothes, and had red hair. I managed to sidle up beside her, make myself known and give her a little well-considered advice, all in one breath." He paused and cocked a sly eye at me. "Poxily dry work this talking," he said. "There is a small but cosy alehouse nearby . . ."

"Go on," I commanded. "Your story—all of it."

He shrugged. "She saw the sense of what I told her. We withdrew from the gate, I thinking to beg the price of a bowl of couscous from her for old scores' sake; and it was then, after much disputation that we made our compact."

"What compact?"

"That I should become her father, and thus gain her egress from the city. Being well-breeched for funds, she accoutered me with the clothes of a Jewish merchant, and dressed herself fittingly as the daughter of such. We saw you several times during the next two days, having divers near escapes from your discovery, and finally we decided to take passage to Smyrna by galley, and from there by Flemish brig the length of the Inland Sea, round the toe of Spain and up to London. I was near dead the whole way with ship-sickness, on top of the weakening effects of my foul mistreatment. I am still an ailing man."

"Thank God for that," I said fervently, "if it serves to keep your lechery within bounds."

"And if it doesn't," said a voice behind me, "I carry constantly a Turkish stiletto in lieu of a pineapple."

I spun round. She was standing in the doorway, clad soberly in a gray kersey gown, plain white collar and cap, all of which became her mightily. I stepped towards her, hands outstretched, my throat constricted so that words would not come—but she ignored me and glared at the Angel.

"There is water to be drawn and the kitchen fire to be made up," she said grimly. "After that you will prepare tomorrow's lessons— and in less slovenly manner than those of today, you idle lout, or not one drop do you get to swill down your lying gullet this night. Begone."

"Yes, Mistress Nixon," mumbled the Angel meekly, and shuffled from the room. I stared after him, then at her, in the manner of one who wakes from a dream and finds himself in a madhouse.

"So you have found me, my Lord Bemforth," she said calmly. "I knew it was but a matter of time, though I had hoped for a few months more."

"But . . . why . . . ?" I managed to mouth, and attempted again to take her hands, but she fended me off.

"Because soon I will have completed the purchase of this house," she told me. "More scholars come to me each week, for that black-guard teaches them well when I am behind him. In a further year I shall be able to repay you the two hundred dinars I borrowed in Constantinople."

"What talk is this of houses and scholars and dinars?" I shouted. "Cloda, don't you realize that I have been near madness this last year, searching for you everywhere . . ."

"Your own stupid fault," she replied. "I told you not to."

"But Cloda, what have I done to you, save love you with all my heart?" I pleaded.

"No more nor less than any other man," she told me. "Don't you realize, my Lord, that it is not you alone of your sex that I take issue with? It is all of you. You who would use me, and take from me my freedom of body and spirit. God's teeth! I could not even move from Constantinople on my own, but was allowed to go without let or hindrance when teamed with that filthy beggar." Her voice rose and there was a catch in it. "Men! Damn you all! I am free of you. I do not need you."

"Less one," I said through gritted teeth, and I swung my arm full stretch, catching her an almighty buffet which spun her on to her comely rump beneath the blackboard. I pulled her to her feet and shook her. "If ever a woman needed a man, it is you . . . if only to pummel some sense into her, you baggage."

She stared up into my eyes, hers blazing the blue fire of rage and indignation. And then she was limp in my arms, laughing and crying alternately and clinging fast to me.

And above us the Star had halted an instant in its course. For here the Road ended . . . and began afresh for us both.